GRIST

A Story of Life in Oregon Country
1835 – 1854

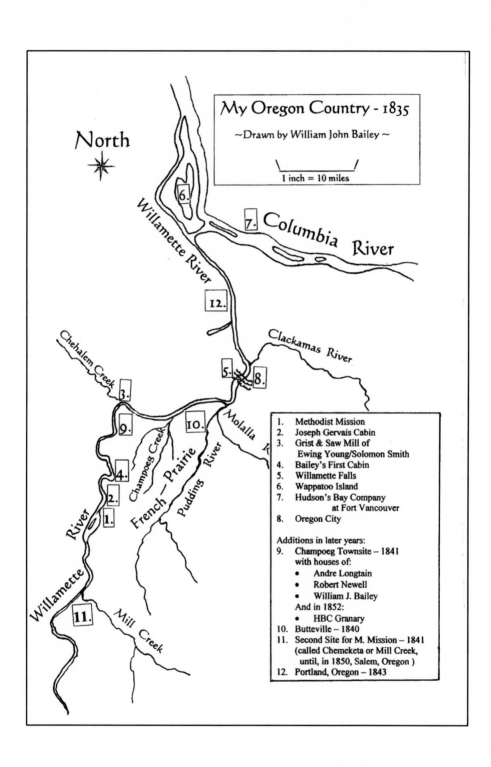

My Oregon Country - 1835

~Drawn by William John Bailey ~

1 inch = 10 miles

North

Columbia River

Willamette River

Chehalem Creek

Clackamas River

Molalla R.

Champoeg Creek

French - Prairie

Pudding River

Willamette River

Mill Creek

6.

7.

12.

5. 8.

3.

9. 10.

4.

2.

1.

11.

1. Methodist Mission
2. Joseph Gervais Cabin
3. Grist & Saw Mill of
   Ewing Young/Solomon Smith
4. Bailey's First Cabin
5. Willamette Falls
6. Wappatoo Island
7. Hudson's Bay Company
   at Fort Vancouver
8. Oregon City

Additions in later years:
9. Champoeg Townsite – 1841
   with houses of:
   • Andre Longtain
   • Robert Newell
   • William J. Bailey
   And in 1852:
   • HBC Granary
10. Butteville – 1840
11. Second Site for M. Mission – 1841
    (called Chemeketa or Mill Creek,
     until, in 1850, Salem, Oregon)
12. Portland, Oregon – 1843

GRIST

A Story of Life in Oregon Country
1835 – 1854

A Novel by

RC Marlen

Selections from *The Grains or Passages in the Life of Ruth Rover, with Occasional Pictures of Oregon, Natural and Moral* by Margaret Jewett Bailey, edited by Evelyn Leasher and Robert J. Frank, with Copyright © 1986 by Oregon State University Press, are used by permission of the publisher.

The Oregon Historical Society in Portland, Oregon, provided the scanned copies of Margaret Jewett Bailey's original letters (see end of book for typed contents).

Books by RC Marlen
may be ordered
through booksellers
or at
www.rcmarlen.com

In this book, historical events, places, and people are presented accurately, although the author created dialogue and some scenes and characters. Thus *Grist* can be considered a historically accurate novel. Readers with an interest in the historical research are encouraged to consult the list of books at the end. All the characters in this novel are authentic, except for those in the Bugat family, who were conceived in order to create a compelling storyline within the flow of history. Scenes with Margaret Jewett Bailey, née Smith, were derived from her novel, *The Grains or Passages in the Life of Ruth Rover, with Occasional Pictures of Oregon, Natural and Moral*; her journal entries and correspondence with her family are indented to indicate her own words. With her above-named book, Margaret Jewett Bailey became, in 1854, the first published novelist in the Northwest. Also, Margaret's discourse about Jason Lee in Chapter 10 on pages XXX was taken from her novel.

ISBN # 978-0-9779752-8-0

Sunbird Press
Salem, Oregon

Cover: Historical Display at Champoeg State Heritage Area, Oregon State Parks
Back cover: Death-Camas Lilies growing among the violet-blue Camas

ALSO BY RC MARLEN

A TRILOGY:

—

Inside the Hatboxes, 2005
The Drugstore, 2006
Tangled Threads, 2008

AND THE PREQUEL:

—

Drop of Fire, 2009

PREFACE

William John Bailey and his future wife, Margaret Jewett Smith, would not have met if another unrelated event had not occurred. It was the journey of two men (some say four men), walking from the western lands of North America to St. Louis, Missouri. The two men were indigenous people – incorrectly called Indians, back then – specifically, of the Nimi'puu tribe (Nez Perce or Flatheads, depending on the source). In March of 1833, at a meeting of those Indians with the noted explorer, General William Clark, they asked to learn about the white man's way of worshipping the Great Spirit and how to join this God after death.

The timing was perfect. The United States of America was fervently working to get rid of Indians. Andrew Jackson was President and supported The Indian Removal Act that was signed into law in May 1830. Aside from Congressman David Crockett, few opposed it. By September of that year, the Chowtaws of Mississippi were exiled from their homelands. Then, in 1832, the Supreme Court passed a ruling in favor of the Cherokees, but President Jackson ignored the ruling; the Black Hawk War began that same year as did the Seminole War. Jackson was reelected and he pushed to expand the United States; in 1835, the Texas War for Independence began, Arkansas became a state, and Michigan was a state by 1837. By the end of the 1830s, the Trail of Tears had driven 46,000 Native Americans – the Cheek, Chickasaw, Cherokees, Seminole, and other southeastern nations – out of their homelands, opening twenty-five million acres, from Michigan to Arkansas and Georgia to Texas, for settlement by whites; at the same time, killing thousands of displaced persons. Six thousand members of the Cherokee Nation alone died during this period.

Amidst all this hate and turmoil, the two Nimi'puu men who walked to St. Louis astounded the Christian community by going thousands of miles to learn of the white man's God. The *Christian Advocate and Journal* and the *Zion's Herald* printed the story. The public was touched by the message and the Methodist Episcopal Church immediately decided to establish a mission beyond the Rocky Mountains for the Flathead Indians.

Jason Lee was selected to head the Methodist Mission in 1834. When he arrived in Wyoming after an overland trip, he found the Flatheads had been decimated in tribal wars with the Blackfoot tribe. Lee also learned that white man's diseases had killed thousands more. Jason Lee was told of more peaceable tribes farther west and better land to farm so he continued on to Fort Vancouver, the Hudson's Bay Company post, arriving in September of that same year.

This started the events that led to the story of William and Margaret Bailey contained on the following pages.

DAVID LESLIE, arrived in Oregon Country on same ship with Margaret Jewett Smith

Wife: Mary (arrived Sept. 1837)

Henry K.W. Perkins, arrived in Sept. 1837 to work for Methodist Mission at The Dalles

Married: Elvira Johnson (arrived May 1837)

SOME OTHER FRENCH CANADIANS LIVING IN FRENCH PRAIRIE: Jean Baptiste McKay, Andre Longtain, Quesnal and his wife Marie Tchalis

THOMAS J. FARNHAM traveled across land in Peoria Party to Oregon in 1839 and returned to publish a voluminous account of his travels

DR. IRA BABCOCK, physician for the Methodist Mission from 1840-1844 and

ROBERT NEWELL, director of the Oregon Printing Association and originator of *The Oregon Spectator* newspaper (in Oregon City). He published MJB's poems, making her the first published poet in the Northwest.

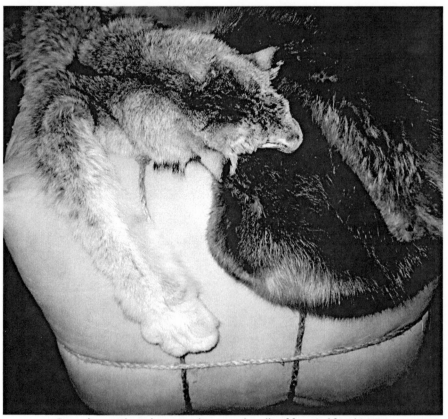

Furs – lynx and two beaver pelts – on a bundle of furs tied for shipping

Champoeg State Heritage Area
OREGON STATE PARKS

CHAPTER 1

WILLIAM
Fur Trapping Trip to Oregon Country in 1835

Taking a deep breath of the crisp air, William J. Bailey gazed around, filling himself with the beauty of the Siskiyou Mountains. But he failed to see the watching eyes. He had fallen behind the pace of the seven other trappers and with none of his party near enough to share his exhilaration, he leaned over the neck of his horse and said, "All this bloody beats New York City." In the past couple of weeks, he had been amazed by the flora of the West and had gathered leaf and needle samples from trees. At the end of this trip, he would learn that he had gathered samples from Coast Douglas Fir, Weeping Spruce, Pacific Yew, and Blue Oak. Grabbing his canteen and drinking, Bailey looked into the distance and drank in the view. Wisps of clouds below him floated and tangled in the tops of the conifers.

Several months prior, in San Francisco, Bailey had sat with these same seven men while they planned this five-hundred-mile trapping expedition on the Siskiyou Trail, going from the central valley of California to the Willamette Valley of Oregon Country. Following foot trails used for hundreds of years by native tribes, they rode a route that afforded the shortest trip, though not the safest. A couple of the men were experienced trappers and had assured Bailey and the others that they could avoid confrontations with natives. Those experienced men were vague when asked how they would avoid any trouble with Indians; over evening campfires, they had talked of peaceful tribes, like the Shookany, Kalapuyans, Coupe, Nawmooit, Shehees, and Peeyou, who were living in Oregon Country.

Ambling along, Bailey's thoughts flew out of his head faster than the little birds he saw darting from the trees. *Never thought I'd find a place like this. Ha! Never thought I'd enjoy eating bear.* Again he took a deep breath and returned the canteen to his saddlebag. Tin clanked against steel, canteen against Colt revolver. He smiled to himself, pleased to know he had the best gun in the bunch, yet he murmured, "It might give me six shots without reloading, but I need to learn how to hit something." Most in this group had single-shot guns or rifles like the Hall breech-loading rifle. Bailey dug in his heels and his horse trotted up to the last packhorse, which was stacked with snares, traps, and furs from beavers, an otter, a lynx, and a black bear. The furs were not the best; this time of year was too warm for quality furs. In Oregon Country, they planned to do serious trapping through the winter.

Riding at the head, the leader John Turner stopped, turned in his saddle, and shouted, "After comin' outta the Siskiyous, we still have a ways to go to the Rogue River. At the Point of Rocks is where we'll stop to camp." They stood in an open grassy area of the Siskiyou Mountains about four-thousand-feet high. In the distance they could see a snow-covered peak. High above, an eagle careened in the winds. "We're almost to Oregon Country," Turner called out. "But don't rush, 'cuz it's a steep trail down from this mountain, and we ain't stoppin' 'til we hit bottom. Like always, we need to set traps 'fore the sun goes down tonight."

Descending, Bailey listened to the clop of hooves and creak of leather from men rocking to and fro in their saddles. He heard the songs of birds, enjoyed the wind whispering past his ears, and gazed at the endless growth of conifers growing to the clouds and crowding the hills. In his calm solitude, he didn't hear the foreboding murmurs. Unseen men watched and sent word across the miles. More than a hundred Indians headed toward the Rogue River, ready to set a trap for these eight men after sunrise.

Once at their campsite, the fur trappers worked quickly, going through the routine they had followed every evening for the last fortnight above the plains of California. Except for the cook, each man took a metal trap or two and set off to the woods or along the riverbank. Within thirty minutes they started to reenter the campsite with their arms full of firewood.

"Where's Bailey?" Turner asked as Bailey appeared in the clearing. "There you are. Take the first turn on watch. Go up that hill over yonder. George'll bring ya some food when he relieves you." George Kirby Gay and Bailey had become friends.

Jesting, Bailey complained, "He'll probably eat most my portion before I even see it. Besides, Gay is scared of the dark so why not send Woodward with him?" John Woodward, one of the more experienced trappers, looked up at the mention of his name and grinned a mile wide. Bailey continued to taunt, "Woodward could guard my food and hold Gay's hand."

The men had started laying down their bedrolls, but stopped to look at Gay. First one chuckled and soon others howled in laughter.

"William, why you no-good skunk of a friend," George Gay hollered as he threw his tin eating plate into Bailey's chest. Then he flung his fork and dove into Bailey's legs. They rolled in the dirt, hitting at each other and laughing.

John Turner pulled Bailey off Gay. "I told you to get on guard duty. When I give an order, do it." Turner was fun loving-like the rest so his men wondered what was bothering him.

Bailey brushed off his pants and picked up his hat. "Yes sir. I need to get my gun." He took his bedroll, and furling the blanket open, threw it around his shoulders before slipping his gun and a worn flask out of his saddlebag.

Turner never missed a thing. "Damn it, Bailey, no spirits on guard duty."

William Bailey nodded and put it back. *Damn liquor! Even when I know better, it calls me. Shit!* He ambled out of camp and up the hill while he tucked his Colt down into his hip pocket. He had decided against buying a holster, not wanting to look like a gunslinger and invite trouble.

Although the last glow from the sun had disappeared hours ago, he walked among shadows: a waxing gibbous moon lit his way. At the top of the hill, he found a boulder surrounded by sword ferns and climbed on top for a better view. Turning to peer full circle, he saw none of the natives who saw him.

An hour passed, and then another.

The chill of the night went to his bones and he felt the ice-cold boulder sapping warmth from his body. He sat on his blanket with it draped over his crossed legs and still he shivered. After a while, he bent his legs to lean his arms and head against his knees. He fought his sleepiness, although from time to time he nodded off. The unseen native men remained alert.

While Bailey dozed, a Great Horned Owl swooped above his head and made no sound in the silent flap of strigidae wings. The Indians saw the bird. A subtle pleasure rippled across their faces as their eyes met; they acknowledged the honor of sharing the night with this regal one. Like the bird, they expected a kill.

George Gay arrived well after midnight to relieve him. Bailey jumped up, hearing the approach of his friend, and took the metal plate extended to him. Before sitting back down to eat, he asked, "Anything happen down in camp?"

"Yeah, after you left, Woodward went back to check his traps. He took so long that Turner sent me downriver to find him. On my way, I came around a bend and saw Woodward comin' with this bundle of fur around his shoulders. Shit! He nabbed a big, blonde beaver! He tol' me that he knew this young beaver was goin' for his trap. So he waited a bit. That's why you got some fresh beaver to eat."

"Tastes good. Especially after having to wait until you decided to get your bloody arse up here to relieve me." Bailey, his black hair glistening in the moonlight and his green eyes twinkling with humor, turned and smiled. He was handsome and the butt of a lot of jokes from the men because of his good looks.

Gay said, "Glad I got to the States when I was ten or I'd still be talkin' like you – a crazy Brit with a bloody this and a bloody that."

Bailey smiled again. "Yeah, you're jealous because you lost your accent." He scraped the tin with his fork and relished his last bite. "I could eat that much again."

Gay squinted, looked around, and wondered, "It's quiet. Shouldn't some frogs or somethin' be makin' noise?"

"Nah, everything knows it's time to sleep. I know I'm going to sleep in just a few minutes. It's a real shame you can't." Bailey got up, picked up his tin plate and fork and straightened his hat. Grinning, he jested, "Hate to go, but I need my sleep to maintain my good looks."

Gay stood and hit Bailey with his hat. "Ain't no women around here so whatta you care?" They laughed. "See you in the morning. At least it gits light early up here. Don't drink all the coffee 'fore I git there."

Bailey started down toward camp and his instincts told him that something was amiss. Gooseflesh rippled down his back as he got to thinking about Gay's question. *It is quiet with no night sounds. Maybe*

Oregon doesn't have all those kinds of critters. But he was a scientist who went to medical school in England, and should have found the situation perplexing. Normally, he had a questioning mind, but he was sleepy and didn't muse about the screaming silence.

At the campsite, he slipped into his bedroll and tucked his blanket around his shoulders. *Oregon sure has cold nights.*

When the early beams of light filtering through the trees, George Gay realized that he had dozed. He rubbed his face with his hands and then, when he looked into the distance, his heart jumped. He saw dark-skinned men coming from the east toward their camp below. Not one or two, but dozens!

Leaping to his feet, he ran to the camp at the base of the hill.

Soon there were more Indians than he could count, and all of the trappers were still asleep in their bedrolls. He had no doubt they meant to kill – tomahawks, knives, and spears were brandished by all of them. They were getting close that Gay could see the small shells sewn around their waists to a piece of rawhide that held their deerskins closed; the skins hooked over their shoulders and hung loosely to their thighs.

Gay began to shake John Turner. Still looking at the Indians who continued to gather around them, Gay leaned down and gave a frantic whisper, "John, wake up! We're surrounded by at least a hundred Indians!"

Although Gay's words had been a soft murmur, others in his party stirred. John Turner jolted upright and saw the Indians.

Like spokes in a wagon wheel, the trappers lay wrapped in their blankets around the hub of the still-smoldering campfire. Each man had his pair of boots standing next to him, some used their saddle as a pillow, and each of them had a handgun or rifle slipped somewhere out of sight. Bailey still had his Colt in his pocket.

As Turner sat up, many of his men were waking and seeing the Indians. He told them, "Men, stay calm. No cause for alarm."

Even the horses sensed the approaching danger and in their frenzy began to pull at the ropes that held them to trees. All the burdens from the horses' backs had been strewn on the ground the night before. Hooves pounded on furs, equipment, reins, and any saddles that had been left there.

Suddenly, all eight trappers were wide-awake. Bailey slipped from his bedroll and stood.

Another trapper jumped to his feet with his rifle pointing at a bunch of Indians walking toward him. "What in tarnation, Turner! Hell, they ain't come for a sit-down breakfast! Don't tell us there's no cause for alarm!"

When the sun breached the top of the eastern hill, the Indians moved faster and circled in a smooth movement, like rising floodwaters, creeping closer to engulf everything. Loud whoops emitted simultaneously at some unseen signal as scores of red men rushed with raised tomahawks and spears.

More than ten to one!

Around the campfire, one trapper squatted and aimed, another reached into his blankets for his rifle, Turner whipped his gun up to eye level, Gay gripped a pistol in each hand, and they started firing. Six Indians fell with the first shots. With no time to reload, the two trappers with single-shot guns began to use their rifles as clubs, flinging the rifle butts left and right into faces and chests. Screaming war cries, many came at them with raised war clubs and soon a couple of red men straddled those two dead trappers to cut off their scalps.

Struggling to pull the Colt from his pocket, Bailey didn't fire with the others. Two Indians, with raised tomahawks, headed straight for him and came close enough to smell his fear before he tipped the barrel up. *This close I can't possibly miss*! He pulled the trigger with his hand deep in the pocket. One dropped. Pivoting to his left, he fired again and the second fell before he ripped the gun from his pocket, tearing his breeches.

Turner screamed, "Run! Just git outta here!" And the six men – five barefooted and George Gay, the only trapper in boots – tried to run, but with every step they had to stop and fight. The air was thick with noise and smoke. Trappers screamed curses and red men bellowed war cries while guns exploded and tomahawks made dull thuds against flesh.

Within seconds, Turner had emptied his gun. Six Indians were dead from his shots, but ten more were coming at him. He turned to run and stopped, seeing George Gay on the ground with an Indian above him, tomahawk raised. Turner was a Goliath of a man; the natives were short.

He seized a huge fir limb from the smoldering campfire and swung it. With a thud and flying sparks, the blow went to the face, demolishing the Indian's features as the rough bark scrapped the skin off; the native toppled into the embers. The end of the limb still glowed red and smoked. Turner used it like a club and two other Indians fell, leaving the smell of burning flesh lingering in his nostrils; having a moment, he snatched a thick-bladed knife from a dead Indian and killed another while one came from behind. He turned and gasped with the sting of pain in his left arm. Taking no time to think about his bloody wound, he took the assailant by the neck and whirled him against others.

Turner found an instant to cry out again. "Run!" He pulled Gay to his feet and handed him the knife. "Go!" Turner took two strides to follow and into his path screaming red men ran. Escape defied him. Standing a head taller than most of the Indians and outweighing them, Turner easily broke the arm of one and seized a spear. He stabbed and left the bloodied shaft protruding from the Indian's gut. Sensing another coming from behind, he ducked down and grabbed a couple of tomahawks from dead warriors; with one in each hand, he began slashing in all directions. Using their own weapons against them seemed to give him more strength. Sweat and blood splattered his face and covered his body – some his, but more theirs. He continued killing and maiming until he saw Bailey on his hands and knees with a muddy pool of blood forming below his head. Bailey struggled to rise.

Turner took hold of Bailey under an arm, pulled him to standing, held on to him, and kept moving toward the wooded area. Bailey's feet trailed in the dirt.

Gay jabbed one Indian in the chest with a force that knocked the man against another and the two Indians fell against each other – seeming to dance for a moment – before falling into the hot coals of the campfire. When Gay turned and slashed the knife across the neck of one with black stripes painted across his face, Turner ran past. "Follow me!"

Turner and Gay sidestepped and jumped over the bodies of downed Indians scattered around the campsite until they found another trapper wounded on the ground. Gay raised him, wrapped the bleeding man's arm around his own neck, and pulled him away from the foray. In the woods, John Woodward plodded ahead of them with another wounded man. The three men hurried with the three wounded in tow until they were far away and in the quiet of the trees. They collapsed beside a creek.

Turner lowered Bailey and turned to listen. He felt in his pocket to make sure he still had his tinderbox. He did.

Gay asked, "Why didn't they follow us? Where are they?"

Woodward commented, "I thought we were goners 'til I saw squaws roundin' up all our horses and ridin' away." During the heat of the battle, while the barefoot men fought the Indians with their knives and guns, other Indians handed saddles and furs to riders who sped out of sight.

Gay said, "How did ya see that? I couldn't see anything but the Injuns coming at me."

Turner nodded. "While I was fightin' I saw two of 'em raise the single-shot rifles above their heads. In their other hands they had the scalps of our friends. They gave out a bloodcurdling yelp."

"Yeah," Gay said, "Come to think of it, I saw the Indians taking all the boots."

As the group of trappers sat at the small stream and washed their bloodied feet, Turner remarked, "Guess that's why they didn't follow us. 'Cuz they just wanted all our stuff – furs, knapsacks, food supplies, and trapping equipment. Once they had 'em, they didn't care if we were dead or alive." He stopped talking a moment and puzzled, "But it is hard to believe that we got away. There were so many of 'em. Those damn Rogue River Indians."

"How do ya know they're Rogue River Indians?"

Turner shook his head and raised his voice. "Damn it all! When ya don't know what tribe they are, ya just call 'em by the place they were. Don't you know that?" He passed a hand through his hair and calmed.

Bailey groaned.

For the first time, George Gay looked at Bailey's bleeding face. "God Almighty, your face!"

Unable to speak, with a wound gaping open from his upper lip through the jaw and down his neck, Bailey took a handkerchief from his pocket, dipped it into the water, and pressed it against his jaw. He groaned in agony – a hoarse sound emitted from deep in his throat. Bailey knew his chances. *I won't make it unless I stop this bleeding. Aghh, I prefer being the doctor than the patient!*

Turner saw Bailey struggling to remove his shirt; he helped ease Bailey's arm out. As Turner walked off to help another, Bailey began ripping his shirt in strips.

The small group rested and soaked their cuts in the soothing water of the stream. Besides blood, they were filthy from mud, ashes, smeared war paint, sweat, and pieces of twigs and leaves. Gay stood, walked out into the water, and fell backward until completely immersed. Others followed. Not Bailey; he continued to tie the shirt strips together and started wrapping his wound. No one talked. They had no food, no containers to carry water, no ammunition for their guns – but worst of all, they had no shoes. They knew they could go nowhere without shoes. Of the six, Turner, Gay, and Woodward had minor injuries; Bailey had a serious wound, and the other two were nearly dead. They listened to the ripple of water and the ripping of Bailey's shirt.

Cooler and cleaner, George Gay left the water. Among the dense scrub bushes and towering trees, the air was pure and clear; the calm view went on and on wherever they looked. Gay pulled his knife from his waistband and removed his leather jacket, saying, "Turner, you're first."

Turner glanced over to Gay. "What?"

Gay spread his jacket on the ground and said, "Put your foot here so I's can cut the leather to your size. I'll make one pair at a time. When I run out of jacket, that's all the moccasins we'll have."

With precision and care, he began cutting. The piece across the top of the foot – shaped like a trapezoid with curved edges – went up to the ankle to cover the whole foot and attached to the bottom by thin strips. Later, when he had finished Turner's pair, they could see that he only had enough leather for one more pair.

While Gay worked, Turner and Woodward walked around the area looking for berries, hazelnuts, or anything edible while the others sprawled on the ground, exhausted.

By afternoon, when Gay finished the first foot on the second pair of moccasins, he took off his leather breeches. He cursed to no one in particular in a low mutter, "Damn it all! Why in tarnation am I doin' this? Shit." At sunset, he still worked on making moccasins from his cut leather, and he continued until dark.

Again, Turner felt for his tinderbox. He squeezed the three-inch metal cylinder in his pocket. "Woodward and Gay, help me find firewood." They went to gather downed trees and limbs in the quiet of the woods.

Bailey sat with his back against a tree and watched the others work. *How ironic, the calm and quiet of this scene compared with this morning's battle scene. Damn. Wish I had a drink.*

After Turner decided that they had enough wood, Gay started cutting thin splints off the logs. Woodward prepared and arranged the wood, breaking some limbs with his knee, until he had a pile with a cavity beneath.

"I think that's good," Turner said and bent down on one of his knees. He unscrewed the tinderbox lid and let it fall – a chain held the lid to the bottom of the metal box. He dumped the firesteel and flint out on the ground and reached in with two fingers to get a bit of the charcloth that was jammed down at the bottom of the box. After placing a small amount of that burnt linen on top of a few wood splinters, all was ready. Reaching for the D-shaped firesteel, he slipped two of his fingers into the center of it and picked up the flint stone with his other hand. The charcloth and wood splinters sat on a stone in the space below the firewood, and he leaned close before he struck the metal against the flint. Two strikes and a spark landed. He bent down and blew – a slow, soft blow. The kindling burst into flames.

Gay added more slivers of wood and soon they had a fire.

Turner commented, "Even in rain, a tinderbox makes a fire."

The six found sleep difficult and curled close together on the hard ground while the cold night air crept over them. Turner and Woodward had brought back some berries to eat and had broken boughs from fir trees to provide bedding to insulate against the cold ground. Some of the branches were used to cover them against the night air. When they laid their aching bodies down for the night, insects found a way through the fir needles to feast on their bare skin. They inched closer to the large fire.

In the darkness, Woodward complained, "Damn it all! How we goin' ta know if those savages ain't goin' to come in the night and slit our throats? They're goin' ta find us fer sure 'cuz of this blazin' fire!"

Gay answered, "Shut up! Hear those wolves howlin'? I ain't sleepin' without no fire!"

John Turner frowned and sighed, "We ain't got nothing left that those Indians want. Sleep, men."

One by one, the six men succumbed to their exhaustion. When slumber took Gay, he tossed in mumbling fits. Bailey glanced at his friend. *He's fighting the Indians a second time. Damn! This throbbing in my jaw is excruciating. And I can't stop worrying about the days ahead. Most of all, I need some booze!*

In the morning, two of the men did not get up to take a pee.

When John Turner squatted down by one, the man whispered, "Let me be awhile. I don't feel so good."

Then Turner went to the second and shook his head. "Shit! He's gone. Gay, come over here and help me drag him up there above the waterline. We'll pile some river rocks on him. There ain't no way we can bury him proper."

While three of them were putting the rocks over their friend's body, Bailey sat at the edge of the stream again with his feet in the water. He unwrapped his wound and dipped his handkerchief into the cool water. Gritting his teeth, he applied it to his face over and over. It stung like the moment the Indian had rammed the tomahawk into his face.

Bailey muttered aloud to no one in particular, "Damn! Wish I had some whiskey to drink." No one would have understood him anyway; his words were slurred sounds, coming from a swollen tongue and immovable lips. *Actually, whiskey poured over my face would be better. Sting like hell but it'd clean out that wound.*

He kept muttering in the same fashion while he rewrapped the torn shirt under his chin and over the top of his head, retying some of the knots to get the length he needed. He grimaced and pulled the cloth tight to hold the wound closed. He took another piece and did the same until he had covered the eight-inch long gap. With his elbows on his knees, he rested his head in his hands and groaned, "Ahhgg." He felt dizzy and nauseated.

Woodward grumbled as he lifted a heavy boulder for the makeshift bier and struggled up the hill. "Whatta we goin' ta do? Thars five of us an' only three pair of moccasins done."

Gay, standing in his underclothing with a big rock in his hands, said, "I always knew you can't count! But can't you see?" Gay lifted his leg before he tossed the rock on the pile. "Those Injuns didn't get my boots. I was wearin' 'em. We need one more pair. I'll make 'em right now."

"Hold on, maybe it ain't necessary," Turner said.

They looked down the hill and saw Bailey leaning over the other man. Turner asked, "He's dead?"

Bailey took a small rock and wrote in the sand. "S-O-O-N."

In a few minutes, Gay slipped into his leather breeches with foot-shaped holes.

Turner asked, pointing to the man soon to die, "Why don't we slip off his pants for you?"

Gay quipped, "Hell, no! Shit, those worn-out wool broadfalls? Wool itches my butt! Besides, my leather ones with holes are warmer and better lookin' than his."

The four left.

George Gay, John Woodward, and William Bailey continued to rely on their leader John Turner to get them to the only civilization in Oregon Country, the area of the Hudson's Bay Company. The four made their way north toward the Willamette Valley, stopping to rest and find food by picking mushrooms and berries or catching a startled snake before it wriggled away. All four had wounds that weakened them and without sufficient food they became weaker.

At least water was plentiful; the rains had started. Water poured from crevices, out of hillsides, and filled the streams everywhere.

After a few days, Turner was healing on his wounded arm. Gay commented that his cuts were no longer hot to the touch. Woodward was on the mend, too. Not Bailey. He tired more than the others, and his wound defied healing. They knew that Bailey was bad off; the gap on his face had begun to fester. And they all knew Bailey's other problem; his body craved liquor.

And it kept raining.

Bailey stopped to drink water often. He kept falling behind. At first, no one complained and they waited for him to catch up. With his wound, drinking water was difficult, but chewing the hard unripe berries, Filbert nuts, and grasshoppers was impossible. When they found food, Gay would chew Bailey's portion and spit it out into Bailey's hand.

"Ain't no other way for you," Gay lamented.

Bailey nodded and with his fingers inserted the mush into the small opening he could make with his mouth.

Though useless without ammunition, they still carried their guns. They had no game to clean, but their knives served them; Gay worked one morning sharpening a stick to spear fish and on another day he tried attaching his knife to a sturdy wooden stake for spearing, but learned that spear fishing was a skill that needed practice. Woodward knew how to build snares for small animals, but he lacked proper materials and his makeshift traps didn't work. Turner tried using his shirt to net fish and had some luck.

At one point, after climbing up the slope of a hill, they found the other side devoid of plants and trees as a result of a mudslide. At that moment, they stood in a slow drizzle with water dripping from their hair, noses, chins, and off their soaking clothes. Hope seemed liquid as well, dripping from them with each passing day and washing away with the rain.

Turner spit and turned to his men to say, "I don't wanna backtrack and go around this. Let's go through the mud on down to that creek." No one said anything so he kept talking, "We'd save time and strength. So let's go!"

They slipped, rolled, and found that their feet became mired in the muck. "Shit, I pulled my foot out and the damn moccasin got stuck down thar," Woodward muttered. He dug his arm down to his elbow in the mud and found it.

Turner, flat on his back after slipping, shouted, "Men, take off your moccasins. We can't lose 'em."

Bailey sat down, exhausted from the effort of moving through the mud, and passed out.

Gay shouted, "Bailey, Bailey! Hell, he's out cold. Turner, help me pull him down this damn hill."

At the bottom, they washed Bailey in the creek, and he regained consciousness.

Turner leaned over to help him up to walk. "Damn it all, Bailey. We can't stop."

As William Bailey stumbled along, he felt his fever rising. By the time they stopped for the night, he was burning.

Every night, someone tossed and turned with nightmares. After the slide down the muddy hill, Bailey's dreams showed a glass of whiskey sitting on a table in front of him and his hands couldn't reach it. His mother stood laughing while he struggled to clutch the glass. Delirious with fever, he hallucinated in bizarre and colorful scenes of reds and purples with her flinging bottles at the trees. A green oozing liquid exploded from the glass on impact, sending slimy chartreuse goop all over the lush forest and covering him. The liquid stuck to him, like mud; he slipped, fell, and rolled, covered with the muck. And she – in a furling scarlet skirt with her hair a bright fuchsia – kept throwing whiskey bottles at him, until his face dripped with mud and green slime. He could not breathe and screamed, "I'm suffocating!"

Turner saw Bailey restless with fever, crept over to him, and touched the burning face. Bailey moaned. Slipping off his own shirt, Turner went to the stream to wet it. He draped the cloth over Bailey's forehead and in an instant the shirt became hot. Turner went to the water to cool it again and returned. This time, Turner talked, "Damn it all, Bailey, you can't die! Fight! Come on, fight this fever!"

Now Bailey began to shiver.

Turner looked over his shoulder at the sleeping men before he slipped off his woolen broadfalls – caked in dried mud. He covered Bailey and began to whisper in his ear as he tucked the dirty pants around him. "Don't die! Shit!" Turner's voice cracked and his eyes moistened. "I knew those Indians might attack us. I was warned that the Rogue River Indians wanted revenge. I couldn't tell any of you." Turner's eyes glazed over, but he fought his tears. "Hell, I never imagined that over a hundred might attack." He took the sleeve of his underwear and wiped his nose. "Bailey, I can't lose another man. Damn it all, fight!" He stood and walked in his long red underwear to the creek again. When he returned, he wiped and dabbed Bailey's face, while he continued assuaging his guilt. "Who woulda thought there'd be so many." He let his dark thoughts disappear into the night; he was getting tired. "Bailey, damn it all, fight!"

Finally the fever broke. Turner took back his clothes and slipped away. He stepped into his broadfalls, hung his shirt on a tree to dry, and put more wood on the fire before reclining to sleep.

Unknown to Turner, Bailey had watched him from half-closed eyes as he dressed and threw wood on the fire. He knew he had not dreamt what he heard Turner say. *I'll fight! Not for you though. I want to live to kill those bloody Injuns.*

After a night with visions of his mother, Bailey would think of her for most the day while the group trudged through the thick undergrowth of Oregon Country. In an endless and silent rant, he complained about his mother: *I can't get away from her. I traveled halfway around the world to California on that bloody ship! Damn! From New York, she harasses me still. Why can't she let me live my own life? I studied medicine because she wanted that. She dragged my sister, brother, and me to North America to get me away from my drinking friends. Didn't she realize I would find more drinking friends wherever I go?*

Then again, I had a good job as a surgeon once on these shores. I let booze destroy that! I had to get away from her to live my own life, but now she nags me in my sleep.

Bailey reflected for a moment. *It's all in my mind. I let her nag me while I sleep, while I walk, and every day while I think because I know I was dishonest by stealing money from my father's account. I could have asked permission, but I just took it. The drink drove me. But I did it. Why did he die before I could see him and make amends? I know the drinking is no good. Look at me, shaking and bawling for a drink!*

On the fourth day, Bailey collapsed at midday.

Turner went to him. "Bailey, you gotta git up," and pulled him up. The heat of the fever surged again. "He's burnin' up. He's got to rest, and we need food. While he's resting we can work on our next meal."

"This is the worst time of day to fish or look for game. Damn, we need to go on."

Turner insisted, "Bailey's got to rest and cool down. His fever's back. Let's find a stream and put him in."

Woodward griped, "Hellfire and damnation!"

Gay gave Woodward a push, and they fell into a brawl.

In disgust, Turner pulled them apart and shouted, "You're fools to waste the little strength you have in a broil. Go practice spearing a fish in that deep pool over there. If the savages can do it so can we! Go on and find something to eat!"

They caught one small fish that afternoon – not even enough to sustain two men let alone four.

Gay cut more holes in his leather pants to replace the soles on three moccasins. He could no longer declare his leather breeches better looking than worn, wool broadfalls.

By the next day, they all started to weaken; they searched, but found little to eat. Without sustenance, their minds began to deteriorate along with their bodies. When they found no other food, snails and insects became their diet. Bickering and contentions increased.

Two men were dragging Bailey between them.

"How'd ya know we're headin' north? We ain't seen the sun fer days," complained Woodward.

Gay retorted, "Shut up, Woodward! Turner's right. We're headin' north."

"How'n the hell do *you* know?"

"I know! Now shut up."

Turner answered, "George sailed on ships for years. He knows his directions. You worked on the ship called *Beaver*. Ain't that right, George?"

"My last ship was a whaling vessel called *Kitty*."

At this point, Gay stood in his tattered long underwear. What had been left of his leather breeches had been swept away in a river they had crossed. But he still had his boots. Woodward always covered Bailey with his shirt at night, but he wanted it back during the day. Turner put his shirt on Bailey during the day. Everything they wore was falling apart from crawling up slopes with nettles and jagged rocks, from stumbling and falling on protruding roots. The thorny bushes seemed alive; they reached for them to scratch and tear.

Gay used his shirt for fishing; after awhile, it went to pieces. At least he had bagged two big fish before it was nothing but shreds. Then they used Turner's shirt to fish. No one knew which roots to eat, although they tried many; without a pot to boil them, they were hard, bitter and impossible to chew. They gave up on roots. As the days passed, most berries were long gone, even the unripe ones had been taken by wildlife. There were slugs – some bright yellow and others slimy black, both kinds as long as a man's hand – but no one could stomach the thought of eating them.

On the sixth day, Bailey still was incapable of walking by himself and Woodward refused to help carry him any longer. "It's too damn hard ta drag him along. Why we doin' it? Let's leave him!"

Turner made clear a rule of his. "We're in this together. While Bailey's alive we help him. If you want to go off on your own, do it! Damn it!"

Turner and Gay carried Bailey that day, but the next morning Woodward pulled Bailey's arm around his shoulder. "Hell, let's git goin'. Someone git on his other side."

After they had been walking for more than a week, one morning they saw a log cabin in the distance. Everyone quickened their pace, but no one spoke. Hope glowed in their faces. *A French Canadian fur trapper might be staying there, although there's no smoke coming from the chimney.* Bailey let his mind reason that at this time of day the Frenchman could be out setting his traps. So, in those few minutes, while they hastened toward the cabin, Bailey brightened and hobbled along seeming stronger.

Their minds began to imagine food, and their tongues began to salivate.

Gay whispered aloud, though talking to himself, "Is that a whiff of bacon cooking?"

Woodward blinked several times, looking at a swaying movement in a tree; he swore out loud and pointed, "Damn it all! I'm seein' a deer hangin' from that tree."

Bailey dreamed of a full whiskey bottle.

Turner said, "Stay calm. We'll be lucky to find a supply of dry grits and a pot to boil them in."

As they walked through the doorway with no door, a gust of wind hit their backs and blew away their hopes. They stopped dead in their tracks while their senses adjusted to the dank and darkness. The cabin stunk from animal droppings, and a broken corner of the roof gave evidence that trappers had long ago abandoned the place. Their anticipation of venison and bacon had let them smell and taste their hopes; their disappointment growled from deep in their stomachs.

As they stood listening to the rumblings inside their bodies, a rustling sound from a dark corner startled them. They turned to see a young squaw coming with a raised stick. Turner seized her stick to block the blow and wrapped his other arm around her waist; he lifted the squealing and fighting girl off her feet. She beat her fists against Turner's shoulder, kicked at him with her knees and feet, and squirmed so much that he fell to the floor. Quickly she straddled him, whacking with her fists at his chest. Though tired, hungry, and disappointed, the men erupted in mirth. Titters and chuckles burst from them until the cabin echoed with loud guffaws.

Confused by the laughter, she stopped fighting.

Smiling, Turner lifted her off his body and set her down next to him. He rolled to his side. They were eye to eye. While the others continued to laugh, Turner and the girl stared in silence. A minute passed before Turner got to his feet and extended a hand to help her up. In a soft voice he talked in English.

Gazing at his face, she listened. She had smudges of dried dirt on her legs where leggings had partially slipped off; she wore a deerskin, stitched from many small pieces, draping from her shoulder. Some seashells were threaded and woven with reeds to make a bracelet and her black hair was tousled from wrestling with Turner. Before long, she looked closely at their gaunt faces and rags for clothing. In her expressive face was reflected the plight of these men.

Calmly, she took a step backwards, searched the dirt floor, and found a smoothed stick at her feet. Grasping her ebony hair and with a twist of her wrist she coiled her tresses onto the back of her head; the stick held it in place.

Turning to his men, Turner said, "It'd be good to sleep here tonight with a roof over us, but it's still morning. We can't lose a day of walking. We gotta move on."

The woman walked to a darkened corner and took a bundle out. Upon returning to the center of the cabin, she kneeled and placed her things on the dirt floor before she reached into a leather pouch. Extending her hand to Gay, she gave him a small gray biscuit-like food.

He took a bite. "Just like bacon!" He grinned.

She pulled some out for Woodward.

He thanked her with a nod. "Shit almighty, mine tastes like venison."

Gay held out his hand for Bailey's portion and she refused. So Gay took a bite of his. "Watch me," he told her. He chewed and reached for Bailey's hand to spit out the mush.

When Bailey crammed the food into his mouth, she understood and handed Gay another portion.

At last, she handed Turner his piece – bigger than the others. While they ate, she removed her loosened leggings and rewrapped them, holding them with strips of rawhide, and then she sat and made two braids in her hair.

Turner told the others, "I'm goin' to talk this pidgin language that's used among the whites and Indians. I ain't too good at it, but I may as well try." He turned to her and asked what they were eating in pidgin.

Tucking a stray strand of hair at her temple, she finished the last braid and a pleased expression filled her face as she told him that they were eating roots that were pounded and baked. While the men ate in utter contentment, she seemed content as well – to talk. Turner nodded from time to time as she rambled in her soft voice.

They finished her dried food and Turner said, "She asked to come along. Let's take her with us. Maybe she's better at finding food than us."

Looks passed between the men until Gay blurted out, "So, Turner, seems like you've taken a liking to her."

"It ain't that."

Woodward said, "Ain't no need to explain. She can come, and we knows she's yours."

A bit of food had brought more than sustenance; hope returned to their lives. Heading north, they continued to talk with Turner about the woman.

"Why she askin' to come along?"

Turner thought a minute. "She told me that she is from the Tetawken tribe; we call them the Cayuse Indians. Her name's Mai-yi. No one from her tribe lives down here; they live far to the north in Oregon Country. So I figure that she's probably a runaway slave. If she is, her owners will kill her if they find her."

"You mean a slave to some white trappers?"

"No, no, different tribes buy or capture Injuns from other tribes to use them for wives or slaves. There ain't no Cayuse down here so she's here alone. It's obvious she's got troubles." Turner looked at the confused faces of his men. "I think she wants to come with us 'cuz she thinks we could protect her."

That night Mai-yi speared two fish and gave them a lesson on how to spear. She served more of her dry biscuits with the fish that she cooked in edible leaves.

On their journey, they saw no white men and they hid from any Indians they heard or saw in the distance. Mai-yi gathered edible insects, leaves, and roots while they walked. One day she found little frogs in abundance; the men called them "little green bandits" because a black eye-stripe extended from the nose through the eyes to the frog's shoulders. She showed the men where to look for the little bandits and they feasted, although the tree frog's legs were no more than the size of the squaw's smallest finger. After a couple of days, they found no more.

Another day, Turner shouted, "Look what I found!" He ripped off his shirt to capture a newt with rough skin. The creature was fat and three times the size of the tree frogs. When Mai-yi saw it, she screamed and told Turner to let it go. In her pidgin, she explained it was poisonous and could kill a man. When the newt fell out of his shirt, Turner exclaimed, "Look, it has one leg shorter than his others."

"It grow new tails, legs, and eyes when it need them," Mai-yi said in pidgin. "That little leg grow to be a new leg now. If you catch one by tail, newt run away. Then you left with only a tail in hand. After that, he grow new one."

Finally on the twelfth day of their trek, they came to a valley with a river.

Turner brightened and exclaimed, "Look! It's the Columbia River! We can use fallen trees to float to Fort Vancouver."

Gay exploded, "Are you crazy? This ain't the Columbia. The Columbia flows east and west. This has to be the Willamette River 'cuz it's flowin' north."

Turner lost his temper. "We've been walkin' so many days. It has to be the Columbia."

"Well, it ain't and I ain't floatin' on no river – don't matter which one it is!" Gay was adamant. "Injuns are goin' ta pick you off!"

Turner retorted, "Well, it don't matter what name it has. It'll git us wherever we're goin' faster. You want to walk? You're the crazy one! In a day or two, floating down the river, we'll reach help. There's a mission I heard about on the Willamette River and Fort Vancouver is on the Columbia. We can't go wrong on this river."

"Hell! I ain't goin' on that river," Gay insisted.

"Well, I am. And I'm taking Bailey. Don't matter if we get to that mission or Hudson's Bay Company. I want to find a doctor for Bailey – at least, medicine and food."

Gay calmed his voice and tried one more argument. "Turner, there are lots of rivers here in Oregon Country; this one could be goin' nowhere you want to be."

Turner was tired of talk and walked away. "Woodward, if you're comin' with me, help me find a downed tree – a couple big ones that ain't gonna fall apart when we roll them to the river. Make sure they have some limbs sticking out so we have handholds." Turner disappeared into the woods and Mai-yi went with him. Suddenly his voice echoed back, "Remember, we need big ones. Big enough for two or three of us on 'em."

Woodward went to look for a trunk.

Gay stood firm. "I ain't goin' with ya. So I ain't lookin' for no trees on the ground! Damn it! I'm leaving."

Bailey heard Gay. Using all his strength to raise his arm in Gay's direction, he pleaded in silence.

Gay saw Bailey's sorrowful eyes, but shook his head and turned to go north by himself.

With Mai-yi, the three men – John Turner, William J. Bailey, and John Woodward –floated north on the Willamette. They traveled the river, floating by the will of the water – slow in the wide, deep expanses, fast in the narrows. They banked each night to eat and sleep. On the thirteenth night, they ate the last of Mai-yi's dry biscuits with a fish. Since they no longer walked, the squaw had no opportunity to gather greens, insects, and roots; they had to rely on fishing when they came to shore for the night. All were famished and weak. On two nights, they had no food so, on the following days, they had little strength to hang onto the floating tree trunks. Bailey had no strength at all. Switching logs from time to time, each took turns holding Bailey on.

Every day it rained now.

On the fourteenth day, a bend in the river appeared ahead. Out of sight and around that bend, white water and boulders awaited. Woodward and Bailey hit the rapids first; they were flung in the air and landed near the shore; their log spun onto the bank below them on the rocks. Woodward jumped up on the shore to warn the other two coming. In the roar of the river, his scream was drowned; the second log, carrying Turner and Mai-yi, hit the rapids. Caught by surprise, they rode the water, going under and popping up several times until they disappeared from Woodward's sight.

"Shit, theys gone! Where'd they go? Don't think they hit those big rocks," Woodward told Bailey, who groaned. "Let's git back on so as we can find 'em."

Bailey groaned louder.

A kingfisher flew past them as Woodward dislodged their log from two boulders where it had wedged. He pushed it to the water. Pulling the trunk a few yards across the rocks was a struggle for Woodward, and he tore a hole in his moccasins. "Damn it all, Bailey, can't ya try 'n help!"

Soon they were floating north again, but Mai-yi and Turner had vanished.

On the afternoon of day fifteen, their situation improved; the sun came out and Woodward saw the log buildings of the Methodist Mission. Since

Indians had attacked them at the Rogue River, they had lived over two weeks in the wilderness and had traveled over two hundred miles.

Straddling his log and paddling with his hands, Woodward tried to turn the log toward shore beneath the Mission, but the river took them to the opposite side. They rolled off the log into the shallows of the shore. Woodward dragged Bailey onto the land where they collapsed.

It was the fall of 1835, and there was activity around the three mission buildings. A handful of native boys – dressed in cotton shirts and worsted pants that didn't quite fit in size or character – were cutting and stacking wood when one boy noticed the beached men across the river. In their native tongue, the boys chattered together before calling out in English, "Look!"

With wariness, the missionary Brother Cyrus Shepard turned from his work in the garden and saw the trappers across the river. He called to Jason Lee after sending two of the bigger Indian boys across the river in a dilapidated wooden boat to get Bailey and Woodward.

Standing stiff and straight in his black coat and white shirt and looking down at the two strangers struggling up the bank with the help of the boys, Jason Lee sounded irritated, "I am Superintendent Jason Lee, in charge of this Mission. This man is Brother Shepard, our teacher. We can't help you. We have no extra food and no space for you to sleep. I'm sorry, but we have our own problems."

The children eased Bailey's arms from around their necks and lowered him prone onto the ground. He collapsed near Lee's feet.

Lee continued, "We erected these buildings for the Methodist Mission last autumn and we are still working hard to establish a livable place. We are struggling to exist, having great difficulty growing food for ourselves and for the few Indian children whom we are trying to convert to Christianity. They are half-breed *Métis* whom no one wants." He stopped to take a breath.

Bailey didn't know if the children spoke or understood English, but he thought, *By the tone of this Jason Lee's voice and the look on their faces, they know he's refusing to help us.*

One of the boys ran into one of the log buildings and returned with a short, older man who stood and listened to Lee.

Lee started again. "Like I was saying, we arrived last fall and nearly starved through last winter."

At that moment, Jason Lee's brother Daniel rode up, leading a second horse. "Jason, we need to leave for the meeting. What's this?"

Lee threw his arms up in disgust. "Daniel, I'll tell you while we ride." He frowned while mounting his horse. "I must leave." The two Lees rode away.

Brother Shepard came forward and squatted near the trappers. "You must excuse our leader. He has many problems. Last winter we had fourteen Kalapuyan children in my mission school and seven of them died. Now I have over twenty and we must use all the food we have to keep these boys alive." He pointed toward a garden. "We planted potatoes and corn but, you can see, the weeds are growing the best." He leaned over to examine the men on the ground and saw Bailey's wound. "My, my, this man is greatly injured. We don't have a doctor here, and he needs medical help. I don't know what we can do. Well, we have extra shirts – I'll go get one. He seems to be shivering from fever even on this sunny day."

The older man, who had been watching in silence, stepped forward. Dressed in moccasins and a worn-out blanket coat, he made a little bow of his head. In a thick French accent, he introduced himself to Woodward and Bailey by saying, "Hello, my name Joseph Gervais." Turning toward Brother Shepard, who was entering the cabin for a shirt, Gervais called out, "If you let the boys help, I take 'em to my house."

Before disappearing inside the building, the missionary agreed with a raised arm. "Yes, do."

Gervais squinted into the sun, adding more lines to his wrinkled face, and pointed north. "My place sits over yonder outta sight and back around a bend in the river. My wife always has food cookin' and you're welcome."

Brother Shepard returned and explained, "Mr. Gervais is a French Canadian who has made some chairs for the Mission. He just now delivered a couple in his wagon over there." He pointed across the dirt yard where a hitched wagon waited. "You are fortunate that he was here."

Gervais said, "We be needin' to git this injured man to Fort Vancouver to the doctor. But I'm takin' them to my place for the night; they need to eat first." Gervais assisted the boys in raising Bailey to stand. "Yes, both of these men need food."

As the boys hobbled with Bailey, they first passed a woodpile, then some discarded iron contraptions rusting under a tree, and finally several broken baskets strewn here and there, until the group walked along the edge of a field. Woodward ran his hand over the wheat heads and pulled off some grains. "Theys got a good crop of wheat."

"I plant this wheat," Gervais said with a big grin. "Maybe you not know that wheat is money here." He hesitated a moment before adding, "So don't be a pulling off the tassels like that."

"S'cuse me." Woodward jerked back his hand and slipped it into his pocket.

They arrived at the wagon and the two native boys started to lift Bailey onto the bed when Gervais stopped them. "Wait, boys! I use my capote." Gervais took off his old blanket coat and spread it in the wagon bed. "My capote keeps him warm. Now put him in." The capote was made from a Hudson's Bay Company blanket with yellow, red, green, and indigo stripes against a once-white background.

Standing in a shirt with holes in the elbows and dark-green broadfalls, Gervais covered Bailey in his worn capote, tucking the tattered edges around him. Then he climbed up on the driver's seat and said, "This fine wagon was built by me." Woodward sat next to him while the boys climbed in back next to Bailey.

Woodward asked, "How's come you got food, but the Mission ain't got none?"

Gervais started rambling while the horses pulled the wagonload along the riverside. "Like I said, wheat is money. I have a one hundred twenty-five acre parcel and lots of wheat from last year; after this year harvest, I'm gonna have more. I can trade for anything with my grain. The Mission have no wheat harvest yet. Maybe this answer is better, Monsieur. I live here for years, and I trap for years before coming to live on the French Prairie. First, I trap for the North West Company and then Hudson's Bay Company. Furs were my money back then. Now I retired from trapping.

"My wife live here all her life and she knows how to find food from the land and how to prepare it for eating all winter. I know how to hunt and fish, besides trapping. Those men at the Mission know nothing and don't like us telling them how to do things." He laughed, showing some missing teeth. "Maybe they no ask me 'cuz I'm Catholic." Dust puffed from his broadfalls when he slapped his thigh and roared with laughter.

They traveled a couple of miles when a homestead appeared in the distance. "There she is – my house and barn. I make all the logs square. It very good house."

Delicious aromas of cooking soup greeted the group when they left the wagon. The two Indian boys looped Bailey's arms over their shoulders again, and Bailey worked on putting one foot in front of the other. His head hung down as he watched his feet – a big toe protruded from one moccasin where it had worn through, and he could feel the ground from a hole in the bottom of the other.

Gervais took his capote and hung it on an iron hook nailed to logs inside the door. "Here, here! Come meet my wife, Mrs. Marguerite. She welcome you, too." With his scarred and weathered hands, he unbuckled a belt of variegated worsted that held his woodworking tools and hung it on another hook.

Gervais gestured to the Kalapuyan boys to take Bailey to a bed and said something in another language before turning toward the table. "Come. Sit. The boys go back outside to unhitch the horses for me.

"We have no lumber mill here. So I made square-hewn logs with a broadaxe and hatchet. See!" Gervais ran his hand over a bench. "I work until they were flat and square to fit together." His home was a two-story log cabin, about eighteen by twenty-four feet, with handmade furniture.

Woodward went to another bench at the table and ran his hands over the small ridges and gouges that still existed on the uneven seat. "It sure's smooth. This were a lot of work, weren't it?"

Gervais sat down across from him and smiled, sending deep creases spreading around his eyes like the opening of a fan. "Yes, sit and make it more smoother. Please tell me what happened to you while she pours soup in the bowls."

Woodward slid in. "We were trappin' when one mornin' bloodthirsty savages attacked us at the Rogue River." With an expression of shame on his face, he looked up at Gervais and over to his Indian wife. "S'cuse me, ma'am."

"No worry, Mrs. Marguerite not a savage and her people not either. She is Clatsop, and her father a chief. But she knows about savage tribes." He pulled out a pipe and began packing it with tobacco while he talked, "I think the man we put on my bed got a tomahawk to his face."

Woodward nodded and stated, "It was a blizzard of a blow."

"I'll have Mrs. Marguerite feed him some soup." Gervais turned and talked to her. She put two wooden bowls on the table and handed bowls of soup to the two native boys, sitting on the floor near the hearth. "She has herbs for his wound, too. I asked her to pack his face with her medicines." Gervais stood and picked up a splint of wood off the windowsill; there was a pile of them. He walked to the hearth, lit the splint in the fire, and then lit his pipe.

"You talkin' like an Injun wit her?"

Puffing, Gervais said, "No, I talk Chinook Jargon. It a mix of some Chinook, Nootka, Chehalis, English, French, Hawaiian, and other stuff. There too many tribes to learn all of 'em so we trappers and the Indians learned this way to talk."

Mrs. Marguerite spooned soup into Bailey's mouth and turned to speak to her husband. Gervais translated, "She say to be careful and eat one or two bites and then stop to rest. Eat your food little by little or you will be sick. How many days since you eat food like this?"

"We walked fer 'bout two weeks." Woodward took two swallows and added, "Had some fish an' frogs ta eat, but mostly snails and hard berries." He took another spoonful.

"Now a bite of bread," Gervais tore a piece from a loaf and said, "and tell me your names. You know ours."

"John Woodward here. That's William Bailey over thar. Two others came on the river wit' us; a man called John Turner 'n a squaw."

The old man, jumped. Excitement filled his face, he explained, "I know about them! They came to Mission yesterday. And like today, Reverend Lee said he had no food and turned them away. I not know they came 'til they were gone. They went north on a log down the river."

"No!" Woodward looked over to see if Bailey heard. "Well, now we know they got this far." Bailey was agitated on the bed; Woodward got up and went to him.

Bailey muttered, "Gay, ask 'bout Gay."

Woodward turned and started walking back to the table. "Thar were another man wit' us. Named George Gay. He took off by his self."

"You mean George Kirby Gay who was a sailor? And last worked on a whaling ship?"

"Damn, ya know 'im?"

Gervais stood and put his pipe down. He leaned closer across the table and tapped on his own chest. "George Gay is my relation. By marriage, but he my kin. Why he not come with you?"

Woodward explained the situation, "Looked ta me that he feared Injuns would pick us off easy with arrows. He headed out on foot. Goin' ta Hudson's Bay Company. That's all I know. Hope he gits thar."

Gervais turned to tell his wife, "When I take this sick man to see the doctor at Fort Vancouver, we tell about George Gay so they look for him."

With the warm soup in his stomach, Woodward sat taller and joked, "Well, we gotta tell 'em to look fer a naked man. Hell, Gay used his buckskins ta make these here moccasins for us." He raised his foot up.

Bailey swallowed a spoonful of the soup broth and noticed that Mrs. Marguerite laughed with the men. *She understands English. I wonder how much.*

Gervais spoke again to his wife and told them, "She get some of my old clothes for both of you. They not fit good, but they cover you. In the morning, we leave early for the Fort in my bateau."

"What's a bateau?"

"It my boat. It look like a fat canoe, but made with wood from a mill. Here in the Northwest, we use this type of boat. Bateaux are wide and float high in the water. They can carry heavy loads like loads of grain or crates full with supplies. The Hudson's Bay Company has big ones – thirty-two feet long by six feet wide. Mine is smaller. I just small person." He laughed, enjoying his own humor again. "No worry! It will fit all of us tomorrow; Mrs. Marguerite goes, too. At the falls, we must leave the river and carry the bateau. Mrs. Marguerite will help." He smiled as he spoke, "She is strong. I don't think any of you are strong enough to help. Anyways, not right now."

Woodward nodded and ate more. "Food sure tastes fine. Thank ya."

"There are still few white men here in Oregon Country. We all help the other. Someday you will come here and help me. That is how we are."

Woodward nodded.

And Bailey, who was still listening, thought back on what happened at the Mission and wondered about the truth of Gervais's words.

"We give you more food in an hour. Now, both of you rest on the extra bed we have over there. Many pass by and need a place to sleep. When many come, we use our barn. Go to bed." In pidgin, Gervais talked to the two Indian boys. "I tell them to sleep in the barn and help with Mr. Bailey in the morning before they walk back to the Mission."

Within a couple of weeks and during that fall in 1835, William J. Bailey was on the mend. He had a permanent scar and a lopsided face with one side of his jaw hanging lower than the other – still a good-looking man, a bit more worn and rugged.

John Turner arrived with the native woman at the Hudson's Bay Company soon after Bailey, Woodward, and Gervais.

While Bailey recovered in the Hudson's Bay Company infirmary, word came that a starving naked man had arrived at Nathaniel Wyeth's Trading Post on Wappato Island about ten miles from Fort Vancouver. When Bailey heard, he knew George Gay had made it.

Bailey looked off to the west as if he could see his friend. *He's only a stone's throw from where I am at this moment. We'll meet again.*

June 1st "'52

Mr Deady — Sir — Enclosed is a notice as you
will perceive for me to appear at Portland on the
9th of June &c. — if I shall please; I am anxious to be
present — & also wish you should be there. Will
it be possible for you to attend? & will you send
me word?

If you write please direct to the
care of Mr Weston — Canemah.

Respectfully — Margaret J. Bailey.

Copy of original letter written by Margaret Jewett Bailey

CHAPTER 2

MARGARET
In Massachusetts From 1835-1836

Turning this way and that, she smiled in approval and then reached out to swivel the full-length mirror to see her hair. She noticed a hairpin slipping from one of her dark brown curls; with one hand holding the hair in place, she inserted the pin again. Still gazing into the mirror with her remarkable blue eyes and smiling at herself, she opened the top mother-of-pearl button and tucked her lace-fringed handkerchief down her cleavage. After buttoning it again, she pulled a corner of the handkerchief back out. "Just a hint of enticing lace to show." Her blue taffeta frock exactly matched her eyes – both were a striking cerulean. She hoped they would elicit some complimentary words.

Her mother opened the door a crack and popped her head in. "Margaret, please, your friends are waiting. Oh, look at your dress! I was surprised your father allowed you to buy expensive taffeta. You do sew beautifully, but stop primping. You're going to church, not to a ball. Please come!"

"Mama, I'm twenty-three, not a schoolgirl who needs to be told this," she complained, picking up her Bible and reaching for her reticule. She slipped the drawstrings of her crocheted reticule onto her wrist. "But I'm quite ready." Walking down the staircase behind her mother, Margaret said, "Mama, you should go to church."

"Margaret, if I may use your logic, I'll say that I'm much older than twenty-three and don't need you to tell me what to do, either." Reaching the bottom of the stairs, she turned and smiled, gazing into the eyes of her daughter. "Don't forget, you promised to help me make apple butter and applesauce with those bushels of apples we collected yesterday."

"Mama, I promised Katie I would spend the night with her because her parents are traveling. She fears being alone. But I shall return to help with the apples tomorrow. And let's make a pie for the evening meal."

Before sliding open the door to the parlor, Mrs. Smith whispered,

"Although I never experienced being saved in the name of the Lord like you, I'm a good Christian. When you have a husband, have raised nine children, and must keep a house with no one to help, you'll understand that there isn't time for everything. And today I must arrange the burial of our boarder."

No longer listening, Margaret kissed her mother's soft cheek, reached for her bonnet, and turned toward the parlor while calling out, "Shall we depart?" Her friends appeared and said their goodbyes to Mrs. Smith.

Once outside on the walkway in Saugus, Massachusetts, where Margaret had been born and raised, she turned to her two girlfriends to say, "You both know how I believe in the manifestation of the providence of God." For drama, she hesitated, enjoying the wide-eyed expressions that her pause elicited. "Have you heard that the boarder in our house died last night? Well, I went into his room."

"What!" interrupted her friends in unison.

"No, no, the body was gone. The coroner had removed it long before. As I was saying, I found his Bible open to a passage that said, 'My son, let tears fall down over the dead and begin to lament as if thou had suffered great harm thyself.' My heart took a frightful palpitation."

Katie asked, "Margaret, what does that mean? Were you afraid?"

"If you cannot grasp the significance, it matters not. You did understand the incident, which occurred at the great fire in New York, some years since, didn't you? I mentioned it last week. Remember?" Seeing blank faces and hearing no response, Margaret repeated what she had told them a week ago, "It was in respect to the Great Fire of New York, and in the Methodist Book Establishment during the fire, a leaf blew open to the verse, 'Our holy and beautiful house is burned,' which was conveyed to Long Island to be printed in the *Zion's Herald.*"

Her friends made no response.

"No mind, it is my belief that God sends us instructions, to comfort or teach us. I always find texts of scripture that fit particular situations, and I feel God is guiding us in our lives," Margaret stopped, but then thought to herself. *Possibly I am merely superstitious. No, the Lord speaks with us in this way! Even if my friends don't have the minds to understand, I know He guides me in my life.*

With expectation, Katie looked about, "Here we are at the church." Her voice changed to excitement. "There he is, Margaret!"

The other girl remarked, "He sees you and is coming. Margaret, you go together; you are so beautiful and he is quite handsome." She giggled, "And he must be wealthy, being the son of a physician."

Margaret replied, "This is the perfect example of the providence of God in which I believe. I met him for a reason. I know it is so because I opened the Bible after our first meeting." She didn't finish because her friends tittered. They saw him coming and hurried into the church.

Jeremy Stone approached and tipped his hat. "Good evening, Miss Smith, I am pleased to see that you have come." He crooked his arm and turned toward the door.

Margaret made a little curtsy and slipped her hand through his arm. "Good evening to you as well, Mr. Stone."

The Methodist Episcopalian Church had evening services every Sunday during the summer months because the days remained light. Margaret always attended and sometimes she went with her brother Isaac; of the nine Smith children, he and she were left living in the house. Her other brothers and sisters had married and moved to other towns – some close, others far; for example, one lived in Boston, eight miles away, and another lived in Illinois, a world away. Margaret was the youngest and the pet of her parents, who were content that she had not married. Her mother looked to her for help in keeping up the house. Her father had slated her to be the one to care for him in his old age. Little did they know that Margaret would decide her own future and was busy searching. She was sure God had unusual and wonderful plans for her life.

When the service ended, Katie approached Margaret and Jeremy, who waited in the distance.

Margaret looked to be in a serious discussion as she said, "It is quite exciting to think of missionaries bringing the heathen over to the Lord. When our pastor mentioned the start of a mission for Oregon Country, I felt it could be my calling." With the arrival of her friend, Margaret turned and stopped speaking.

Katie made a simple curtsy by bobbing slightly with a bend of her knees.

"Hello, Katie." Margaret introduced her friends to each other. With an excited glow on her face, she told Katie, "Jeremy has invited me to his house. I shall not be long, I am sure. We shall walk you to your house, and after passing a small time at Jeremy's, I shall return to spend the night with you. Will you be all right until then?"

"Of course," Katie smiled at the thought of her friend meeting her beau's parents. The group of three walked on. Margaret, in the middle with her arms locked in theirs, returned to the topic of missionary work in Oregon Country. In Margaret's opinion, a good conversation was one with a topic of her choice and her doing most of the talking. The two listened to Margaret's chatter, the sound of her taffeta skirt rustling, and their heels clicking against the wooden walks, until they reached Katie's house. The evening air held the scent of flowers and the sky glowed a deep blue with clouds of raspberry swirls.

"I shall return within the hour, Katie," Margaret reiterated and turned to Jeremy to confirm. "Does that seem possible to you?"

"Yes, I live two blocks away." Jeremy tipped his hat as they turned to leave.

Within minutes, Margaret entered his family's white Cape Cod cottage with red roses entwined over the doorway. After she removed her hat, Jeremy escorted her to the sofa in the parlor and then went to light some lamps.

"Why are the lamps not lit? Where are your parents?"

Jeremy replied, "My parents are on a trip."

"They're not here?" Margaret was indignant, "How dare you bring me into your house without a chaperone here!" Wanting to leave, she stood up, bumping the serving table in front of the sofa and overturning a vase with roses.

Jeremy was grateful that she had not bolted. In the time it took her to right the vase, he arrived to her side and took both her hands and bent onto his knee. "Please, give me a moment." Astounded to see him kneeling before her, Margaret hesitated and he blurted, "You are so beautiful and I would be so proud, hmm, what I want to say is simply, will you marry me, Margaret Smith?"

"Oh!" She floated back onto the sofa and used the moment to pull the lace handkerchief out from her cleavage. She dabbed her upper lip and cheeks.

Jeremy got to his feet. "I have something for you," and scurried to a desk in the corner of the parlor. The lamps were still unlit and the light in the room was waning when he returned. He slipped next to her on the sofa. Holding his palm open, he held a silver sewing thimble with intricate designs curving around flowers. "May I place this in your hand to signify our promise to each other? It is the thimble my father gave my mother, and my grandfather before him used the same to profess devotion."

"I am finding it difficult to think. I did not expect this. I thought I was to meet your parents, have some tea, and return to Katie's house. But I must say I found myself attached to you at first sight."

Jeremy interrupted to proclaim, "I felt the same!" He took her hand, slipped the thimble onto her palm, and closed her fingers over it. Then he took her face in both his hands and kissed her with the soft touch of their lips. Waiting a second, he kissed again with much ardor.

Margaret was strikingly attractive and had garnered the interest of several men in her young life. She had enjoyed the attention of those men, but soon was bored with their advances. Of all those men, none had kissed with such fervor. *Kisses from others had been unlike these!* Sensations were developing and traveling to private places in her body. She saw him opening her mother-of-pearl buttons down the center of her blue frock and didn't want to stop him. "Jeremy, I swear my life to you. I can marry no other." His touches flooded her with pleasures that she never thought possible. She lost all her inhibitions.

Without seeming to notice, they slipped off the sofa to the floor, and Jeremy searched among layers and layers of skirt and petticoats with his hands. Margaret helped to separate the yards of fabric from her open-drawers and rolled to him belly to belly. In an instant, she had her first explosion and knew not what to call it. But she knew that she wanted it again. Soon Jeremy followed her ecstasy, and they collapsed apart on the Persian rug.

Panting to get her breath, Margaret said as if to herself, "This is how Adam and Eve experienced each other the first time. What a gift God has given to a man and woman who have chosen each other." She sighed and had an opposite thought that she stated in a puzzled manner. "My one sister told me this was uncomfortable and at times disgusting. My mother said it was a marital obligation that one had to put up with. My other sister hates it." She rolled onto her side to face him. "What are they talking about?"

Jeremy had no idea what she was saying and had no interest in her conversation. He was spent.

"Oh my, could I be pregnant?"

Now Jeremy reacted, "I have overheard my mother telling the importance of washing afterwards. You understand, I didn't mean to eavesdrop, but the walls between my bedroom and theirs are thin."

Margaret, with wide eyes, exclaimed, "Yes, quickly, tell me."

"Well, she called it a douche with vinegar, and I could hear her open a drawer in their dressing room. Let me go see if I can find what she used."

Still buttoning the front of her dress, she hurried to follow him, while talking, "I think my mother does the same."

In the dressing room, two wooden chests of drawers, standing three feet high were opposite a sturdy chair with a hole in the seat for the chamber pot. Three small picture frames containing pressed flowers, hung above the chest Margaret choose to look in. The other chest, where Jeremy looked, had a vase of dried hydrangeas on top. Jeremy turned to her with something in his hand. "Look!"

When she saw the rubber bulb-shaped contraption, she looked relieved. "Yes, now where is the vinegar. And how much should I use?"

"I don't know. I don't know what you will even do with this." Jeremy said as he dropped the rubber bulb into her waiting hands.

They found a bottle of vinegar in the kitchen. "I am going to mix half and half, I think. Please leave me alone." She went back to the dressing room.

In a few minutes, she appeared back in the parlor. "I hope I did that correctly. I didn't notice where you found this." She handed him the douche bulb and went to return the vinegar to the kitchen. Speaking as she walked, she tittered, "I poured the liquid from the chamber pot out the window onto some rose bushes."

Not thinking, Jeremy set the rubber bulb on the side table next to the sofa, intending to return it to the dressing room later.

Coming from the kitchen, Margaret commented, "I must discreetly ask one of my sisters how this douching is done properly. For now, we must get to Katie's house. Does everything look in place?"

Jeremy was puzzled.

"Is my hair in order? Are all the buttons closed? Do I look proper?" She twirled and he wrapped his arms about her again. "Oh no, Jeremy, you are making things happen in me again!"

He grinned.

She pulled away. "No, no, next time. Yes, when can we meet and be together again?"

And so began Margaret's relationship with Jeremy, and Margaret thought that she had found heaven on earth.

The next day, when Margaret took a moment between cutting and cooking apples, she went to her writing table to record in her journal. She reached for her ink box next to her Bible. The ink box was her most prized possession and was made of dark, polished wood with carvings of rosettes and small filigree lines in each corner of the cover. A beautifully crafted brass clasp, with exquisite rosettes that matched the floral design on the cover, held the box closed. The cover slipped out from grooved slots and could be used in Margaret's lap for a writing surface when she had no desk. Inside the box, there were little compartments of different sizes and shapes for extra nibs, two wooden holders, finger-sized red sealing wax, drying powder, a curved blotter, a pen knife, and two ink bottles – one blue ink and the other black. Not everyone wrote with metal nibs; many wrote with goose quills. The bottom of the ink box had a thin sliver of a drawer for sheets of paper; the length and width of the whole ink box was that of a sheet of paper and the thickness was wide enough for an ink bottle. She caressed the smooth wood of the box and let her fingers run over the rosette carvings before she began to write:

One does not think that a person's proper character, as it will appear in the day of judgment, is to be determined by the feelings of the present moment, or the transient experience of some gracious visitation of divine mercy, for though we are unquestionably pleasing or displeasing to God every moment, the present is a state of warfare, in which the Christian is the subject of fightings without and fears within. One considers therefore that a man is not to be judged so much by the temper, words, and action of any given moment, as by the steady purpose of the soul.

They went to the woods the next time and there, with birds above and leaves beneath, they spread a blanket and made love. Afterwards, Margaret told of finding God at a camp meeting in Cape Cod in 1829. "I was seventeen and had felt the need of religion for some years."

Jeremy lay unmoving, and to Margaret he seemed to listen with rapt attention; in reality, he was dozing. She continued, "The first night, when we were on the campground, the Lord appeared and blessed me. I felt the burden of sin removed, but not until the next morning did I feel the bright evidence that I had indeed been forgiven. Oh, what joy I found in my breast when, on awakening, I heard saints – some singing, some praying – while all the woods echoed with the songs of the redeemed!

"I had been converted and baptized by immersion. Now I feel I am near God again with our promise. I know the Lord led me to you."

For the following tryst, they were more brazen. They made love in the library at a friend's house while everyone gathered on the terrace having finger food and wine. No one missed them during those fifteen minutes.

Sunday evening arrived again.

Jeremy walked from the church with Margaret on his arm and explained, "Every Sunday, my parents go to Boston to stay all day with my sister's family, and they always return on Monday afternoon. We have the house to ourselves again."

Margaret squeezed his arm. "I must tell you that my mother expects me home soon after this service. If I stop by Katie's house when we finish, I can tell Mother that I went there. And we must plan for you to meet my parents to tell them we are betrothed."

Jeremy chuckled and said, "Thinking about parents, you must meet mine as well. But let me tell you what happened. I forgot to mention this when last we met."

"Tell me. Tell me."

"Well, last week, I did not replace my mother's douche bulb in her dressing room. I forgot! I had put it on the table in the parlor when you handed it to me."

Margaret gasped.

"So, one night while in my bedroom, I overheard my mother trying to find it. She puzzled where it could be, because she was sure that she had put it away last time. My father grumbled that she must have mislaid it. I could hear them looking in the bedroom, moving things, opening drawers, and looking behind doors. Finally my father said, 'Remember when you couldn't find your book and eyeglasses and had misplaced them in our dressing room? Let's look in other rooms.' Well, my mother protested that she would never remove it from their private area.

"Everything was quiet for a while until I heard a loud squeal from my mother when she found it next to her book on the table in the parlor. My father was sure she had walked out there and absentmindedly left it," Jeremy laughed and Margaret joined in.

When they entered his house and closed the door, she said, "Tonight, I brought my mother's. She hasn't used it in years." She opened her teardrop-shaped reticule and pulled out a similar contraption for douching. "But I still will use your vinegar in the kitchen."

Enveloping her in his arms, he whispered, "Enough talk!"

About a month later, Jeremy met Margaret's parents, and they announced their intentions. Having had the experience of many daughters announcing a plan to marry, Margaret's parents were calm, discreet, and demonstrated no disappointment until, in private, her mother told her husband of the difficulty she would have in keeping a house.

He interrupted in a gruff voice, "Well, woman, you can't die before me now! Who will care for me?"

On a Saturday, a week later, Margaret let some of her friends know of the engagement. Throughout the day, she chatted with her girlfriends, one by one, and all of them gushed with excitement about her coming marriage. All, that is, except Katie.

Katie and she were alone in the park, watching the swans on a lake, when Margaret told of the pending marriage. Katie gulped and put her hand to her mouth.

This startled Margaret, and she turned to face her dear friend. "I dare say, Katie, what is the matter?"

With her fingers still covering her mouth, Katie muttered, "Margaret, I can't. Please don't make me be the one to tell you." Tears came to her eyes.

Margaret pulled out her handkerchief for her friend to use. "You must! No one else has said anything. You are my best friend. Please tell me what troubles you."

Upon hearing Katie's words, a thunderbolt went to Margaret's heart; she learned that Jeremy had, before her, proposed to another.

Katie twisted the handkerchief. "I wanted to tell you when I heard a couple of days ago, but I could never find you. I even went to your house, and your mother said that you had gone to my house. I knew what that meant! You had to be with Jeremy."

"I cannot believe it! He proposed to my sweet friend Molly? What if I had told Molly about him proposing to me! She would have died. What am I to do?" Not expecting an answer, Margaret continued, "Molly is an excellent young lady. What could have happened that he discarded her?"

Katie hesitated before saying, "What I heard is that they had a slight misunderstanding, and he ceased to even visit her. Molly told me that he had sworn to marry no other but her. After their misunderstanding over something trivial, she never saw him except from a distance. Molly never told me what the trivial matter was."

"When did this occur?"

"You will not like to hear this, Margaret."

"Tell me!"

Katie swallowed, cast her eyes down, and wound the handkerchief tightly around her finger as she said, "It was a little over a month ago. And about the time when you and Jeremy met."

Margaret gasped, "Oh! I must go to Molly now," and hurried off.

With all confirmed by Molly and even another thimble produced from a small box that Molly carried with her always, Margaret assured her sweet friend that she would forever decline his addresses thereafter. Margaret took her thimble from her reticule and dropped it into the same box; they rolled and tinkled.

Margaret asked, "Did he say your thimble was the one his father gave his mother?"

With a tear trickling down her cheek and a trembling chin, Molly nodded. Margaret hugged her friend, and they wept together.

That day Margaret sent a note to Jeremy accusing him of lies and deception to Molly and her. She ended the engagement.

Without delay, Margaret told her mother that the engagement had ended and that she wanted to go to the home of one of her sisters for a time. "Discretion keeps me from explaining why this occurred. Please understand, Mother, and 'tis useless to attempt to portray my sorrow; I must go from Saugus for a time. I shall omit telling you to which sister I am going because no one is to know where I am. I cannot open the possibility for Jeremy to learn where I am and go to me. So, if you learn where I am, promise to breathe not a word to my father. Please give me your word. I shall write to you. Do not worry."

On the next morning, Margaret rode away in a coach for her sister's house with her most treasured possessions on her lap – her Bible and ink box. For hours, she listened to the torment of her own mind. *By my own foolishness, I am deprived of going to church, and O! My wicked heart, how much must I suffer? How long, because my carnal nature is not subdued, must I be led captive at Satan's will? How long shall I feel the corruptions of human nature springing up within?*

Her incriminations toward herself continued at her sister's house. Margaret had no desire to venture outside and spent most of her time in a bedroom alone. Lost in her thoughts, while she sewed a dress for her sister, she pondered. *When shall I be renewed in the spirit of my mind so that every desire of my soul will be drawn out after the Lord? I have of late more than ever felt an awful influence from my foes within. What have I done to myself?*

After a few weeks and while paring peaches with wormholes for jam, Margaret confided all to her loving sister. The confession relieved much of her torment. They sat outside in the shade where the ripe fruit dripped onto the dirt. In gingham aprons and with sticky hands, Margaret talked of her impulsive and imprudent behavior. Her sister listened, responding with short replies as "I see," while Margaret told the details of her relationship with Jeremy from beginning to end.

That evening, she wrote in her journal:

> My pride has led me to be vain – to speak vain words and to think vain thoughts, which should be placed on God alone. The fear of man has kept me from doing my duty – and unbelief has kept me from the throne of grace. O! cursed roots of inbred sin, how long will ye torment me?
>
> Yet, perhaps, the Lord led me to this man and ended it to teach a lesson. My Lord knows I want to do something important with my life. No, He has a plan for me to do something with meaning. I was not on the right path.

She began to heal and told her sister, "A few days ago, I had a very humbling view of myself. My weaknesses and sins seemed all arrayed before me – and then came the question, 'Can you thus, with all your vileness, cast yourself on Jesus?' It seemed a wicked thought, at first, to suppose that He would receive me, but in an evening meeting at the church, I beheld such fullness in Him. I was able to cast myself upon His mercy, all sinful as I was, and believe He received me."

"Margaret, I am so happy for you."

"I shall be returning to Saugus. I have decided to return to school and with the Lord's direction, I shall find what my life is. I learned that the Missionary Education Society of my church is being organized for the purpose of educating teachers of both sexes for missionary work. I feel there are many young females who are desirous to sacrifice every earthly object to become teachers in heathen lands. I am one. This is my remedy."

"How will you pay for this schooling?"

"My hopes are that Father will assist me."

"Margaret, you are well aware that you are our father's pet, and while he has indulged you in many more clothes than I ever had, not to mention, trips and outings with your friends, I doubt he will help with this endeavor since he yearns to have you care for him as he grows older."

Margaret agreed, "I realize this, and we both know that he has never favored education for females. I shall look to the Lord to guide me, if Father fails me. Nevertheless, I shall ask him and give him the opportunity to help me or deny me. Tomorrow morning I shall return to our parents' home in Saugus, and I want you to know how deeply I appreciate all your concern and our conversations. I enjoy time in your home and thank you for always opening your door to me."

"I enjoyed having you. And thank you for sewing such a lovely dress for me."

They embraced a long time before Margaret excused herself to go pack.

On the returning coach ride, her thoughts gave her strength. *My disposition seeks to bear some nobler part in life than the mere rounds of domestic duty. My situation is, I think, singular. I know of no Christian that ever felt as I do. I sense that some unseen hand is leading and directing the events of my life.*

She had confidence that, even if her father refused to pay, an answer would fall into her lap.

Stepping from the coach in Saugus, she motioned to a couple of the numerous young lads waiting to earn pennies. "The brown trunk is mine, and I shall pay two pennies to each of you to follow me to my home." The boys scrambled up the wooden docking platform to get her trunk. Margaret held her handkerchief to her nose for the ten-minute walk. *I can understand why those ragamuffins have dirty and tattered clothing, but why do they not bathe when it is warm, like today? I find that bathing must be a natural desire for humans. Surely the indigenous peoples, when I am a missionary, will be desirous of being clean. Thankfully here is the house. Their odors are not masked sufficiently with my handkerchief, and I feel nauseated.*

No one was home when the boys hefted her trunk up the stairs to her bedroom. She stayed in her room to think. *How shall I present my ideas to Father?* She opened the windows to rid the room of any latent odors from the boys. With the lace curtains billowing in the breeze, she reached for the key on a cord around her neck and unlocked the trunk. This time she had packed her Bible and ink box and was relieved to see that they had traveled without damage. She placed them on her writing table and unpacked her clothing and toiletries.

When she finished putting things away and reclined on her bed, her mind raced in thought. She decided to make some entries in her journal and rose. As soon as she dipped the nib into the blue ink and began to write, she relaxed. *What would I do without words? Such pleasure I get from writing all my thoughts and ideas on a page.*

After she filled the page, she returned to her bed and slept, until her mother called her name from the foot of the staircase. "Margaret, oh Margaret, you are here? I see your hat and coat. Margaret?

"I am coming, Mother."

While they prepared dinner together, Margaret told about her visit with her sister, avoiding any discussion of her future plans. *I do not think Mother will want me to leave to become a missionary. So there is no need to upset Mother now. I may as well address both of my parents at the same time.* She bit her lip and frowned. *I hope they will understand my desires and help me. But, if they decide against me, they can be upset together at the end of a filling and calm dinner.*

After their dessert of rice pudding, Margaret asked her parents to allow her some time for a talk.

"Father, last Thursday, I offered my services to Brother Lindsay who is a member of the Methodist Executive Committee of the Missionary Education Society." Margaret inhaled deeply and finished, "I offered myself as a missionary teacher." From the expression on her father's face, she knew that she needed to say more, "And I want you to know that he said he considered me a suitable person to be devoted to this work. He also said that as soon as he could see the agent he would make my case known."

Her mother blurted, "What does this mean, Margaret?"

"Mother, it is my greatest desire, and has been for quite a while, to become a missionary. I care not where I am sent, let me but go where God would have me."

Her father leaped from the chair and shouted, "What? I have had my daughter returned to me from a disastrous engagement and a lengthy trip to her sister's to heal, and now, am I to understand that you have another ridiculous adventure in mind? Who is this man? This Brother, what was his name? Never mind! His name doesn't matter. Does he even know you? How did you put it? Yes, 'he considers you a suitable person to be a devoted missionary.' My goodness! What have you ever done to make him think that?" He banged his fist on the table, causing a glass to overturn and the spoons in the empty pudding bowls to tinkle, and ranted, "Don't you know this home is where your responsibilities are?"

Her mother jumped from his loud voice and reached over to set the glass upright. She sighed and turned to face her daughter. "How does one become a missionary teacher, Margaret?"

"This Mr. Lindsey has led me to presume that I would be accepted in the school and would need to go for a year to learn how to teach indigenous groups about the Lord."

Her father retorted, "And does this Mr. Lindsey pay for your year?"

"No, Father, I had hopes that you might."

He laughed and sat down. "Pay for something that, by the time you finish the school, you will have changed your mind. This is probably my fault because I have given you whatever you wanted. I have spoiled you." He stopped and stared at his youngest child. His eyes and face reflected his mind wandering back in time. "Everyone had always told me how sweet and pretty you were. I had always told everyone that you, my youngest, were the joy of my life." He stopped again and a minute passed before he came back to reality with a jerk of his head. He stood again and raised his arms, straining his waistcoat; a button popped off. "No and no! Not this time! Margaret, if you persist in this ridiculous resolution I shall disinherit you."

Margaret's mother gasped, "Mr. Smith, do you hear your words?"

"Mrs. Smith, by hard work I have saved a little to leave to my children. But Margaret was my hope for care in the last days of my life."

Pouting, Margaret told him, "Father, I have the deepest hope you will live many years. In the Missionary Society, I shall be engaged in my work for a term of only six years and would return to devote my entire self to you for the remainder of your days."

"Six years!" he roared. "Long before six years are ended I shall be sleeping in the ground. You know my health and energy have been failing me. I have great difficulty walking to the town center and home again without arriving here short of breath and with heart palpitations." He started to leave the room, but stopped and turned to make his point. "If you go out of the country on this missionary business, you need never write me. I'll not answer you a syllable. And as I said, I will disinherit you."

After he had gone, Margaret turned to her mother. "What think you about my desire to help others learn about our Lord?"

"Margaret, at this time, you belong to this world. But this life, with all its flickerings and vanities, is but a prelude to eternal life. Whether you spend this life in joy or sorrow, it is soon past. Hence, the best way to spend it is in preparation for that which is to come for all eternity. You must decide on this subject in accordance with your conscience and the obedience due to Him."

Margaret kissed her mother. For quite a while, they sat holding hands. "Thank you, Mother. Maybe I should not have mentioned my hopes until I knew that I could attend the missionary school. All this upset with Father and I have not been accepted into the school. I have put more strain on his poor heart. I shall go to my room to think."

In her bedroom, she opened the Bible for guidance and saw her destiny. She read a lengthy section from Jeremiah 1:19 that ended: *And they shall fight against thee; but they shall not prevail against thee; for I am with thee, saith the Lord, to deliver thee.*

She knelt to say her prayers. "For two weeks my mind has been troubled in view of my unfaithfulness and weakness. I thank thee Lord. Ye called after me while in sin and caused me to love the Lord even more. The Lord is my father and friend, and I am His child and servant." Margaret had a sound sleep that night, knowing the funds for her schooling would come to her in some form because she had faith in the Lord.

The next morning, she had doubts – doubts about all aspects of becoming a missionary – and doubts about her belief in the Lord. Also, she questioned her behavior with Jeremy and admonished herself, although when searching her soul, she realized her feelings might be more embarrassment than guilt. This troubled her. So she decided to go every day to the church when empty – to pray in privacy.

As the days passed into a week, she vacillated back and forth between knowing that everything would work out and wondering if she had any faith at all. While sitting in a pew she sulked and her impatient nature surfaced. *Nothing is happening. There are no funds appearing, and no signs from the Lord.* She stood and walked from the church, deciding that she must make it happen for herself.

Back in her room at home, she pulled her savings out from behind a drawer in her chest where she kept it in a stocking. She closed her bedroom door and dumped the coins on her bed, frowning and whispering to herself, "How meager!" She turned with slumped shoulders and plopped on the side of the bed. "What am I to do?" Not one to cry easily, she covered her face with her hands and pouted again. Soon, the sun came streaming in through the lace curtains, inviting her to fall back on the quilted spread. She fell asleep.

And, during her thirty-minute rest, things began to happen.

"Margaret, Margaret, are you upstairs?" her mother called. "A letter has arrived."

With her hair in disarray from resting on the bed, she arrived at the bottom of the stairs and took the letter. "Oh, I hope, Mother," she said with the letter clutched to her chest. "See, it is from Missionary Education Society. I believe I shall learn if I have been accepted or not."

"Well, open it!"

"No, you must open it and read it for me. Please!"

Mrs. Smith broke the wax seal and unfolded it. Margaret could hear pedestrians passing outside, a bird singing, and her heart pounding. After a moment, her mother, saying nothing, locked eyes with her daughter's pleading blue ones and smiled.

Margaret squealed and hugged her mother. "I'm going! Oh, I am so happy, Mother." It lasted, but a moment. Margaret's glee dissipated from the room and her groan filled the air.

"What is the matter, Dear?"

"Oh, Mother, just now, I was counting my money, and I have very little. I don't know how I shall eat and pay rent while I am going to school."

Mrs. Smith pursed her lips and blinked. She took her daughter's hand. "Come!" They went to the kitchen, and Mrs. Smith pulled the lard bucket off the shelf and placed it on the cutting board table before she stretched to reach back up to the shelf and slip some bricks out of the wall. With one more stretch and with her hand reaching into the dark space, she produced a canvas bag. "Never tell your father about this," she insisted. "Never tell him that I helped you, and never let him know that I keep some funds for a rainy day. Promise!"

As Margaret agreed to keep the secret, church bells started ringing. *A sign from God!* Margaret knew the bells may have been ringing for a wedding or funeral, but she was sure that the Lord had timed them for her, too.

"Thank you, Mother. And I must go to church right now and thank the Lord." Margaret squeezed her pudgy mother for an extra-long hug. Then, with a little peck to her mother's cheek, she rushed out.

With rapid little steps, Margaret hurried to the church. Halfway there, she saw dark clouds rushing across the sky and lightning arcing. A second later the thunder exploded. As fast as the clouds had come in, they started to move out. An opening appeared between clouds and the sun shot out several glowing rays; the golden beams reached to the earth. It had all occurred in the few minutes it took for Margaret to arrive at the church doors.

Inside the chapel, Margaret prayed and then sat on the pew to think. *The Lord has appeared for me today. He has removed my burden of unbelief that I felt for so long, and now I rejoice in God. I thank God that He ever called after me in sin.*

Soon Margaret found herself living in Wilbraham, Massachusetts, at the Wilbraham Academy; established in 1815, it was the oldest institution of the Methodist Church. She didn't struggle with the classes and her grades were good. Nevertheless, she struggled to find money to make ends meet. She tutored fellow students besides taking a three-month leave from her studies to earn more funds. Although she earned enough for a few months of room and board, she still lacked enough money for all her books. She talked with an administrator, and after he made her case known to the executive committee, a collection was taken at a prayer meeting in Boston. They collected eight dollars and twenty cents – the amount needed for her books.

And then, out of the blue, she was called to have a short interview with one of the Society's members who agreed to assist her with a loan for all her needs. She knew his decision was a godsend.

On trips back to Saugus for holidays, Margaret's father treated her with disdain. He used sharp words, "You are not welcome here. It is not my wish to provide food for you in this house." So she stayed with one or the other of her sisters who were kind, although they also did not approve of her going into the missionary life. No one in her family encouraged her efforts.

A letter came from her brother Samuel in Illinois, who begged her not to squander her life on the heathens. Margaret read the word "squander" and was infuriated.

She wrote a letter back immediately, berating him for assuming that her endeavor would squander her life. She posted the letter and returned home, but she could not suppress her upset.

"Mama, you are the only person in my family who hasn't complained to me about my desire to be a missionary. Samuel thinks I am squandering my life. How dare he!"

"There, there, Margaret," Mrs. Smith said as she reached for Margaret's hand to pat.

Margaret pulled her hand away. "Mama, don't patronize me!" She huffed from the room, yanked her bonnet off the hook, and left the house.

The walk to her sister's did not help calm Margaret and she decided to write another letter to Samuel. Out came her ink box and a sheet of paper. She wrote, "I was called by God to go to the heathen" and "Someone like you could never know how deep my faith is" as she scrawled her frustration onto the page. With shaking hands, she folded the letter and addressed it on the back. Again she left with her bonnet and banged the door on her way out to post it.

For the rest of her holidays, she wrote letters to Samuel and to her other siblings. She seemed obsessed, tossing in her sleep and waking with the need to write another letter in her defense.

Her mother was concerned. "Margaret, don't you think that you are exaggerating Samuel's comment?"

"*Et tu, Brutus?*" Margaret blurted.

After all her family's discouragement and her obsessive behavior, she returned to the academy at the end of the Christmas holidays feeling despondent. Margaret found herself wandering deep in thought one cold evening when she came upon one of her professors.

"Good evening, Miss Smith. Is it not late to be out and about?"

"Thank you for your concern, but I was in need of some cool air to allow myself to think more clearly on some family matters."

"Come, join me for a tea and some sweets. Oft times, talk soothes one's family matters."

And Margaret agreed before she realized that he was taking her to his quarters for the refreshment. When he held open the door to his place, she hesitated a bit, thinking, *I need some kind words tonight after a week with the recriminations of my family. I consider him my best professor, and I do so enjoy his class.*

While he busied himself in the kitchen area next to a tiny room with a table and two chairs, they were in full view of each other. She strolled around his small living quarters and looked at book titles. He was a biologist who taught Natural Science to the future missionaries, giving them some rudimentary concepts of flora and fauna to help them understand the importance of learning about the natural surroundings of wherever their mission took them.

"Which books interest you, Miss Smith?"

She wanted to tell him that she hoped someday to write a book herself, however, she answered, "I find interest in most things, and I love birds. I see you have books by Alexander Wilson. Do they show prints of the birds he drew?"

"They do. I have six volumes of his work." The professor came with a tray of cups, saucers, spoons, and a plateful of scones. He returned to retrieve the teapot. "Come sit."

Margaret set out the cups and reached for the teapot. "May I pour?"

"Of course. But back to birds, do you know of Audubon?"

Margaret inquired, "Who might that be?"

"James John Audubon has far surpassed Wilson. He has volumes that hold images of birds that raise the quality of anything produced before. He uses a process called lithography to make the plates. There is a show of his work in Boston next week." The professor hesitated and turned to face her before saying, "I plan to go."

"How exciting for you. Would you like sugar?" she asked.

"No, thank you." The professor continued, "Audubon's works are in natural poses of the bird; Wilson's are stiff. I understand that Audubon takes his kills and poses them himself before painting."

They continued in general conversation for the time it took to drink their tea and eat a scone. After he removed the dishes and teapot, he returned and stood behind his chair with his hands grasping the top rung on the chair back. His next sentences surprised Margaret as he proclaimed, "Your tall and stately charm moves me each time you enter my classroom. I find you irresistible. Would you consider bedding with me tonight?"

Stunned, Margaret sat looking into his face; she appeared frozen in place although her senses began to heat and her mind flowed in thoughts. *My first instinct is that he insults me. Nevertheless, is this not how I think that men and women should be? Equal in most ways! He should not have to court me to know me; do I not prefer a higher level of intelligence on which to converse and share myself? Is he not a wonderful specimen of a man?*

Margaret merely stood and offered him her hand. He took it, led her to his bed, and with an "Allow me," began to unbutton, unlace, and disrobe her. She found the exercise to be a breathtaking thrill. He refrained from kissing her or touching her skin until she stood dressed only in her hair, which he had let down. Then he arranged her hair down her back. She closed her eyes because, with every slight brush of his fingers against her, she tingled.

Holding all her hairpins and clasps, he asked, "Where shall I put these so as not to lose them?"

Margaret nodded to his side table next to the bed, and he proceeded to undress himself. When he finished, he said, "Next time, you might help me."

She had never seen a naked man. Jeremy had always worn all his clothes, and the sexual act always ended in a flash, leaving no reason to undress. Margaret wondered why she had lacked curiosity to see Jeremy because, seeing the professor's manliness, she was quite amazed.

He held out his hand and the touch of her hand in his was more sensual than anything she had felt with Jeremy. To Margaret, everything happened in slowed motions and progressed from soft, gentle, and smooth to hard, deep, and hot, until the experience became a sensation like immersing oneself in a hot tub of water where one's breath is a gasp followed by complete pleasure. When they finished, she lay soaking, and they fell asleep.

Such intelligent conversations she had with the professor. She relished the topics they covered: during a walk in the woods, he showed her the native plants versus invasive species that had been brought from afar; on a walk in the center of town, he explained how the trees along the streets were pruned incorrectly; in his lab, he talked of his rock collection from this area in the northeast and how they were formed; and he had her start a list of all the birds they saw.

A week before he was to go and see Audubon's bird plates on display in Boston, he invited her on the trip. They went by train and stayed in a plush hotel as man and wife. On observing her wardrobe, he bought her a gown that, as he put it, was more acceptable for such a prestigious show such as

Audubon's. They stayed the weekend and dined in fine restaurants.

Margaret felt she had found her destiny in this professor. Making love upon waking and again before sleeping satisfied her. *I desire him as much as he does me; when I want him, he wants me. We are destined to live a life together.* That he neither spoke of marriage nor their future seemed unimportant to Margaret because she was sure he was planning to wed her after all they had done. *How could he not!* She was lost in happiness and her future missionary plans rarely came to mind.

Upon their return to the academy from the Boston trip, he invited Margaret to his quarters with less frequency – only every other week. Once he took her to a concert in a nearby town, but, other than that, they never went to public places together. She yearned for him every day but he made excuses that he lacked the time with his busy teaching schedule. *I know he can't devote his every moment to me as he did for the Boston weekend.* On a couple of occasions, they went to look at the springtime birds and the semester progressed in this form with them meeting every so often until mid-May.

One evening in his bed, she asked, "What are our plans for this summer?"

He turned toward her, adjusting the sheet that covered them. "I don't believe there are any plans."

With enthusiasm, Margaret suggested, "Shall we make some now?"

"I think not." He answered as he arose. "I best walk you back to your place before it is too late."

And that was that. He never met or talked in private with her again.

The semester ended. When she was bidding a girlfriend goodbye, she asked, "Have you seen our professor of Natural Science lately? I wanted to ask him a question."

"I do believe he left with his latest conquest. I think she is the redheaded girl from the third row of our lecture hall. Or it could have been any one of them. Someone saw him board the train with a lovely woman, so I heard. I really don't know who."

Margaret stood dumbfounded.

"Didn't you know about him?"

Margaret looked up and shook her head, speechless.

She wrote her prayers that night in her journal and they were lengthy:

O! God, I come. To whom else shall I go, for thou alone hast the words of eternal life. I am weary almost of life – tired of sin – cast down with sorrows, and buffeted by Satan. Can I expect mercy at thy hand? Can a God so supremely glorious for a moment regard me? Can I come to Jesus all guilty as I am and cast my burden on him? Will he receive me? My soul is struggling to know – I cannot rest short of brighter evidence! Never let me rest in carnal security, fancying I am on the road to heaven, when, in fact, I am in the broad road to hell.

At the end of May, she completed her missionary education; however, she learned there were no openings. Disillusioned in her quest to teach the heathen, in debt to her benefactor who had helped pay her bills while studying, and having no place to call home, she wrote to her sister in Gloucester in the County of Essex to see if she could live there until she found a job teaching school.

While traveling to her sister's home, she ran her fingers over the textured cover of her inkbox in her lap and began to daydream. As the carriage went around a curve a bit too fast, her thoughts came to an abrupt end, and she became disgusted with herself; she had been indulging in scenes from the past with the professor. *Where will this wicked heart lead me? It seems that everything unholy is centered within me. 'Tis good to live for heaven; I desire never to rest until my carnal nature is subdued and I am prepared for heaven. Lord, I am back on the path you have planned for me; I shall do something in my life of significance.*

Soon after she arrived at her sister's house, it seemed that she was back in God's graces, because she found a teaching job for the fall. Not only did she have a job, but also it was in the same County of Essex near her sister and on the seashore: a beautiful small town called Lynn.

At first, feeling grateful to her Lord, she recorded in her journal:

> While in Wilbraham Academy, if I did not make great proficiency in
> Natural Science, I did in moral; and what I learned of my own heart
> has nearly discouraged me. I find my mind weak and easily affected,
> and I have suffered extremely with temptation and disappointment.
> But hitherto the Lord helped me, and I discovered much wisdom in
> the arraignment of providence, and only regret that I have not been
> more submissive and relied with more confidence on God.

But soon after the semester began, she was restless. She told herself that she wanted to be off in a foreign land at some mission station teaching the word of God to heathens. She told herself that her teaching job was something anyone could do. *I know I am destined for something more.* She felt impatient with her life.

To add to her confusion, she met a man.

He wasn't someone whom she could picture being part of her future. He was a Baptist, after all. Yet she encouraged his advances and became sexually involved. *I have not discovered much wisdom about myself. When temptation knocked at my door again, I answered. I have desires that are not satisfied with my own efforts.* Although she would never say it aloud, she realized that her sexual desires overpowered her.

She wrote in her journal:

> While in Gloucester, I consented to receive the addresses of Mr.
> D.O., a member of the Baptist church. Considering that there was
> no longer any probability of my going to the heathen, I did this the
> more willingly. I never thought to be engaged to marry him. And
> now I must part with him. As he is a man differing in many points of
> doctrine from myself, I think we should not live in perfect harmony
> together as married persons should be. I don't have great feeling
> when with him and soon will let him know.

She wrote a letter to him and ended their relationship.

Her inner restlessness was more than she could bear. After one term in Lynn, she quit her job teaching school. The teaching was interesting; the schoolhouse was pleasant and possessed a fine large library; an excellent Christian family had provided her board; and her acquaintances were intelligent, but still she had to leave. Although she was disturbed by her confusion, she knew that there had to be more for her in life.

So she made plans to live with another sister in Malden and to work on a manuscript for her future book. She knew she was flitting here and there in her plans so she prayed for help. But before her move, a surprising event happened. This time, before she completed her packing, something other than physical desires came knocking at her door.

Two men arrived from the Mission Society to ask if she still wanted to become a teacher to the heathen. One of the men, David Leslie, said that he had a dual purpose to his offer, "I am going with my wife and three children, and I have come to ask that you assist my wife on the lengthy journey on the ship."

Margaret objected, "I am wanting to serve the Lord through teaching the heathens, not wanting to be a servant to your family."

Mr. Leslie rephrased his proposal. "As there is not time to obtain an appointment for you from the Board in New York, you should accompany my family and depend on me for your financial and proper support. I am sure you are aware that an unmarried lady cannot travel alone. I am willing to help you in this manner and do not wish or expect you to serve my family or me, however, my wife is not well, and it would benefit her to have a female associate on board – merely, a lady for companionship."

Margaret agreed and soon after this visit, a pledge arrived in her hands:

Lynn, January 16, 1837
To Margaret Jewett Smith:

Dear Sister – We, whose names are undersigned, do hereby pledge ourselves that you shall be employed and sustained as a teacher in the Oregon Mission, when you shall, by the providence of God, arrive in that station. If the board at New York does not do this, we pledge ourselves to do it.

Timothy Merritt
Thomas C. Pierce
N.S. Spalding
J. Horton
R. Spalding
K.S. King
David Leslie
H.K.W. Perkins
A. Stevens

To her, the incident confirmed that Margaret Jewett Smith was destined for greater work with the direction of her Lord.

One week later, on January 23, 1837, Margaret boarded the ship *Peru* in Massachusetts to go to Oregon Country and save the heathens.

Corncracker's metal grinding plates Thompson's Mill in Shedd, Oregon

CHAPTER 3

WILLIAM
End of 1835 Through 1836

Everyone living or working in Oregon Country eventually found their way to Fort Vancouver or, one should say, to Hudson's Bay Company. But most people called the place, the Fort. If wheat and furs were the money of the territory, the Fort was the place to cash in.

The Hudson's Bay Company was a thriving kingdom in the wild. Inside the Fort, where Chief Factor John McLoughlin controlled the establishment, were forty buildings – housing for McLoughlin's trusted men and their families, storage for grain, a school and library, a chapel, a pharmacy, a blacksmith, and a large manufacturing facility. Enclosing the entire fort were palisades – walls made of 20 feet tall vertical logs, 750 feet long by 450 feet wide – protected by armed men. Outside the walls were fields and orchards, a dairy and gardens, a tannery and shipyard on the Columbia River, a distillery and sawmill, and also Kanaka Village, which comprised homes for workers of all these enterprises.

Recovering in the infirmary of Hudson's Bay Company, William Bailey knew little of the busy community beyond his sight; his room was small with one window showing a view of the blacksmith's workplace. He watched the smithy repair ploughshares, hammer harrow teeth, make chains, and mill irons. Each day, he heard the Fort bell when it clanged at dawn, at eight in the morning for breakfast, at mid-morning and afternoon for two work breaks, and the final ring of the day at dinnertime. Until he was able to get up and around, the complexity of the Fort was left to his imagination.

After a couple of weeks on his back, his surgeon allowed visitors, and John McLoughlin came to meet Bailey.

With his six-foot-four stature, McLoughlin ducked through the doorway to enter Bailey's room in the infirmary. His coarse, long white hair flew in all directions and the grip of his handshake was strong. "I wanted to meet this man who took a tomahawk blow to his face during an attack from a hundred of the Shantes, yet lived. I am Dr. John McLoughlin and wish to welcome you back to the land of the living. My surgeon tells me you were near death and have a face to remind you of that."

"A pleasure to meet you. I thought I should view myself in a mirror, now that I know I'll live, but decided to wait a while longer. I understand the wound is ugly."

"Yes, that is one reason I didn't come to greet you until now. No, no, not the appearance of the wound. Until I was assured that you would get well, I saw no reason to meet a dying man." He nodded to agree with himself and gave out a powerful guffaw.

Bailey remained with a stoical face. "I avoid laughing or even a smile. I sneezed yesterday and cannot describe the pain. But, to change from this topic, I heard you say the Indians were of the Shante tribe. How do you know that?"

"It is my job to know everything. If I want to keep my organization running efficiently, I must work at balancing animosities between all the groups surrounding me – natives of many tribes, my superiors the British, the French, the French Canadian trappers, and the white men who are starting to wander here in greater numbers than ever before. Tell me, why did you decide to come? You don't appear to be the trapper type."

Bailey bobbed his head and pursed his lips. "Yes, why did I come? I have asked myself that question all my conscious days here in this room. I have no good answer. As vague as it sounds, I am looking for my life. I don't know where or what it is."

"I see. Well, you have chosen a difficult one to try. Tell me, what are your thoughts at this time about the attack you experienced?"

"What do you mean?"

McLoughlin's face lost the smile and pleasantness that had prevailed since he had entered this room. "Don't play with my intelligence or pretend to be naïve."

Bailey's eyes narrowed. With a slow nod, he leveled, "Yes, I am angry and want to kill those bloody savages who attacked us without cause. I am glad to know whom they are."

Pulling out a chair, McLoughlin sat, although he remained with his back rigid. "I guessed as much. Let me suggest that 'knowledge is power' as Sir

Francis Bacon succinctly put it. I tell you that you have something to learn from every man you meet here in the Northwest. There are no white women here, and I don't think you will take the time to learn from the women of the tribes. So I suggest learning from men. And may I be the first? Nothing you see is as you think until you have lived here for years. You know nothing about this place. A seaman knows how to read the sea after years of sailing the waters, but he knows not to look only at the sea. He looks at the sky, at the wind, at the birds and fish as well as the water; then and only then, can he draw conclusions.

"You have only seen the water rush over you and nearly drown you. You know nothing else." McLoughlin stood. "I suggest you study the sky and wind."

Bailey was peeved, "And how does one do that?"

"Seek out a scoundrel whom I know. His name is Ewing Young. You will find him somewhere in the French Prairie area, I believe."

"That is rather vague," Bailey raised himself onto his elbow and furrowed his brow.

"May I invite you to learn all you can here at Fort Vancouver when the surgeon allows you to walk outside. You might enjoy a trip up to our tower to see the view from there. It is quite impressive. I'll let everyone know that you are my guest, and I welcome you. Of course, you will need supplies to live, at the very least, clothes and a horse; pick what you like and know that your credit is good here. If I can be of any other service, please come visit me. I always enjoy a chat with a well-educated person. Until then." With a slight nod, John McLoughlin disappeared, ducking out the door.

Bailey slipped back down on the cot. *Interesting character. I don't know if I should be grateful or irritated. Well, I know I can't leave here how I came. I had nothing, not even a shirt on my back when I gave back Gervais's shirt. McLoughlin is quite a businessman, it seems. He doesn't know me, but will support me until he can learn who I am. He appears to be fair. I shall be fair as well. I'm not going to be grateful or irritated until I learn more about him.*

By the time Bailey's face was scabbed over and no longer filled with pus or hot to the touch, the rains of winter had started. He had only to sign for anything he bought and was allowed to stay in a small room at the Fort on that same credit. He spent the winter wandering about Hudson's Bay Company in the drizzle and finding interest in every corner. Back wearing a pair of good boots and outer clothing made of leather from the general store, he strolled out of the Fort's gates to see the Kanaka Village – so named for the large numbers of Hawaiian people who had come to work and had stayed. The place bustled. Trappers were riding up with furs piled high on their packhorses, shouting greetings to friends not seen in months. A cooper was making barrels for packing furs; he made others for pickled salmon. One could hear the creak of the barrel slats, as they were pulled tighter. A barefoot child of ten years old or so and in ragged clothing was herding a dozen cows toward the dairy; he used a switch three times his height to flick the flanks of any cows that started to stray. The streets were mud and inches deep; the cow's hooves made sucking sounds as their legs were pulled from the muck, and they bawled, but plodded on. A wheelwright was making a wagon on the side of his shop. His hammer pinged and banged nail against wood. Some Indians with flattened foreheads were squatting and puffing on their pipes, while they watched in silence among the din. Bailey stopped to observe an old man standing by a buckboard while he bargained for some nails in trade for his squawking chicken that he clutched by the feet. Small buildings in dire need of repair were used as homes or shops and for animal housing; they stood here and there, not in neat rows, but as if dropped from the sky with the rain.

People came and went, doing business at Hudson's Bay Company. Bailey saw Jason Lee walking into the Fort one day. Remembering their first meeting, he saw no reason to greet him. Yet he thought, *How does a man of God, such as he, explain to himself and his God how he treated us when we arrived at the Methodist Mission? Hasn't he come to spread the word of God and goodness? All of those young Indian boys saw what this pious man of God did that day. Jason Lee is a very tall man, probably over six-feet tall, but inside he is very small.* But William Bailey kept those thoughts to himself.

Off and on, he went to the office of John McLoughlin to chat and learned that the Chief Factor was quite the opposite of Jason Lee. In fact, McLoughlin's generosity and code of fair play would eventually (but not until 1845) cost him his position, because being fair did not make profits.

During this time, he was there for everyone – the men who worked for the Hudson's Bay Company, the men who had retired to settle in French Prairie, the Indians, and the arriving Americans, like Bailey.

"Glad you dropped in, Mr. Bailey. I want to introduce Webley Hauxhurst. Webley, this is William John Bailey. I need not say more because his face and the rapid rumors tell all. Am I correct?"

Hauxhurst stood with outstretched hand. "Dr. McLoughlin's got that right. Heard all about your troubles on the Rogue River, Bailey."

Bailey greeted Webley and turned to the Chief Factor, "Before we go on with this conversation, I have a question. Are you a physician, Dr. McLoughlin?"

McLoughlin chuckled before explaining, "Here in Oregon Country we informally give out that title to some men who have saved some lives or bandaged up wounds. But I actually studied under Sir James Fisher of Quebec for four years to become a physician. I no longer practice because of the demands of my present position."

Bailey nodded, "I see."

McLoughlin continued, "As I was saying, since Webley knows all about you, let me share some of his background. Webley arrived here in October of 'thirty-four, I believe."

He nodded.

"And within a year, Webley had built his gristmill on Champoeg Creek, north of the Mission. It was quite needed. I understand all the settlers living in French Prairie had to pound their wheat and barley in mortars."

"Actually," Webley explained, "the folks at the Methodist Mission had a cast-iron corncracker they used for their wheat. Weren't too good, but it crudely done for them until my gristmill was up and running." He gestured to Dr. McLoughlin while facing Bailey, "The Chief Factor here furnished all I needed to git this done. I can't thank him enough."

"Webley, you have been a service to many."

Webley offered to Bailey, "Come on down and stay at my place to see the mill."

"Thanks, I will."

McLoughlin mentioned, "One more fact, Webley came up from California, like you. He and some others were bringing horses and some mules. He came with Ewing Young."

In an instant Bailey was both quiescent and astir, yet he showed no emotion. McLoughlin, with intention, had dropped another tidbit, and Bailey's ears tingled at the sound of that name – Ewing Young.

That night, spread out on his cot with the shutters thrown open and the crescent moon hanging with Venus, Bailey thought about McLoughlin. *He keeps dropping the name of Ewing Young, not knowing that I already know that bag of worms. I'm not too eager to seek him out, but it seems that no one else is going to tell me what it's about. When Hauxhurst and I walked out of McLoughlin's office, hmm, how did he say it when I asked if he knew anything about our attack at Rogue River? Yeah, "Gotta talk to Young on that one." Guess I need to take a trip down to the French Prairie. It would be good to see Gervais anyway to thank him and his wife.*

He turned on his side, with the unscarred face resting on the pillow. *How long has it been? Over six months, or is it eight months? Haven't been drunk for that long. It feels good. My mother was right again. I seem to need other chaps who are friends before I get falling-down drunk. I lose my memory at those times, but many have told me that I am mean and ornery in that state. I hope I might.*

And he fell asleep.

In the spring of 1836, Bailey went out to walk around Kanaka Village. Out of the blue, up rode George Kirby Gay on a long-necked sorrel mare.

"It ain't, is it?" Gay shouted. "Well, if I'd be hit by lightning, I couldn't be more surprised. Bailey, where'd you come from?"

"Now, that's my question. I've been here over six months, waiting for your bloody face to appear. Where in the hell have you been?"

Gay slipped off his horse down to the muddy road and answered, "I was just over yonder at Wyeth's Trading Post. Waitin' fer you!"

They punched each other and hugged and then punched again.

"Why you walkin' in this crap? Don't you have a horse? Ya can't be without a horse here." Gay lifted a boot and mud hung to the bottom.

"Damn it! It wasn't 'nough that I carried you miles and miles and ruined my favorite ol' boots, now I muddy my new ones on accounta you. Shit!"

Within the week, the two of them were outfitted and riding out of Fort Vancouver, heading for the Willamette River. Bailey mentioned, "I figured that I needed to go and thank that French Canadian down by the Mission – his name is Gervais. I already told you all he did for Woodward and me. Right?"

"You gettin' old or somethin'? Course you tol' me. Don't you remember? I'm comin' 'cuz you said this Gervais is my cousin or some relation. And I want to meet this Ewing Young. Like you, I heard that he can tell us why those Injuns attacked us."

His gut turned. Bailey hated to hear the name Ewing Young, and he wasn't sure what he would do when face to face with the man. For the moment, Bailey pushed away his upset and made fun of Gay, "Your English is worse than the last time I saw you. Are you really sure you were born in England?"

Gay took off his hat, leaned out from the saddle, and reached over to hit Bailey, who took off in a gallop. Off and on, their time together continued like this – two friends, enjoying horseplay.

Soon they were at Willamette Falls and headed south toward the French Prairie.

"Got any plans on how to live here in Oregon Country? You know, since we lost everything to those savages." Bailey asked.

"Nah, I ain't thought that far just yet."

Bailey had some ideas. "I understand that this Ewing Young has built a saw and gristmill on some creek near the Mission. He built it with a man named Solomon Smith. I thought they might need some help."

Gay grimaced, "Doin' what?"

"Drinking, George, I thought they might need help drinking. Humph! I know you could do that. I sure can!" They laughed for the next mile or so until Bailey got serious. "What I meant was that we could help cut the wood, if the sawmill is done. If not, we could help with the construction of the buildings and other jobs like that. It's the same with the gristmill. I'm willing to do anything."

"What's grist?" Gay asked.

Bailey looked hard at his friend. "You're kidding, aren't you?"

"Nope!"

They passed areas of wetlands and meandering streams, rolling hills covered in pines, and marshes.

"Well, to tell the truth, I don't know either. But I do know that a gristmill is where they grind up wheat into flour, corn into cornmeal, and things like that. Don't know what grist is though." Bailey grinned and retorted, "Why don't you ask them when we get there."

"You want me to look stupid when you're just as dumb. No sir! You ask yourself."

After traveling more than ten miles and talking nonsense most of the way, Bailey decided to be serious again. "I know a little about these people. Not much about Ewing Young,"

Bailey wasn't telling everything; when he had crossed paths with Young in California, he was left with a bone to pick. "But I learned a lot about Solomon Smith at Hudson's Bay Company. He's an educated man."

"No! I'm going to shit in my pants. I have to put up with another one like you?" Gay ragged.

"As I was saying, I'm going to tell you some things so you don't look so dumb." Bailey made a toothy smirk – a painful one with his stiff scar.

Suddenly Gay's face looked pained, even without a wound.

"Sorry, I was joking." Bailey reached into his *parflèche* and pulled out some dried meat to eat. He passed a piece to Gay. "Anyway, this Solomon used to have a school up at Fort Vancouver. He taught all the children and the native wives of the men at the Fort."

"I'll take another piece of that *charqui*? Hey, that sure is a good-lookin' saddlebag."

"It's called a *parflèche* and Indians made it. Look at the design on it." Bailey pulled out another dried, blackened strip of meat for Gay, and pretended to be irritated, "Would you stop interrupting me?"

Gay ignored the comment and took a bite, yanking hard before looking to Bailey with a grin. "Come on, go on with your lesson, Professor."

"Well, this Solomon Smith taught for a couple of years at Hudson's Bay

Company and during that time I heard that he fell in love with a beautiful Indian girl, whose father is Chief of the Clatsops. Get this: I met her sister – Mrs. Marguerite – she's the wife of Gervais. Remember, she took care of me and brought me to the Fort. So, back to Solomon Smith, he moved down to this French Prairie and they started their own school. The schoolhouse is at Gervais's place. Interesting story, isn't it?"

"Yeah, it is. I wonder if Smith's wife is really beautiful. Was the sister?"

"Not on the outside. Well, those are our white man's standards. I know she's beautiful on the inside. She fed me with a spoon and put a poultice of herbs on my wound. When we went down the Willamette River, she held my head on her lap. At Fort Vancouver, people called her sister a queen of a woman. If I were a religious man, I'd say Gervais's wife is Saint Marguerite."

Black cottonwoods and willows reached across the Willamette River and brushed their new leaves against the other trees in the narrows; cedars spread out on the upper banks. Fir and oaks filled wooded areas until the prairie appeared; it spread out for twenty miles in length and fifteen miles in width. When this flat land of French Prairie opened to their view, they stopped in a meadow filled with violet-blue flowers undulating in the breeze as far as they could see.

"That must be the camas lily I heard about," Bailey said. "The folks at the Fort told me that I'd see it coming down here. I read in Meriwether Lewis's journal – there were excerpts in the newspapers back east – that it looked like a lake of fine clear water in the distance."

Impressed, Gay said, "There sure is a lot of those flowers."

"I heard that the natives set fire to dead grasses in the fall to make for a better crop of this camas. The roots are the main food supply for them through the winter. They make little loaves with it. Don't know how. Maybe that's what Turner's squaw fed us when we found her in that abandoned cabin."

They started moving again and traveled more than an hour across the lake of camas.

Bailey pointed, "Look, that's Gervais's cabin up there. I think I can smell some of Mrs. Marguerite's soup."

"Hope you're right, I'm starving."

Dismounting and tying his horse to the porch post, Bailey turned to Gay, "Looks like they have a visitor." He gestured toward a buckboard with a horse still hitched. "If I'm right, that isn't Gervais's buckboard. I seem to remember his looked different. I could be wrong because I was plenty sick when he transported Woodward and me."

"Look at those horses! No one leaves horses hitched and sweated up like that."

They started toward the house and saw a trail of blood. "Someone's hurt."

Gay shouted, "Hello, anyone home?" More blood covered the porch planks and doorframe. The two walked into the cabin.

Gervais jumped up from a chair. "William Bailey!"

"What's happened here?" Bailey could see that Mrs. Marguerite was busy trying to cover a wound on a man's thigh. The blood flow was profuse, covering the herbs and bandages faster than she could work. He bent to get a closer look and stood again. "I can help. Mrs. Marguerite, get his breeches off, even if you have to cut them off. Gervais, help her. I need to get my things outside." Gay walked over to the bed.

"Yeow!" The injured man screamed when they pulled to remove his pant leg, "Son of a bitch. You bastards!"

With both his hands, Gay reached for a tear in the pants and spread his arms, ripping the pant's leg from top to bottom. Gervais pulled out his knife and slit the waistband open. They left the other leg covered.

Bailey was back with a flask and bundle. "Gay, give Ewing a swig of this."

Gay took the tin flask, looked at Bailey with curiosity, and asked, "Ewing Young?"

Bailey turned to the injured man and knelt beside him. "Hello, Mr. Young. Meet my friend George Kirby Gay." Bailey continued talking as he set his bundle on the bed next to Ewing and unrolled the small bundle. "We been looking for you, but we'll talk later. Let's see how I do with my surgery so maybe next time you'll give me a better recommendation. Of course, if you die, we both lose. You better hope I'm better than what you said in California." Bailey clenched his jaw, remembering the tomahawk coming at him and quickly made an effort to remove the scene from of his mind. As a doctor, he must put aside all distractions. Besides, he knew that understanding the connection between Ewing and his disfigured face could wait. Inside the bundle were surgical tools slipped into little pockets and all in neat rows.

Ewing took a gulp of the laudanum. "Damn you, Bailey. This tastes like shit! I thought it was whiskey. Hope it ain't poison!"

Bailey said nothing.

"Aghhh," Ewing screamed in pain as Bailey started to work.

"Mrs. Marguerite, bring me a pot of boiling water."

She went to her cast iron pot over the fire, clutched the bail, and lifted it off the hook.

Bailey nodded when it arrived. "Just set it here. Gay, give him another shot from the flask. Gervais, can you tell me what happened?" Bailey dropped his instruments into the still-bubbling water. *I may as well test my idea to kill little bugs I can't see.*

"Me and my wife went to this new mill of his to get some flour made. We went in my bateau down the river. Mr. Young worked feedin' the hopper on the floor above, while I used the hoist to get sacks of wheat up to him. We suddenly hear this scream and see his leg and boot pokin' through a broken board in the ceiling. That board was rotten. It splintered into a long jagged knife-like piece when his leg went through. He couldn't get himself out, and nobody else was there but us." Gervais took a deep breath, "So we went up to git him out. We tore him up more doin' that, but we couldn't do nothin' else. Then we used his wagon and horse to bring him here. Solomon and his wife were gone, and we saw nothing at the mill to take care of his bleeding leg. Besides, my wife has all these herbs here at our cabin."

Bailey pulled another long splinter out. "This one looks to be four inches."

Ewing groaned in a stupor from the laudanum. But Gay and Gervais continued to hold him down while Bailey removed all the wood fragments.

While Bailey worked, he commented, "It's a bad wound, I can see bone."

After twenty minutes, Bailey began to sew. He sutured the torn muscle first. Ewing passed out. "He bled a lot, but the main artery in his thigh wasn't severed. He would've died."

When applying the last stitches to the skin over his thigh, Bailey looked up to Mrs. Marguerite, "I know you must have some plants to help this heal. And I sure would like to learn about your medicinal herbs, but not now. I'm starving and could eat something."

She smiled and said, "I have beaver stew. Still hot and good. We all eat."

Bailey put all his tools back into the cast iron pot. "Boil these again, if you will."

Gervais put bowls and spoons on the table.

Bailey called to Gay, "Help me wash up this mess off the floor."

Bent over, while they cleaned up, Gay asked, "Are you a surgeon?"

Bailey nodded.

"Why didn't I know that?"

"I never said."

"Where'd ya get all those tools and stuff to sew him up?"

Bailey sighed, "I told the new doctor up at the Fort, a Dr. William Fraser Tolmie, that I had been educated in the medical profession in England, and he gave them to me. He told me that I would find some use in my travels around here. Damn, my first day out of the Fort and I needed them."

Gay asked another one, "I didn't know you knew Ewing Young."

"Yep, I do. Met him down in California. Tomorrow when he's awake, I might sock him. Don't let me. He's too sick. Tomorrow, when we talk with him you'll understand what I mean. I don't want to explain right now." Bailey turned to Mrs. Marguerite, "I brought you something. Hope you like it." He went to his *parflèche* sitting by the door.

When Bailey came back with the gifts, the bowls of stew were steaming on the table, with Gay and Gervais shoveling it in. "Mrs. McLoughlin thought you would like this color." He held up a bolt of bright red fabric with a smaller yellowish-gray piece on top.

Mrs. Marguerite put her hands to her mouth in little fists and simpered. She hugged Bailey, standing only as high as his chest. Carefully, she passed her hands over the red fabric with her eyes sparkling like riffles in a stream. She opened the red fabric and draped one end over a chair and the other over the woodpile. "Mrs. McLoughlin tell you right. I like. It so big! I thank."

"Mrs. McLoughlin said the color is called turkey-red, and she said that it would make a fine cotton dress. The other piece is called linsey-woolsey and could be used as a blanket. Or you could sew a warm shirt for him," Bailey pointed to Gervais.

Gervais beamed. "Thank you for bringin' a gift to my woman."

"I remembered you, too." Bailey handed him a pouch of tobacco from England. "A ship from London brought this and other supplies to Hudson's Bay Company. Joseph, I thought of you when I saw this tobacco. You and your wife probably saved my life with your kindness. My meager gifts are nothing." Bailey squeezed the small man's shoulder. "I'll always owe you more."

In the morning, when Bailey went to let the horses out of the shed to graze, he saw Indians along the riverbank. He turned and reentered the house. "There's Indians out there!"

"Yes, Kalapuyans come to mark camas," Gervais said. And noticing Bailey's alarm, he explained, "They gentle people and do us no harm. They come every year to mark camas."

Bailey interrupted, "Mark camas?"

"Of course, you don't know. They harvest only roots of the blue flower 'cuz the leaves and roots of the white camas are poison. We call it Death-Camas because it can kill a man. Mark the camas means that the Kalapuyans dig up all the white poisonous plants – down to the bulbs. In a few weeks, when the petals fall they can harvest everything 'cuz they dug out poison ones.

"My Mrs. Marguerite go out to help today. She wants white camas for medicine. It good for boils and rheumatism. And I sick with both sometimes, especially when rains come for thirty days when no sun."

Bailey went out with Gervais to watch.

"Kalapuyans have no horses and no boats. And they never use tents. You watch. Later they sleep under the cedar where they unloading what they carried. This ain't all of them." Gervais went on talking to explain how many years ago, before many white men lived here, there were two large Kalapuyan villages nearby with large lodges on both sides of the river. The scattered groups would come to these big lodges in the spring before the time to spear salmon, in the fall before game hunts, and in the winter to live. Sadness came into his eyes as Gervais added, "Now they have only one lodge, and they disappearin' fast."

Bailey's face looked puzzled, "What do you mean?"

"For ten or fifteen years, they is dying with ague and fever and scabs on their skin. It horrible for all tribes. Thousands are dead. And when sick, they have no one to hunt or gather food. So they starve sometimes. I know some kill a child to have food. And I lay no blame on them 'cuz the white man and his diseases caused it."

Gervais remained quiet with his memories for a while, before saying, "Looks like only few families, surely more nearby. Most probably up yonder workin' more camas. S'cuse me, I want to greet them." Gervais called his wife before walking out to a cedar tree fifty feet from their cabin.

Gay came outside as a rider approached the house.

"Mornin', I'm Solomon Smith and found all the blood at the mill this morning. I knew Gervais was coming with some wheat so I came to see what happened." He dismounted. "I see Gervais and Mrs. Marguerite over there. Who's hurt?"

"Ewing Young. He's inside."

Bailey and Gay shook Solomon's hand and introduced themselves.

"His leg went through a board up in the hopper area."

"Damn, I told him to burn those old boards. Cut wood had been scarce around these parts until we built our sawmill. Ewing saved some old boards from a wagon that the Hudson's Bay Company tore apart." Solomon shook his head and sighed, "I'm going in to see him. He okay?"

"Yep," Gay answered. "He's all sewed up and still drugged on the laudanum, but you might git him to talk some."

Pointing to the Kalapuyans, Bailey inquired, "Before you go in, can you tell me what's on their heads"

Solomon turned to look. "All the Kalapuyans wear a bonnet of *wattap*. That's their word for the reed or grass that they weave to make a hat."

"They look like the short Chinamen I saw in San Francisco. Well, except for the skins they have draped over their shoulders."

"Let me go see Ewing. I'll be right back, and we can talk more."

Gay and Bailey sat on one of Gervais's hewn logs on the porch. Bailey commented, "Gervais hacked this out to make a bench. Look how he left places for our arms to rest." They leaned their backs against the hewed log. "Here in his home everything is simple but functional. Well, this bench isn't too comfortable, but it does what it's supposed to do. I like this life."

Solomon came back out. "Ewing didn't say much, but it don't look like he's in pain. I was thinking that you ought to come up and see what we built. The mill is on the Chehalem Creek that runs into the Willamette River. It's close. Gervais needs the rest of his wheat ground anyway. Why don't we load up the buckboard and bring the flour back later? Mrs. Marguerite is a good cook. I always like to have some of her supper. If Ewing is better, I can take him home on the buckboard."

They hauled three more sacks of wheat to be milled out to the buckboard and rode away. Riding his horse at a slow gait next to the wagon, Solomon asked to hear their story of the Indian attack at the Rogue River. Gay told the story, ending with, "I don't imagine that many have been as hungry as I was when I got here."

"That ain't so. Why, most of us arrived that way. I came in the spring of 'thirty-two with Nathaniel Wyeth."

Gay blurted, "You came with Nathaniel Wyeth? The man who owns Wyeth's Trading Post on Wappato Island where I stayed?"

"I did. He's brought many settlers here. Like I was saying, in Boston we had a party of twenty-one men who went down to the city of Baltimore, across mountains to the Ohio River, sailed down to the Mississippi and up the Missouri River to Independence. That's where we struck out over the monotonous plains of Nebraska. It was difficult going. By the time we got to Pierre's Hole, we'd lost many in our party – only twelve were left. At the Continental Divide in the Rockies, we were desperate and starving to death. Men were dying from lack of food. We decided to split into two groups, going two different ways, so the little food that we'd find could be divided among fewer.

"Food, I say, but we were eating mostly rosehips. The snails and insects you ate sound delicious. We found no snails and few insects.

"Then we were saved. A mile before we saw anyone, we could smell the elk meat boiling; we came upon an Indian lodge. We would have died if we hadn't happened on those Indians. We were lucky that they welcomed us and fed us. In November we arrived at Fort Vancouver. Eight months that trip was."

For a short distance, they rode in silence until Bailey turned to talk, "Like you said, most white people here in Oregon Country have a story like ours to tell. Nothing seems to come easy."

"That's right. Hey, there's my mill up ahead." The vertical wheel turned from the force of the water in Chehalem Creek. "Look! There's my wife." He raced ahead with his horse. His wife was as beautiful as Bailey had heard. Solomon slipped from his horse and pulled her close. When Bailey and Gay pulled up in the wagon, he introduced Mrs. Ellen.

She spoke English well, wore a cotton dress with Indian neck beads, and seemed to be an educated woman. Bailey saw how the two of them could be teachers.

Looking to her husband, Mrs. Ellen asked, "What happened in the mill?"

In a few words, he explained about Ewing.

"Why don't you come in the house for some berry juice I made?"

Solomon answered for them. "We need to get back to Gervais with all his flour. And I want to check on Ewing. We'll drink some water from the wheel."

"I cleaned all the blood up. We didn't need to have our neighbors finding blood in their grist. Now, if you will excuse me, I have chores in the house and must see how the children are doing." She started to leave and stopped, "Solomon, I received Mr. Longtain's wheat an hour ago. Please grind it. He's going to return before dark. My, you have so much to do and that broken floor to mend."

"Gay and I don't mind helping."

Gay didn't hesitate, "Yeah, show us how to help."

She gathered her skirts to leave, "We appreciate your help. Please come and stay longer when we aren't so busy."

Solomon talked about mills while they worked. "Hoxie had the first gristmill. Do you know Webley Hauxhurst? His friends call him Hoxie."

Bailey mentioned that he had met him in McLoughlin's office.

Solomon continued, "Anyway, Hoxie had the first mill in these parts, but it can't do what ours does. See this pit wheel mounted on the axle of the waterwheel? It drives a smaller wheel called a wallower, running vertical to the top of the building. This makes for the main gear to go faster than that slow movin' waterwheel outside, which turns at ten revolutions per minute. This here millstone needs to go at one hundred twenty revolutions per minute to make good and fine flour.

"Not only that, I can use this driveshaft to do other things like hoist the sacks of grain up to the hopper on the other floor or drive the saw to cut wood."

Gay asked, "How do you do that?"

"See this huge bottom stone? It's attached to the floor, but the top stone is the runner and runs off the main shaft. I can move this top stone outta the way, leaving the main shaft ready to run other machinery, like the hoist and saws."

Gay marveled, "It's amazing! A change from ten revolutions per minute of the waterwheel to a hundred and twenty."

After a few hours, with the three of them working, they finished milling sacks of corn, wheat, and barley from last year's crop. Bailey asked, "Do you have work here for George and me until we can figure out how to make a go of it?" Looking like white-haired old men, the three of them brushed the fine dust of grist from their hair and eyebrows.

"I could use you from time to time. Not steady, but like today. I appreciated your help. I'd let you bunk in our barn, that's not a problem. Like I said before, Webley Hauxhurst built the first gristmill a couple of years ago. We'll ride over there to see if he could use some help, too."

Bailey dusted off his hands and they shook. "It's a deal."

"Well, the sawmill is where I need more help."

Gay slapped his pants to get the fine grist off. "I hear there ain't never been any way to cut a log and plane wood around here 'til now."

"That's right." Solomon talked as they walked to their horses. "Ewing wants to build a house for himself on the west side," he pointed across the creek, "and I know a lot of other folks who want to make houses or barns and sheds."

At Hauxhurst's place they were offered more work starting the next day.

They didn't stay long and went to mount their horses out under a huge, sprawling oak. Hearing about Ewing's fall, Hauxhurst saddled up to ride back with them and came out of his barn on a shining black gelding.

Curious, Gay wondered, "Why'd you cut that fine lookin' horse."

Hoxie said, "Only way to tame 'em. Ain't he a beauty?"

After going a distance, the four men came upon Kalapuyans working the camas fields. Bailey noticed two women with flattened foreheads working with the others. "Isn't the Flathead tribe different from the Kalapuyans?"

Solomon explained, "Yeah, you're right that those women are not Kalapuyans, but they're not from the Flathead tribe either. Someone misnamed the Flatheads, who are found near the Rocky Mountains. Our local Chinook, livin' north of the Fort, are the Indians who flatten their foreheads. And only the upper class Chinooks do it. I know this is confusing to someone new around here."

Bailey looked at him and nodded.

Solomon continued, "I'll try to explain. Like most tribes around here, the Kalapuyans have a class system. There are three levels, with the highest class being the noble, wealthy ones. Next are the commoners, and slaves are the lowest class."

"Slaves!" Gay exclaimed.

"Yes, slaves are Indians from other tribes, usually *Métis*. Around here we call the half-breeds *Métis*. The French Canadian trappers started the use of that word." Solomon pointed, "Those you see with flattened heads are *Métis* slaves."

Hauxhurst added, "Noble ones are born into their class, but a commoner could acquire wealth and move up. There ain't much hope for slaves. Do you know that these tribes – all of them around here – are traders? Peaceful people who trade with us and with each other. So the Chinook traded away those *Métis* women you see over there." He hesitated and then started laughing. "Those women were probably bought by the Kalapuyans with blue beads. They love blue beads." Hauxhurst kept chuckling. "Blue beads!"

Solomon joined in, "Do you have some blue beads? You could trade them for a camas cake or a woman."

Bailey answered, "At Hudson's Bay Company, while I was getting outfitted at the general store, they suggested that I take some of those blue beads. So I do have some. I was only obliging the man." Bailey shook his head. "It's strange that they value something so simple."

Solomon contradicted him. "If you think about it, those beads are anything but simple to them. They can't find 'em or make 'em."

George Gay asked, "I'm confused. Why do ya call those flatheaded slaves *Métis*? I thought you said they's Chinook."

Hauxhurst found humor in Gay's comment, but hid his smile behind his hand while scratching his nose and said, "Well, those two women with flattened foreheads who we saw have mixed blood. Their mothers mixed with the white man. Couldn't you see they was? The natives don't like half-breeds anymore than most white folk. They's born slaves in their own tribes and are traded to other tribes 'cuz nobody wants 'em."

That evening after eating, the group sat around the hearth and talked. The topic returned to the *Métis* and slaves. While Gervais translated, Mrs. Marguerite explained that all the nobles have slaves to do their work. "The *Métis* make good slaves. I come with two when my husband trade for me."

Gay interrupted, "Gervais, you bought yourself this wonderful woman?"

"No man got such a deal like me."

Mrs. Marguerite said for herself in English, "Yes, he trade for me. I bring two slaves because I daughter of Chief. My father Clatsop Chief. My name *Yi-a-must*. My slaves *Métis*."

Just then, Ewing Young stirred on the bed and muttered, "I'll be damned. Is that you Solomon and Hoxie? You two come to get the body? Well, I ain't dead yet."

Everyone went over to the bedside. Ewing's friends greeted him and started joking around. Bailey and Gay stood silent. After a while, Ewing became aware of the two. He looked at Bailey – their eyes locked – and he lost his smile and all his good humor. "If it ain't the drunkard William J. Bailey."

"You bastard, Ewing!"

Ewing said in disgust, "What you doin' here? Back in California, I knew you wouldn't get that doctoring job after I told 'em you were a damn drunk. I thought you'd board a ship back to your mama."

With that, Bailey grabbed Ewing at the top of his shirt and raised him off the bed, cocking his other arm to make a blow. Hauxhurst and Gay jumped to pull Bailey away.

Solomon had to hold Ewing down on the bed. "What's going on with you two? Ewing, he saved your life."

"Like hell he did!"

Gervais nodded his head. "He did," and pulled back the cover to show the wound on the thigh.

Ewing raised himself to his elbows to look. His expression showed he was trying to grasp what had happened. "Shit! It's nothin'. I just fell through the mill floor." He took his hand and brushed the poultice from his leg and screamed in pain.

Mrs. Marguerite pushed through the men. "I make again with more herbs. All men get away!"

Ewing stared at the jagged ten-inch long wound, closed and all stitched up with tiny, neat sutures. He looked at Bailey. "I didn't know you could stay away from booze long enough to do something like this."

Bailey lunged at him. "Young, I should've let you bleed to death."

Hauxhurst and Gay seized Bailey again and held on while he squirmed,

"Hey, I gave you a compliment," Ewing said, "let bygones be bygones."

Bailey jerked one arm loose from their grasp and then the other. "I'm calm. Let me be. I'm not going to kill him yet. I need to find out why everyone says that Young is the cause for that Rogue River Indian attack against Gay and me. No one else will explain so I can't kill him yet." He sat down.

Ewing frowned into Bailey's frown and neither said a thing.

Gay leaned toward Ewing and broke the quiet, "I gotta know, too. I was there. We lost everything – horses, equipment, grub, just everything." Trying to lighten the air, he jested, "Well, that ain't quite right. Maybe I arrived here naked, but I still had my boots."

No one laughed, but the tension subsided. Everyone sat down.

Without really seeing her, Ewing stared past Mrs. Marguerite packing his thigh and said nothing.

This time Webley Hauxhurst broke the silence by saying, "I was with Ewing and know the story." He began the tale. "For years, I had a dream to start an American colony in Oregon Country. It weren't easy to interest men and harder to do. In California, I met Ewing. Then, in 'thirty-four, I organized a group with Ewing, me, and five other men, to herd a hundred horses to Oregon Country. Ewing knew the trail from his trapping days. We had a rough trip – lots of setbacks.

"On the way, nine men with fifty horses joined us. It wasn't until later that we heard they stole those horses. We didn't know it but Mexicans were trailing us to get those horses back. They saw us all together so the Mexican government in California decided that we were part of the horse thieves. They sent word to John McLoughlin that we were comin' with stolen horses.

"It didn't take long 'fore we heard the horse thieves talking. Little by little, we figured out what they'd done. We were madder than hell! So we told 'em. They left, heading south, knowing we could give them trouble. Besides problems with those horse thieves, one of our men was nearly dead. We kept having other hardships, and it put us in bad spirits. By the time we got to the Rogue River, the men were edgy."

Hoxie stopped talking. Everyone turned in their seats to look at him. Hoxie looked at the bed and said, "Ewing, you need to tell the rest."

Ewing didn't move on the bed. Now he had his arm across his forehead, covering his face, while Mrs. Marguerite finished up. Bailey knew Young had to be in extreme pain without the tincture of opium since last night. Ewing muttered, "They ain't human."

Hearing those three words, Bailey looked at Ewing with a different eye.

Hauxhurst went on talking, "Well, I'm going to tell about our arrival at the Fort. John McLoughlin let the sick man among us stay there, but the rest of us were considered outcasts. Especially Ewing. It took me quite a while to get in good with McLoughlin. He finally believed me that I didn't know those horses were stolen. But Ewing still is blacklisted." He hesitated before saying, "Come on, Ewing, look at Bailey's face! He deserves to know why those savages did that to him!"

Mrs. Marguerite stepped away from Ewing's bedside. She had finished.

Bailey reacted to Ewing's silence, thinking, *Don't give the bastard any laudanum. He doesn't deserve it!* But he found himself saying, "He needs more laudanum. I'll get it." He walked to get his *parflèche* and retrieved the flask.

Ewing hesitated and looked Bailey in the eye, before he lifted his arm and took the flask. He gave a nod to Bailey and put it to his lips.

"Careful, that's enough." Bailey took the flask back. "Give it ten minutes and you won't feel much pain. You need to sleep again. Besides, I want to see Mrs. Marguerite's herb collection so I can learn what she knows. Whatever she's using, it seems to be helping the wound."

Ewing nodded a second time. Bailey could see hostility drain from Young's face.

"Before that laudanum gets me, let me tell you. Everyone, especially McLoughlin, is angry that I shot two of those savages. You can't tell me they're like us; they're closer to animals. But this is what happened.

"Approachin' the Rogue River, first two Injuns showed up on horseback, asking to trade some of the horses. I told them no, but they're so stupid. They kept followin' us and pretty soon more came and were askin'. This went on all morning, until I was fed up. I raised my rifle and shot two. That's all. The others ran off. Hoxie got all excited and said we had to run with the horses. So we ran for a couple of hours. Everyone was so damn angry with me. I only shot a couple savages. I'm tryin' to make this a place for white man. Hell, I don't see why everyone was so damn mad."

At that moment, knowing the laudanum had removed the armor that hid Young's weaknesses, Bailey peered deeply into Young and pitied him.

Solomon finished the story, "It wasn't long after that incident that word came north from the Shante tribe. They let it be known that they were owed two lives and planned to take them."

This time Bailey nodded. He had nothing to say to Ewing and walked away. "Please show me your medicines, *Yi-a-must.*"

Her face beamed upon hearing her Clatsop name. She led Bailey outside to see some of the plants that she had grown near the cabin.

A few minutes later, Hauxhurst and Smith followed them outside. "We need to get back to our mills. Can we take Ewing?"

Sketching a plant in his notebook, Bailey looked up and responded,

"Tomorrow! Let me watch him one more night." Then he stood and walked to the two men. "We'll take care of Ewing. Good to meet you." They shook hands. "See you tomorrow."

A little later, Bailey sat at Gervais's table with Mrs. Marguerite. From her cupboard she took tins with dried leaves and shriveled flowers – skunk cabbage, stinging nettles, yarrow, western red cedar, sword fern, and more. He said, "I know the yarrow. What do you use it for?"

"I show one by one." She picked up a tobacco tin and opened it. "These I use for leg of Mr. Young. They heal and stop pain."

Bailey nodded and took out his pen. *A violet! That will put it in the genus of viola; I'll look it up to see if it's in my plant book.* He began to sketch the dried leaves and flowers. Like two medicine men, they shared knowledge for a couple of hours.

Most days Gay and Bailey worked in one of the two mills. The summer passed with them bedding in Gervais's schoolhouse or sleeping at the mills. They were welcomed for meals where they slept. On free days, they traveled around the French Prairie trying to decide where they could build their own places. A percentage of all the grain and wood that they handled was their pay; they had piles of flour and stacks of lumber stored at the mills, waiting for them to take it to the Hudson's Bay Company to pay off their debt.

During this time, Bailey and Mrs. Marguerite often talked about medicinal plants.

She had gathered some Western White Clematis plants. "With leaves I make what you call poultice, for chest pain. Also, I take white parts of bark, boil, and let soak for two days."

After she explained that herb, Bailey wrote: *Febrifuge: Make two-day infusion of clematis ligusticifolia (white portions of bark) for fever reduction.*

Mrs. Marguerite dumped little faded cloth bags – the size of acorns and tied close with reeds – from a leather sack. "Look! New plants," she motioned for him to see. "When he make chairs for Mission, he take." Using the tips of her fingers to untie, she opened a little square of cloth to expose a bunch of seeds nestled inside.

To explain, Gervais walked over to the table where the round little sacks were scattered. "I take a few seeds from each plant in the Mission's herb garden. They plants I never see before."

Later, when they sprouted and grew, Bailey recognized mint, rosemary, comfrey, tansy, and others. He could tell her how to use these. Like the plants growing together in the herb garden, a friendship grew between Bailey, Gervais, and Mrs. Marguerite.

One day after supper, Gervais got out his jug of spirits. "It's my birthday. I always have drinks on this day. Would ya join me?"

Bailey sat up straight and rubbed his scar with his hand. *I knew this day would come. I don't remember when the craving for a drink stopped. Maybe one wouldn't hurt.*

Gay didn't hesitate, "Why sure. Good way to spend a birthday!" And he held out his tin cup.

Gervais filled the men's cups and told them, "Everybody on French Prairie have code not to give spirits to Injuns. They go crazy when they drink. Somethin' about Injuns can't drink liquor. Mrs. Marguerite tasted it one day and don't want it anyway, but she like to sit and talk with us. Hope you don't mind. She like you, Bailey."

After they drank down the first cupful and then another, Mrs. Marguerite asked her husband to find out if Bailey and Gay would like to sleep with a Kalapuyan woman.

Gervais looked at the two men and explained a custom of most tribes in the northwestern areas to share their women with visitors. "Well, I told Mrs. Marguerite I not put up with that. She's mine. So she never went with any man but me." He filled the cups a third time and said, "Happy Birthday to me, again."

They raised their glasses and drank.

Gervais talked some more. "Now you know you can trade a woman to be a wife, like I did. But maybe you not know this." He took a swig. "You can trade a woman for a night or a week or more, too. Mrs. Marguerite want to get a woman for you both."

Bailey straightened his back and spoke up, "No offense, and I can't say what Gay feels, but I don't want to get sick from an Indian woman. If she has a disease from sleeping with men, most of the time you can't see that she's sick. I won't take the chance." Then he laughed, "I would need a virgin, I guess."

Mrs. Marguerite understood the words and asked, "What plant stop the red sores on skin that you talk of? The red sores that kill."

Bailey had to ask Gervais what she meant.

"She mean the sickness that kills many of her people. They never had it until white man came. When she a little girl, tens of thousands got a horrible skin rash. Soon they started dying. By the time I came to this territory, half were gone. Other sickness killed many, too. Now there are few red men. Only hundreds are left, if that many."

Bailey responded, "Yes, the doctor at the Fort told me of measles, smallpox, malaria, whooping cough, and influenza that the trappers brought with them. But maybe she is asking about syphilis that comes from the men sleeping with the native women. I hear that the babies are even born with syphilis. It sounds horrible."

Mrs. Marguerite looked confused with all the complex words.

Bailey turned to Mrs. Marguerite and looked her in the eye. "Gervais, please explain to her that no cure exists. There is no herb or medicine to help with syphilis or measles or smallpox. There is only one way to prevent syphilis. Don't sleep with someone who has or had the rash."

After her husband explained, Mrs. Marguerite frowned with disappointment in her eyes. She sat for a long time with a sober face while the men talked and joked with each drink.

After an hour or so and before the three were flat drunk, Mrs. Marguerite took the jug. "We have deal. I not sleep with other men. He not to drink too much."

Bailey would be grateful the next day but, at the moment, he protested, "Mrs. Marguerite, just one more."

Gay held out his cup.

"No!" She walked toward the door, saying, "You sleep now. Bailey and Gay go to schoolhouse. Thank you." And she left.

"Where she goin'?"

Gervais shook his head. "She will hide it. I never can find it. Best to go sleep, I think." Without undressing, he went to his bed and plopped down – snoring in an instant.

"Well, Gay, guess it's time to go." Bailey jerked his head in the direction of the door. They headed to the schoolhouse a few yards from the house.

Bailey spread out his bedroll while Gay leaned against the wall complaining, "She could've let us have one more drink," when they heard a knock at the door.

Bailey opened it. Gervais stood there with his wife and two female natives.

While swaying on his feet, Gervais explained, "She made me git up to tell you that they's both virgins. So they's safe. Now, I'm going back to bed."

Mrs. Marguerite took the girls hands and walked past Bailey, who found himself without words. Gay got up, came forward, and needed no encouragement as he took the hand of one and walked with his bedroll to the other end of the classroom – past tables and benches to the far corner.

To Bailey, she said, "This one called Sawala. Her name mean seed of the sunflower." Mrs. Marguerite turned to face the girl and pointed. "Bailey," she said before turning to walk out into the night. Mrs. Marguerite's gift to Bailey and Gay cost a chicken. The chicken went to a Kalapuyan woman designated as the leader of the group of workers in the camas field.

Sawala was small and looked like a child. She repeated his name, "Bailey," in a thick accent.

With the night breezes, a loose doeskin flapped against the glassless window opening, letting the moonlight shine and disappear with the flip of the skin. The girl had a flattened head and blonde hair in two braids – one down her back and the other hung over her bare shoulder. In the usual fashion, she wore a fur from a black-tailed deer that tied at her waist and tied again over her shoulder where the tail was still attached.

His gaze followed her as she went to his blanket and sat on her heels, saying something in soft vowel sounds while looking at him. He heard "Bailey" mixed with other words in her language. Again the wind whipped the doeskin from the window; it flew toward the ceiling and moonlight spread over her. She had blue eyes.

"*Métis*," he whispered to himself. The situation sobered him a bit. Her flattened forehead made the top of her head narrow – it angled upward. She had a short neck and a body rather thick and chubby. He puzzled why Mrs. Marguerite had brought him a child; yet, when she loosened the fur from her shoulder, she exposed two small upturned breasts. Bailey knew she was old enough.

At the window, the doeskin blew open and closed, again and again. She would appear and disappear until his vision adapted to the darkness. After loosening her braids, her blonde hair glowed in the moonlight. She spoke again in meaningless words that told him that she was ready.

On the other side of the room, Gay and his woman were making grunting noises and bumping into pieces of furniture that squeaked against the floor. The grunts and verbal noises increased, a chair toppled to the floor with a crash, and then there was silence inside the schoolhouse. Night sounds drifted in through the window, but Bailey only heard Sawala's breathing and his chest pounding.

Bailey still stood where he had been since she arrived. He decided that he had been there long enough. *My friend Mrs. Marguerite would not lie to me about this girl. She must be a virgin. I'll treat her as such.* He moved toward his bedroll.

Now, with him by her side, she whispered her many thoughts, and he saw tears in her eyes. Her voice held a sound of apprehension. *Or, is it fear?* She appeared upset and confused about something. He knelt on his bedding, wrapped his arm about her, and caressed her hair until she quieted.

"Sawala, Sawala," he said, over and over. "Sawala is a beautiful name." Then he undressed himself and rolled beneath his blankets, pulling her in with him. Her fur slipped off completely. He found her to be soft and supple with a compliant nature. She smelled of cedar and felt small.

She touched the scar on his jaw and asked some question. He decided to try kissing her to quiet her talk. His tactic did stop her speech, but it aroused him and he found that too much time had passed since he last had a woman – for it ended as soon as he was within her.

He fell away from her, drained. For a while, she waited without moving. When she started to say something, he touched two of his finger to her lips with a "shh" sound. She waited again.

If this is her first time, she probably wonders why it ended so fast.

When she would no longer be silenced, her whispering voice told him that she was determined to have more of an experience than he had given her, and she began to explore his body with her hands. She mounted her stallion, and this time they took the journey together. They rode across a sensual valley, shared the beauty of all they touched. Nearing exhaustion, they galloped onto the highest mountaintop and hung suspended in pleasure until she lowered her chest to his. Then they spread huge wings to soar like eagles into ecstasy.

On this moonlit night, he had silenced her talkative nature, taken her virginity, and given her something to last beyond her lifetime. She was pregnant.

Burden Basket of Kalapuyans

CHAPTER 4

SAWALA, THE *MÉTIS*
Life Among the Kalapuyan Indians in 1836-1837

Like everyone else, Sawala had always called her mother Waqa, not knowing at first, that it meant "slave." Sawala never knew her mother's real name, because soon after Sawala had been born, they both were traded to the Kalapuyan tribe who forbid them to speak anything but the language of the Kalapuyans.

During all of Sawala's life, her mother had repeated upon waking, "This day, I greet you and remind you that I am a slave because you came from my body with hair the color of the sun. My people did not like this and traded me to the Kalapuyans. Now we forever are slaves." Both Sawala and Waqa had the flattened brows of their people, the Chinook tribe. Waqa carried her high and flattened forehead with pride. For her daughter, who could remember no other life except her time among the Kalapuyan children, who taunted her for her blonde hair, blue eyes, and flattened forehead, her brow was a burden.

Sawala was a gentle soul and always wanted to please. She worked hard and with pleasure: she liked her life. She enjoyed gathering the blackberries, elderberries, huckleberries, and salmonberries when those seasons came. She picked hazelnuts and acorns in the late summer and fall. She liked the travels to different places to search for berries and nuts as well as the trips to catch salmon. But her favorite time was the harvest of the camas that grew in the rainshadow climate on the savanna.

The morning dawned with a drizzle. Sawala rose and braided her hair; even in a braid, it fell past her waist. She remembered being in this camas field weeks ago when they had removed all the poison camas and when she had slept with the man called Bailey. She donned her deerskin with the black tail draping from her shoulder. She secured the skin around her body with a strip of rawhide and slipped out from under the tree. Away from the others who still slept, she lifted her face to the falling rain, enjoying the coolness, and then she circled around the camp to greet the birds. She returned after a few minutes.

Upon seeing her daughter, Waqa turned to say the usual, "This day of soft falling water, I greet you to remind you that I am a slave because you came from my body," and she finished her recitation as she tied her fur to her waist.

And Sawala returned the greeting as always, "Forgive my birth, Waqa. I try this day to make it up to you."

Sawala and Waqa walked with a group of six other women, in cone-shaped hats made from woven grasses, to a field where the camas had dropped their violet-blue petals. None of the noble women came to the harvest; only the commoners and slaves worked on the camas. One of the commoners was designated the leader, and she was called Tkoopa.

"The plant waits to give us food. Dig with the speed of a diving eagle." Waqa reminded her daughter, "The slaves with the fewest bulbs are struck by the leader."

"I know," said Sawala. What they both accumulated went to Waqa's quota because Sawala was still considered a child.

On her knees, Sawala reached into their basket to get her digging tool made from deer antlers. Some were made from wood and broke easily; her noble family had given her this prized tool because she always dug many bulbs. It came in two parts, a long and curved digging stick with a hole at one end for the handle, making a T-shaped implement. Clutching the antler handle, she thrust the long, curved point down into the soil along the stem of the plant and twisted it to loosen the small, egg-shaped white bulbs. With a flip of her wrist, the bulbs were thrust up and out of the soil. Bulbs were chosen for size; the smaller ones were returned to the hole to grow another season. Waqa and Sawala dropped their harvested bulbs into the burden basket that they had woven from thin green branches.

They worked all morning gathering bulbs. While they worked, Sawala talked, "Listen to the life-in-the-sky, the one who has a breast the color of blood." She stopped her digging a moment and removed her hat. While shading the sunlight from her eyes with her hand, she saw the bird. "Look. He sits at the top of the tree, close to us. He sings like my heart feels." Not wanting to take too much time looking at the robin, she donned her hat and returned her gaze downward to jab the antler point into the soil again.

And she stopped her words, working quietly and watching her mother move away.

Waqa began to work her way between the other women, farther and farther from her daughter.

Sawala glanced at her mother and saw the familiar look of torment in her face. At these times, the girl surmised that her mother dwelled on memories of her life before becoming a slave. Sawala accepted her mother's need for quiet and watched as Waqa moved away, putting the bulbs into a small skin pocket that Sawala had made for her from discarded scraps of leather. Sawala saw moisture glistening on the backs of all the women; the day was getting hot. After a while, Waqa moved back to Sawala's side and the girl continued her cheerful chatter.

"Waqa, did you see the black-noisy-ones soar from the cedar tree? I think there were more than my fingers and toes. Look at the size of this camas root! I have never seen one this large. It is like the egg of the ones-who-float-on-water." Sawala held up the bulb that looked like a duck egg for her mother to see.

Their basket filled quickly. "Let's go together. Our basket is heavy, you take one side," Waqa said. They proceeded to an area where older women were beating boiled bulbs in the shade. Boiling rendered them soft and the women pounded them until sticky and dough-like. Then the pulp could be shaped into rounds of ten-by-three-inch cakes. During the day, dozens of cakes were carried one by one to a pit to wait to be baked.

When Sawala and Waqa had first come a month ago to dig out the poison bulbs, the large pit had been dug in preparation for this harvest. At that time, the slaves had searched the riverbed for flat stones, just the right size, to line the eight-foot-wide pit – an earthen oven. Today, after an overnight cooking, workers opened the pit by removing the charred logs, dirt, and any leaf remains – leaves of skunk cabbage were preferred and placed over and under the camas cakes. Women hung the roasted cakes from tree limbs in loosely woven reed baskets to cool. A few of the small and broken cakes were given out to the workers.

"Look, Sawala, let's go to the hole-with-rocks-on-fire! They're passing some of the fresh, baked cakes to be eaten now. Hurry, Sawala so we get some."

The mother and daughter took their small portions of cooked cake over to the riverbank and sat. Words bubbled up and out of the girl. "Hmm, it is sweeter today. Why are they sweeter some days? Why is some food sweet and other not?"

Waqa raised one hand, "Quiet, Little One, eat!"

Sawala smiled. Her mother had used the endearing term of "Little One" and the girl's heart grew large and warm in her chest.

When all of the cooked camas cakes were removed, women made a new fire on top of the stones to heat the rocks again. The daily harvest of bulbs ended when the rocks were hot enough and the newly formed cakes, wrapped in skunk cabbage leaves, were placed on top of the hot rocks in the pit. Dirt was spread over the leaves and a fire started on top of the dirt for the night cooking. An abundant amount had been harvested that day, making the pit fuller than normal; two days were needed to cook this amount. So instead of digging the next day, the women would walk to the winter lodge with finished cakes.

When Sawala finished eating her camas cake, she looked toward the pit. "Waqa, I see a piece of cake on the ground." And she ran to get it.

The leader Tkoopa saw her coming and picked up a stick. "You filthy slave, you think you can eat more than others?" She struck her with three blows.

Sawala saw no pity in the eyes of the many slaves who watched. Even among the slaves, a hierarchy of worthiness and camaraderie existed between those from the same tribe. Waqa and Sawala were the only two with flattened heads and were thought to be the lowest of the slaves. Tkoopa finished beating the girl, threw down her stick, and walked away.

Waqa went to her daughter and helped her up. Sawala whispered, "The stick was small. I pretended that it hurt more than it did. I am fine."

Tkoopa was the commoner who had received the chicken in trade from Gervais's wife for Bailey and Gay to sleep with the virgin slave girls. Waqa said to Sawala, "I think that Tkoopa watches the house to see if the two men might arrive again. Be prepared to go and bed with a man again."

But Bailey and Gay didn't come that night. Sawala saw Tkoopa's disappointed face when she finally gave up her watch to go to bed. *She wanted to eat chicken again.*

On the following morning, with the dew still beaded on the grasses and the light a soft glow, Tkoopa loaded many camas cakes in a deerskin bag on Sawala's back. It was the custom for the largest and strongest slaves to carry the heavy camas cakes back to the lodge, but Tkoopa included little Sawala in the group to carry a load of the winter food on this two-day trip. Waqa watched. When Tkoopa left, Waqa whispered to her daughter, "Your load is too many for one so small, and we will have nothing to eat until the time comes to take the first rest – a few hours away."

Sawala saw the worry in her mother's eyes and whispered, "I can do this. Maybe we will walk past some berries. I can pick them for us to eat." When they trudged away, some birds were beginning to praise the day; Sawala smiled to hear their songs. She saw something small and furry disappear into the undergrowth and watched the grasshoppers jump with her every step. Then the group walked through a field of lupines and tiny sparkling blue butterflies fluttered everywhere. The wings were edged in black and white. Sawala watched one blue butterfly land on Waqa's back and fold up its wings to display an arch of black speckles. Not until the next hour would her load distract her from these joys. She held her tongue to avoid giving anyone a reason to beat her, and she found it more difficult to not talk than to carry her load – at first.

When the rest time came, they sat by a stream away from the others and ate a portion of camas cake that had been doled out to them. Waqa's eyes darted back and forth in fear, hoping no one would see as she took two cakes from her daughter's pack and placed them in her own. Soon they were walking again.

The rain started. Waqa held her breath when Tkoopa came down the line of walkers to make sure the cakes were not getting wet; she pulled the flap down farther on Sawala's bag.

Pivoting toward Sawala, Waqa asked her daughter, "Sawala, check my bag." No one noticed the mother's bulging load and Sawala's light one.

The terrain changed to hills. They crossed creek beds, scrambled up rocky banks, walked among slippery mossy paths of the black-tailed deer, and passed under waterfalls. As the young girl tired, she tripped and fell a few times. Waqa pulled her up each time. "Come, Little One, the day is almost ending." Sawala's feet were not tough and callused like the feet of the older women; she had blisters where her moccasins rubbed.

As the sun dipped low in the western sky, dropping below the distant hills, a group of Kalapuyan men on horseback approached. Waqa motioned with a bob of her head at the men coming toward them. "Look! Those men will want to eat some of the fresh camas cakes and bed with us tonight. I think the leader will tell us to stop now." Then she saw the sky and pointed to the first evening star in the west. "Now that the sky darkens, do you see the one bright light? We have been given a blessing from that drop of light above. We will pass a pleasant evening."

Sawala nodded. When they stopped near a stream, the girl put her sore feet into the water. The blisters on both heels had burst and were bleeding. She sucked in her breath with the pain the water caused, but in minutes the cold water soothed the open sores. She relaxed and looked in wonder at the night sky, a cloudless space with many stars. To Sawala, it appeared that a large elk skin had been pulled across the sky; an old, worn skin with little holes where the light shined through. So deep in thought was she that she jumped when Waqa came to her side and gave her leaves to use on the sores. With a grimace, Sawala tore off the flaps of loose skin from the broken blisters and placed leaves over the open wounds. Next Waqa arrived with their dinner. Sawala ate a leg of a squirrel and more camas cake. The men had been on a hunting outing and had rabbits and squirrels to share. "Waqa, you were right! The bright light gave us good food and a pleasant evening."

Now that Sawala was old enough for men, there would be many times she would be glad to be different – a blonde *Métis* – because the men of tribe had no desire to bed with her. She saw they were rough to her mother, batting her head and striking her, before they inserted their manliness. Sawala remembered the gentleness of Bailey, the thrilling ride to the sky in his bed, and her final flight like an eagle. She did not yearn for any of these men.

The next day, Waqa told Sawala, "This day, I greet you and remind you that I am a slave because you came from my body." Waqa omitted the rest. Instead she told her daughter, "We are almost to the lodge. Today, the march is a half-day. Make a lining in your moccasins with these leaves I gathered. They will help the sores."

The men rode off toward the lodge with a few bags of the camas cakes. Waqa was a lucky one; they had taken her bag. So she swung her daughter's bag onto her back. They looked at each other and hid a smile. Yes, the evening star had blessed them.

Sawala pulled her mother to the back of the line to talk a little, "Waqa, you always said that one day when I was old enough you would tell me why I have hair the color of the sun and eyes with a drop of the rainless sky? Can you tell me now?"

Waqa hesitated and then nodded.

Sawala beamed and asked another question, "I never see others like me. Have you?"

"Yes, I see others with hair like yours. Sometimes the white man who beds with us likes to play tricks. Sometimes they trick us and a child is born with eyes and hair like yours. I think they like their trick and laugh."

Sawala asked, "You told me that your mother bedded with a white man and you were born. You don't look like me; except for your forehead, you look like a Kalapuyan."

With the pace of the walking slower than yesterday, Waqa had time to think before she answered, "I do not know everything, Little One. Maybe, the white man who made me in my mother did not play tricks. But you are wrong; look, I have nose of the white man and my hair is soft like hair of the white man." She took her daughter's hand and put it to her hair. "But few have eyes of a hawk to notice this."

Sawala delighted in hearing her mother call her "Little One" again; she knew the time was right to ask many questions, while Waqa's heart was soft. "Waqa, my forehead is not as long as yours. Did the white man who made me grow in you cause this?"

"No, I lived with our people for many moons before they noticed your hair. I placed you on the board and bound your head because I was among the noble Chinook. A flattened head prepares you for afterlife. I wrapped and wrapped, pulling it tighter and tighter each day, to make you grow a beautiful long forehead and also to cover the sight of your hair." Waqa took a deep breath. A dark look fell across her face and her voice cracked to tell about the day, "One day a woman saw your hair when I unwrapped you to dip you in the stream. Always I hid you from the others, but she saw. She yanked you out of my arms and ran to show everyone. They called you the ugliest thing they ever saw. That is the day we were traded to the Kalapuyans, who would not let me wrap your head anymore." With a sad face, Waqa stopped her story. Finally, she whispered, "They beat me. My own people! I came to my new home with deep cuts and dried blood on my back."

Puzzled that shame and pain could happen from the tricks of the white man, Sawala wanted to touch Waqa to make her feel better. She took her mother's hand. Not wanting to cause her mother more pain – for Sawala had seen torment in Waqa's face – she walked in silence, wondering to herself. *Why would a white man play tricks? Once the white man is gone, what pleasure would his trick give him? How would he even know? Did the white man know the life of pain that he gave to Waqa? Was he pleased?* Sawala looked up into the face of her mother, wanting to tell Waqa, *I am happy that I am here. I am glad that you are my mother.* Sawala had one more question, but she could not bring herself to ask it. *Do I make Waqa happy that I am here even though she lives with the shame of my hair and eyes?*

Three months would pass before Sawala would question whether she had a small one growing in her or not. At that time she would wonder whether Bailey, who flew with her and the eagles that night, played a trick on her.

Waqa told Sawala, "We will receive a special greeting because our walking group carried the first load of camas cakes to the village." But nothing occurred when they walked into the village. The celebration had happened hours before, when the horsemen took the glory with the camas cakes they had brought. Unnoticed, the walkers went to hang the cakes to dry in the lodge.

Their winter lodge was a large pit house. The ground had been dug out and the dirt piled around the edges to form a wall, making the pit deeper. They dug until high enough for a man to stand; the center was deeper for ceremonies with the audience elevated around the walls. Timbers supported a roof of fir bark that was covered in dirt with a center hole for cooking smoke to escape. Inside, the rafters supported the roof and made a place from which to hang the cakes and other foodstuffs to dry. Noble families claimed spaces where they stored their food and huddled to sleep in winter, separating themselves from others by long, woven mats suspending from the ceiling. The Kalapuyans were expert weavers and women made woven items year-round. One area of the lodge stored dried reeds, grasses, long and thin twigs, and other materials to create baskets for all kinds of tasks – winnowing trays for grains, seed beaters that were the size and shape of a hand, cone-shaped burden baskets, long and thin baskets, squat and fat ones, some with handles and others without.

When Waqa and Sawala finished hanging the cakes in the lodge, Sawala selected a special moist and large one to present to her noble family. The two tired woman searched for their owners and found them beneath a tree with a fresh kill – a prime buck of three summers hung from a limb – all were enjoying the special cuts of liver and other edible innards that had spilled upon the grass.

Their family greeted them in happiness. Sawala passed the special large camas cake to her noble woman and received a smile in return. Soon, Waqa and Sawala were given knives to help skin the black-tailed deer. They divided the deer between the families of the three hunters who shot their arrows into the buck. But two of the hunters were commoners, so the best cuts of the meat would go to Sawala's noble family. The nobleman's wife stood to watch and make sure that the less delectable cuts went to the other two families. She picked some poorer cuts for the men who helped load the carcass onto a horse and for the men who hung the animal to drain.

Off to the side, the men from the hunt were dancing in celebration. Two were wearing hollowed heads of bucks that had been dried years ago when they were made to fit the head of a man. During the hunt, this is how they attracted the game to come closer.

They assigned Sawala the task of scraping all fragments of fat and flesh from the underside of the hide. She sat down to work near a blackberry bush whose flowers were blooming. She liked to hear the buzz of bees and hoped she could find the hive and honey later that summer. While thinking about the delicious honey, she heard a different buzz; she looked up to brush flies away. "You are pests, but look how you glisten with colors like the arc that glows across the sky in the sunshine after a rain."

Waqa came to Sawala and said, "They gave me many of the cuts of meat to prepare for winter. I go to the lodge to get some herbs to put on the drying meat. Put some of the fat that you scrape from the deer hide on your blisters."

The slaves worked long after dark until the littlest girl of the noble family called to Sawala to come to bed; they slept together because the little girl liked the stories Sawala told her to help sleep come.

This little noble daughter wore a lynx fur – the softest of furs, with long hairs. Both girls removed their fur clothing to make themselves a bed in their corner of the lodge; they would sleep naked. They nestled in their furs and snuggled. The Pacific tree frogs were singing in the night. The chorus gave Sawala an idea for a story. As always, she reached out to touch the lynx before beginning the tale:

> The Kalapuyans have lived and died in this green valley for more seasons than there are leaves on the largest oak tree. And all your ancestors live with you still, because after they were placed beneath the grasses into the earth, they enjoyed living again as the mushrooms and the lupine and the camas. Others became bushes with berries, and some became trees with acorns; these were the ways that they shared their body with you, as their flesh disappeared to become rich earth for things to grow. But it must be told that your ancestors were sad they could not sing to you and send the sound of their voices to you to remember them.
>
> One day, the Maker of All saw the sadness of your ancestors and decided to make a new little animal. First the Maker painted him green and then painted some brown. While painting, a stroke of black was swished from the nose across the eyes to the neck and little green bumps of paint were dropped all over the back. "I am going to make your legs good for jumping. I'll make sticky pads on your feet to climb trees." The Maker made the little tree frog and was happy.
>
> Now the Maker said to all your ancestors, "Every spring, while you rest deep in the earth eager to sing to your people, you can send your voices up and into the throat of this frog. I have made a throat

sac and painted it black; you need to fill this frog with all your songs so your people can hear you again.

With the end of the story, they listened to the tree frogs. Within minutes, sleep came to both, but for different reasons. With the arrival of camas cakes and the killing of a deer, excitement had tired the noble child; the long trek with a heavy load, followed by hours of scraping, had exhausted Sawala. Both girls liked to sleep touching the lynx fur. Although Sawala was years older, she was nearly the same size, and they huddled together like two cubs snuggling for warmth.

The season of the camas blended into the season of the berries. The Kalapuyans busied themselves and were thankful for the food they had. Berries were placed on a large flat boulder to dry in the sun. If the sun refused to come out to help, the berries were dried in long flat baskets over embers.

By the end of the summer, the lodge was full of cooked acorns ready to grind into flour; dried wild cherries, thimble-berries, raspberries, and many other berries; baked sunflower seeds and wild squash seeds; and strips of smoked bear, rabbit, elk, deer, beaver, gophers, and squirrels. They ate their last meals of freshly cooked grouse, pheasant, quail, robin, and pigeon and prepared for the season of the salmon.

The Kalapuyans had been fishing for salmon in rivers and streams on the east side of the Willamette River since springtime. The men chose a narrow spot in the water and put in wooden stakes. Then the women entered the water with strips of bark to weave around the stakes and make a mesh for the water to pass, but not the salmon. When many fish were trapped behind the woven gate, the men speared the salmon and they were eaten fresh.

In the fall, during salmon season, they would go to Willamette Falls to catch hundreds of fish and dry them. Then they would have enough to last through the winter. Many families moved to the area of the falls. Sawala went with her mother and their noble family.

The noble wife told her, "Instead of making baskets like you did in prior years, this year you can help turn the drying fish."

The men had made spears with tips of obsidian, bone, and hardwood and they often lit torches to spear the fish during the night. Everyone worked long hours and the tasks were never-ending – collecting wood for fires to dry the fish, repairing baskets and spears, sharpening knives, preparing food to eat, packing dried fish between leaves, loading baskets onto poles to drag back to the lodge, making trips back and forth to the lodge, and more. Each day dawned with everyone scurrying. Sawala was proud to work with the drying of fish.

"Waqa, it is hot work. By the time I have walked around the whole pit of embers, to reach and turn every fish, the shadows from the sun shorten this much," and she held out her hands the width of her growing waist. Still no one had noticed she carried a child, not even she did.

One reason she liked the work was that she could talk all day. She talked to those working with her, anyone who passed, and others when she sat to eat. And she liked to hear what others had to say for there was much gossip at this time.

One told her, "That one sneaks away at night to bed with him," and she pointed. "Her mother would be angry, if she knew, for the mother likes to bed with him herself."

Another slave by her side explained, "I collected petals from the death-camas. They are dry and powder now. When I am angry with my owner, I sprinkle a bit on his food. He doesn't know why it burns his mouth when no one else has problems."

Then one day, a rumor circled the camp about an unwanted birth. "They will crush the child's head to be rid of the half-breed." Sawala knew of such a practice. "Today, they will do it here for all to see. The nobles are tired of all the ugly mixed children in our lodge. They want all women to rid themselves of these unwanted babies."

Sawala wondered why her mother had not crushed her head. Without words, she glanced at Waqa in the distance and thanked her.

A couple of hours passed and soon a horseman approached the center of the work area, holding a newborn upside down. The child screamed. He threw it to the ground and called for the mother. She came forward with a heavy stone larger than the child's head.

The man slid from his horse and put the still-wailing child on a boulder next to the river. The mother came to the boulder and lifted her rock. At that moment, something inside told Sawala, *Close your eyes. Don't look!* She heard the blow, but saw nothing except the smiles on faces when she opened her eyes.

That night, while a mock-orange bush bloomed nearby and filled the air with its fragrance, Sawala had a dream of the afternoon demonstration. In her dream, when the child's head was crushed, the intense smell of the bush erupted into the air. And tiny teardrops of blood along with little white petals splattered everywhere – red and white sprayed above the crowd. Everyone smiled.

When the leaves turned to colors and the days grew shorter and cooler, Sawala noticed she was getting fat and remembered not having the days of bleeding for a long time. Covered with the loosely draped fur around her body, she looked the same as always. But she began to think. She remembered tiring after simple tasks, being dizzy for no reason, and having flutters inside. She made a little gasp at the realization that she might be carrying a child. A child from a white man! Bailey's child! In a flash of heat, sweat covered her.

Within a few days, when Sawala awoke and got to her knees to cover herself, the child of her owners said in a loud, surprised voice, "Sawala, you are fat!" and poked her tummy. Since all families slept together in the lodge, they heard and looked. Any adult who saw the bare belly knew she was pregnant.

The noble wife took Sawala and Waqa aside, "What is this? When did this happen? Tell me. Tell me. You deceived me? I am to be paid when you sleep with a man."

Sawala stammered, "At the camas harvest."

"Yes, yes, what happened at the camas harvest?"

Waqa answered, "One night, out of the cabin came the woman who is daughter of the Clatsop Chief; she asked if she could trade a chicken for two virgin girls for the night. Sawala was one they picked."

The noble wife was indignant, "Who gave permission? Why was I not told? Where is my chicken? I'm going to the Chief!"

An hour later, everyone in the tribe came to see this injustice settled. The Kalapuyans sat on the tiered stairs that circled the center of the lodge, where the Chief sat with the group of men in his council as well as the nobleman and his noble wife. Those who had no place to sit squeezed together and stood.

They called Tkoopa, the commoner who had given the girls away and who had eaten the chicken, into the center. She groveled on the ground, asking forgiveness.

"Stand up, you fool. So you thought I would never know," the noble wife said, and spat on her.

"Silence," commanded the deep voice of the Chief. He said, "To make this right, you must pay these nobles their chicken."

The woman stuttered, "But I ate it."

Laughter passed through the crowd until the Chief ordered again, "Silence!" He sat with the quiet for a whole minute while the commoner stood shaking before him. "What have you to replace this chicken?"

All the food, whether gathered or killed, became community property for everyone in the tribe, including the commoners and slaves. But the noble ones could store their own stock of food in their area. The commoners owned nothing of value unless they had found a way to accumulate furs, food, or beads, at which point, they could move up to the noble wealthy class. The Chief knew that Tkoopa had nothing.

"I have only the furs I wear."

The Chief nodded and said, "Then you must work as her slave, until the end of the next camas harvest."

The noble wife was not pleased. She leaned over and whispered to her husband, who whispered to the Chief.

The Chief continued, "Yes, now there is the problem of the unwanted half-breed. Where is the girl with this child?"

Sawala had not expected this. She looked to Waqa, but her mother could do nothing. Waqa stood with her gaze forward and a tear in her eye.

Sawala went to the center of the lodge.

The Chief demanded, "Remove your fur for me to see that you are truly with child."

When her fur slipped around her ankles, a little gasp was heard around the room. The Chief held up his arm to quiet them again. "And is the man who did this a white man?"

Sawala nodded.

"Tell me!" He insisted.

And she said in a strong voice, "Yes."

The Chief turned to the commoner, "You caused this. You must stop this child from being born. Take the spear in the corner and hit her belly to kill the child within her. Do not stop until I tell you." The six-foot-long spear had a smooth and round shaft an inch in diameter.

Sawala moved back. With pleading eyes, she looked right and left. The Chief motioned for two men to step forward and hold her against one of the main posts in the center of the lodge. Tkoopa returned with the spear and grasped it with her two hands. She took a wide stance and whirled the shaft into Sawala's belly.

Sawala screamed in pain and doubled over. The men righted her and another blow came. The Chief made lines in the dirt at his feet until there were five lines for five blows to the belly, and then he shouted, "Enough!" When they released Sawala, she collapsed to the floor in a faint. The Chief demanded, "Take her outside under the trees for all to see. She deceived her owner. Give her no pity." He turned to the Medicine Man, "Try your herbs. I know these brews have the power to kill the child only sometimes, but try them!"

Men grabbed Sawala by her arms and pulled her across the ground like a dead deer. Though conscious her head hung. In anguish, Waqa took her daughter's fur and followed in the shadows along the earthen walls of the lodge. The men were rough and heaved her below a pine tree.

Sawala remained in a daze and naked under the tree until darkness came; Waqa watched from a distance and crept to her daughter with her furs to cover her. "When they dragged you, with each bump of your body over wood or rocks, I had a jab of pain inside my heart. Little One, I am sorry this happened to you." Waqa cried while she smoothed Sawala's braids and brushed dirt from her face. Sawala said nothing and moved nothing except her eyes. Waqa stayed and placed her hand on Sawala's chest to feel the rise and fall of shallow breaths.

The next day, Waqa told Sawala, "I went to our noble's wife to plead. I told her that you are one of her best workers. I reminded her that her daughter loves your stories. She said that I could care for you and bring you food. She does not want you to die."

Sawala looked at her mother, but still remained silent.

With tears rolling down her cheeks, Waqa said in a soft voice, "The noble wife said to tell you that she knows you are a good girl. She did not think they would beat you."

Days passed and Sawala hurt too much to move, but the baby did not abort. Waqa brought food and helped her daughter go to the place to relieve herself. Those passing spat at her or kicked dirt on her. The bruises across her belly turned from blue to green and still the baby remained within her. During a waning gibbous moon, the council had met. So when the moon disappeared into a new moon, the Chief came with others to declare that it had failed. He stood before Sawala and gave the command to kill. "You will crush the skull of your child at birth."

Sawala knew that she must agree and said, "Yes."

Now Waqa moved Sawala's resting place farther from all the activity. Sawala could not walk without help and told her mother that she had a great pain inside. She thought her ribs may have been cracked or even the hip bones bruised because many days passed and she still could not walk unassisted. Sawala would lay curled beneath the trees and take her mind from the pain by watching and listening to the sounds of the life of earth.

And her child gave her joy with his kicking and moving inside her. Sawala knew she carried a boy and would talk to him, "When you come into the light of this earth, you will smile at all you see. Here," she picked up a ladybug, "you will see this funny one that has black spots on its back and is the color of the harvest moon. And you will love to watch this one roll into a ball when you pick it up." As long as she rested on her side and did not move, she could watch the insects in the dirt, touch the grass, smell the moisture of the woods, and feel no pain. As soon as she moved, even a slight turn, she hurt.

Finally, the Kalapuyans rested; the berries were picked, the salmon's eggs were laid, the birds had moved to warmer places, the world of nature grew quiet, and Waqa had less work. She spent most of her time with her daughter.

When Sawala healed enough to speak without pain, she had many questions, "My head asked many things, while here with no one and no work. Will you tell me more about my birth? Waqa did you bed with a white man with hair the color of mine?"

"Yes, for many months. He traded furs to have me. His hair looked like the dry grass that sleeps in the time of cold and his eyes had drops of the sunlit sky, like yours."

Sawala asked, "What happened to him?"

"He took me back to my people one day and left. He had seen that you were growing in me, maybe that is why. Or, maybe because he had trapped many furs at that time of cold and it was time for him to return to his people. I do not know why; I never saw him again."

"Oh," Sawala wondered many things from that story and started to ask another question when her mother began to talk.

Waqa said, "When you appeared from my body, I saw the trick he had played on me. I was surprised. My mother had told me that she had lived from camas harvest time to the next harvest with a white man with eyes and hair like yours. Like my white man, he left her, but he did not play tricks because, look at me, I have hair and eyes the color of night." Waqa smiled, "Not many see my different nose."

Sawala reached out and touched the special nose that looked like a white man's nose. She grinned at her mother and told her, "Your nose is warm."

Another new moon came and then a full moon brought cold, cold nights. At last, the noble family gave permission for Sawala to be brought into the lodge with them at night. The noble wife came to her and took her hand to help her walk to the little girl. "I hope you are better; I did not mean this to happen." When the lady took her hand away, she left a small bag of dried berries in Sawala's fist, but said nothing more.

Sawala found happiness to have the lynx fur to touch again and the opportunity to make stories for the little child again. That first night back in the lodge, with her fingers caressing the lynx fur, Sawala planned how to take it for her son.

She healed from the beating; nevertheless, her time of sleeping on the ground, her time of no exercise or movement, and her time in the cold nights had started a sickness that would never heal.

And the months passed.

There came a day when she could walk by herself and she felt great joy. But she noticed that the sharp pain in her chest remained, when inhaled deeply. I must walk every day and grow stronger," she told Waqa. She began walking a bit longer and farther each day. During her walks, she planned for the time when her son would come to see the light of the day.

Winter came like an angry bear, rushing at the Kalapuyans when they went outside, and biting their ears and toes.

With the cold, the noble ones handed out extra coverings to the slaves. They gave Sawala furs and strips of rawhide to wrap around her legs, binding them against the sting of the icy wind. Each day, with a belly the size of a hornet's nest, she would adjust the leggings and go for her walks. She added extra fur scraps into her moccasins and Waqa helped to wrap her arms in the same fashion as her legs. The cold crept in the lodge and stayed. Everyone slept with the coverings on their arms and legs.

"Waqa, when I am all wrapped in these deerskins, do I look like a doe?"

Her mother answered in a jovial tone, "No, a fat bear!"

Sawala's eyes twinkled at her mother.

And Waqa smiled, but neither laughed at the little joke. Sawala saw the worry in Waqa's eyes with the time of birth drawing near.

Waqa suggested, "Let's walk to the stream, Little One." They walked away from the ears of others and Waqa asked, "When it is time, do you want me to crush with the stone?"

Sawala's body tensed. The soothing sounds of water flowing over rocks helped relax her and she unclenched her teeth to say, "No, I am a woman and do the work of a woman. I can do whatever I must." A harrier landed in the top of a tree above them. He made a rasping whistle, falling in pitch, *sheeeeew*.

"The bird says your eyes mock you with a different meaning than your words. Sawala, do not do anything against the wishes of our Chief. You could be killed!"

Standing as tall as she could, Sawala nodded, "I know this. Do you think I am stupid?"

"Again I see a different meaning in your eyes. Because I know that you are clever, I worry." Waqa waited a moment before she said, "I think the council and our Chief would give the command to kill me, too."

With the longer nights, frost was common, but this year was unusual and snow came. In the darkness of the morning hours on January 23, 1837, Sawala woke with the pains of contractions and knew she needed to be brave – not only to bring her son into the world but also to complete her plan to escape from the Kalapuyan tribe.

During the night, Sawala left the lodge to relieve herself with more frequency since being pregnant. That morning, she hoped anyone who saw her would think she was leaving for that reason. She waited until the time was very short between contractions before she sat up in her fur bed; she tightened her leg and arm furs before wrapping other furs around her body and feet. Then, before she stood, she slipped the lynx fur, little by little, away from the sleeping child and stuffed it into her breast area, hiding it beneath her deerskin, mumbling, "For my son." Like an animal in the wild, moving with speed and silence, she left the lodge and headed away from where one goes to relieve oneself.

Waqa saw her go and dressed, knowing that the snow would leave tracks for her to follow.

Heading in the direction of the river, Sawala stopped to retrieve a sack of food and things that she had kept hidden in the hollow of a tree. She thanked the animals for not eating any of her food and scurried off again, slowing or stopping when the pain was great. She wanted to be near the river for the birth, because she had made a soft place with leaves, hidden in bushes. But she changed her plans when she felt a powerful contraction. *Time to stop. I am far from the lodge.* She squatted with her back against a fir tree, pulled the lynx fur out, and placed it at her side. "This for you, my child." She opened her sack of food and found the strip of rawhide and sharp-edged rock, one to tie and the other to cut. She placed them on the lynx fur. She felt the ground for a stick, found one she liked, and placed it between her teeth as she felt a painful contraction starting.

Biting hard on the stick to stop her screams, she pushed and pushed until her hand could touch the hair of the head of her son. "Push more," she mumbled through the stick. In one smooth motion, the child slipped out onto the bed of needles under the tree – into her sight. The stick fell with her smile. Sawala hugged him to her chest at the same moment that he sucked in air and began to breathe. She moved into the light of the moonshine to have a look at her little man. He had a birthmark on his scalp; Sawala ran a finger over the black oval mark. It was the size of the joint of her thumb. She placed him on his lynx bed. "Greetings, my son, how do you know it is best not to cry?" She tied the cord in two places and reached for the sharp rock.

A twig snapped!

Sawala stopped and didn't move. Silence. But she knew something or someone was there. With shaking hands she put the cord against the tree and jabbed the stone to cut it, making a muffled thud sound. She began to close the lynx fur around her son when Waqa stepped into her view.

Without words, Waqa reached down, snatched the child, and hurried toward the river where there were large stones and boulders. The child started to cry.

"No, Waqa, no, please, leave him." Sawala knew the afterbirth must be expelled, but she seized the lynx fur and ran after her mother. "No," she cried out.

Only minutes away, Waqa came to the river. She placed the baby on a huge boulder and bent down to look for a rock to kill. Finding one, she stood up straight hefting an oval stone – heavy and wide.

Sawala could not run fast and saw her mother walking the few feet toward her baby on the boulder.

Waqa strained to raise the weight above her head. She froze!

Sawala stopped, too. Something was wrong! Sawala saw fear on her mother's face while she held the uplifted rock. She sensed danger. Above the sound of the river, she heard a thundering.

Out of the darkness two horsemen came at a gallop.

At first, Sawala had puzzled over what she heard, until she saw the silhouettes of two men on horseback approaching fast. The child, on the cold stone, screamed. The path of the horses went straight toward Waqa.

Waqa looked this way and that, not knowing what to do, until the men reined in their horses a step away. She cried out before dropping the stone and turning to run.

One man shouted to the other as he slipped off his horse and lifted the child. His eyes grew wide and Sawala, who was hiding behind a tree, saw the puzzlement on his face. Again the man shouted to the other who remounted and rode after Waqa.

At that moment, Sawala squatted, like before, and the afterbirth oozed out, noiseless like a slug, slipping across the earth beneath her feet. She closed her eyes to tell herself to make no sounds. When she opened them again and peeked around the tree, she stood amazed to see the white man slipping her son into his shirt, against his skin, and closing his shirt and jacket.

The other rider returned without Waqa. The men talked. As the moon passed into an opening in the trees, the man with the child mounted his horse to leave. With the moonlight, Sawala saw who he was.

She whispered his name, "Bailey."

Statue of Dr. John McLoughlin on grounds of Oregon State Capitol

SALEM, OREGON

CHAPTER 5

THREE JOURNEYS –
WILLIAM, SAWALA, AND MARGARET

In the darkness before dawn on January 23, 1837, Sawala gave birth to her son. During that same morning, William J. Bailey saved his son's life and Margaret Jewett Smith boarded a ship on the east coast bound for Oregon Country. These three events happened at almost the same hour – on the east coast, Margaret sailed out of the port of Boston at eight in the morning, which was a still-dark five o'clock in the morning in Oregon Country.

On January 23, 1837, Margaret and William Bailey knew nothing of each other or what the future held for them. Yet if Margaret had known of this coincidence, she would have opened her Bible to read what the words of her Lord had to say about all of this.

If Bailey had known that he had his son in his arms, he would have puzzled at the ways of the universe, for he should have been on a ship sailing to California. In fact, he had boarded that ship, but an event of nature had caused a setback and delayed the trip.

Both Margaret and Bailey would later agree that the three events were a godsend.

Sawala accepted this day in 1837 as her destiny. She knew that all who live on earth connect to each other – giving and taking – to balance the existence of one with the other. She knew that even the smallest event had meaning in the cycle of life. All living things entwine. Even in death, there was importance when one life disintegrates to become soil for another life to begin and grow. Sawala loved the trees, the birds, a blade of grass, and her son.

Now these three were starting on journeys that would eventually bring them together. Margaret and Sawala began on January 23, 1837, but one must go back a month to understand William's journey.

William J. Bailey Begins his Journey

Having been in Oregon Country for over a year, Bailey had many friends. For him, friends meant drinking. Although he believed he had more control than before, he was wrong. He still got stinking drunk and was obnoxious, but his friends helped him because in Oregon Country, knowledge and experience among the few white people was a resource for all. Whether a man was a blacksmith, miller, farmer, boat builder, or doctor, their abilities were shared and needed by all. Each person became an asset for others.

Knowing this to be true, Ewing Young and William Bailey put aside their differences and learned to work together for the good of Oregon Country. They had all kinds of ideas and schemes to better their lives.

"If we're ever going to make it here, we need to go down to California and get some cattle," one of them said over drinks one night. Bailey and Young would argue for years about who thought of this idea. Whoever had said it first, mattered little; whoever could get the venture started, mattered a lot.

Soon after the idea was hatched, George Gay, Solomon Smith, and Webley Hauxhurst joined them for drinks. All of them agreed that bringing cattle to Oregon Country would help not only the five of them but the other settlers as well.

Webley held up his glass to make the toast, "When we prosper, Oregon prospers!"

"That damn McLoughlin pretends to help us all, but he has all the cattle in these parts and we pay an arm and a leg to eat a steak," Ewing complained. "He's got a monopoly. Let's break it."

"Yeah, I'm tired of renting a cow from Hudson's Bay Company when we need milk. I want to have my own."

"To make this work, we need to find a lot of money."

None of them had much money. Each of them had some land. A settler could claim land by building a house, living on it, and working it for three years. Because of Ewing's and Smith's sawmill, all of them had access to wood, and they built houses. But they were just eking out a living.

Ewing announced a plan to build a distillery to sell alcohol to the Indians, "I'll make money selling spirits from my still!"

Hauxhurst stood up abruptly, knocking over his chair. He leaned over the table with his knuckles pushing on the tabletop. "Ewing, you can't do that! For years there's been a policy not to sell spirits to the natives." He banged one of his fists against the table. "They go crazy if they drink."

Ewing seemed to disregard the comments and took another swallow of his drink. When he set the glass down, he retorted, "That's McLoughlin's policy, ain't mine. I'm sick of him controlling everything. I'm surprised McLoughlin don't have a rule about when we can take a shit." He drained his glass.

Bailey agreed with Ewing on this, "There's no law. Ewing can sell his booze to anyone who wants it. Well, he doesn't have any yet," Bailey chortled, "and what he makes may kill a man. I'm going to wait and let him drink his own before I try it."

That brought some hearty guffaws from all, even from Ewing, who said, "I may have to experiment for a while before I get the recipe right. That's for sure."

Just talking about the still, Hauxhurst bristled. "Damn it, Ewing, build your still, but don't sell to the natives."

Bailey used Hauxhurst's nickname, "Ah, Hoxie, I heard that you joined that temper-thance shociety at the Mission. Whath you doing here with us?" Bailey had drunk until he couldn't see straight. "You drinking with us or here to preach?" Bailey turned to Gay to ask, "Is Hoxie drinking?"

George Gay leaned over to look at Hoxie and answered, "Well, I ain't here to keep track of the drinks, but I think he ain't even sipped anything outta his glass all evening. He uses it to make a toast from time to time. By the way, I heard that he visits the Mission a lot and has found his Lord."

"Hey, don't talk about me like I ain't here."

And Bailey started to repeat what he had said, "I know he is in the temperance so, sho, soci – damn it, you know what I mean."

Hauxhurst urged, "Hey! Just ask me if you want to know something."

Ewing reached over and picked up Hauxhurst's glass. "We emptied the bottle. Hoxie, if you ain't goin' to drink this, I sure as hell will." He lifted the glass with an approving nod from Hauxhurst and drank it down. "Whooee, that had a kick. Did you spit in it, Hoxie?" Not waiting for or wanting an answer, Ewing continued, "Come up to my still and spit in it once in a while. I think it would make the spirits better."

Webley Hauxhurst never minded friends making him the butt of jokes. He had a rough exterior, but was a fair and just man. He never judged anyone, even before he had learned "Judge not that ye be not judged" from the Bible. He saw worth in most, but he was frank. "Look at you, Ewing, you sound like a fool! And Bailey, you're so drunk you can't talk. Let's call it a night, but tomorrow come to my place. I want to talk more about goin' to California for cattle. You got a good idea there. I'm going to invite some others, like Philip Edwards, Calvin Tibbets, Pierre DePuis, Williams, and Emert Ergnette. I think they'd be interested in joining up with this drive."

News traveled fast in Oregon Country, courtesy of the Willamette River and as a result of all the comings and goings to the Hudson's Bay Company. People talked while they headed to the Fort to sell their furs, wheat, corn, *parflèches*, baskets, and whatever else they had. Everyone – white men, missionaries, Indians, French Canadians, and Irish settlers – had to travel to Fort Vancouver. There was some trading not involving the Fort, but if you wanted a gun or powder to shoot it, nails or a hammer to use them, gingham fabric or thread to sew a dress – nowhere except the Hudson's Bay Company had those kinds of supplies.

So on the rivers, canoes passed bateaux; on the trails and roads, wagons passed horseback riders; people met others at homes, mills, and the falls; and everyone talked about these two schemes. Both were big news – not only Ewing Young building a still for selling spirits to the natives, but also men starting a cattle run to bring stock from California. It took less than a day for these pieces of news to reach the ears of John McLoughlin and only a moment to raise his fury.

Like glittering winged termites, coming from who knows where, people appeared overnight. Some had sparkling gold coins; others had paper money from the United States; people brought gold dust and silver, furs and grain. And after they invested in the cattle run, everyone complained about Ewing's still. People dug deeply into their pockets to have the opportunity to own a few cows from this cattle scheme; but, like termites, they came to gnaw down the idea of selling firewater to the Indians.

About this time, a naval ship from the United States sailed up the Columbia River to the Hudson's Bay Company. Lieutenant William Slacum commanded the ship and took an interest in the cattle venture; he wrote into his report to the War Department:

> Nothing was wanting to insure the comfort, wealth, and every happiness for the people of this beautiful country, but the possession of meat cattle. And the Hudson's Bay Company, who refused to sell under any circumstances, owned all the cattle in the country. The people had to rent the animals to use them.

Hence, the Lieutenant assisted in the formation of the Willamette Cattle Company in 1836. In the estimation of Lieutenant Slacum, Ewing Young was the only man with sufficient experience to lead this whole expedition. Young had connections in California for purchasing cattle, he had had dealings with the Mexican government, and he had been a trapper trekking through the Siskiyou Trail between California and Oregon Country.

At the first meetings of this newly formed Willamette Cattle Company, Lieutenant William Slacum of the United States Navy sat listening to the disorganized discussion.

"Money ain't the only problem. How we going to get to California?"

Not waiting for someone to respond, another man complained, "A trip down is costly and time-consuming. Who can walk away from their life for months and months?"

"Yeah, I've got a business to run," said Webley Hauxhurst, "but I want to help."

Someone else said, "I want to help 'cuz I want to git some cattle, but I ain't got no money."

Hauxhurst suggested, "We need drivers for the cattle, and I would think that we could pay a dollar a day."

A man shouted, "Hell, that's crazy. We can't guarantee wages when we ain't even got money to buy the animals!"

Hauxhurst complained, "You interrupted me, 'fore I was done. Course, not in cash, we could pay in cattle at the end of the trip. Would that help ya?"

"Sure!"

Another man worried, "We got to time this right to not come back when the snow closes the passes through the Siskiyous. We need to go now so we's got time to buy enough cattle and be ready to leave at the right time. And who even knows when the right time is?"

Ewing replied, "Those are legitimate worries. I know 'cuz I've come through the Siskiyou Trail many times."

Throughout the evening, more problems were discussed than solved.

Finding the right moment, Lieutenant Slacum stood to talk, "May I have the floor?" He hesitated until all eyes were on him. "I have been given the authority to assist the people of Oregon. So, to you eleven men here tonight who volunteered to go on this cattle run, I can offer free passage to California on my ship the *Loriot*."

Cheers went up in the room, and men started applauding before he had finished.

Ewing hollered, "Quiet men! Let him go on."

The Lieutenant raised his hands. "Yes, I have more to say and remember that nothing is final at this time." He pulled on the bottom of his coat to straighten the uniform and then cleared his throat. "Humph! The help I can give you on this cattle run is one example of the advantages you would have if the United States government took possession of Oregon Country."

"Hell, this ain't the time for politics," Bailey murmured to Ewing. "Don't let him get started on this."

A ripple of talk washed through the room. Some stood.

To stop the talk, Ewing hit his fist to the table. The room went quiet. He said, "Men, sit back in your seats. Lieutenant Slacum, we respect why you were sent to Oregon Country, but this is not the time to talk about that."

Slacum returned to the topic of this meeting and let it be known, "In my opinion, the choice of a leader on the cattle run is most critical. You need someone experienced in all ways to benefit your efforts. According to the facts I have learned, Ewing Young has the qualifications."

Again he was interrupted; this time with disgruntled words. Voices erupted with "No!" A flurry of complaining circled the room, and bits of the griping were heard, "No good can come of it," "liquor for Indians ain't," "crazy scheme," and "it's gonna be nothing but trouble."

The Lieutenant turned toward Ewing and asked in a loud voice, "Mr. Young, would you please stand?" After Ewing stood, Slacum turned back to his audience and bellowed with a stiff back, "I believe we all know why these men object to you being the leader." The men continued to talk between themselves as the Lieutenant came to the point in a louder voice, "And it is not about your experience, Mr. Young." He hesitated a moment and took a deep breath before riding into the storm, "I hear that you are fitting up a distillery with the purpose to sell spirits to the native people hereabouts."

The room quieted.

"Yes," Ewing stated, "that is true."

"Do you realize that most people admonish you for this endeavor?"

Ewing feared no one. "I do. But it ain't none of their business."

Murmurs started circling the room, and the talk grew louder until one man jumped out of his chair and shouted, "You're crazy! It's all our business."

Slacum shouted, "Mr. Young, you have missed the point! Please everyone calm down, so we can talk." The men settled down again and gave Slacum their full attention. He continued in a compassionate tone, "Don't you see, Mr. Young, that your pursuit of that endeavor does and will continue to affect *your* businesses? I imagine that you are concerned about your own businesses."

Ewing, still standing, threw up his hands. "You're not makin' any sense."

"Let me make it clearer to you. Those who disagree with you about selling to the natives can't stop you. Like you said, it ain't their business. But they can stop coming to your gristmill. I understand that Webley Hauxhurst has one, too. His is old and may not be as good as yours, but they could go to his instead because of your decision. People who owe you for wood from your sawmill could be late in paying, to make a point. Before long, you will have a lot of drunken Indians around your place, sleeping it off under a tree, fighting, and breaking things. Is that what you want?" Slacum hesitated and turned to the crowd before continuing to make his point.

"Oregon Country is being made by each of you. You need to work together. These men need you and your experience to have a successful cattle run." Slacum turned back to face Ewing. "A leader is someone who demands respect because he deserves respect."

Someone agreed with a "Hear, hear!"

"This cattle run will be a more profitable enterprise than selling spirits to the natives. And what these men want in a leader is someone who knows this cattle run will benefit not only him but everyone else."

Ewing flung his arms wide and blurted out, "You've said enough! I'm beginning to think I won't have time to build that distillery after all."

Hats flew to the ceiling, hurrahs bounced from the walls, and applause erupted to fill the room.

Ewing raised his hands to quiet everyone, "The Lieutenant is a generous and logical man. If you men would ask me to be your leader, I would accept and tell you that I think we need to get down to California as fast as we can."

Again the room filled with clapping hands and shouts of enthusiasm.

After another hour of talk, men began to leave. Hauxhurst approached Ewing, who was talking with Lieutenant Slacum, and waited to ask something, "Ewing, did you get that letter from the Temperance Society?"

"Why yes, I did. And I happen to have my reply here in my pocket. Would you take it to them?" Ewing pulled out a paper, and Hauxhurst opened it.

"Ewing, you son of a gun!" Hauxhurst turned to the Lieutenant. "Yesterday we sent this communication telling Ewing that if he abandoned this enterprise forever, we would reimburse him for some of his expenses." Hauxhurst walloped Ewing on the back. "Look here, before this meeting he had already written this letter and decided not to go ahead with his distillery. And he declined any of the recompense we offered him for his cost already spent."

The Lieutenant took the letter, and read:

Gentlemen, I accede to your request to abandon the distillery forever. Nevertheless, I do not feel it is necessary to receive any recompense whatsoever for expenditures. I am thankful to the society for their offer.

I remain yours,
Ewing Young

Now the Lieutenant turned to shake Ewing's hand.

And Webley Hauxhurst followed, taking Young's hand and pumping it with force. "This is such good news. I put five dollars in the fund to pay you. Now I can get it back." He grinned a big one, "Ewing, you sure were pullin' our leg at this meeting tonight."

Four days after the meeting, the men headed north on the Willamette River to the Columbia River, where the *Loriot* stood. They boarded on January 21, 1837. By the next morning, they were ready to sail, having raised $1,600 to buy the livestock. At the last minute, McLoughlin decided the idea would benefit him and added $900 to buy cattle for the Fort. Lieutenant Slacum advanced $500 to Jason Lee on behalf of the Methodist Mission. Along with the money, people had a deep hope for a promising investment. Now Ewing had a total of $3,000 to fulfill those hopes with cattle in the Willamette Valley.

When it was time to raise the sails, Reverend Jason Lee gathered all the men of the Willamette Cattle Company on the quarterdeck and offered prayers for the success of the undertaking and for Godspeed, and then he left the boat.

On the *Loriot*, Lieutenant Slacum sailed west down the Columbia River toward the Pacific Ocean, with a sister ship close behind. This river was known for its rough waters and the dangers it posed to ships, but there was smooth sailing that day.

The day was January 22nd and the sun was popping in and out of the clouds. They sailed in good spirits, with the anticipation of success. Bailey and George Gay hung over the port side of the ship and waved to natives on the shore. Excitement filled the air as the wind whistled in their ears; they couldn't remove the grins from their faces.

When the *Loriot* reached the mouth of the Columbia and headed into the Pacific, the sun disappeared, dark clouds rolled over, and the sailors started shouting. Immediately, they encountered rough seas. The ship rolled and tossed from side to side. Bailey and Gay kept falling on deck as they tried to make their way to the stairs to go below. Then the wind increased and rain plummeted.

Gay saw disaster approaching and shouted, "Bailey, get down below! I'm going to help these sailors. We must get the sails down!" Gay clutched a lifeline – a rope strung along the ship for men to grab in situations like this – and headed to the stern, leaving Bailey foundering near the railing.

A gust of wind increased to gale speed and forced Bailey to lose his hold. He toppled from port to starboard, rolling across the deck; the rain stinging like splinters. He got to his knees to get up just when a sailor, holding on to a line from one of the masts, swung over him. Bailey ducked down flat on the deck again. One of the sails started flapping. A barrel rolled by Bailey and just missed him.

Another gust, and the ship shifted again. Bailey slid back to port side and landed against the wooden slats with a thud. He held on to a metal fitting, feeling secure for the minute and glad that his back had taken the force of the impact instead of his head. Within seconds, he heard a crash and the sound of splitting wood. A cable came loose from its mast, crashing with its metal gasket into the wheelhouse. Then another cable broke from the deck and the ship reeled, spinning onto the shore.

With the vessel driven ashore, the sailors managed to bring down all the sails and secure the lines on the damaged *Loriot*. The sister ship waited for the storm to pass and then came to their aid. Lieutenant Slacum announced that the trip was postponed until repairs could be made, "I'll stay on board and hobble the *Loriot* back for repairs. Maybe the work can be done in Baker's Bay near Astoria. You men from the Willamette Cattle Company must return to Fort Vancouver on the other ship. Wait there for me. I don't know how long it will be, but only a week or two, not months. Don't be disheartened, I'll get you to California."

Once they were back at the Fort, Bailey suggested, "Ewing, let's not sit here. They said it would be at least a week, or maybe two. Let's borrow some horses from McLoughlin and ride south to raise more funds. Remember, before we sailed, you regretted that we didn't have time to get in touch with everyone. Here's our time!"

They saddled up and rode out late in the day. Snow began to fall like sifted flour, dusting the edges of trees and grass, the horses' manes, and their hat brims. At first, body heat melted the flakes that fell on their clothes until the wind blew colder on the French Prairie.

Before they got near their cabins, all was white and Ewing said, "Let's stop here at my neighbor's. Their house is warm inside, and I can smell somethin' cookin'. At my place, I ain't got nothin' to eat." Without dismounting, they rode their horses up to the porch and called, "Anybody home?"

A dark-haired boy in a green shirt with Indian beadwork came to the door. A smaller boy's head poked out under his arm, and whatever he chewed was smeared around his mouth. They both wore knee breeches. The older boy said with a smile, "Hello, Mr. Young and Dr. Bailey. My ma and pa went to help Mrs. Bugat have her baby 'cuz something was wrong. They been gone a long time."

Bailey turned to Ewing to suggest, "I'd better go see what the problem is. I might be able to help."

"Yeah, let's go." They thanked the boys and rode away.

Everyone knew everyone in Oregon Country. On January 22, 1837, fewer than one hundred non-native men lived there and no white women had yet arrived. Of those men, most were French Canadians who worked for the Hudson's Bay Company or retired from it; some were *Métis*, children from the men who had native wives; four lived at the Methodist Mission; and the others were a handful of men like the eleven going on the cattle run – men who were trying to make Oregon their home. Thus no one had to tell Bailey and Ewing how to get to the Bugats' homestead. And no one needed to tell Bailey that Mrs. Bugat had lost her three-year-old to measles last year and a younger child to influenza. She had no other children. It was obvious that this new baby meant a lot to the family.

Upon arrival, Bailey removed his medical bundle from his *parflèche*, "Ewing, will you tie up my horse?" Heading toward the door, he didn't wait for Ewing's reply or for an answer to his forceful knock.

With a gasp, Monsieur Bugat said, "Dr. Bailey, how you know?" He fell to his knees and looked to the ceiling. "Thank you, Lord, you hear my prayers."

"Mr. Bugat, good evening, sir," Bailey said before he turned to greet the two neighbors as well. The neighbor's wife wore a gingham dress with beadwork on the bodice. Both she and Mrs. Bugat were from the Chinook tribe, but their heads were not flattened. Mr. Bugat and his neighbor were retirees from fur trading and from the hard life of trapping. They had lived a life exposed to wind, rain, and cold, and their stories were etched in the creases and crevices of their weathered faces. Even their handshake told of hard work; Bailey felt as if he clutched the backside of an uncured hide.

Bailey said, "Now let me see this mother."

In bed in her cotton nightshirt, Mrs. Bugat lay listless and covered with sweat. Bailey asked Monsieur Bugat questions and learned that her contractions had started yesterday. He listened to her heart but heard no fetal heartbeat. The three adults leaned over to watch and Bailey asked, "Please everyone go sit over there for the moment and get ready to help when I need it."

When Ewing came in, he saw Bailey examining the woman. Bailey looked at him with an expression close to fear and motioned Ewing over with a slight movement of his head.

In a soft voice, Bailey asked Ewing, "Do you still have some booze from your distillery?"

Ewing nodded.

"Go get it for me." Then he turned to the group, "I'm ready for your help. First, find me clean cloth. A lot of it." Bailey turned to the woman and asked, "Can you make some soup or food for all of us?" Bailey went to the hearth, dropped his instruments into the hanging water kettle, and swung the arm over the fire. When Ewing returned, Bailey asked everyone to step outside and he explained, "I didn't want Mrs. Bugat to hear, but I think the child is dead. And the mother may not make it." Bailey placed his hand on the shoulder of Monsieur Bugat. "I am so sorry I had to tell you this. But I am going to do my best to save her."

The man began to cry.

"Mr. Bugat, I am going to do a caesarean operation."

Puzzled faces stared at Bailey.

"To save her life, I must cut her open and take the dead child out of her."

The woman gasped.

Bailey led them back inside. "You three men help me move her from the bed to the table. It's higher." After they moved her, Bailey urged, "Mr. Bugat you stay away. This is not for you to see. Actually, it's best that everyone stay away from the table while I'm working. Except you, Ewing! You come help me."

Ewing started to complain.

Bailey cocked his head and pointed to his jaw to emphasize, "You owe me."

"Can't I help?" The neighbor man asked.

Anxious to remove the stillborn, Bailey pointed across the room. "You can keep the fire going, stack more firewood on the porch, go milk the cow, you know, things like that." He pulled the man close, with a grasp on his arm a bit too tight, and pleaded in a low growl, "Get Mr. Bugat out of this house! He shouldn't see. I'll call if I need something."

And so Bailey began. He had Ewing expose her distended stomach and she groaned. "Mrs. Bugat, we're going to help you with your baby. It won't be long," he lied.

Bailey washed her belly, first with soap and water. "Ewing, take a clean cloth and wipe the sweat from her face, then get my flask of laudanum out of my *parflèche*," he nudged it with his boot, pushing it across the floor to Ewing. "And give her a good drink."

Mrs. Bugat gagged on the laudanum and coughed. "Ahggg," she cried out in pain.

Bailey retrieved his instruments from the boiling water and poured them into a bowl to cool. He motioned to the woman. "Fill this kettle again and put it back on the fire."

Ewing was rocking from one foot to the other.

"Stop that dancing, Ewing. If you have to pee, do it now and git back here."

"Damn it, Bailey, I don't need to pee!"

"Okay then! Pour some of your firewater over my hands and on her

135

belly. Then go hold Mrs. Bugat down by her shoulders. Stand out of my way. Up behind her head."

Bailey wanted to wait for the laudanum to sedate her, but her life depended on him getting the baby out as fast as possible. He picked up the scalpel. "Okay, Ewing, hold her good and tight." He made an incision down the midline of her stomach to her pubic line and then, from the gap, up to the navel. He took care to avoid making a deep cut that would injure the displaced organs such as the bladder.

She shrieked!

Anguish filled Ewing's eyes and sweat poured from his underarms.

In deep concentration, Bailey ignored her scream. *Damn, why didn't I ask more questions back in England when that cadaver was on the table, and they opened her?* He hadn't cut deep enough! He sucked in his breath and cut again. Mrs. Bugat went limp and lost consciousness. Satisfied with the incision and feeling content that there was little bleeding, he pulled her stomach muscles open with his hands and saw the uterus. *Damn, it's good she fainted.* He tucked some folded clean cloths beneath the wound. *The cadaver didn't have liquids; I don't want blood or amniotic fluid inside this woman.* He started to cut again – this time into the uterus. He punctured the uterine wall in the center and slipped his fingers in before he sliced upward and downward from that hole. He made a twelve-inch opening. *If the child is alive, my fingers will prevent me from cutting him.* He reached into the uterus to grasp the baby's feet. Slipping the fetus out, he was sure that the child had been dead for hours. The baby's body had a blue sheen and no heartbeat. He draped the little lifeless corpse across his mother's chest. *Glad she can't see this!* The umbilical cord extended from the child's belly back into his mother; he tied and cut it, as in a live birth.

Bailey reached back into the incision and massaged the uterus to encourage the afterbirth to release. This gave him a moment to turn to his friend and say, "Ewing, she fainted. You don't need to hold her down. Get over here to help me. Put a cloth down so I can get the baby out of sight. It will be less than a minute before the afterbirth releases. Hurry!"

Just as Ewing arrived and spread a piece of red calico cloth, the bloody sac of afterbirth detached and Bailey pulled it out of the uterus, splashing Ewing. After Bailey placed the child and placenta onto the cloth, he glanced to Ewing and said, "Now pick up that bulb with a tube attached. I may need you to suction liquids out of this wound."

Under his breath, Ewing complained, "Damn you, Bailey."

But Bailey didn't hear, and he stretched her abdomen open to look inside to see if all the membranes had released. *It looks clean.* He placed another absorbent cloth on one end of the incision and began to close the other end with a needle, curved and thin like a fishhook. Without looking up, Bailey ordered, "Ewing, suck up this blood and liquid. Quick!" Under and over he sewed from one side to the other until the deepest flesh of the uterine was closed. Then he started on the next layer. To close the uterine muscle took three rows of catgut sutures. Finally, he was ready to stitch her stomach muscle. Beads of sweat rolled down his face and onto his beard, but his concentration didn't wane. His hands were steady and worked faster than he had thought possible. When he was finally closing the peritoneum layer and her outer stomach skin, he could relax a bit. *She hasn't bled much. What luck!*

The neighbor woman went to door to motion for Mr. Bugat and her husband. In murmurs, she told them what she had seen. Monsieur Bugat sat and cried.

The passage of time had no meaning to Bailey; he didn't know if thirty minutes had passed or hours, but he had worked through the night. At last, Bailey turned and said, "I'm finished and Mrs. Bugat's heart is beating stronger than when I came."

The neighbors left to go home to their boys. Monsieur Bugat came forward.

"Please don't touch her. But you can pull up a chair and talk to her. It would be good for her to hear your voice. Talk softly and calmly. Don't mention the child. It's my job to tell her about that." Bailey picked up the bloodied bundle – heavy with all he had taken from her – and went outside. "Ewing, pick up the last of those clean rags and come with me."

They walked toward a creek that ran alongside the house. Bailey took the child out, cut the cord off to the belly, and washed the baby. "I know they will want to bury him." He set the child on the largest piece of cloth he could find and wrapped him up in a blue and green wool plaid cloth that looked like it had once been one worn pant leg.

Ewing was squatting and washing his hands. "Damn, I feel sick. I can't believe that you made me do that. There's even blood on my shirt. Damn you, Bailey."

"Shut up, Ewing. I still have to tell that mother that her child is dead. She has lost three children. You think I care that you feel sick?"

Later that morning, before it was light, Monsieur Bugat made them a breakfast of bacon and fried cornmeal. His wife was not better, but not worse.

"My neighbors will come back again today. My wife will need a woman to cry with."

Bailey promised to stop back later in the day. "We want to go talk with Longtain and a couple of others. Then we'll be back to see how your wife is doing. Don't let her get up. And bring her a lot of water to drink." He ate his last bite of fried cornmeal and said, "Please don't tell her about the baby unless you have to. She's had a lot of laudanum, so she is going to be sleepy and drunk-like. I should be the one to tell her, so I can answer any questions she has." Bailey had another problem to tell them, and he hated the thought of it. He needed to advise her not to get pregnant again because the wall of her uterus could have weakened. He figured he'd tell them both at the same time. *Time! I need some time to figure out how to explain this to them.*

Leaving the Bugats' homestead, Ewing and Bailey rode out into the darkness under a bright moon that had not yet set. They didn't talk much at first. Then Ewing asked, "Why did you use my liquor to pour over your hands and her belly?"

Bailey lifted his hat to scratch his head and got an idea how to explain. He looked at Ewing as they rode. "Well, for a long time I've had this notion that those little bugs like lice and fleas aren't suppose to be inside a wound. Just now, I scratched my head. If I had lice, they'd be under my fingernails and on my hands. I figure that those bugs could cause problems with the healing. I knew your spirits would kill 'em. That stuff nearly killed me when I tried it!" Bailey grinned and Ewing pulled back his arm to sock him. But Bailey dug his heels into his horse and took off at a gallop. Ewing followed fast on his tail. They both were laughing, but not for long.

Just ahead, they could see the silhouette of a woman with a huge rock above her head. At that moment, Bailey heard the cry of a newborn. Both he and Ewing knew, without a doubt, what the scene meant. One could not live in Oregon Country and not know how the natives rid themselves of unwanted half-breeds.

The path of the horses went straight to her. Waqa looked this way and that, not knowing what to do, until they reined in their horses a step away. She cried out in fear and threw the huge rock down before turning to run. With a thud, it fell, hitting other rocks on the ground.

Bailey slipped out of his saddle and lifted the still blood-covered newborn. He saw that someone cared – *the cord is tied and cut. That woman running away surely didn't do that!* "Ewing, ride after her and bring her back."

Ewing remounted his horse and disappeared into the trees.

Bailey pulled the child close and began to unbutton his shirt. The snow had started to fall again and there was a cold wind. He slipped the child – feet-first – into his shirt and couldn't stop talking to him, "Take it easy, little fella. There, there." When he was ready to tuck the head, he stopped. "Look at that! You have a birthmark up here in your hair. Looks like a scrub oak leaf. It sure does, but it's black." He pulled his jacket closed to get them both warmer, cradling the child with his arm on the outside of his clothes and jostling him to calm him. The crying stopped. "If that damn savage, trying to crush your head, isn't your mother, she won't have any milk. But don't you worry. I know a woman who does have some."

Ewing returned. "Don't know where she went. Couldn't find any tracks either."

Bailey put his foot in the stirrup and pulled himself up into the saddle. "Guess you know where I'm going now."

"Where?"

"Ewing, a few hours ago I removed a dead baby from a woman. Where do you think?"

They turned their horses around.

The Bugats would have a son.

Sawala's Journey

Sawala stood up as the horsemen rode away. Fighting her dizziness, she leaned against the tree and inhaled deeply, ignoring the pain in her chest. "My son, where Bailey go with my son?" The lightheadedness was passing as she reached for the lynx fur and tied it around her head for warmth in the wind and snow. After walking back to get her food pouch and securing it inside the fur around her body, she started out. "I must find my son. I cannot live not knowing."

She knew the tracks of the horses would be easy to follow, so there was no need to rush. She also knew her body needed rest. "But later."

She began her journey to her new life, knowing that she could never return to the Kalapuyans. Leaving the only life she had known made her think of her mother. *When Waqa gets to the lodge, will she tell everyone? No, no, she will not. She must pretend to not know where I am so they will not kill her.* Sawala noticed that the riders were disappearing in the direction from where they had come. "Waqa, I am sorry to leave you, but now my life is a journey to my son. I go to his new life." She would never know what happened to her mother.

Sawala found the walking exhausting. She rested often, although her maternal instinct drove her on. The pain in her chest, with each deep breath, started hurting more as the day progressed. Exhausted, she stopped and welcomed the early darkness of January. She took her cutting stone and chopped boughs from the fir trees – six limbs full of thick needles – to make her bed. Choosing an oak tree that stood next to a fir tree, she pushed the fallen leaves beneath the oak into a pile under the evergreen. The standing fir would stop the snow from falling on her; an oak would not do that. She placed three of the cut limbs on top of the soft oak leaves and set aside the others to cover herself later. She found a stream and drank for a long time before returning to her spot. Sitting on her bed with her back against the tree trunk, she opened her bag. As she chewed a camas cake, her eyes took in the beauty in the shadows of the moonlit night, and her ears enjoyed the sound of the breeze, water, and animals – a coyote, an owl, and some little creature squeaking. After eating, she scooted down into her bed, covering herself with the lynx fur and the three boughs. Soon she slipped into a deep sleep.

During the morning hours, while it was still dark, she heard the leaves rustle and something scurry away. Her mind needed a moment to clear the slumber before she understood what had happened. Her first thought was that the Kalapuyans had found her and her heart jumped. But then her eyes grew wide as she heard the noise of an animal. She sat up. "My food!" Sure enough, a raccoon had snatched her pouch and opened it. She had put it under her head, but she must have rolled away from it during the night. She stood and saw the tracks and followed. A few feet away she found the pouch with nothing in it. "No! I must eat like you," she said to the raccoon. And then she saw a large chunk of camas cake on the ground. "Thank you." She sat back down and ate some.

More snow had fallen while she slept, but not enough to cover the deep tracks of the two horses. She noticed that it was warmer than the day before when she had started out. Then she noticed other tracks. Cougar! Fresh and huge paw marks crossed her path. She stopped to gaze around, knowing she would never see him. So she whispered to him, "I am small and not too tasty." And she spoke to the wind, "Blow my scent away from this mighty cat," and to the trees, "Hide me among your shadows," as she hurried off.

She traveled faster than she should have and was soon tired. Next to a creek bed, she stopped, panting. *The pain is worse in my chest.* She drank from the water and noticed a beaver dam a few feet upstream. Two beavers slapped their tails at her intrusion and disappeared under the water. Sawala smiled.

She bent down for another drink and froze in place. She saw and heard nothing in particular, but knew danger was near. Maybe she smelled the cat without realizing it. *Maybe*, she thought. *Maybe the warning signal of the beavers was because of the cougar. Maybe the lack of bird chatter meant he was there.*

Her heart pounded against her chest and fear oozed from her pores. She knew she could not hide: her smell was like a strong silent scream. She turned from the water's edge.

There he was – majestic, magnificent, and deadly!

Above her on a ledge over the water, the cougar sat poised to leap. She gave a small move to the right, hoping he would expect her to go right, and then she jumped to the left and ran as the huge cat hurled in the air toward her. She saw him airborne in the other direction. It had worked!

Suddenly there was a deafening clank and screech – the scream of an angry cougar! Sawala could not grasp what had occurred behind her back, but she knew her life had been favored over his. She stopped to turn and saw the cougar caught in a beaver trap. He lunged at her. His one back leg was clamped halfway up. He whipped his front paw out and caught her leg as the chain holding the trap stopped his momentum. Sawala fell backward and pulled herself across the ground with her arms to widen the distance between her life and possible death. Their eyes met, and as she stared into the depths of his amber iris, his eyes spoke of determination to fight and live.

She blinked from his gaze. *I am too close! The teeth of this magnificent animal look as long as my hands.* He lashed out at her, missing and screeching. She thought her ears would explode from the noise. "But you can no longer reach me," she whispered to him. To make sure, she stood to run, because the trap seemed small against his powerful strength.

She ran and ran, not thinking to look for horse tracks, not heeding the pain in her chest. She ran unaware of her bleeding leg. She ran until she collapsed in a faint. And there she remained, unconscious.

When she awoke and opened her eyes, she found herself in a bed inside a cabin with a native woman in a green cotton dress placing a cool wet cloth on her forehead. Sawala burned with fever and a pain came from her leg. She looked down at her thigh, wrapped in a poultice of leaves, and remembered that she had looked a cougar in the face and lived.

The older Indian woman spoke to her in pidgin that Sawala understood. She told Sawala that she would heal. "My name is Mémé. You fought the king of cats. I see by marks on your leg."

Sawala knew that few lived who could tell their story of facing a cougar. With these thoughts, her eyes beamed.

"Here drink some of my broth to help you sleep again."

Sawala drank and nodded her thanks before closing her eyes.

Her fever raged as the claw marks festered deep in her leg. During her sleep, Sawala's pain created nightmares. The throbbing in her thigh created a dream of dancing in the Kalapuyan camp and she became the drum. The nobles sang and chanted to the beat of her throbs. Everyone danced and as they passed they hit her thigh. With more pain, the chanting in her mind was louder. She awoke in a sweat and Mémé was there with water and soup.

Several days passed in this way. She needed sleep, not only for her abused body to heal but also to assuage the pain of her last months with the Kalapuyans.

During her time in the bed, Sawala felt her breasts swell with milk and she saddened to think that she could never suckle her child. She yearned for her son. She wondered if he was warm and safe, but decided he was. *He's with Bailey.* She wondered how his skin smelled, how the touch of his hands on her face would feel, and how his cooing voice would sound. *Since he came from me, I have a hole inside to fill. I must know where he is.*

January ended and February came before she left the bed to walk and talk. At first, Sawala spoke little.

"You say your name is Sawala. Call me Mémé," the old woman told her. "It means mother of your mother. And you can call my husband, Monsieur. He speaks little pidgin. I speak his tongue of French with him. I tell him what you say, if you like."

Sawala nodded.

The old woman sat beside Sawala and said, "We like to know what happened to you. A story of living after an attack from the king of cats must be told."

With a somber face, Sawala said, "I was attacked by a cougar. The world smiled on me that day and I kept my life. A white man's trap caught the magnificent cat by the leg and let me go free."

Sawala feared being traded as a slave again so she mentioned nothing about her past life. Although Sawala said little, she knew that her body shared her story: her forehead told that she was from the Chinook tribe, and her hair showed that she was *Métis*. Sawala was grateful when the old woman did not probe.

When April came, Mémé and Sawala went out walking to see the spring flowers, buds, and the unfolding of the leaves. While they walked and enjoyed the fragrances of spring, Mémé confided, "You are almost well. I want you to know that I saw the milk in your breasts and know that you had a child before we brought you here."

Sawala made a little gasp.

Mémé took her hand while they sat upon a large rock. "Do not worry. The moon has been full three times and you see that we do not harm you." She patted the girl's hand. "I know the life of a slave and know you must have been one. We will not send you where you do not want to go. In fact, Monsieur and I invite you to stay. I am getting older and we can use the help of another. But I need you to tell me what you plan and where you were going."

Sawala rarely allowed herself to have tears, but she wept. "I must open my heart to someone and believe someone is good. I think this of you, Mémé. I tell you all."

With patience, Mémé sat ready to listen.

And Sawala began her story, "Last year at the time of digging out the death-camas, I was asked to bed with a white man called Bailey."

When she finished her tale, she confided, "Mémé, I want to find Bailey and find my son. I have no way to care for my son, but I must know he is with good people. I hope he is with Bailey who made him grow in me."

Mémé hesitated, "I don't mean to worry you, but we know all that happens here on the prairie and I know Bailey. He is a good man. But I do not know where your son is."

Sawala cried harder.

"Do not cry, Little One," Mémé told her.

The endearing words brought calm to Sawala, and she hugged the old woman. "I like that you call me Little One."

From that day forward, they shared with talk as they did their daily work: grinding corn kernels with a stone, making flatbreads on a skillet, milking the goat, fishing, picking berries, and crushing them for juice. Sawala learned to love this woman.

During this time, a plan came to Sawala – she would learn to speak the same tongue of Bailey. "Then I could ask him about my son."

Mémé said, "There is a mission school not far from here. They take native boys to learn about their god, and they teach them to talk like Bailey. I'll ask Monsieur to go to his friend Gervais to ask if you could go. This is the only way for you to learn the tongue of the white man."

In May 1837, the Methodist Mission welcomed the first reinforcement of missionaries, bringing the first three single white women to Oregon Country – Anna Marie Pittman, Susan Downing, and Elvira Johnson. With them was a doctor, Dr. Elijah White, who came with his wife Sarepeta and their two children. On the same ship were others: a farmer, Joseph Whitcomb; a carpenter, William Willson, whom Dr. White tried to train in medicine on the voyage; a blacksmith, Alonson Beers, and the blacksmith's wife, Rachel.

With women working in the Mission, the missionaries granted Gervais's request to bring the *Métis* girl called Sawala. That May, when the camas lily bloomed, Gervais fetched her. Sawala arrived with a deerskin around her waist, the lynx skin over her shoulders, and contentment on her face.

William J. Bailey Continues His Journey

After Bailey nestled Sawala's baby into his shirt and mounted his horse, the two men separated. Ewing Young rode away to raise more money for the cattle venture, and Bailey left with the child.

The snow rose in windy swirls and dropped from the fir trees, making plopping sounds as Bailey returned to the Bugats' cabin with the newborn. The day was bright even with the sun behind clouds and Bailey glowed as well, elated with the idea of bringing a child to the Bugats. He rode at a steady pace.

Upon entering the cabin, the same neighbors greeted Bailey; they had returned to help. Bailey looked toward the bedroom and saw Mrs. Bugat sleeping in her bed. Monsieur Bugat came in with a burst of wind from the open door and brought a pail of milk from the barn.

With the child still out of sight and sleeping in his shirt, Bailey blurted out, "I guess you've heard that some tribes crush their half-breed children at birth."

Although confused by the topic, Monsieur Bugat did not bother to question the doctor. He nodded and said, "*Oui, Métis.*"

Baffled, the neighbors nodded as well.

Bailey took off his coat and draped it over a chair with his free hand; his other still supported the child. He continued talking to his puzzled audience, "Not long after Ewing and I rode away from here, we saw in the distance what looked like a woman ready to crush a child with a stone. Probably she was the mother." He started unbuttoning his shirt and three curious faces watched him. With his shirt open, he adjusted the hand that cradled the unseen child, slipped his other hand under the baby's back, and brought out the child.

He said, "This is the child."

Stunned faces peered at the sleeping baby.

Bailey turned to Monsieur Bugat to say, "He is for Mrs. Bugat and you to raise. Would you do that?"

With his hands to his cheeks and eyes wide, Monsieur Bugat muttered his amazement in endless French, talking on and on. The neighbor couple came closer, chattering also.

Turning to the woman, Bailey asked, "Could you wet a cloth with warm water so we can clean the dried blood from his birth? I'll slip him back into my shirt until we have blankets. Surely you have clothes for him."

"Oui, my wife made new ones, and we have old ones from our other children. I get," Monsieur Bugat went to the other room as the woman spread a wet cloth on the table.

Bailey wrapped the warm cloth around the baby. With a gentle touch, he began to wipe the blood from the matted hair and little face. The child awoke and peered at Bailey's face, only inches away. Bailey stopped his cleaning captivated by the child's concentration. The child didn't cry. Motionless on the outside, Bailey peered into the little face, experiencing an excitement and feeling a familiarity. They furrowed their brows at each other until Bailey felt uncomfortable with his own actions. *How long have I been staring at this baby?* He glanced to the other adults and said, "My, my, this little one doesn't look like an Indian. And look at all his hair. It was black from the blood and as I clean, it is turning red." Now the child cried.

Happiness flowed through Bailey as he worked faster to clean the baby while listening to cries of "oh" and "ah" coming from the others around the table. The three talked between themselves in words Bailey didn't understand, Chinook Jargon, French, or some native tongue. Whatever language, it didn't matter; he heard their excitement and happiness.

When Bailey's hand touched the infant's cheek, the child turned to root for a nipple. Bailey put his little finger out and, with a jerk, the child sucked it into his mouth. Bailey blushed and his heart seemed to burst inside his chest. "Without a doubt, he is a redhead." Bailey fingered the birthmark again in his hairline and showed the others. "He has this special mark like a black oak leaf, but it's nothing to worry about. He has all his fingers and toes."

This brought laughs.

"Can you put some clothes on him?" Bailey asked the neighbor woman. "It's time for him to meet his mother."

Once dressed and wrapped in a small blanket, the baby was placed next to his sleeping mother.

Mrs. Bugat opened her eyes with the touch of the child and saw her redheaded boy. A pleased smile spread across her face. She pulled him closer to suckle and began to talk in Chinook.

Monsieur Bugat explained what she said. "The Chinooks believe that babies come from the sun, and if they die as a baby, they return to the sun to be born again to the same mother. My wife thinks this baby looks like one from the sun. She is happy."

The other Chinook woman went to the bedside, and Bailey walked away.

When away from the bed, Monsieur Bugat whispered to Bailey that he had buried the stillborn in the back corner of their barn, without his wife knowing. "Outside, I could not dig frozen ground, so I dig in barn. I make a wooden cross and put it up when you are ready to tell her what happen."

As Bailey got ready to depart and join Ewing, he explained, "I'll return tonight to spend the night here and will come tomorrow night, too. I want to watch Mrs. Bugat and check on the condition of her wound."

"That good idea,"

By the first week of February, Bailey knew that Mrs. Bugat's caesarean operation had been a success; she was without fever and healing. At that time, he told her of her dead child and finding a new baby for her. She held her son sent from the sun and accepted what life had given her.

Now Bailey and Ewing were ready to ride north to board the repaired *Loriot*.

On the ride, Ewing started talking, "Do you know that McLoughlin still thinks I'm like shit? He blacklisted me here in Oregon because of a lie. A lie! He thought I stole horses back in 'thirty-five. So like you, I know how it feels to have a lie spread against you." He paused for a long while before continuing. "Also, I need to say that you sewed my leg as good as new. Now that my hair has grown back on my leg, I can barely see a scar. So I thought I should say something." He inhaled through his nose and clenched his teeth, finding it difficult to say these words. "Especially now that I've seen you perform a miracle with Mrs. Bugat, it's time I tell you I think you're a gifted surgeon. What I said years ago in California when you lost the job because of me." He gritted his teeth. "Well, it weren't true except for the drunken part. Bailey, this is as close as I can get to an apology."

Bailey understood. "Thanks, Ewing. I deserved not to have that job. I was drinking so much back then. And I know I shouldn't drink, but sometimes I need to." He laughed. "And this is as close as I can get to talking about my drinking problems."

Without any more words, they rode for miles, animosities blowing away in the breeze.

On February 10th, twenty men sailed from Fort Vancouver. Nine days later, they arrived in Fort Ross, California. Ewing suggested to the men that they go find work at a mill while he inquired about buying cattle. "It'll take time for me to arrange everything. Remember, I'm paying you to drive cattle, so you gotta earn your own victuals until the cattle run is ready." Eight of the men went to Cooper's Mill and were hired.

Ewing Young, George Gay, William Bailey, and John Turner took some upstairs rooms in the local hotel, which was also the local tavern – and claimed to be the local restaurant because they served food. Over dinner the first night, they talked.

"What you going to do first, Ewing?" Bailey wondered.

"I'm goin' to see General Vallejo. He helped me years ago when I bought horses, so I figure he's the place to start."

Gay said, "What do you want us to do to help? I know my way around here, too."

"Well, we're lookin' at buying six to seven hundred head. We won't get them all at once; I imagine we'll buy a few here and some more there. Gay, why don't you, Turner, and Bailey see where we could start corralling them." Ewing gave them a list of some ranchers to ask.

After Ewing's meeting with General Vallejo, all the business dealings turned into a political and religious battle. It turned out that the Catholic missions in California owned most of the cattle, and buyers had to be granted permission from the Mexican government to drive the herd out of their territory.

A month went by, and then two months. Ewing tried to explain to the men, "Something ain't right. I asked what's taking so long and General Vallejo avoids answering me. I think he's dealing under the table. Another man – I don't want to name him – said that the Catholic missions are fighting the sale because they think the government's going to cheat them by taking some of the cattle as their own and selling 'em to us. I ain't quite sure what's goin' on, but they promised we would have a hundred and fifty head this week."

"Only a hundred and fifty head! Damn! So we gotta herd a hundred and fifty of 'em somewhere to get fed 'til you git the rest. That costs money!" Gay stopped to think, "And, damn it all, they're wild Mexican stock and not used to men herding 'em. Right?"

By June 22nd, they had finally assembled eight hundred head of cattle, many of which had arrived starving. It was time to start the drive north. The men headed out and ran into trouble every mile of the way. This venture was the first time beef stock had been driven all the way from California to Oregon Country, and these were difficult trails even without cattle. With twenty men working day and night, they lacked enough men necessary to keep the cattle together. Every day, the men searched for wandering bovines to be herded back.

One week, the problem was not enough water – the next week, too much water. When they reached the San Joaquin River and drove the animals into the rushing river, most of the cattle turned, refusing to swim across.

Ewing screamed. "Lasso that damn animal and pull him over! Who in the hell is out there pullin' one by the horns?"

That night the men divided up and slept on both sides of the river, one group with the swimmers who had crossed. The other group spent the night planning how to get the rest across.

Someone came upon an idea. "Let's build some rafts to pull across with ropes while men on the rafts hold on to those crazy cows by their horns." They tried it and it worked, but the going was slow. They lost a week crossing the San Joaquin, and sixteen animals died. A lot of the men's enthusiasm was swept away with that river.

Quarrels cropped up with more frequency as they approached Oregon Country, and fear of Indian attacks rode with them. Bailey and Gay didn't help the situation, telling of their experience during the surprise attack of a hundred red men when Bailey got the tomahawk to his jaw.

Together Gay and Bailey drank too much every night. One such evening at the campfire, Ewing pulled them off to the side to complain. "Damn it all! Look at the two of you. You're drunk again and talking too much. Besides workin' yourselves into a crazy state of mind, you're worryin' the men. And I'm hearin' in your words the want for revenge. Git into your bedrolls and shut up!"

Weaving on his feet, Bailey put his face in Ewing's face. "You can'th tell me thath."

Ewing gave him a push, and he fell backwards. "Bailey, you're disgusting when you drink." Ewing walked off.

Adding to the men's jumpy nerves, natives frequently wandered into their camps to sit with them. Never had the red men seen cattle being moved like this or so many cattle in one place; they were curious.

One night when the air had a cold edge to it, a pair of Indians came riding on one dun mare. The two rode around looking at the herd before approaching the campsite and slipping off the mare. Talking among themselves they laughed as they walked over to the fire where the men sat. One Indian squatted near the fire and held out his hands to warm them; the other sat on the ground next to a cattle driver playing his mouth harp. A tune twanged out into the night. Neither red man had any weapon, and they behaved in a friendly manner trying to converse with the men. No one was saying much, only listening to the tune, when Gay pulled out his gun. For no apparent reason, he shot one who sat ten feet from him.

The wounded man sprang up to run, and Bailey put a second shot in him. Bleeding, the native ran twenty paces and fell down a hill. The other red man stood and froze in fear. Bailey and Gay shot him.

Philip Edwards, one of the drivers, jumped up. "What a dastardly act – how mean and base! Why'd you do that?"

Gay replied, "I told you they killed a couple of our men two years back. They attacked our men while still in their bedrolls. Now we're even."

Hearing the gunfire, Ewing came running. His fury was like waking a sleeping bear during hibernation. He socked Gay and demanded, "Gimme all your liquor. And let's go git the rest." The three walked over toward the horses where they stashed their gear by some trees. They were far enough away that the other men couldn't hear when Ewing exploded, "This was revenge! Don't tell me anything else! I don't like these stinkin' Injuns either, but we ain't even near where you were attacked. That place is days ahead. You killed savages from a different tribe, you idiots!" Ewing put his face inches from Bailey and gave him a little push in the chest. "Do you know what trouble you've caused?" Bailey teetered and fell back against his horse's rump. "No, you can't understand 'cuz you're falling over drunk again!" In disgust, Ewing ended the conversation, "I'm takin' all your booze! And I'm goin' to dock your profits here for endangering lives and putting the whole investment in jeopardy."

Within days, a group of natives in war paint came at them in a narrow ravine. The warriors wove in and out of the cattle, shooting arrows and stampeding them. No men were killed, but Gay took an arrow in his back. The red men disappeared as fast as they came, leaving a dozen animals down – some dead and others wounded.

Even with the Indians gone, it was chaos. The men took off to overtake running animals. They needed to maneuver ahead of them to slow and stop them. The longer horns of one animal ripped into the side of another and bloodcurdling bawling followed. The bellows from the wounded echoed among the running animals' pounding hooves. In the narrow passage, the noise was deafening and dust obscured vision. More than thirty minutes passed before they calmed the cattle.

When Bailey didn't see Gay anywhere, he went to look for him, asking other men as he passed, "Have you seen George Gay?"

Finally, someone knew something. "He's up yonder on the ground. Don't know what's wrong."

Peering into the distance, Bailey saw someone prone in the dirt, with Ewing riding fast toward him from the opposite direction.

Bailey took off at a gallop, riding until he was close enough to see Ewing's face twisted in anger. Ewing reined in and slid off his horse where Gay lay on his belly. The whole arrow jutted up from Gay's back, with the arrowhead embedded in his spine. Gay was reaching around with one of his arms, groaning while he strained to clutch the arrow.

Ewing shouted, "They should've killed you!" and kicked Gay who screamed with pain. "See what you caused? You think that little kick hurts? Here, I'll pull out the arrow, and I hope it hurts like hell!"

Bailey rode up. "No! Don't touch that arrow. Let me look at where it is." The nostrils on Bailey's bay flared and narrowed; the animal's eyes looked wild as he pranced in all the confusion. Not waiting for his horse to stop moving, Bailey dismounted.

Cattle continued to bawl, and dust from the stampede still swirled. Men whistled and twirled lassos while trying to contain the herd; kerchiefs were pulled up over their mouths and noses against the fog of dust from the dry creek bed.

One man rode over to Ewing. "So far we found three dead animals and more than twice as many wounded ones. No men killed. What'll we do with the bleeding cattle, Ewing?"

"What do you think? We'll have to shoot 'em."

Bailey stood. "Wait! Let me go see, but don't anyone touch this arrow in Gay. We can't take it out because it might paralyze him." He mounted his horse and told Ewing, "I want to see the wounded cattle before you shoot them. Maybe I can do something." He rode off, shouting, "Don't touch Gay and don't let him move until I get back."

Bailey pulled arrows out of a couple rumps and shoulders before stitching up a few animals. They had to shoot a couple of others.

Ewing rode up at the moment that they killed a cow. "Bailey, you're good with a knife! Cut 'er up and let's have steaks tonight."

"I need to get back to Gay."

Ewing shouted, "That's an order, Bailey. You caused this, now pay these men back with some good cuts of meat." He rode off to check on more of the stock and called back, "Gay can wait awhile longer."

That night around the campfire, the men were sullen and quiet. Even having steaks didn't lift their spirits. Without any breeze, a cloud formed above the fire and hung there; the smoke eddied toward any movement made by the men and stung their eyes. Left to their own thoughts and worries, many were praying to make it home alive.

Bailey had worked on Gay and cut off the wooden shaft of the arrow. Gay hadn't bled much, but the ends of the obsidian arrowhead jutted out alongside his spinal column.

Gay sat next to Bailey and under his breath whispered, "Just take it out. I'll take the chance."

"No! Listen, you don't understand? If I take it out, it's not that you might die. You could be left a total cripple. Damn it, Gay! That's worse than dying." Bailey calmed a bit to say, "Just take a swig of the laudanum from time to time. You can make it back. I want to talk to Dr. Tolmie, the physician at Hudson's Bay Company, to get a second opinion."

Bailey hadn't been sleeping well since Ewing took away all his booze. More sobering than the lack of alcohol were the workings of his mind as he realized the implications of his actions. *Am I losing my ability to reason? How could I not see what killing those two Indians would mean? Two years ago, I was angry at Ewing for causing an attack that left my face lopsided, and yet here I do the same thing. I killed innocent natives for no reason. Damn that booze! If I drink again, I am a fool!*

In September 1837, nine months after the Willamette Cattle Company first hatched the plan to bring cattle to Oregon Country, the herd of six hundred bovines arrived.

When they reached the Methodist Mission, Ewing and his men counted out Jason Lee's share of cattle. They next went north to distribute cattle to the settlers in the French Prairie and other homesteads all the way to Fort Vancouver. With the many unanticipated expenses and the losses of cattle, the purchase price of three dollars a head rose to a cost of eight dollars to the settlers. No one complained though, because owning cattle was going to better their lives.

The Hudson's Bay Company had bought a third of the herd and when the final cattle were driven into the area surrounding the Fort, a large crowd, including Chief Factor McLoughlin himself, gave the men a grand welcome.

While in California, Ewing Young had worked to clear the false charges against him, and word had been sent from the Mexican government that he was innocent of horse stealing. McLoughlin retracted his former accusations and exonerated Young, removing him from the blacklist. Moreover, after hearing the stories of Ewing Young's leadership and seeing the large importation of cattle, McLoughlin commended him as well.

On the first day at the Fort, Bailey accompanied Gay to the Fort's physician to see about the arrowhead in Gay's back.

"Dr. William Bailey, welcome back. It's good to see you," said Dr. Tolmie. "I heard that you put the medical tools I gave you to good use. I knew you would. Without a doubt, they need a doctor down in the French Prairie."

They shook hands, and Bailey introduced Gay. "You may know George Kirby Gay," Bailey said as they sat down. "I'd like you to look at Gay's back. He's got a souvenir from an Indian attack."

After Gay removed his shirt, Dr. Tolmie suggested, "Bailey, there's someone I wanted you to meet anyway, but I think we need him here now. This past May, Dr. Elijah White came on a ship from the East. He's working for the Mission. I want him to see Gay's wound and help us decide what to do."

Dr. White arrived in the infirmary a few minutes later and the three medical men agreed that the arrowhead should be watched, and not removed. They knew that paralysis was more probable than death in spinal surgery.

Gay would have that black obsidian point in his back for five years before it would be taken out.

The men from the cattle drive spent a week celebrating and drinking at the Fort, but Bailey didn't join them. At dinner that night, while a guest at the Chief Factor's table, he learned of two reasons to abstain from drinking forever.

It happened like this:

After Gay left the infirmary, Dr. White extended an invitation. "Join us for dinner tonight, Dr. Bailey. John McLoughlin requested that we invite you to his table. I have my wife with me and would like you to meet her. What's more, I want to talk more with you and make you a proposition."

Dr. Tolmie offered, "You can wash up in my quarters, Dr. Bailey. If you need a clean shirt or anything, I can lend you some of my clothes."

Upon entering the dining room, William Bailey looked around with amazement. The quarters of the Chief Factor John McLoughlin were elegant. Knowing McLoughlin's annual income to be £720, Bailey should not have been surprised, except that this was Oregon Country, and he didn't expect the décor he saw – velvet draperies, cut glass, fine china, and a mahogany table that seated twelve. Nor did he expect to see a woman as stunning as Margaret Jewett Smith. After the introductions, he found his eyes kept returning to gaze at her. When he realized that he was staring at her and not hearing the words of his host, he stopped staring. *Thank goodness she didn't see my impertinent looks!*

Dr. McLoughlin spoke to Bailey, "Why don't you sit between Dr. White and his lovely wife Sarepeta? I think I shall put Dr. Tolmie across from you because I know the three of you have some business to discuss. And this way, I'll have more lovely ladies surrounding me. Miss Smith, I think you might enjoy talking with my wife and Mrs. White."

Bailey stood still and let McLoughlin pull out the chair for Mrs. White. He had heard the words "Miss Smith" and worried that if he didn't remain still, he would be jumping with elation, upon the discovery that she was not married. Slowly, he turned his head to look at her again as she sat two seats away from him on the same side of the table. *Perhaps it's best. I won't be able to stare.* Miss Smith was out of his line of vision.

During the evening, Bailey learned from the Whites that, a few days ago,

Margaret had arrived on a ship with a family called Leslie and that they were going to work at the Mission. Then Dr. White started discussing happenings at the Mission and Bailey lost interest. Instead, Bailey strained to hear Miss Smith's conversation down the table until he realized that Dr. White was addressing him.

"Excuse me, Dr. White, would you repeat that?" Bailey asked, a bit chagrinned.

"You may not be interested, I realize. But I think that your talent should be utilized to its fullest. I have been here three months and everyone talks of Dr. Bailey and his medical miracles." Dr. White lifted his brows before he continued. "You would be welcome to live with me while we work together. Since you only returned today, I'm sure you haven't seen the hospital that we recently built; we completed it with cut boards now that there is a sawmill. To call it a hospital may be a bit too grand a word; it has only two cots, an examining room, and an office. Nevertheless, I consider it quite handsome, although small. Since you have been out of touch with practicing medicine for a while, I know I could help you review the medical studies you learned in England. I heard that you lost everything during that horrible attack by the savages. I have brought all the latest medical books as well as some journals and will make them available to you."

With a look of surprise, Bailey reiterated what he had heard, "You are offering to coach me and work with me in a medical capacity?"

"Yes, to help prepare you to take up the practice of medicine again. Dr. McLoughlin thinks it a wise idea." Dr. White turned to his host. "Do you not?"

"Really, Bailey, I think this is an offer you cannot refuse," the Chief Factor responded. "You must know that we need your services, practicing medicine full time, not only helping out like you have been. Dr. White cares for the medical needs of the missionaries and the Indians at the Methodist Mission. We need someone for all the others in French Prairie."

Bailey considered the possibilities and asked, "This is quite an interesting offer. Where are your home and the hospital located?" He hoped the answer to this question would be what he wanted to hear.

"On some high ground not far from the Methodist Mission."

What two better reasons than this to stop drinking? A good job and a beautiful woman close at hand!

Margaret's Journey

On January 23, 1837, Margaret Jewett Smith began her journey from Massachusetts to Oregon Country. It would take nine months for Margaret to arrive, and her journey would be full of frustration and pain, but she omitted those details from her correspondence – at first.

After two days at sea, Margaret opened her ink box, mounted a nib in the wooden holder, and began a letter:

Brig Peru, January 25, 1837

Beloved Sister and Brother Isaac:

The most keen and painful feelings I felt at parting were realized when I took the last look at Boston, when the vessel left the wharf. I had left a large circle of true friends, to whom I was much indebted, and whose kindness I expect to be never able to repay.

I wish I was near enough to you this fine morning to converse without having to wait for my pen to commit my words to paper, and then some months, perhaps, before I shall receive your replies. In a ball of yarn I found, today, a scrap of paper concealed by you, my dear sister, on which you had written many assurances of your love to me and regrets at my leaving.

Off and on, Margaret thought about the comment her brother Samuel had made about her squandering her life, and she swore to herself that she would never write to him again. *Only letters to my other dear brother and sisters.*

Weeks passed as Margaret continued to add to her letter. She considered what topics to share and decided to not include everything. *Oh, my seasickness! I abhor it and refuse to write about it. I know the Leslie family experienced it as I did during the initial rough weather while going south. I only hope they did not write home to worry our friends and family.*

Margaret added the following to her letter home:

> I take much pleasure in working for those on board who cannot use the needle. I have made for the steward, cook, and waiter, each a cloth cap; have made a new coat and mended old ones – and have made aprons for the steward, et cetera. The rest of the time I employ in working for myself, reading, writing, painting, drawing, studying, stargazing, and exercising on deck and in the cabin. So you see I need not be idle.
>
> I have seasons of devotion, when I am peculiarly favored with the Spirit's influence, and find my mind greatly invigorated by meditation on divine subjects.
>
> We have all things in order on board, I assure you. The steward tends the table, which is set in style. The knives ever shining like polished silver, and the spoons and castors glowing with brilliancy. Our food is well prepared, and relished with smiles and compliments from the officers and passengers.

Margaret dotted the period in her last sentence and the ship rolled. Not only did her ink box slip to the deck but she was tossed from the lounge chair as well. Instantly, the wind began to whistle and whirl with such a force that her hair was undone and swirled free in the air. All hairpins disappeared in the gusts. She scrambled to gather her pen and ink box, feeling fortunate that she still held her letter in her hand as she slipped it into the drawer of the ink box. She stood and managed one step before she careened into the railing. The ship continued to heave to and fro as she tried to hurry to her cabin. The sun disappeared between darkened clouds and rain came in sheets at the moment she arrived to her door. In sopping clothes, she entered her cabin.

At some point most days, Margaret experienced sudden wind, rain, or sleet. She found writing to be impossible, and after losing many pages to downpours, she discontinued writing until she reached the calm waters off

Brazil:

March 6th

Yesterday we had religious services for the first time since we have been out. Mr. Leslie spoke on the topic, What is truth? The gentlemen spread an awning over the deck to screen us from the sun, and we found it very pleasant to sit thus quietly in a fine day, on the smooth ocean, and listen to the words of divine truth. I find a sweet submission of my own will to the will of God. So judiciously has my heavenly Father ordered the events of my life; and O! how I mourn that I was so repining and unbelieving in those times when thick darkness covered my path.

We are within a few miles of St. Catherine's. The view of the coast is very fine indeed, and if it were not the Sabbath day, I would give you a sketch of it.

Margaret stopped writing a moment and thought. *It's Monday! Why do I lie? I could tell the truth that I am upset. But, no, I cannot tell my sister that I am hiding in my cabin and don't feel like sketching. I cannot bring myself to write about this other family in my midst – those Leslies! If I write about my hurts and frustrations, I shall be more upset. No, I shall only write about happy occurrences. Yes, like the Captain and crew.*

Margaret continued writing while docked in Brazil:

You cannot imagine how pleasantly we pass our time. Occasional accidents and exposure to dangers cause us, when free from them, to rejoice in the many mercies and favors which we receive. The anxieties and cares which devolve upon our captain, are very great, and I never knew a Christian who conducted himself in seasons of trial with more prudence, or sustain himself amidst difficulties with greater composure and fortitude than does Capt. Kilham.

A squall of wind has helped us into the harbor of St. Catherine's, and we have just dropped anchor. I really wish I could describe to you this beautiful coast. On the mountaintops rest the clouds – their sides and valleys are admirably covered with green shrubbery and grass – and occasionally appears, near the water's edge, or on the mountainside, a neat white cottage.

Capt. Cathcart, said to be from Nantucket, who resides on the Brazilian coast – having married a Portuguese lady – earnestly requested us of the mission family to take up our residence at his house, while the brig proceeds to the island to make repairs.

Mrs. Cathcart does not speak English, but renders herself very agreeable by her attentions and acts of kindness to us. She will have her slaves wait upon us, taking all our wardrobe to the springs in the mountains for washing, and returning them beautifully fresh and clean, and refusing any compensation. Every day I wander around the plantations, seeking and finding ever-new delights in this enchanting place. The air is filled with birds of every variety of colored plumage, and with insects of rich and varied luster. Wild flowers, which no art or cultivation can improve in splendor; insects, astonishing you with the order and occupations of their lives – in short, every delight to make the place a paradise, is here.

Here are found oranges, lemons, and limes in great abundance – the ground almost covered with those, which had ripened and fallen from the trees. The orange blossoms follow the fall of the ripe fruit almost immediately, and hence, on the orange trees may be seen at all times flowers and fruit of different degrees of perfection, from the smallest to the perfectly ripe. This tree knows no change of seasons.

The coffee and cotton plants are also novelties to me; and the pineapples I have never seen growing before. The prickly pear is also a curiosity. That frightful looking plant, which in Boston you cultivate with so much care in your parlor window, grows here a large tree, the bulk of the size of a person's waist, and is as ugly looking as anything you could wish to see in nature. The fruit, however, is delicious.

I often observe, in my rambles, processions of emmets [ants], one following another, and each with a bit of orange leaf in his mouth, for a distance of a quarter of a mile or more and to which I never find the end. Spiders, too, would frighten you from the size. I have seen them three or four inches in length. Butterflies are numerous and are a splendor I never before saw equaled.

Mrs. Cathcart will take this letter. She can send it sailing back to you on the next ship that docks and goes north.

Your loving sister,
Margaret

Eventually, three months later, Margaret confided to her sister some realities of her journey. The *Brig Peru* carried another person, destined for the Methodist Mission; besides the Leslie family, a Reverend H.K.W. Perkins was aboard.

June 1837

To my beloved sister:

How much I wish I could see you, and to you confide all my troubles. I am unpleasantly situated in some respects. The many little petty annoyances, which one unavoidably meets on a long voyage, cannot in a small vessel be shook off by an occasional visit to a friend, or a walk, or a ride, but we must bear them, hoping for the time when we shall be again on *terra firma* and free as birds. Among other disagreeables, which I have to encounter, are the infidel conversations of Mr. Perkins. He ever seems to think he can convince me that our faith is erroneous – that he has discovered a new and a better way, and urges me to read the books that have fallen into his hands. He says that I am not "logically qualified enough to contend with those who have received collegiate education!" – and I know I am not conceitedly qualified enough to argue with one so superior in point of intellectual acquirements and capacities. He calls himself a Utilitarian.

Our captain has been during the voyage very anxious about the event of passing Cape Horn – even saying that if he were only safely past it he would be happy. We did safely pass that point, and attempt to run up along the coast of Patagonia. The captain was in high spirits – came below and offered the passengers extra refreshments and delicacies, but while partaking a head wind met us and blew us far south, where we had to remain for three weeks and endure the cold, the rain, and gales, so common in these latitudes.

Besides the stormy days, the nights were rendered unpleasant and sleepless by violent winds and the rolling of the vessel. With all my efforts to retain my self-possession, I have sometimes become disconcerted. I had flattered myself considerably in my adroitness in preparing for the violent motions of the vessel, so as to preserve myself from accident, but I must resign the palm to others, for I have many times had my work-basket upset and all its varied contents thrown about the cabins—have found myself, when dressing, thrown immediately before the open door, in view of the gentlemen—have spilled my plate of soup time and time again, and been thrown from the table, food in hand, against the side of the cabin, and had the vexation to perceive, on recovering myself, that the captain was laughing at me. I have made up my mind that I, too, must be submissive to old Neptune, and think lightly of his wayward habits.

Having arrived in Valparaiso, I shall mail this to you and start another letter afresh.

Your loving sister, Margaret

In June, the *Brig Peru* arrived at the Port of Valparaiso. It seemed that Margaret had shared all her problems – rough seas, the differences of opinion with Mr. Perkins, and some insults to her intelligence from him. But in addition, Margaret was experiencing a disagreement so intense it would shadow her life for years to come.

I know many of the incidents that upset me might seem trivial to most; however, after months at sea with one's every movement in view of all and with restrictions on where one can go, I crave privacy. Perhaps I am spending too much time alone in my cabin, and I do know that I dwell on simple happenings – thinking too much and too long – and work myself into a state of extreme upset. Oh, what am I to do? By nature, I am overly sensitive. And I know my parents spoiled me. I was always their pet and got my way. But surely everyone knows that I am not selfish, or am I? Surely, people can see that I am devout and sincere.

Margaret's traveling companions didn't know what to make of her when she hid in her cabin. By the time she arrived in Oregon Country, many in the Missionary Society would see her as a maniac.

Again in her letters to her friends and most of her siblings, she reverted to sending descriptive messages detailing her delight with all the sights in her travels, omitting her burdens:

To my family and please share with my friends:

Valparaiso is very singular in appearance, viewed from the harbor. Built upon the side of a mountain the houses appear to be contiguous, and you obtain the idea that a heavy shower of rain would wash them all into the sea. They are built mostly of adobes and never of more than one story on account of frequency of earthquakes, which happen in this region.

We took lodgings today with Mrs. W-----. The wife of Capt. Scott has just called and invited us to her house for tea. There are but three American ladies who reside here. Gentlemen, however, from almost all parts of the world throng the place on matters of business, and soldiers numbering about seventeen hundred are everywhere. The Chileans are also making preparations for war with Peru, and I can find no time for walking but early in the morning. The scenery here is grand, but there is little of that luxury in the productions of nature, which is so manifest at St. Catherine's. The mountains are almost barren of vegetation, but in a few nooks and crannies of the valleys I have seen very good plants. The native women, however, cultivate flowers to a great extent, in their small door-yards.

In truth, what had been happening on the voyage was a growing conflict that had started in the boarding house months before as they had waited for the *Brig Peru* to be ready to sail. The quarrel involved the Leslie family. On the first evening, Margaret had been requested by Mr. and Mrs. Leslie to eat at the second table with their three children because other guests from the boarding house had filled their table.

It was how he phrased the request that rankled Margaret.

Mr. Leslie had said, "Since our table is full, please sit with our girls to assist them and converse with them."

Margaret made no comment in response, and with no other place to sit, she went to the children's table and made a point to pay no attention to the children. While eating, she fumed in silence. *I specifically told Mr. Leslie that I would not be a servant to his family. If he thinks I am a nursemaid for his children, he will soon see he is wrong. Being a single woman, I agreed to be a part of his "little family" since I could not travel alone, but I shall not be his servant.*

The journey began in choppy waters as did her interactions with others.

To make her point, Margaret avoided and often ignored the Leslie family. Everyone had been seasick from the start, and Margaret offered no help. Frequently, when someone suggested that she assist the Leslies, she made the same response, "I am as ill as they are. I must go to my cabin. Excuse me."

Mr. Perkins took it upon himself to be an intermediate and after a time he asked, "You knew that Mrs. Leslie was ill before we left, why don't you help a bit? For example, you could help with the children's clothing."

Margaret became indignant. "I beg your pardon? I don't know if you mean to have me wash or iron, but I am here to become a teacher of the heathen, not a servant of spoiled rich people." And off she huffed.

Weeks passed with Margaret reading, drawing, writing, or otherwise occupying her time away from the others. Most of the time, she took her meals alone in her cabin or avoided eating because of her seasickness.

Mr. Perkins wrote to her:

> It has come to my attention that you were not made aware
> of my situation before Mr. Leslie asked you to come on

this voyage. If you had understood, I believe your position would have been more apparent to you. I had been selected to go to the Mission in Oregon Country for this trip with the Leslie family. They had missed going with the group that left in May, a few months before us, because of Mrs. Leslie's health. Mr. and Mrs. Leslie thought I had a wife who would be coming. Alas, I am not married. So they were concerned about some companionship for Mrs. Leslie and someone who would be gracious enough to help, if needed, with the three girls.

Mr. Leslie refused to go unaccompanied by another female for his wife. Then he proposed to the Board to take a single woman on his own responsibility; he offered to provide for her maintenance. You were recommended.

I had supposed you understood these circumstances. It appears that you do not consider yourself a part of his family and responsibility, but it is my understanding that all your friends and family back home were told you would be as one of his family. Without another guardian, it would be imprudent of you to disclaim Mr. Leslie's offer.

You will soon mingle with strangers. Mr. Leslie considers himself bound to furnish you with a house and things comfortable. If you disclaim any connection to his family, of course his obligations will cease and whatever he may do then will be a matter only of courtesy.

Respectively,
Rev. Perkins.

Margaret read and reread the letter in her small compartment. *How dare Mr. Perkins think he is in a position to interfere with my affairs – how dare he!* She tied her bonnet and left her cabin to find him. *His interference does not deserve a written answer. How presumptuous of him to address my situation.*

Margaret's relationship with the other passengers was like the sea: it continued to be rough and many dark clouds hung over them.

On her way to meet Perkins, Margaret was thrown against a railing, and she continued to complain to herself. *Where is the sun? Don't I have enough dark clouds with my companions?* A large wave washed over the deck and soaked her skirts, shoes, and under things. *Oh, no! There are always more than dark clouds to contend with.* Through a porthole, she spied Mr. Perkins alone, except for a steward, in the dining area. *I will not let this opportunity pass; he will have to accept me talking while soaking and dripping wet.*

Margaret stumbled upon entering and held tight to the door handle to brace herself. Then the brig shifted the other way, and she careened against a wall. Both men jumped up to assist her; she slapped at Mr. Perkins hand. "I don't need your help. I am fine, thank you!" The steward had her elbow and steadied her. She knew that she would have fallen without his strong hold.

Mr. Perkins responded, "Forgive me. You looked in need of a hand."

"No, no, no! I want to talk with you in private. Would you accompany me outside?"

The steward interrupted, "One cannot walk and talk easily in this sea. I'll leave you here, sitting in privacy. I can straighten up later. Excuse me." He left the dining area.

Once seated, Margaret clenched her jaws and pursed her lips before beginning. "In reference to your letter, Mr. Perkins, you talked about matters of which I may not have been aware." Sucking in air and sitting straighter, she said, "But it was you who are not aware that months ago I objected when Mr. Leslie's asked me to come to help his family. It is true I have no appointment, but I have a pledge signed by ten or more men on the Mission Society Board. It stated nothing about any responsibilities to the Leslies, only an assignment as a teacher in the Mission once I arrive."

Mr. Perkins felt seasick. He looked a bit green against his black suit. His neck bulged out around the tight starched collar. Both his hands held fast to the table and a chair to steady himself as he listened and swayed with the boat. He cleared his throat. "Excuse me a moment while I get a glass of water. Would you like one?"

Margaret huffed, "No, thank you." *He looks as if he has not even been listening to me.*

Upon his return, Margaret continued, "You say in your letter that he promised that he would provide for me like one of his family, but he does not. Why, I asked Mr. Leslie if I might have a bar of soap and towel from the supplies he is taking to the Mission. He refused me. He told me that I had no more right to those things than any other stranger." She straightened her back while waiting for a reply.

Mr. Perkins took another sip from the glass.

She reiterated, "What do you make of that? Would he have refused his daughter or wife a bar of soap from the supplies?"

He stuttered a bit, "I, I know nothing of that occurrence nor, nor the rules of supplies for the Mission."

"Well, you must admit that he did not treat me like family or provide for me. How did you put it?" Margaret opened his letter. "Ah yes, he was to 'provide for my maintenance,' it says here." Her face got a haughty look, and she thought of another example, "When we got to Valparaiso and were going ashore. Mr. Leslie informed me that he had a place for his family to sleep on shore, but nothing for me. I slept on a couch that night!"

The ship had stopped reeling and Mr. Perkins's color returned a bit. He cleared his throat. "I thought you stayed with Capt. and Mrs. Scott?"

"Well, I did, after the Scotts learned I had spent a night on the couch and had no bed in which to sleep." She held her head high, knowing he should see her justification.

Again he cleared his throat. "Miss Smith, I have seen you on this journey so infrequently; it seems you avoid all of us. This is why Mr. and Mrs. Leslie are upset. You often take your meals alone in your cabin. It is disconcerting. And you don't come to services."

"Sir, there were no services for more than a month into our journey. When a Sunday arrives, who knows whether there will be a service or not? It is all very irregular. I became accustomed to making my own religious service and reading the Bible. Mr. Leslie, I believe, was lax in his duty to give services on the Sabbath." She stopped for a moment remembering herself standing in her cabin listening to a service on deck while she stood at her cabin's skylight. "I have always done my prayers and observed the Sabbath." She felt the impulse to point her finger at him as she blurted, "Why, you yourself could have given service, but didn't."

"All of us were quite ill at first." He stood. "Forgive me, but I must take leave from you. It seems I am still not quite well." He left and she could hear him expelling his discomfort over the side of the vessel.

Within the day, the vessel stopped in Chile again, north of Valparaiso in Callao. The passengers were to go to shore overnight while the crew took on a shipment and made ready for the trip across the Pacific to the Sandwich Islands.

Margaret resolved not to go on shore and remained on board with the Captain and some of the crew. *Now that I see that they are all against me, I know I would have an even more unpleasant situation here in Callao. Thus far, the Lord hath led me on the path he desires.* She knelt next to her bunk and clasped her hands. *O Lord, lead me in the true path. I am here to do what you desire. I desire only to please. Amen.*

As she rose, she realized, *Again I have been panting for my God. Only he can fulfill me and satisfy me. Take my hand, Lord.* She reclined on her bunk for a while and then sat up to write:

To my sister and brother:

June 2, 1837

Our ship anchored in the harbor of Callao, Chile. I have begun to read the New Testament again, and it never before was attended with so much pleasure to my mind. I never so loved, so adored the Son of God. With the Bible for my treasure, I find the yoke of Christ is easy, and his burden is light. My whole soul is alive to the sentiment when I repeat:

> I thank thee, uncreated Sun,
> That thy bright beams on me have shined;
> I thank thee who hast overthrown
> My foes, and healed my wounded mind.

I thank thee, whose enlivening voice
Bids my free heart in thee rejoice.

June 10th

I am glad to find myself on the passage to the Sandwich Islands, for which we left Callao last evening. While at that place we were requested to visit the sloop-of-war North Carolina, and were much pleased with the appearance of a school on board of her. There are two able teachers for the instruction of sixty boys and twenty midshipmen.

We crossed the equator last night. We have the finest weather imaginable, and are making our way rapidly and pleasantly.

This day has been exceeding pleasant. Just enough clouds have floated in the atmosphere to prevent the rays of the sun being too warm and bright; and a good breeze has filled our sails while the ocean's wide and beautiful expanse, with its surface alternately variegated with black fish, whales, and flying fish, and the scenery above us rendered beautiful by the appearance of tropical birds, have produced in my heart grateful adorations to Him who made them all...

Sitting in a deck chair in the sunlight with a large-brimmed straw hat, Margaret stopped writing and mumbled to herself, "I'm bored with trying to write happy words." She sighed, leaned her head back on the wooden slats, and closed her eyes. *When will this excruciating journey end?*

At dinner on the eve of the Fourth of July everyone discussed plans to celebrate the holiday. Everyone knew about the pending celebration except Margaret. No one had told her and when she heard celebrating the next day, she was incensed. *How could they neglect to invite me?* She went to her cabin and did not leave the whole day. Her upset grew to anger. *How utterly cruel of them! I would have liked to celebrate. The Leslies are with their whole family. Can't they imagine how I miss mine on such a special day? How could no one think to invite me?*

July 29th

Arrived at the Sandwich Islands this morning at the Island of Oahu after having been on our passage one hundred and eighty-seven days, and in two hours found the Presbyterian missionaries on board to welcome us to their homes. I shall write you the particulars in another letter because I can seal this one and have it go off to you in the ship that is near ours.

Your loving sister, Margaret

Since Callao, Margaret had not spoken with the Leslies or Mr. Perkins except in passing to say "Good morning" or "Good evening." She had avoided them for a month. Margaret took her breakfast before her companions had risen from their night's sleep; she ate a light lunch alone on deck with her head in a book or her journal, never looking up at passersby; and she had dinner alone in her cabin. Her message became clear to all. And she justified it to herself. *If they really wanted to be with me, someone would come knock on my cabin door and insist. The Captain, who has been such a gentleman and so gracious to me, should do that. But I am so tired of Mr. Perkin's talk. He knows nothing, yet continues to chastise me in my manners toward the Leslies. He who knows nothing!* And when she felt self-pity, she recalled: *A bar of soap! How could he refuse me a bar of soap?*

And so, with her arrival to Oahu, Margaret eagerly accepted an invitation from the local Presbyterian missionaries with whom she stayed for a month. She had promised her family a letter from the Sandwich Islands:

To my beloved sister and brother:
Sandwich Islands
August 2nd

Throughout our voyage I have admired the wonders of the mighty ocean as well as the beauties of the firmament above; I have adored that providence has protected and blessed me; and I have constantly rejoiced at the step I have taken. Our captain, one of the most agreeable of men, has exceeded, in his kindness and attentions to us.

This day I have been to the top of Punch Bowl Hill, which is very steep and of difficult ascent. Long before I reached the top I found it quite necessary to climb with my hands as well as feet. On the top are placed several cannons for the defense of the island.

Accompanied by Mr. Hall of the mission here, I took a ride the other day, on horseback, to what is called the Pari. It is truly a delightful and romantic spot, on the opposite side of the island.

I am not pleased with the scenery of Oahu about the town. The mountains are very rugged in appearance, probably thrown up by volcanic action; there is but little shrubbery apparent – a few cocoa nut trees with their scarcity of foliage. I walk the dusty streets and scarcely see the indications of a resident's house, the high mud walls so completely screening them from view.

The missionaries and many of the residents have excelled, in their efforts to benefit us, beyond our conceptions, and we cannot soon forget them.

Tomorrow we leave on another ship *Barque Sumatra* for the Columbia River that cuts into Oregon Country. My journey is not yet over; we must return the long distance over the Pacific Ocean again and up the river Columbia, which, I have been told, can be very difficult to navigate.

I am sending this now since many ships, coming and going in the Sandwich Islands, can take the mail.

Your loving sister,
Margaret

While the ship *Barque Sumatra*, owned by the Hudson's Bay Company, was docked and being loaded in Oahu, Margaret experienced her final and greatest disagreement with Mr. Leslie. Compared with her other trivial faultfinding, this incident caused her the most discomfort. But as with her other complaints, she could not help exaggerating the error that Mr. Leslie had made. She let this problem became a huge fire in her soul. Like all fires, it needed tending and somehow she kept feeding it more kindling until it burned bright and hot for all to see. Yet she did not seem to notice that it was she who was burning. Years later, she would admit that she exaggerated these trivial matters, building this huge fire with the devil's helping hand.

The incident began in the morning before her trunks were taken to be loaded onto the *Barque Sumatra*.

Changing ships meant moving all the supplies and trunks. Wanting to avoid her companions, Margaret petitioned Mr. Hall, the Presbyterian missionary who had been so kind to her on the islands, for help. She asked him to be in charge of the removal of her trunks stored on the first ship, and to see that they were placed in an accessible location on the *Barque Sumatra*.

Mr. Leslie overheard and said, "Miss Smith, please entrust this to me. It is quite unnecessary to trouble Mr. Hall. I know how they should be arranged, and I must be there to oversee our trunks and the Mission's supplies."

Margaret hesitated a moment before saying, "Why, thank you, Mr. Leslie. I am entrusting you with caring for my belongings. And I thank you again."

Nevertheless, it wasn't long after they sailed from the Sandwich Islands that Margaret discovered that her belongings were indeed on the ship, but stored under the hatch and not accessible. To make matters worse, while she searched the closets and storage in her cabin trying to locate some of her items, she saw all spaces filled with items belonging to the Leslie family. None of her clothes, books, or writing materials could she locate.

Margaret then approached Mr. and Mrs. Leslie, who were strolling on deck.

"Look at me, Mr. Leslie. I am dressed for a tropical island, and I have nothing else to wear for the twenty or thirty days we have ahead on this leg of our journey. After I went to get a wrap for the cold air and found none of my belongings, I had to talk with the steward to learn where my trunks had gone. I entrusted you to make my belongings available to me and you failed."

He stammered, "I, I am so, sorry. There was, was so much to, to do. I didn't realize until too late that your trunks and boxes were put below into the hatch. There was nothing I could do at that point."

"It seems all your family's clothes were put into convenient places. My closet is full of your own wardrobe. Here I stand freezing with no wrap against this coming gale. It is no wonder that there is a lack of union in our midst, while selfishness is apparent."

Mr. Leslie stood a bit taller and huffed out his chest. "If you are accusing me of being selfish, you are wrong. I just explained it was a mistake in all the hustle and bustle of transferring everything."

"I think you have been selfish, not only in this affair, but also in other ways since we left Boston."

Mr. Leslie raised his voice. "You offend me to a great degree. We shall soon see our brethren in Oregon and let them decide."

Margaret agreed with him, "Very well, we shall let them decide."

He added, "I should also say that this will need to be decided before we come to the communion table together."

And thus the fire began to catch and burn hotter.

Now Mrs. Leslie put her hand on her husband's arm to suggest, "My dear, my dear! Do be careful what you say." And turning to Margaret she said, "I have some beautiful warm cloaks. I'll get you one right now. It is so cold. But I do not want either of you to discuss this further until you have both calmed."

He stated to his wife, "I don't enjoy being interrupted. I do know what I am saying." He walked off.

His wife touched Margaret's arm. "I'll be only a moment. When I return, you must let me know what else you are needing. I am so sorry you have been inconvenienced." She rushed away, not waiting for Margaret's wrath to surface again.

The next day, Mr. Leslie had a letter delivered to Margaret – a letter five pages long! Margaret had called him "selfish" and his anger was festering. His position in the church had required that he take an oath, and his brethren could take severe actions against him if he lied, was dishonest, or showed selfish traits. She had accused a well-respected man of the church, one with a reputation for writing moving sermons and converting many who heard his words.

Margaret held firm. *He was selfish to me. Nothing he can say can change what he has done.* In his letter, after much preaching, he opened his heart and told her:

> My dear Sister Smith, my heart bleeds! My spirit weeps!! And shame mantles my cheek!! That I am connected with a scene so revolting – so derogatory to the Christian name.
>
> Your needs must perceive, my sister, that there is something wrong – radically wrong – and that this wrong must be righted. I am not disposed to exculpate myself and cast the blame on you or any other person – but there is blame somewhere. It may rest wholly on me – if so, the greater the work of repentance before me; may God grant me grace to perform it.
>
> I wish to assure you, Sister Smith, my object is not to cause you unnecessary pain. I am still your friend and harbor nothing other than the best of feeling towards you. I wish, however, to be understood as decided in my feeling that this state of things referred to must be put away, and to this I'm sure you will not object.

Margaret stopped reading at the above sentence. Her hands fell to her lap. *I do object!*

To no avail, Mr. Leslie went on for a couple of more pages, asking for Christian frankness and tenderness. But nothing could put out the bonfire burning inside her.

In the following days, she ignored Mr. Leslie even though he had admitted possible blame.

More correspondence went back and forth while they traveled across the Pacific Ocean toward Oregon Country; however, their words kept repeating what had already been said.

Margaret held firm even when Mrs. Leslie, in pure sweetness, put her arms about her and spoke like a mother, "My dear, you are going to teach the heathens, and it is good that you are strong because life will be harder there. But Margaret, remember that you are young and lack experience in life. Sometimes it is best to forgive and forget."

Years later, Margaret would understand what Mrs. Leslie had tried to teach her and would write in her journal:

> Energy and firmness of character are admirable in some circumstances, but when youth and inexperience resolve that they will accomplish certain ends, without knowing what will be the consequences, and in spite of all the admonitions of experience and suggestions of wisdom, 'tis very lamentable.

When she sailed up the Columbia River in September 1837 and arrived at Fort Vancouver, she had not yet learned this wise lesson.

Margaret accepted Chief Factor John McLoughlin's invitation to dinner and arrived in her blue taffeta gown with mother-of-pearl buttons. Standing tall above all the women, though not as tall as McLoughlin's six-foot-four, she met William John Bailey for the first time and took little notice of him.

Ghost Mission – Metal Replica of Original Cabins at Methodist Mission

Willamette Mission Park
OREGON STATE PARKS

CHAPTER 6

HEADING SOUTH
TO THE MISSION
September 1837

As had been agreed, William Bailey, Dr. Elijah White, and White's wife Sarepeta left Fort Vancouver the morning after the dinner party. They headed south to the Methodist Mission on horseback – a forty-mile trip. It was September 16th and a typical day for that season, with a sky full of clouds and the sun peeking in and out. Dark clouds would blow under the others and drizzle on the travelers for a few minutes before the sun would burst out again. Their trip was uneventful, and by late afternoon, they arrived at Dr. White's home. Soon the two doctors sat together in the hospital, getting better acquainted and planning their work while Sarepeta prepared the evening meal with her *Métis* helper.

Meanwhile, Margaret remained behind at the Fort, enjoying herself as the guest of the Chief Factor. She went horseback riding with Dr. Tolmie. She helped Brother Cyrus Shepard sort through all the supplies that had arrived on the ship. The next day she and Shepard placed all the clothing supplies in a field to air in the sun – there were colorful shirts, common factory gowns, crash pants of durable linen, woolen socks and caps, and other articles that Margaret believed to be suitable for the indigenous people she was to teach. On another day, they organized china, pots, and other paraphernalia that had been purchased for the Mission's store. She had dined with the McLoughlins each evening, from September 14th until she departed for the south. During these four days, she found everything to be comfortable and proper.

Early Monday morning on September 18th, two bateaux from the Fort were loaded with trunks and supplies for the Mission. On board were three children and six adults: Reverend Daniel Lee, Reverend and Mrs. Leslie,

Margaret, and two paddlers – one a Chinook and the other a Cayuse. Everyone stepped down onto the flat-bottomed bateaux and squeezed between the baggage to find a space to sit. Soon, with brisk winds and a drizzle, they were gliding westward on the Columbia River toward the Pacific Ocean. Daniel Lee and Margaret were in the first boat; she held her crook-handled umbrella with both of her hands while he paddled. Mrs. Leslie, in the second boat with her children huddled around her, held her yellow flowered umbrella and Reverend Leslie sat behind her. It seemed a calm and easy trip with the mesmerizing sound of water, views of many seagulls swooping above, and black-tailed deer appearing in riverside meadows from time to time.

After ten miles, they turned south into the Willamette River, and the travel became difficult. Going south on this river meant going upstream, and the men strained with their paddles, heading for Willamette Falls.

Suddenly, the lead bateau struck a submerged stump in the center of the river. The pointed front cracked apart and boards ripped away. Heavy trunks and wooden cartons jolted with the impact, shifted, slipped out from their rope bindings, and careened against the low wooden sides. Some of the smaller boxes and tools toppled into the river. Margaret fell to the bottom of the boat; her umbrella sailed high into the wind before it fell into the water and floated downstream. Daniel Lee jumped to her side, wedging himself next to her with his shoulder against the boat's side and his feet extended straight out to block a huge wooden box that was toppling toward her. Margaret saw the box coming at her and screamed as she doubled into a fetal position; her bonnet fell over her face and slipped off her chin before blowing up and out to join the umbrella, gliding high between gulls. Her petticoats and skirts rose like sails and flapped in the wind, covering her head.

Screeching erupted in the air as the children screamed when their bateau headed for the back of the sinking boat. Mr. and Mrs. Leslie wrapped their arms around each other and the children to brace against an impact, but the Cayuse paddled with expertise around the sinking bateau and headed toward the shore.

Both ends of a bateau are pointed, like canoes, and it has no rudders, so as Margaret's broken bateau was taking water, the Chinook sitting in its stern turned himself around and began to paddle the unbroken end toward the shore. Daniel Lee grabbed his own fallen paddle and helped maneuver the boat closer to shore. One steamer trunk with Margaret's belongings slipped out and floated downstream. Then another trunk slowly inched down the slanting boat toward the open gap.

Margaret righted herself and fought to move her skirts away from her face, crying out, "My belongings!" On her knees, she reached out for the leather strap of her second trunk, grasped it, and held tight. With her free hand she reached, here and there, searching for the side of the boat to secure herself, but began to slip with the trunk toward the opening. "Help me!"

Daniel Lee and the Chinook strained against the waves and wind with each stroke. They dipped into the depths of the water with each paddle thrust; their frowning faces concentrated with clenched jaws. The rain began to pour as they progressed toward the shore.

The others watched in terror while Margaret held fast to her trunk, which reached the edge of the broken boat bottom and began to tilt over the side. Mr. Leslie called out. His words lifted into the wind, like the umbrella and hat that had floated up and away, unheard by the passengers of the other bateau.

The children were hysterical and crying. Everyone was soaked from the downpour. Mrs. Leslie had her arms wrapped around all three of her girls and screamed, "God help us. God help us," over and over until their bateau reached the shore. The Cayuse, followed by Mr. Leslie, jumped from their boat into the shallows and pulled it up on land.

The distressed bateau was nearing the shore fifty feet farther down river from the grounded one with the Leslies. Margaret's trunk continued to slip over the open end, lifting vertically and raising her from her knees to a standing position. She refused to let go and held the strap with both hands while she pleaded, "Help me! Help me!" The big bulky trunk pulled her closer and closer to the water.

When her bateau bumped the ground of the shore, reeds and cattails enveloped the boat. Margaret lurched and was jabbed by a low hanging bough of a cottonwood. She flew over her trunk and into the mud and water of the shoreline. Trying to stand, she slipped and landed face down. Her trunk, one corner wedged in the mud, leaned from the bateau but remained intact.

At first, the watching Leslies gasped. But when Margaret somersaulted over her trunk and stood in the distance dripping with slimy debris, one child snickered and exclaimed, "Look at Miss Smith!" The whole family laughed.

Wiping muck and green slime from her face, out of her hair, and off her clothes, Margaret heard the laughter.

Daniel Lee and the Chinook had no interest in Margaret's appearance. Knowing she was safe, they left the bateau to rush down the shore to retrieve floating articles. The Cayuse jumped into the water when he saw that Margaret's drifting trunk was moving toward land. He swam out, got behind it, and pushed it to shore. They saved all the articles except the umbrellas and Margaret's hat.

When the two groups gathered on the shore, Daniel Lee gave directions to both Indians, in pidgin, before turning to Margaret and the Leslie family. "All of you are to remain in this spot along the river while we reorganize." He moved wet baggage to the good bateau as he spoke. Lee and the two natives worked with speed, filling the good bateau and leaving room only for two persons.

Margaret approached and pointed. "May I remove clothing from that trunk you just loaded? I am in need of a change of clothing."

Daniel Lee looked at the trunk located in the middle of the bateau. "I am sorry, Miss Smith. We have much to do before dark. For your safety, I cannot delay."

Margaret stood dumbfounded and dripping as he turned and continued to load.

Daniel reached to a stack of blankets bound with belts and tossed them on shore. "Wrap yourself in some of these blankets for now and dry your clothes by the fire." The Chinook and Daniel jumped onto the overloaded bateau and left. He called out as they drifted away, "We're going to the falls where Brother Shepard waits."

Margaret looked for the fire that he had mentioned. Puzzled, she turned back to watch Daniel disappearing.

Mr. Leslie approached her. "Brother Shepard is waiting at the falls because we have to portage around the falls. With only one boat, we don't all fit. We must wait to see what develops."

While Mr. Leslie spoke, the Cayuse man began to make a fire in preparation for them to stay the night.

Margaret went to the river's edge to wash while the Leslies stayed dry and ate lunch under a large willow tree. Margaret muttered to herself and wiped the slime from the front of her dress and face, "He saw how I look, yet would not let me get into my trunks for other clothing. He wants me to undress in front of the Leslies and this native. How dare he tell me that!"

Margaret jumped and made a little squeal when the Cayuse approached her from behind and tapped her shoulder. She turned to hear his words, which were without meaning until he pointed to the fire. She saw that he had made a place to dry her clothes; stuck in the ground were small green limbs that had cross sections bound to them with reeds.

"Yes, yes. I understand." She waved her hands for him to go away. Shivering with the disappearing sun, she relented, took a dry blanket, and hid behind a tree to remove her dress, petticoats, stockings, and shoes. She remained in her chemise, corset, and drawers. *I refuse to get naked! My underclothing will have to dry on me.* Wrapped in the blanket, Margaret hung her clothes to dry. The Leslie family was finishing their meal when Mrs. Leslie brought some food to Margaret.

Tears welled up in Margaret's eyes. *No one told me to bring my own food. Mr. Leslie was so unchristian, telling me that they packed only enough for themselves. Mrs. Leslie is truly Christian-like, always exhibiting meekness and love. What would I have done without the piece of bread and cheese that she gave to me?*

With all the exertion of the day, Margaret was exhausted and found an old tree with roots to make a pillow. She collapsed on pine needles and dirt, tightened the blanket around herself, and slept.

During the night, the rain abated and the good bateau returned empty. In seconds, and without discussion, the two men changed positions – Daniel got out and the Cayuse got in. The two natives paddled toward the Fort to get another boat, leaving Daniel Lee with the Leslies and Margaret.

Daniel crept over to Margaret to throw another blanket on her and open an umbrella over her. He had taken her dry clothes from the campfire area and rolled them up, placing them near her head. She opened her eyes.

He suggested, "These rolled clothes would make a good pillow, if you are warm enough."

Too tired to talk, she nodded and pushed the roll under her head. The clothes smelled of smoke.

Margaret was starving the next day, but no bateau had arrived.

It was afternoon before their two bateaux appeared. In haste, they left to join Brother Shepard at the falls. The air felt damp and the trees dripped from yesterday's storm, but the blue sky peeked between fluffy clouds. They sped down the river without cargo. Margaret's heart lifted when she saw a tent in the distance. In minutes, they were on shore at Willamette Falls.

"I cannot tell you how grateful I was to see your tent, Brother Shepard. This tea and bread is most welcome. I feel civilized again." They sat on boxes while a trunk served at a table for the tin cups with tea.

Daniel Lee chuckled, "Don't expect that feeling to last for long. With every turn there could be another surprise. Oregon Country has a way of jolting us into its reality."

Shepard agreed. "Yes, expect the worst and then these experiences will seem smaller. Life is not easy here. I hope that the beauty and duty to our Lord will fill you with enough pleasure to distract you from situations like yesterday." He turned to Mrs. Leslie to ask, "Would your girls like the last of the bread?"

"Why, thank you. I know they would."

Margaret walked a distance to some bushes to relieve herself.

Shepard confided to Mr. Leslie, "We welcome your family and Miss Smith, but I was not told that you had a grown woman in your group. Please forgive us that we have little space at the Mission."

"Miss Smith has come without an appointment from the board, and I do not have a clear idea what she intends to do."

"Really!" Brother Shepard said with a look of surprise. When Margaret walked back, Shepard asked for clarification, "I understand that you were not hired for a position before you came."

She sat back down on a box. "What situation could you give to me?" Without waiting for a response, Margaret suggested, "If I could have a school."

Daniel Lee interrupted, "We have no particular job to assign you. We were not expecting you. Brother Shepard runs the school, and I already have more females than jobs." He looked to Mr. Leslie. "I do not understand. I sent for no teacher."

No one said anything.

Daniel Lee blinked his eyes in thought. "Mrs. Lee is assigned to cook and wash dishes. I imagine you could help her."

Margaret straightened and declared, "I am unwilling to work in the kitchen. I was given a pledge that I could work as a teacher to the heathen."

"Let's not dwell on this now," interjected Brother Shepard. "We will talk later. It is not as if we are going to send Miss Smith back downriver by herself."

Daniel Lee maintained, "Between here and the Mission, nothing is going to change. If Miss Smith will not accept the employment offered, I cannot consider her to be a member of our mission family. But you're right. Let's have no more discussion today and be on our way. It is getting late."

On September 20th, the group again left the water at a small community in the French Prairie fifteen miles north of the Mission. The trip had taken longer because of the accident with the destroyed bateau and food ran short; they had been eating only bread and dried meat. They were thankful when Jean Baptiste McKay, a French Canadian living there, invited them to eat at his house while the two natives continued south on the river, paddling the supplies and trunks to the Mission. The natives went faster without the weight of the others, even though they paddled against the current and without a second paddle.

In the house, McKay told the missionaries that he had settled there seven years ago. "I am doing quite well with my farming," he told them His wife approached with a steaming tin kettle filled with tea and two tin cups dangling from her fingers. McKay continued, "I used to work for the fur trading company in Astoria. Let's see, I started working with them back in 1814. I have been here a long time." He took the cups from his wife and placed one in front of Mrs. Leslie and the other in front of Margaret. His wife poured.

Looking around the sparsely furnished cabin, Margaret sipped her tea while the others talked. Besides the table and chairs where they sat, there was a bed, covered with furs and blankets. A fire in a large hearth warmed the room. Hooks on all the walls held articles of clothing, hats, a shovel and hoe, pots, rope, and empty baskets. Other baskets with dried mud on the bottom and bulging sides sat in corners. *Maybe there are potatoes in those baskets*, Margaret thought.

When Margaret finished her cup of tea, Monsieur McKay took it and poured tea in it for Brother Shepard. When Mrs. Leslie finished with her cup, it became a cup for her husband.

Margaret's eyes opened wide.

Soon Mrs. McKay placed on the table a tin plate containing meat surrounded by vegetables. She walked to the hearth and came back with two loaves of bread; she put these on the bare wood of the table, one at each end. A stack of three tin plates and several crockery bowls were on the table and Monsieur McKay took one of the bowls to begin serving.

Margaret could no longer remain silent. "I find it astonishing that you and your wife choose to live so – without proper dishes for yourself and guests."

Monsieur McKay looked up. In a soft voice, he answered, "We use what we can get here. Forgive my lack of a more formal table."

Margaret made a polite smile. "I feel so much gratitude for your hospitality. I shall bear your needs in mind, and if I can obtain any things at the Mission for you, I certainly shall." She remembered all the wares and china that she had seen when she helped repack everything from the ship with Brother Shepard. Margaret smiled at McKay's wife and turned to take another morsel from her tin plate.

The others said nothing. Mrs. Leslie had a look of pity as she gazed at Margaret. Shepard blushed.

Margaret sat and dabbed her mouth with her handkerchief. *I was raised to be proper. I am twenty-five years old and have seen these rules followed in Massachusetts, during my travels on the Brig Peru, in the Sandwich Islands, and even in the presence of the Chief Factor at Fort Vancouver. I shall help the people here learn how to live properly.*

But Margaret would soon learn that in Oregon Country, these rules and proper ways were meaningless most of the time and sometimes made her appear a bit crazy as she tried to maintain them.

After the meal, with thirty minutes left before sunset, the group mounted horses to begin the last leg of their trip. They left McKay's house and traveled in the moonlight over both rough and level country before arriving, past midnight, at the Mission. The hour mattered little as the missionaries sought their letters from home with eagerness. No one introduced Margaret at this late hour; instead, she was shown to a room with a bed while the others shared news from the East.

In the loft above Margaret, where the native girls slept, Sawala listened to all the talk downstairs, wondering how long it would take to know what the sounds meant. Four months had passed since she had come to the Mission, and still she spoke no English. She turned over, tucking her lynx fur under her head, and nestled her baby doll under the covers. She liked that the missionaries had given her a doll; she took it everywhere. In all that time, she had not seen Bailey because he had arrived only a week ago. *Many moons have gone. Will my heart know my son? My eyes will! He holds a black leaf on his head.* She touched the head of the doll on the spot of her son's birthmark.

At the mission hospital a mile away, William Bailey was awake as well. He had been out with Dr. White at the home of a sick neighbor. As he placed his head on his pillow, he remembered that he and Dr. White were going to ride over to the Bugat home to see how the mother and child were doing. Dr. White had heard they were fine. *The boy is eight or nine months old now!* Just before he fell into an easy sleep, he wondered if the beautiful woman called Margaret had arrived at the Methodist Mission.

Early the next day, Drs. White and Bailey rode out toward the Bugat homestead. Unnoticed by them, Margaret had gone out exploring the mission grounds and came upon a shelter the natives had made by placing blankets and skins over some bushes and branches. While the two horse riders passed fifty feet away, she squatted in front of the dwelling, trying to communicate with two women. For the moment, Margaret was happy to be able to point and tell them some words in English like *baskets*, *mats*, and *furs*. In the future, Margaret would find that she could never speak to them about her Lord in the way she desired. Their tongue had no words for soul, sin, repentance, salvation, hell, heaven, and so on. The natives would have difficulty grasping the fundamental concepts of Christianity.

The two doctors were deep in conversation, talking medicine.

"You did a caesarean operation and she lived! Do you know the probabilities?"

Bailey confided, "Yes, in school we learned that ninety percent of the women die, and our instructors admitted that they often did the operation on the destitute women to learn more. Typically, the women bled to death or, if they lived for some days, died of peritonitis."

"I know, I know." Dr. White paused to think. "But I don't know if I would have done what you did with Mrs. Bugat. We should do nothing that might harm the patient."

"I agree, but this situation was different. Remember I knew the child was dead, so I spent no time on the infant. Time is the factor that determines success or failure. I knew that suturing the wound and stopping the bleeding as fast as possible was of the highest priority. Dr. Tolmie has given me the finest catgut sutures that I've ever seen. I can work so quickly with them. He brought them when he came from England a year ago. I carry a supply at all times."

They rode in silence for a while.

Then Bailey added, "She was dying already with the stillborn in her. I really had nothing to lose."

"That does make sense."

Bailey decided to mention his ideas on the importance of cleaning everything. "And I did something else. Living conditions here are not the cleanest, and I got to thinking that if anything like small bugs or dirt entered the peritoneal cavity it could affect the recovery. So I boiled all my equipment to kill any little bugs. Knowing that tiny insects like gnats, fruit flies, and fleas exist, I surmised there might be smaller ones we don't see. I cleaned my hands and her skin with spirits before making the incision – and I even doused the sutures. I don't know, but I think there is a relationship between this procedure and her surviving."

"I would like to see the wound, and how it healed."

Bailey turned and grinned, "Me, too. I've been on the cattle run since I operated on her. We'll ask her if we can examine her abdomen." He hesitated a moment. "I haven't told you that she has a baby."

Dr. White's eyes filled with confusion.

Bailey continued. "Have you heard that some Indians kill their newborn half-breeds?" Seeing White's quizzical expression, Bailey explained, "The half-breeds are the lowest class in their societies. The mothers are disgraced to have a mixed child and crush the infant's head at birth. I came upon this situation after Mrs. Bugat had her stillborn child. I startled the squaw before she could kill the baby and took the Indian child to Mrs. Bugat to raise."

The wind picked up. Bailey pulled his collar higher, and Dr. White tugged his hat tighter on his head.

Bailey had to shout over the wind to be heard, "The baby didn't look like a native in any way. I don't think they told anyone about this. Please, would you keep this in confidence?"

Dr. White shouted back against the wind, "Of course, a doctor's pledge."

Once inside the Bugats' home, Bailey found the little boy sitting on the floor playing with smooth, river rocks, too big to swallow and small enough for his pudgy hands. The child looked up and smiled, extending his hand with a rock to show Bailey.

Dr. White introduced himself to the Bugats.

Without hesitation, Bailey swooped up the child into his arms. "Look at his size! He certainly looks healthy and happy." The baby dropped the rock on Bailey's foot and squeezed the doctor's nose in his little fist. "Ouch! My toe! And, my nose! You have a strong grip."

The room filled with laughter.

"Oui, he a little bear cub. And he eat more than mama's milk. He want my food, too. I cut off little pieces and let him eat with me."

Bailey exclaimed, "What a head of red hair! And look at his blue eyes."

Monsieur Bugat had a twinkle in his eye. "Dr. Bailey, I must tell of my great, great grandmother from Scotland all the time now. People ask why his hair red. You see I have lots of curls, but no red. My grandmother had curls and red hair, I say. At least I have blue eyes, and I no need to explain that."

Mrs. Bugat asked, "You like tea? I have hot water."

As they sat drinking the tea, Bailey continued to hold the baby. "And what do you call him?"

"His name you say R-No."

Bailey looked to Mrs. Bugat and questioned, "Is that an Indian name?"

Monsieur Bugat raised his bushy eyebrows and frowned. "No, it French, not Indian. Why you think Indian?"

Dr. White explained, "I don't think Dr. Bailey knows his French. Am I correct that one spells the name A-R-N-A-U-D?"

"I don't spell. Well, I don't write or read either." He slapped Bailey on the back. "You like my little joke?"

They spent a long while with the Bugats. After examining Mrs. Bugat's healed incision, asking some questions about her health, and finding everything fine, Bailey went back to the child. He couldn't keep his hands off the boy or stop talking to him. "Guess I'll have to come and teach you how to read and write. Would you let me do that, Monsieur Bugat?"

Bailey turned to Dr. White to quip, "Did you hear? I'm learning French. I called him Monsieur, for the first time."

Bugat answered, "Oui, teach him to read. Why not? Start next week." He burst out laughing and slapped Bailey's back again.

Bailey went back to visit the Bugats the next week, and often after that. Dr. White asked him why he went so much and Bailey couldn't explain in words what was pulling him toward the child. But he realized something about himself, *Sobriety opens a world of joy that I never had when drunk. If I can only stay on this path! Dr. White doesn't know, but he is doing more than reviewing my medical knowledge with me; he has made a life of sobriety possible for the first time.* Bailey answered, "The boy seems to be bright, and I want to help teach him things." After a minute, Bailey added, "Besides, I like children."

Margaret liked children, too. There were thirty living at the Mission. Her first few days were spent outside, drying her soaked articles, and exploring the countryside near the Mission. The children watched her in all her tasks and followed her. She began to teach them.

Holding up one of her damp hats, she said, "Hat," and placed it on her head. None of the children wore their native clothing any more, but she pointed to an old Indian man walking in the distance wearing a hat woven from plants. Then she pointed to her own head. "Hat," she said again and pointed to the man with a hat.

They understood and told her, "*Wattap.*"

Margaret shared her room with another woman, Elvira Johnson, who had arrived four months prior. One evening as they prepared to go to bed, Margaret asked Elvira, "Do any of the children understand English? I can convey only the simplest concepts to the ones I have seen."

In the dark, the two women could hear the other missionaries talking in the next cabin.

"No, the Indian children do not speak any English or understand when we talk to them. I have been here only since May, so we have not been successful at giving them instructions on the scriptures. There is one little girl with blonde hair, who seems to want to learn more than the others, but we are so busy here. There has not been time to plan lessons for them."

Margaret seemed appalled, "What does everyone do if they are not trying to teach and convert these poor heathens? Isn't that the purpose of the Methodist Mission?"

Elvira sighed, "Every day is so difficult. Maybe you don't realize that there were few people here before I arrived in May. Four men, to be exact, – the two Lees, Brother Shepard, and Philip Edwards. They had to do everything to make this Mission – I mean everything! Cut down the trees, build these three cabins that you have seen, plant the crops, harvest, and cook. Now there are more living here, but it is getting late in the season. We are all working to prepare food for the winter." She sighed and said, "When we came, there was no room for us all – two married couples with five children, six single men, and three single women. Now there are more people – twenty-five missionaries and their families – living here. We have sixty to feed, including the Indians who are sleeping outside all around the Mission and the Indian children in the cellar and lofts."

"If everyone is so crowded, how can only two of us be sleeping in this room?"

"So much has changed since I came. You have seen only the three buildings that were here when I arrived. These three buildings have four rooms for sleeping – two bedrooms in each of the two cabins. The third building is for everything else – eating, Sunday services, a school, and storage for all food and supplies. Each of the two families took a bedroom. Look at the size, a mere fifteen by eighteen feet! And a family of five had to sleep here. We three women went to the third bedroom. The six single men were in the fourth bedroom; they were very crowded.

"Immediately, they started building more – two buildings and a hospital, where Dr. White lives now. Reverend Leslie moved into a square-log house formerly owned by one of our French neighbors. Then south of the Mission, they built a log house and shop for the blacksmith, Mr. Beers. All of the men worked on these buildings. They had no time for teaching and converting."

"I still don't understand. Why are we only two in this room?"

Elvira laughed, "Reverend Jason Lee married Anna Maria and Brother Shepard married Susan. Yes, there were two weddings in July, two months ago. All the sleeping arrangements changed. Reverend Daniel Lee often isn't here because he comes and goes between here and the Hudson's Bay Company. Do you remember he went to assist you with all your supplies? Soon he will be going to The Dalles to start a mission. And there is much more space now that the three families with children are in their own houses. Have you been up to see the hospital and houses built for Mr. Leslie and Dr. White? They are only a mile away."

"No, I haven't. I will go find those places tomorrow. Thank you for all the information. Good night," Margaret said before she fell asleep.

While Margaret slept, three of the men – Jason Lee, Brother Cyrus Shepard, and David Leslie – had gathered in the largest cabin to talk about her.

Mr. Leslie repeated what he had said on the boat trip, "Yes, she came without an appointment, and I do not know her intentions." He chose his words with care, making no lie other than the lie of omission.

Jason Lee asked, "Do you suppose she came to find a husband? I do not want someone who comes without being requested and seeks a man."

Brother Shepard leaned closer to say in a softer voice, "From what I saw of her during our meal at McKay's home, she appears to be a maniac. She actually said she would send them dishes and other things from the Mission."

Lee shook his head. "She seems to be a bit overzealous and a weak-minded enthusiast. How is it that she has traveled so far from her home without authority? I certainly do not want to give her any encouragement."

They discussed possible alternatives.

"We can't send her back. We would have to pay for that out of our budget. She seems capable and intelligent, though strong-willed. We must talk with her before we decide anything. Now that she has arrived, it may not be to her liking. Maybe she will want to leave."

Mr. Leslie remained silent and finally excused himself, "I don't know of anything to add. I am quite tired. Please excuse me."

The following day, Margaret met Reverend Jason Lee. When he asked her why she had come all this way to the Mission, she produced her pledge. He read it and saw the name of David Leslie, signed at the bottom with the other board members.

Lee leaned toward her raising his voice, "But he declared he did not know what you intended to do here. What is this about? This makes no sense."

Margaret told him there were difficulties existing between Mr. Leslie and herself, "And until they are settled, we cannot meet at the Lord's Table together."

Lee became irritated, "No, no, no! Not this again. My young lady – yes, Miss Smith – you have no idea the stories I had to listen to when the others arrived in May. I shall not go through that again. I refuse to settle the disagreements of adults acting like they are children."

Margaret sat up straighter. "Would you please then tell me what is my proper course of conduct if I believe a preacher is guilty of uttering falsehoods? I have made mention of none of this to anyone, and I am asking your advice in private."

Now Jason Lee was angry. He stood and slammed his fist against the table. "Speaking untruths? Speaking untruths by a preacher is a criminal offense!"

Margaret gasped with her hand to her mouth. "I only said," she began.

"Don't interrupt me, Miss Smith. If I know of anyone speaking falsehoods, it shall not be concealed and the scriptures must be read. You must tell me the fault between you and Reverend Leslie, and if he is found guilty, I shall tell the church. His punishment will be severe!"

Margaret stammered a bit and refused to convey the problem, excusing herself.

As soon as she could talk to Mr. Leslie in private, she said, "When we were on the vessel coming here, I had no idea the seriousness of this. What should I do?"

They agreed that a letter to Jason Lee would end the problem. Margaret wrote one but made matters worse. Now, on paper, she stated that untruths had occurred in two instances:

Rev. J. Lee:

Respected Sir: I have had an interview with Mr. Leslie, and I think proper to inform you of the conclusion of our conversation. He declares he knows no reason why I should not be received into the mission family and into the church here, to enjoy the privileges of the same as I have been accustomed. He was able in some instances to lead me to suppose I might have been mistaken on the subject of his speaking untruths, but in two instances, at least, my impressions remain as they were. I however told him that I now had done what I considered my duty and I should trouble him no further – the matter now rested with him and his God.

Very respectfully,
Margaret Jewett Smith

Days passed. After observing everyone working so hard, Margaret volunteered to do anything to assist the good of the Mission. Daniel Lee, William Willson, and Philip Edwards sent their clothes to her to be washed and mended. Even Jason Lee sent work – material to make bags for wheat, his clothes to be mended, and some sewing for the Mission's native cook. Few knew of her difficulties with Reverend Leslie and as she assisted with many tasks, everyone welcomed Margaret to the Methodist Mission.

Oldest and Largest Black Cottonwood in USA (sprouted circa 1735)
Trunk Circumference: 26 feet 3 inches
Height: 155 feet
Spread: 110 feet

Willamette Mission Park (Located near original Methodist Mission)
OREGON STATE PARKS

CHAPTER 7

A TIME FOR
WEDDINGS
End of 1837-1838

On her knees, Margaret finished placing the pins in the hem of Elvira's wedding dress and said, "Now turn slowly again so I can see if it is even." Margaret stood up and said, "Oh, you look beautiful!" She offered her hand to help Elvira step off the chair but decided otherwise. "No, wait. We would be wiser to remove the dress while you are still above this dirt floor. Look how dirty my dress has gotten!" Margaret tried to brush the dirt from her skirt, to no avail, and then picked up the lantern to extinguish the flame. "It's so dark in these cabins even during the day, but we're finished."

Elvira glowed, "It pleases me so to have a wedding dress. Wasn't I fortunate that Anna brought this one? Of course, some of us think that she was chosen back east to wed Jason Lee. Well, that's a rumor. She has never said. I was told that there were men here in need of wives, but I didn't know that I would be so honored. Margaret, next you must marry. Of the three single missionary men – William Willson, Philip Edwards and Joseph Whitcomb – whom do you find interesting?"

"I have no plans to marry. I am here on a greater calling – to teach the natives about our Lord."

"I know, Margaret, but every woman needs to be married. You can be married and still be a missionary." Elvira sighed, "And you don't know how it feels. I am so happy."

Margaret patted her hand. "I understand."

"You came with my Henry, I mean, Mr. Perkins," Elvira giggled, "and you must know him better than I. After all, it is but November – less than two months ago, I made his acquaintance. Don't you find him to be wonderful?" The bride-to-be carefully slipped the dress over her shoulders and placed the white satin and lace gown into Margaret's waiting arms.

Margaret ignored the question. Mr. Perkins's interference in her dispute with Mr. Leslie still irritated her, although she was working on forgiveness. She placed the dress on her bed. "Elvira, with the material I must cut from the skirt to shorten it, I'll make some rosettes for your hair. What do you think?"

"Margaret, would you? You sew so well. Satin rosettes! With no flowers growing outside now, I would be so pleased," she sighed.

The mention of flowers gave Margaret an idea. "And I could make a few extra rosettes for a bouquet, with some real ferns between them. How divine this will be!"

Elvira dressed and then turned to let Margaret button the back of her cotton day dress. She clapped her hands together and gave a little jump. "I forgot to tell you. Earlier today, Brother Shepard came to my table where I lunched; he was so excited. He said that the little girl with blonde hair gave a greeting of "Good Morning" to him." Elvira giggled again. "He said it didn't matter that it was afternoon. He commended you on your achievement with this child. What name did you give her?"

Margaret picked up her books and papers. "My! She is such an eager little girl and is learning well." She hugged the stack to her chest and enjoyed the moment, knowing that she was appreciated among the missionaries. Margaret then voiced a question that had been bothering her for some time, "Why don't we have any full-blooded Indian girls here?"

"It seems that the native tribes do not want the half-breed children and send them to us. They keep the orphaned children who are full-blooded Indians. Dr. McLoughlin often gets unwanted half-breeds and sends some down to us. Did you know everyone calls the half-breeds *Métis*?"

"Yes, I learned that French word. Oh, it is time for me to teach." Margaret had informally started teaching English to the *Métis* girls and had made progress where the other missionaries had not. Rushing out the door, she stopped a moment to answer Elvira's earlier question. "The little girl who speaks so well has the native name Sawala. No one has given her a proper English name yet. She learns so quickly that I give her private lessons sometimes."

In a few moments, Margaret sat under a tree for her afternoon class as William Bailey passed by on his horse. Again, they did not see the other.

Bailey was heading out to visit his friends. Dr. Elijah had urged that he take a free day from doctoring, so Bailey decided to go to the mill owned by

Solomon and Ewing. However, before Bailey left the mission area, he went to visit the sick Kalapuyan family he had seen earlier in the week. Scattered around the mission area were a dozen temporary huts made with discarded wood from the sawmill – six-foot-long thin slices of fir with bark edges. The boards leaned against tree trunks with blankets draped over them. Bailey walked his horse close to the ashes of one of the campfires where two men were sitting on their haunches. Some horse hooves were scattered in the ashes and entrails from the large animal lay near a tree a few feet away, covered with buzzing flies. Charred bones were smoking in the embers.

The men looked up and greeted Bailey in Chinook Jargon. Bailey answered in English, "Good afternoon." He didn't understand much of this *lingua franca*. Raising his black bag, Bailey pointed to the lean-to where the family of four was sick. He smelled death as soon as he lifted the blanket and bent to enter. He almost stumbled on a four-year-old child sitting with a blank stare. Dr. Bailey felt the child's forehead. *He is better!* When Bailey's eyes adjusted to the dim lighting, he saw the father sweating with fever. He spread a crumpled blanket over him and tucked it under his chin. The man did not respond. At last, he saw the cause of the stench: the dead mother lay on her side on the dirt floor, her arm still cradling the baby who sucked on her breast. The woman's mouth and eyes were open. Bailey stepped over her husband and crouched close to her before lifting the child; he had to press on her breast near the nipple for the child to release. The child began to wail.

With the infant in his arms, Bailey left the hovel holding the hand of the four-year-old. He looked around and saw a group of women near the river. They sat weaving baskets and looked up when he approached. "I don't speak your language, but," he stopped to point to the home of these children. "What do I say to you?" He noticed that one woman sat with a child to her breast. He went to her, placing the crying infant on her crossed legs. He patted his chest and pointed to the baby's mouth; she put the child to her other breast. He pointed back at the lean-to and shook his head.

Another woman jumped up and hastened to the hovel. Upon entering, she cried out and clamored in frantic sounds. Others rushed to see. Bailey remained, watching and holding the older child's hand. Glancing down to the little boy, he inquired, "What can I do with you, little guy?" As one woman passed, he reached out and took her hand, placing the little boy's hand into hers, saying, "He is yours now." Bailey's eyes told her what he meant. She nodded.

Bailey was filled with gloom when he rode away from the Kalapuyan site. For miles he was pensive. But his somber mood broke when he saw Solomon in the distance, in front of his mill, loading sacks of flour onto a wagon. Bailey spurred his horse and hurried to his friend. "Solomon, here, I'll give you hand."

"Why, look who it is!" They hugged and slapped each other's back. "I heard you were down at the Methodist Mission working with Dr. Elijah White. Did I hear right?"

"Yes, you did."

They finished loading. "Let's go in my house and have a cup of coffee. I know Mrs. Ellen wants to see you. Here comes Ewing. He must have seen you ride up; he was working on our records. He looks glad to see you." And he was.

Ewing inquired, "What's that fur you got on your face, Bailey?"

Bailey reached up and ran his hand over his beard. "My scar was a curiosity to children and some folks. Scared them! So now that I'm a practicing doctor, I have to look more refined."

Ewing quipped, "You wanted to have that handsome look back. Hey, look at his emerald eyes, Solomon. Ain't he a pretty one?"

They entered the Smith's house with loud voices and laughter. "Ellen, come see who rode up."

After talking about sawmills, gristmills, and doctoring, Ewing slapped his thigh and let out a "Damn, I forgot!" He stood and pointed to Solomon. "Bailey, have you heard what Hoxie and Solomon did while we were sweating and working to get the cattle up here from California?"

Bailey looked at Ewing and then to Solomon, who beamed with a grin.

Ewing blurted, "They both got married! They said that they needed to be at peace with the Lord. So they went to the Mission to git married."

Solomon stood and went to his wife, putting his arm around her shoulder. "He's telling the truth. On February 11th, Reverend Jason Lee married me to my Clatsop princess."

Bailey scooted his chair back to stand and congratulate them. He pumped Solomon's hand. "May I kiss the bride?" Mrs. Ellen stepped toward him, and he placed a kiss on her cheek.

"And there's more news!" Ewing announced. "Hoxie found the Lord. He goes to services at the Mission most Sundays. I think we were still on the boat waiting to leave for California when he found his Lord. Then he goes and gits married, too."

Solomon beamed, putting with his arm around his wife again. "Hoxie has a woman from the Yamhill tribe. Miss Mary is a wonderful woman like mine."

Bailey added, "I've met Miss Mary and agree. I'm happy for all of you."

Ewing turned to Bailey. "You ain't goin' to go and git married on me, are you, Bailey?" Not waiting for an answer, he commented, "Even George Gay has a woman now."

Solomon said, "We don't know her yet, but her name is La Louisa. Isn't that pretty?"

Mrs. Ellen explained that she saw La Louisa and George a few days ago and learned they were planning to marry.

For the moment, Bailey wasn't listening. He had sat back down when Ewing asked if he was getting married and an image of Margaret popped into his head. *My heart jumps just thinking about her, but she didn't seem to take much notice of me at McLoughlin's dinner.* The others were still talking and his mind went to Jason Lee marrying his friends. *How can he be a man of God? Woodward, Turner, that squaw, and me were turned away with nothing to eat. He sees the Indians as "degraded red men" and I heard he refers to them as "filthy and miserable" people. No, I can't find anything in Lee to like.*

Soon the conversation turned to business.

Ewing said, "Bailey, this mill is going good and my cattle are making money for me. We've been back here for only two months, and I have five calves." He grinned, "That ain't fate working for me. When I picked cattle from the herd, I looked for cows ready to bear."

Solomon agreed, "Now all of us settlers are getting richer like McLoughlin's been doing with the Hudson's Bay Company." Solomon hesitated, and then said, "McLoughlin is a mystery. He encouraged us to make the cattle run even though he had the monopoly on cattle and rents his animals. Why'd he do that?"

No one commented.

Solomon continued, "Every time I think about us having to rent cows for milk, I get angry. Well, now that's over."

Ewing stood. "Hey, Bailey, let's go over to my place. I'll show you my next plan to git rich."

Bailey wanted to avoid going to Ewing's place. He knew that Ewing would get out a bottle. So he suggested going where no liquor would be offered. "Let's ride over to Hoxie's mill. I haven't seen him for a time. Let's talk about your get-rich ideas as we ride."

On the ride, Ewing gave a discourse on Oregon needing leadership and never shared any get-rich schemes.

After spending the day with his friends, Bailey stopped at the Bugats' home in the early dark of the November evening. He had dinner with the family and played with Arnaud. *This child gives me so much joy. I should have some children of my own.*

And the months passed.

During those months, Margaret was learning the Kalapuyan language as well as Chinook Jargon. Languages came easily to her. Out walking one afternoon, she saw a Kalapuyan working with a plow and horse in one of the Mission's fields. He glistened in the sunlight with the sweat from his efforts. Suddenly, he threw his arms in the air and walked away, leaving the horse and plow in the heat of the sun. He stalked across the furrows, complaining in his native tongue. When he got closer, she recognized him. She asked in Chinook Jargon, "Oofaaf, what is wrong?"

"No more! I plow no more!"

"Why? What is wrong?"

Now Oofaaf was at her side in the shade of a tree; he wiped sweat from his brow. "I want sugar and asked how to grow it. Brother Shepard say he teach me to grow."

"Oh, I know how you love sugar. Everyone knows." She patted his hands. "Let's go sit by the stream so you can cool yourself and get a drink.

Tell me more."

Seated with his feet in the water, Oofaaf continued. "You crazy. All of you. I want sugar, but not enough to work so hard. Why you pale ones work so hard? There is food to pick from a bush or spear in the river or gather from the trees. No work. It easy."

Margaret reflected on his words. "I never thought about what you are saying. Yes, there is an abundance of natural food in Oregon." She hesitated, but decided to tell him about growing sugar. "We cannot grow sugar here. It comes on a ship from places like the Sandwich Islands where it is warmer."

Oofaaf jumped up, looking surprised.

Trying to make amends for his disappointment, Margaret suggested, "I'll trade you sugar from time to time. You bring me a basket, a fur, or something you make. But I can only give you a little bit at a time."

He furrowed his brow in thought and then said, "I like that better than plowing."

"Come, we must get the poor horse out of the sun. Help me and then you can go."

Another fine day, Margaret gathered all the natives – adults and children – at the Mission. Outside on benches that were used for Sunday services, she gave her own service. Later the *Oregonian* newspaper would print the details of what she said.

She began:

Mican tum-tum cloosh? (Your heart good?)
Mican tum-tum wake cloosh. (Your heart no good.)
Alaka mican ma-ma lose. (By and by, you die.)
Mican tum-tum cloosh mican clatamay Sakalatie. (Your heart good, you go to God.)
Mican tum-tum wake cloosh mican wake clatamay Sakalatie. (Your heart no good, you no go to God.)
Mican Clatalmay sayyah; hiyas wake cloosh schochen. (Go ye great way off; very bad devil.)

Sakalatie mamoke tum-tum cloosh. (God make heart good.)

Wah-wah Sakalatie. (Speak to God.)

Sakalatie mamoke hiyas cloosh mican tum-tum. (God make very good your heart.)

Hiyack wah-wah Sakalatie. (Quick speak to God.)

Some of the missionaries observed the service and were impressed with her achievements, but Margaret was starting to have problems again. The missionaries were irritated with her meddlesome ways.

In private, Brother Shepard complained to Jason Lee, "She rearranges everything. I can never find something when I want it. She did it in the kitchen, and the other women asked that she be relieved of helping them. She went to the shed, where I keep the broken or unused things that we use for repairs. Now I can't find anything there. She went to the storerooms, where we keep clothing to give to our Indians or to sell. and she refolded and stacked it all. And I might add that she took at least one shirt to give to a boy. And the sugar supply is dwindling. I have no proof, but I fear she is in some way to blame." He stopped to wipe his forehead. "This is all so upsetting." Then he sat taller and huffed, "Giving away the clothing is not her job. I decide what and when to give."

Jason Lee nodded, "This woman is so very headstrong. What can we do?"

They both sat quietly for a moment.

Shepard admitted, "She is so good with the native children. But I am assigned the boys. She is assigned to teach only the ten girls. I saw her working with one of the boys, and as I mentioned she gave him the shirt without my permission. She didn't even tell me. I heard it from the boy. He can't speak English, but he pointed to her when I saw the shirt and inquired."

Jason Lee brightened. "I have an idea. Let's get her away from the Mission. She can keep her room and sleep here, but I'll tell her to go help Dr. White in any way he needs. She could help his wife cook or sew." Lee made a sly grin. "She could work in the hospital and help him organize his medical supplies." They nodded with enthusiasm.

"Yes, that is a good idea."

Lee continued, "I'll tell her to have her board with the White family and to come here only for the girls' lessons and to sleep." As an afterthought, he said, "I wish she would marry someone, so he could control her."

Shepard agreed, "Yes, I agree. I know William is interested in her."

Lee looked surprised. "The doctor?"

"No, no! I mean William Willson, the carpenter."

"I see." Lee ordered, "Tell everyone to encourage her to marry. We shouldn't have a single woman here. It isn't proper."

So Margaret began to spend time with the two Williams – William J. Bailey and William H. Willson.

The first time that Margaret noticed William Bailey was on the day she went to the White's place to help. Rain came in a downpour as the doctors finished seeing the Kalapuyans who had come to the small hospital. The two doctors ran to the house and went to their bedrooms. Margaret was in the pantry and didn't see them enter.

"Let's eat in an hour." Mrs. White said and then suggested, "After you prepare the table with plates and cups, why don't you ask Dr. Bailey if he needs any mending done or something sewn? This is a good evening to sit and sew."

Margaret knew she would like working in this house and told Mrs. White, "It is a pleasure to walk on wooden floors. I don't know why they don't get some boards to put down in the Mission, now that there is a sawmill. Actually, I do know. They fear the Mission might be flooded away. I have heard that the river has risen too close many times."

"Yes, I heard as well."

Margaret arrived at Bailey's door and knocked.

"Come in."

"Hello, Dr. Bailey. Mrs. White thought I might ask you if you have any," she never finished her sentence. Her curiosity was piqued by what she saw. Since she entered, he had not moved; he was hunched over his desk. She wandered closer to look over his shoulder. "You collect plants?"

He finished gluing a plant to the paper and looked up. A heat came to his face upon seeing Margaret so close. He could smell her sweet dusting powder. *She is close enough to kiss!* But he nodded and cleared his throat,

"Yes, this is a hobby of mine."

She had so many questions. "What do you do with them? Why? I mean, my oh my, the whole plant is as flat as a sheet of paper."

He relaxed and grinned. "What do you want to know?"

"This is so interesting. I love plants and would like to know more. Well, I like birds as well. I saw this hummingbird that I never saw before – brown and so tiny." She stopped herself. "I'm making no sense. I guess I was wondering why you collect plants."

He stood and said, "Let me get you a place to sit."

He left the room and Margaret looked at a map on his desk until he returned with a stool. She asked, "You drew this map? It's interesting."

"Yes, I wander around this area so much, I decided to map it. Here, you sit on the chair and I'll take the stool. Until you, I knew of no one interested in my hobby." He reached up to a shelf and took down a stack of papers.

She could see that there were pages and pages of plants. "Oh, my! You have collected so many."

"You asked what I do with my plants. If it's a small plant – like the one I was gluing when you came in – I carefully dig up the whole plant, taking care not to mar the leaves or cut off a root. I press it into one of these thick books that Dr. White has lent me to study. When it has dried – and each plant takes a different amount of time to dry – I glue it to a sheet of paper." He turned over sheet after sheet until he came to a leaf from a tree. "If I have only the leaf or needles from a tree, I draw the flower and fruit on the same sheet and save the actual fruit, if I have it, in my tobacco tins. He reached up and took down a tin box filled with acorns of all sizes and shapes. "See, each acorn has a number I wrote on it. Let's see, this is number thirty-nine." He rummaged through the sheets with pressed leaves until he came to the thirty-ninth page. "This acorn goes with this leaf of an oak tree."

"What do I smell?"

Bailey flipped back a page and the fragrance increased. "These are leaves and flowers from the mock-orange bush. Even dry, they still smell like orange blossoms. Did you smell any real orange blossoms in your travels on the Sandwich Islands?"

"I did. What a marvelous smell. And I saw the oranges on the tree with the blossoms at the same time!"

"Yes, well, this mock-orange bush may be a new variety here in Oregon. It blooms at night and is from the genus *philadelphus*. There are many varieties of this bush. I understand that George Washington planted one in his yard."

"This is amazing." Her face was glowing. "I know you said this is your hobby, but do you plan to do anything with all this?"

Bailey turned and looked into her eyes – her bright blue eyes. He rubbed his beard, hesitating to tell her what he had never said to anyone. But then he said it, "It is my dream to find plants that no one has seen in the United States. I plan to take all my work back, if I ever return to the States, and give it to a scientific institute."

She sensed that he had shared a secret dream. "That is a fine ambition. I dream that I'll write a book one day. Some of my letters and articles have been published back in the Boston. But I want to write a book."

And so their friendship began.

"Have you collected the camas plant? I heard that the natives dig them up and make a bread-like cake."

"I do have the camas lily," he answered, fingering down his index. "Here it is, number nineteen. That means I collected it very early on.

"I see."

He adjusted how he sat and moved a little closer as he showed her. "Here in my index, I noted where and when I found the plant." His face brightened as he talked. "Of course it was impossible to press the bulb root, so I drew the root system on the paper with the pressed leaves and flowers. See? The flower still shows its color of violet-blue."

Not giving it any thought, he did not show her the white flower of the death-camas plant. Next spring, she would learn its poisonous qualities when someone dies at the Mission.

After that first talk, Bailey often invited Margaret to go horseback riding with him. In the East, a chaperone would have been required. In Oregon Country, life was harder but freer, with rules more lax. In Oregon Country, even the spirit of the wind blew freer, with few buildings to stop its course;

the human spirit had the same freedom to fly with the wind. Bailey and Margaret took their outings alone.

One such day, Bailey told her that he wanted to go plant collecting. They rode south from the Mission. "First, I want to show you this black cottonwood tree that looks to be over one hundred years old. It's less than a mile from the Mission."

As their horses trotted at a leisurely pace, a meadowlark sat in the clearing and sang. They glanced at each other, acknowledging their pleasure.

When he pointed to the black cottonwood in the distance, Margaret exclaimed, "Oh, I know this tree. That's the tree the native boys were hanging on when they broke that limb. Do you see?" She rode a little faster to get to the tree.

He smiled and watched her ride away, reflecting. *I am not surprised that she noticed this tree, like I had.*

"Look how they damaged this beautiful tree! I was angry with them. And now I feel even worse, knowing it is so old."

Bailey arrived and looked at the broken limb. He reached to see if he could touch it while he sat on his horse, but it was out of his reach. He commented, "It will heal itself. See, there is a small twig growing up and out where the break occurred. It is going to make a right-angle elbow in the coming years. Eventually, the bark will cover the break."

"That makes me feel a little better. Do you have a sample leaf from this black cottonwood?"

"I do. And I have noted that the original seedling probably sprouted sometime between 1730 and 1750. It is a grand tree." He thought a moment. "I hope the floods never take it out. It is quite close to the Willamette River."

"I think I shall write a poem about this tree." Her voice lifted and filled with excitement, "Oh, by the way, I brought a poem that I wrote. Would you like to read it before I send it to some newspapers in the East?"

"Of course. Give it to me and I'll read it tonight." He took the folded paper and slipped it into his pocket.

She had the words memorized so while they rode side by side in silence, she recited them in her head.

INDIAN MISSIONS

We call them savage – O be just;
Their outraged feelings scan;
A voice comes forth, 'tis from the dust –
The savage was a man!
Think you he loved not? Who stood by,
And in his toils took part?
Woman was there to bless his eye –
The savage had a heart!
Think you he prayed not? When on high
He heard the thunders roll,
What bade him look beyond the sky?
The savage had a soul!

Alas! For them – their day is o'er,
Their fires are out from shore to shore;
No more for them the wild deer bounds;
The plow is on their hunting grounds;
The pale man's axe rings through their woods
The pale man's sail skims o'er their floods.
Their pleasant springs are dry;
Their children – look – by power oppressed,
Beyond the mountains of the west,
Their children go to die.

His heraldry is but a broken bow,
His history but a tale of misery and woe,
His very name must be a blank.

Moving his horse closer to her, he said, "Usually, I stop and gather plant samples whenever I see an interesting one, but today I made plans. So now I want to return to another tree, a maple tree. I need both the leaf and some seed samples."

Although he had not thought to tell her yet, they trotted toward the

Bugats.

He continued talking, saying, "I am excited for you to see the gigantic leaf on this maple tree. It was too big to glue on one sheet of paper. I ruined the first leaf I had, so I need another one to replace it."

She noticed how his face shone with enthusiasm.

He peered ahead, searching for the big leaf maple tree. "There it is! Isn't it beautiful? Wait until you see the size of these leaves. I don't think it grows in the East. Some of the leaves measure a foot across."

Without dismounting, Bailey reached up to gather some samples. "Look at these double-winged samaras. Aren't they colored beautifully? I'm sure the *genus* of the tree is *Acer*." He stopped talking a moment and looked at her. "Do you know that all flora and fauna have Latin names?"

"It was mentioned in one of my classes."

"It's used for world-wide classification. With the names in Latin, all cultures can use the same naming system." He carefully placed the seeds in a tin. "I'm going to roll this leaf into the tin for now. It's soft and green so it shouldn't tear, but remind me to check after we leave the Bugats so I can get another if needed."

"The Bugats?"

"Since we are so close to their place, I would like to stop and visit. Do you mind? They have a little boy. In a way, I helped with his birth. He should be walking now. I want to see him."

"In a way? What do you mean?"

Bailey finished packing his specimens. "It's a long story. I'll tell you some other time." But it would be years before she learns the story of Arnaud and the Bugats. And by then she would have heard parts of the story from Ewing Young.

When at the Bugats' cabin, Bailey was surprised that little Arnaud was walking; he encouraged the child to come to him. With babbles and giggles, Arnaud teetered this way and that, heading for Bailey's waiting arms. Margaret could not help noticing the excitement the child had for William Bailey. But what interested her more was Bailey's enthusiasm for the redheaded child.

He explained to her on their ride home, "Maybe I'm attached to Arnaud because we have redheads in my family. I am of Scottish ancestry. I think my great-grandmother on my mother's side was a redhead."

And then there was the other William in Margaret's life.

Whenever Margaret went to the Mission to teach the little girls or went to Sunday services, William Willson found her. During her classes in the outdoors, he watched nearby. She noticed, with a certain amount of uneasiness, that during Sunday services he always sat one row behind her. She sat with the White family. If she noticed him approaching or if he appeared to want to speak to her, she quickly walked the other way. She wanted to give him no encouragement.

Nevertheless, his opportunity was to come. When Margaret's troubles with Reverend David Leslie surfaced again, William Willson would be standing next to her.

During Margaret's first spring, Sawala went to get her to show the camas lilies blooming in a long meadow not far from the Mission. Sawala was blooming as well; she was bursting with simple English words. When they returned to the mission area, Margaret sat with all the *Métis* girls under the trees while they stitched on samplers to learn their alphabets and sewing.

After a time, Margaret reviewed the samplers and said, "Sawala, come with me." She let the other girls go play. They walked out into the camas field between the jouncing blue flowers. Margaret spoke in simple words and enunciated each one. "Time for your lesson. Just you and me," Margaret pointed to herself and Sawala, to help the girl understand. Then Margaret added, with a playful poke to the doll's stomach, "and your baby."

Sawala beamed from under her bonnet, one that Margaret had sewn especially to fit her pointy forehead, making it longer and with a wider brim than the other girls' bonnets. Sawala bobbed her head to show she understood. But her joy was in knowing the word to call her son. Sawala held her doll in the air, and repeated, "Baby."

Margaret said, "Yes, please talk. Say more."

"No can talk." Pulling a topic from the air was beyond Sawala's capabilities.

"All right. Show me your sampler."

Sawala handed the embroidery hoop to Margaret.

"Look. It is beautiful. Do you think it is beautiful?"

Sawala nodded with enthusiasm and said, "I like sampler. See flower. I sew. It beautiful."

Margaret was ecstatic and hugged the girl. "Oh, Sawala. Why can't the others learn like you? Your words make me so happy."

Sawala looked puzzled. "No can talk."

Margaret put her hand to her chest. "I am sorry." She enunciated each word, "I talked too much and too fast."

"Too fast. Yes."

"Sawala, why do the girls not talk English like you? No, no, this is too hard." Margaret moved her hand in the air to erase what she had said – a signal she had taught Sawala that was like erasing on their slate board.

"Again," Sawala said.

"Yes, again I talk." Margaret pointed to Sawala, "You talk English." Then Margaret pointed to the children behind them in the distance, "Why they no talk?"

"They play. They little girls. No interest. "

"Sawala, very good answer. Now teach me. What is your word for this?" Margaret pointed to the camas flowers.

"*Pookwa am plaatowa.*"

Margaret smiled. "Thank you. Flowers are *pookwa am plaatowa*. Or is this the word for a camas flower?"

The question was too complex for Sawala. Margaret understood this, so she merely added, "Thank you."

"You welcome."

"Sawala," Margaret said with slow enunciated words, "say 'you *are* welcome' and smile."

Sawala smiled and looked to Margaret before she repeated the correction with eager and grateful eyes. Sawala took Margaret's hand and hugged it to her chest. "I like talk."

"And I like to hear. Sawala, can you make food from *pookwa am plaatowa*?" Margaret pointed to the camas lilies.

"Yes."

Margaret was excited, but wanted to clarify her question, "Food to eat?"

"Yes."

Margaret stopped. "You show me how to make?"

"Yes. When ready. Not now."

"You tell me when to dig?" Margaret bent over and moved her hand like digging.

"Yes. I show."

They walked without talking for a while.

"Sawala, I hear girls call you a name." Margaret repeated and pointed to the girls in the distance, "Girls say name to you. What does it mean?"

She giggled, "Me 'old woman' to them."

Margaret asked, "Why?"

"No can talk." Sawala could not explain that the children knew she was older. She could not explain that she carried her baby doll everywhere to remind her of her son. Sawala could not explain why she wanted to learn English. She still did not know the word for "doctor" or "birth" or so many things she wanted to ask. And Sawala had still not seen Bailey.

Weeks later, when Sawala said it was time for harvesting, they both donned old clothes. Sawala had planned for the day and brought two digging sticks that she had made in advance. As always, she brought her baby doll with her.

Sawala could not explain to Margaret that they went to a special part of the camas fields where she had removed the poisonous white plants a month ago when the death-camas bloomed between the violet-blue.

They worked all morning until Sawala thought they had enough to make one big cake. That afternoon, they boiled and pounded the bulbs in Mrs. White's kitchen. The three women sat at the table and pressed firmly to form the ten-inch cake.

Sawala didn't know that Bailey lived there and would not see him that day.

Margaret took a little taste, "Oh, this is horrible."

Sawala laughed, "No eat now."

"What?" Margaret asked, "Not now?"

"No eat now. Cook and eat tomorrow."

Sawala took Margaret's hand. "Come." She picked up her doll and waved to Mrs. White, "Goodbye." Outside, she explained, "We dig hole. Now. With rocks." The rest of the afternoon they prepared a pit oven – a small one to bake the cake overnight. They lined the pit with river rocks and built a fire in it. It was dark when Sawala decided that the rocks were hot enough. They extinguished the first fire and put dirt on top of the rocks. Margaret and the girl worked like natives to finish preparations and started a new fire on top of the cake wrapped in green leaves.

The next day, Sawala and Margaret removed the cooked camas cake from the hole. Sawala told her, "You eat. Not now."

Margaret figured it was too hot and said, "I eat it later."

That evening, Margaret cut wedges of the cake to share with Bailey and the Whites. They enjoyed the new food, but Dr. White said, "I wouldn't want to have to eat these every day."

Bailey agreed, "Yes, they have a very unusual taste. I prefer baked bread from flour or corn bread."

Mrs. White shared her thoughts, "These camas cakes are more work than making bread. For one thing, with our bread, we don't have to dig a pit and fill it with rocks. Yes, I prefer our breads."

Margaret was so excited that she wanted to make more. "To me, it is exciting to know about the food that has helped the Kalapuyans exist through winters for hundreds of years."

Later that day, Margaret went to harvest more bulbs on her own. Without asking for Sawala's help, she went to another part of the camas field and dug, not knowing that some were poisonous roots from the white blooms.

This time, Margaret made more cakes that were smaller. The next day, after they had been roasted, she took them to her students during class.

Sawala looked surprised; obviously the small cakes were not the one she had made. Margaret placed a cut piece in front of each girl. Sawala stood and said to Margaret, "No eat!" In Kalapuyan, she told the other girls that they could be made from poisonous camas. The girls sat with their hands in their laps and would not touch them.

Margaret came to Sawala. "What did you tell them?"

"No can talk."

Many times Margaret had heard Sawala use these words when the girl could not explain something, but today Margaret took them to be words of defiance. "Why can't you tell me?"

"No eat. No good."

Margaret became upset and objected, "Yes, good."

Sawala told all the girls to leave, and they ran out.

Margaret called out, "Stop, come back!" Margaret put her hands on her hips and turned toward Sawala who was rushing around the room, gathering the camas cakes in her skirt. Before Margaret could cross the room to stop her, Sawala left, heading toward the river.

Margaret followed close behind Sawala.

Sawala said, "No! Bad!" Because Margaret would not stop reaching into the girl's bunched-up skirt, Sawala started to run and one fell out, unseen by them. Soon Sawala reached the river and tossed them in.

Margaret stood speechless, not understanding. In anger, she turned to Sawala and slapped her. "Why?" she cried out.

Sawala lifted her hand to the wounded cheek. With her other hand, she lifted her skirt to flee and crossed the fields through the golden wheat, disappearing into the woods. She ran until she could run no more. Collapsing in a meadow of yellow flowers, she felt the pain in her chest that always came with exertion. With her head among the tiny flowers, she stared at one to forget her pain. She saw the beauty of each tiny fuzzy knob protruding from the middle. The petals shone like reflecting quiet waters in a lake. Seeing such a wonderful little part of nature made her think of her son and her pain passed.

Meanwhile, a *Métis* boy picked up the camas cake and ate it.

That night, Brother Shepard went to Dr. White's darkened house. He knocked hard and called out, "Dr. White, Dr. White." He opened the unlocked door and called inside.

The doctor came from his bedroom.

"One of the children is sick. A *Métis* boy at the Mission, please will you come? The boy vomited and then began to shiver."

Bailey heard and came from his bedroom. "Dr. White I'll go. You only now got back from seeing Mrs. Leslie. By the way, how is she?"

"Mrs. Leslie is the same." Dr. White turned as his wife appeared and said, "I'm going. Let me put on my pants."

"I'll come, too," Bailey told him.

When they got to the Mission, all the boys were awake. The sick boy had vomited again before they arrived. "Let's take him to the hospital where we can watch him. He's still shivering. Get some blankets to wrap him in."

As they walked back to the hospital, the boy started wheezing.

Bailey carried the child. "Go ahead of me and get things ready."

"Yes, I'll make sure there's hot water to help him breathe." Dr. White hurried ahead.

Within the hour, the boy had gone into a coma; concerned, both men slept at the hospital. In the morning when they woke, they found the boy dead.

"What do you make of this?" Bailey asked.

"Vomiting, dropping body temperature, and difficulty breathing seems like poisoning to me."

"That's what I thought, but who would poison a child? Usually the children know the poisonous plants to avoid. It must have been an accident. No one else got sick, so he must have ingested something that no one else ate."

At the Mission later that morning, the children whispered between themselves about Sawala saying that there were poisoned cakes; chaos filled the air. The girls told the boys that Sawala had thrown away the poisoned cakes. The boys told the girls that a boy got sick and vomited. In fear, five of the boys ran away as did two of the girls. The remaining children were confused and upset, not knowing if the poisoning was an accident.

The missionaries saw the upset in the children who would not eat. Brother Shepard suggested, "Get Miss Smith, maybe she can understand what the children are saying."

Jason Lee was angry. "I am trying to get ready for this trip back East, and this has to happen. Why would seven of the heathens run off? Do they know that the boy died?"

"No, I don't believe they do. They only know he vomited and went to the hospital."

Margaret could not understand the words of the children; however, she noticed that Sawala was not among them. Confused by Margaret's interrogation, the remaining children left the Mission for the Kalapuyan camp across the field at the edge of some evergreen trees. They did not return.

No one could complete the normal tasks of the day. Margaret and Brother Shepard could not teach; there were no children to attend classes. Mr. Whitcomb, the farmer, was busy digging a grave for the boy, so he wasn't tending the crops. William Willson, the carpenter, was making a coffin. The women in charge of the evening meal didn't know whether to make food for the native children, who had not eaten their lunch. And Mr. Leslie was at his house with his sick wife.

Late in the afternoon, Solomon Smith and Mrs. Ellen arrived with a wagonload of sacks of grain that they had ground for the Mission.

Shepard pointed to the Kalapuyan camp. "Can Mrs. Ellen talk to the children to learn why they are upset? We can't get any of them to eat anything. Not even sweet cakes. They won't touch their food and are staying with the adult Kalapuyans over there." He sighed and with all the confusion, forgot to mention that a boy had died.

Mrs. Ellen agreed to walk over and ask the children what was bothering them.

While she talked with the Kalapuyans, the mission's blacksmith rode up at a gallop. Everyone saw him coming and stood transfixed. He was waving his arms and shouting. He reined in his horse and cried out, "Fire at Leslie's house! Fire!" The Leslies lived a mile away.

People turned this way and that. Some took off running on foot and others saddled horses.

"Grab buckets and go get water at the river!" Some did, but the water sloshed out when they ran. Others put the buckets of water in the wagon and took off. Soon, everyone from the Mission was running or riding the mile to the fire. The Kalapuyans saw all the smoke and joined the rush to the Leslie house.

Before the confusion of the fire, Mrs. Ellen had learned about the poisoned camas cakes that Margaret had served, but she didn't know a boy had died. With everyone running to the fire, she had no one to tell.

Ten minutes earlier, Mrs. White, who had been hanging clothes to dry, saw the smoke billowing into the sky. She rushed to tell Drs. White and Bailey, who were seeing Kalapuyan patients.

"Heavens! Let's go!" They ran to saddle up.

Bailey pulled the straps tight and put his foot in the stirrup. "Could the Leslie place be burning? It's not the time for the burning of the camas fields."

Dr. White pulled himself up and into his saddle. "Let's hurry. Mrs. Leslie was so sick yesterday. If it is their house and she's alone with her three little daughters, I don't think they are strong enough to pull her out."

The doctors arrived at the fire before the others. Flames shot fifty feet above the cabin. Ever so often, a gunshot was heard from inside the house.

"Must be some bullets in the house."

"Look!" Dr. White hollered as he began to dismount. "That looks like Leslie and his daughters on their knees in the grass all huddled together."

"Yes, he's praying. I don't see his wife."

As the doctors dismounted, Leslie got up from his knees and rushed to them. Leslie reached for Dr. White's jacket and pleaded, "Help us! She's still in there. I came out with my girls. Mary fell, but I didn't know. I couldn't see." Leslie's shirt was ripped and his forehead had a scrape. His girls' clothing was blackened in areas and burned in others.

Bailey pulled a blanket off the line. It was still damp.

Leslie was still explaining as Dr. White examined his bleeding head, "I rolled the girls in the grass to stop the fires in their dresses. I tried to go back, but with the heat I couldn't."

Bailey threw the wool blanket over his head, covering his body as well, and went through the flaming doorway. One step inside, he tripped on Mrs. Leslie. Bailey dropped down to wrap the blanket around her body and stayed low. He could hear things falling as he started to exit. While dragging her, all of a sudden one of the sidewalls of the cabin collapsed out onto the grass, with a whoosh of flying flames. Bailey was thrown into the air by a blast of hot air from the falling debris. The heat of the burn increased.

Dr. White ran up and pulled Mrs. Leslie away and kept dragging her until they were far from the heat.

The three girls clamored, "Mama, Mama!" One by one they threw themselves onto their mother.

Dr. White gently pushed them aside. "Let me see her. Go to the well over there and get water. Go on. Your mother needs water!"

Though dazed, Bailey heard and righted himself in the yard. He ran for water, ripped the bucket from the chain, and came back to pour it over Mrs. Leslie to cool her down. "Doesn't look like she's burned. How could that be?"

"I don't know. Maybe because she was down low and on a stone floor."

Leslie was crying as he came to his wife and went down on his knees again. "Thank you, Lord. Thank you." He reached for her hand. "Mary, Mary."

Dr. White poured a little water on her face and asked, "Mrs. Leslie can you hear me?"

She coughed and coughed before opening her eyes. Her husband sat on the grass and pulled her into his arms. "Mary, I thought I lost you."

Another wall fell, and another gunshot went off. Then several more shots exploded as the people from the Mission arrived.

"Stay back," Bailey shouted. But he didn't need to say anything. No one could stand the intensity of the heat. Bailey's beard was all singed.

Everyone stood mesmerized when another wall fell and the roof caved in with a sound like thunder. Everyone jumped back to avoid the sparks and debris that flew up into the air and drifted in all directions. Soon, the whole structure was a heap of black burning wood and orange flames that turned to blue and red as they lapped at the edges of furniture and logs.

The cabin burned quickly, but the smoldering continued for hours.

Margaret wandered over to Bailey. "Are you burned at all? I saw in the distance that you were thrown out of the house."

"I'm fine."

While Margaret and Bailey talked, they didn't hear Mrs. Ellen talking to Solomon, saying, "It's strange but the children said that Margaret serving poisoned camas cakes." The couple walked over to where Jason Lee stood with Brother Cyrus Shepard and explained to them.

Lee asked Shepard, "Do you think that is what killed the boy?"

Mrs. Ellen emitted a frantic, "What boy? A boy died?"

217

Solomon exclaimed, "No!"

With grave faces, they nodded.

The group of four walked over to Dr. White, who stood near Bailey. Jason Lee addressed the doctors, "We've learned that there may have been some camas cakes made from the poisonous variety of the plant. Is it possible that the boy ate this?"

Margaret didn't hear, but Bailey did.

Frowning and taking time to think before answering, Dr. White said, "I would need to investigate, however, Dr. Bailey and I did think it could have been poisoning."

Bailey asked, "How is this possible? Who would do that?" Margaret stood confused at his side.

Jason Lee turned to Margaret. "Did you serve camas cakes to the children?"

Her mind raced with questions. *Why were they asking? How did they know? What did this mean?*

She replied with a simple, "Yes."

Bailey turned to her. "Where did you get these camas cakes?"

"I made them."

"Did you know that the white flowering camas is poisonous?"

Her eyes went wide. "No!"

Jason Lee interrupted their conversation, "We must meet *now* to discuss this. Dr. White, I want you present." With frustration, he turned back to tell Margaret, "My dear, you certainly know how to give me headaches." Shaking his head, he marched away.

Bailey called after him, "I'll come, too."

Jason stopped in his tracks. His body tensed as he pivoted around to face Bailey and said, "No, you will not. This is Methodist Mission business, sir." He turned back around and continued taking long determined strides.

Bailey put his hand on Margaret's arm. "What happened?"

Agitated and confused, she pulled a handkerchief from her sleeve to dab her face before explaining to Drs. White and Bailey, "I had no idea about poisonous ones. After we ate the camas cake that the girl helped me make, I made more by myself."

Sensing that Margaret didn't know a boy had died, Bailey told her, "Last night we were called to the Mission to attend a sick child. He died during the night."

Margaret wrapped her arms around her waist as if in pain. "No, no! How is this possible? Does everyone think my cakes killed him?" Her heart pounded and her cheeks flushed. She looked to Bailey for an answer.

He nodded.

Margaret covered her mouth with her hands. "But I only teach the girls. I don't even know the boys. How did he get a cake? Oh, and I struck the little girl in the face when she took the cakes away. She tried to prevent this. I didn't understand at the time."

Dr. White put his hand gently on her shoulder and suggested, "Come Margaret. We had best be going to this meeting. Bailey, will you help the Leslies to my house, using the wagon over there? Please put Mrs. Leslie in the hospital and stay with her. Would you mind giving your room to the rest of the family?"

Still thinking about the camas cakes, Margaret's face contorted in pain. "The little girl ran away, and I haven't seen her since." Disturbed, she turned to walk with the doctor toward the Mission. "I don't know how the boy could have gotten one of the cakes. The girl threw them all in the river. I couldn't have caused his death. No, it's not possible."

On the edge of the woods, a few yards from the doctors and Margaret, stood Sawala watching. After noticing the smoke from the fire, she had come. Although many were still wandering around and looking at the burning embers of the home, Sawala recognized Bailey from afar, even with his beard. Her little hand went to her eye to brush off a tear of joy. Seeing Margaret leave with Dr. White, she decided to follow Bailey to learn where he lived.

At the Mission, the group sat at a table. "I'm at the end of my rope with you, Miss Smith!" Lee hissed. In disbelief, he shook his head. "How could you have done this?"

The mission leaders – Lee, Shepard, Perkins, and Dr. White – sat on one side of the table with rigid posture and stoic faces. Margaret, sitting opposite them, held her trembling hands in her lap. She had explained everything, including Sawala's disappearance.

"Deplorable behavior. You constantly think you know more than others and do what you think is best. Now a boy has died, and all of the children have run away."

Margaret had not heard that the children had left. "Oh no! Others ran away?"

Lee leaned across the table and stared directly into her face. "Do you see? Can you finally see? You do not know more than we do! We are in charge! All I ever asked you to do was to help the Whites with whatever they ask of you and teach the girls about our Lord and our language." His face turned red as he raised his voice, "*Not* to do whatever you wish!" He inhaled with force.

Margaret dropped her head, finally convinced that she had caused the boy's death. If the other children had run away, they knew what she had done. Something inside her was starting to change. *I have taken a life. I have caused a death. A little boy! Lord, will you forgive me?*

Lee flung his hand out. "Go now! We men need to talk in private and come to some conclusion about you and your behavior." He sighed, "My wife is pregnant, and I am leaving her in a few days while I go on a long trip to the East. And we lost a whole cabin to fire! Why today? I am busy with important things, and you cause more problems. You exasperate me, young lady."

Wanting to be alone, Margaret rose to go to her room. For the first time in her life, she had a glimpse of her egotism and a view of her faults. She understood that she had caused a child's death. Remorse crept through her.

She walked through corridors that had been built between the cabins to her room in the far cabin. Traveling past the quarters of others to get to her bedroom, the light was dim, but she clearly saw a white piece of paper on the ground near the wall. On the dirt floor, the folded paper almost glowed. She picked it up.

Until she opened her door and light from her window flowed into the corridor, she had no way of reading it. Standing in her doorway, she heard someone coming, but the shocking contents of the note made her oblivious to the man who arrived at her side. The note read:

To Whom It May Concern

We, the undersigned members of the Oregon Mission, in view of the statements and representations made by Margaret Jewett Smith, viz; that she believed Mr. David Leslie guilty of selfishness and falsehoods, do hereby certify that it is our opinion that those and any other statements made by her, tending to injure his character, are groundless.

Jason Lee
Daniel Lee
H.K.W. Perkins
Alonson Beers
Joseph Whitcomb

Given in the Mission Hall
December 13, 1837

This was written months ago! I feel faint.

She gave out a little whimper and swooned into the chest of William Willson. With his strong arms holding her up, she placed her head onto his shoulder and started to sob. "Lord, what have I done for you to have forsaken me so?"

"Now, now, Miss Smith. Nothing can be that bad," he told her as he walked toward her bed, bumping the door. It creaked shut and closed with a click. Willson sat on the bed with his arm around her while she cried.

Bending to her lap, she mumbled into her hands, "Yes, yes, everything is that bad. A boy has died. All the other children have left in fear that I might poison them. And a very special girl has run away because of my behavior. I slapped her." She added, "The Leslies' house has burned completely. I wonder if I did something to cause that as well."

He patted her on her back. "Don't be so hard on yourself."

"And now I find a note stating that, months ago, the missionaries ruled upon me without my knowledge." She sat up and looked at him. "Worse than that. They ruled on me without hearing my words, without asking me to explain."

"There, there, it will be all right," he put his arm around her shoulder again and squeezed. "Cry it out."

But she no longer wanted to cry. When he pulled her tighter, she found her face inches from his. A moment passed with their eyes locked, until finally, she kissed him.

More than a year! She had not had physical contact with a man for more than a year; every nerve in her body tingled. At this time, it didn't matter that the man was William Willson; she simply needed and wanted. She didn't think. She only reacted.

Fort Vancouver 1845, Author Lt. Henry Warre

CHAPTER 8

DISCOVERING SOME, LOSING OTHERS
1838

Upon waking, Margaret was relieved to see that Willson had had the wisdom to disappear from her bed sometime during the night. Recalling the encounter, she felt her desires aroused and thought, *Actually, at this moment, I would not mind if he were here for me again.* She allowed herself to loll in bed for a moment, until she realized, *Oh, dear, I didn't douche last night! I must get some vinegar from the kitchen and keep it in my room. I am so glad that I brought the douche bulb with me.* When she heard others up and about, she suddenly remembered all the horrible events of the day before. She went to a bowl of water that she had put in her room for washing her face in the mornings. *I wish I could wash away all the disagreeable happenings of yesterday. I must find Sawala.* She dressed hastily and then sat to compose a note to Jason Lee about the Declaration that she had found.

Any regrets, she had experienced yesterday, concerning her selfish ways, were forgotten. The dead boy had not even entered her thoughts since waking. Her mind dwelled only on the paper that she had found.

In her note, she asked for the Declaration to be withdrawn or, if Lee felt that he must submit it to the Missionary Society, that her name be removed because it conveyed an impression that she was guilty of falsehoods. In her closing, she stated:

I am unprepared to continue my labors in the school until one of these particulars I mention before be attended to.

With respect,
Margaret Jewett Smith

She went to the main cabin and placed her letter in the box for outgoing mail. Although she did not notice, her letter rested on top of one that William Willson had put into the box a few days before. He had written a letter proposing marriage to a Miss Chloe Clark, knowing that Jason Lee would leave soon for the States and deliver it.

Margaret hurried outside to avoid talking with anyone.

She started walking at a fast pace toward the White's place for breakfast. Suddenly, she realized she hadn't even thought about the dead boy. *What is wrong with me? Lord, forgive me.* But her thoughts stopped abruptly.

Sawala sat on a bench under a tree, working on her sampler, with her book and baby doll at her feet. Margaret ran to her. "Sawala, Sawala."

The girl looked up with a pout, but managed to say, "Good morning."

"Sawala, I am sorry." Margaret kneeled in front of her without concern for the dirt. "Sawala, thank you for taking the camas cakes. Now I understand."

Little blonde wisps of hair crossed the girl's frowning face. Margaret tucked them beneath the bonnet. "I worried about you."

"Why?"

Margaret touched Sawala's cheek where she had struck it. "I am sorry I hit you. Thank you for taking the camas to the river."

"You are welcome."

Margaret remembered her note to Jason Lee and told Sawala. "No school today."

"Why?"

"No school."

Sawala wished she had more words to talk. She picked up her book. "Me read to you?"

"Maybe later. I must go." Margaret stood, and waved as she walked away. "God be with you."

In minutes, Margaret had walked the mile toward the hospital and sat with the Whites and William Bailey.

She described her problems and lamented, "Nothing is normal. Now I have no classes to teach, and Reverend Lee will not listen to my side of the conflict. He declares he is tired of so many problems to resolve between the missionaries."

226

Dr. White responded, "I'm afraid what he said is true. When I came in May of last year, I arrived with a disagreement between myself and Alonson Beers, the blacksmith. Jason Lee, the bastard, was really no help to me."

Bailey laughed, "Yes, there is no love lost between Lee and me either. He is a pious hypocrite."

Margaret gasped at their comments, "My goodness. Why do you say that, Dr. Bailey?"

"You know about the attack from Rogue River Indians when I got this wound?"

She nodded.

"After fifteen days with no food, the first man from our party arrived with a native woman, and Lee would not give them food. The next day, I arrived with this horrible wound and another starving man. Again, he would not give us a morsel of food. Is that a Christian?"

Dr. White shook his head. "He came to convert these natives, but I have heard him describe the Indians as filthy and miserable. I can't help thinking he has prejudices. He told me once that the French Canadians have belittled themselves by taking native wives and not having the union sanctified in an official marriage. How could they marry? There were no priests or ministers here until he came. Does a religious ceremony make these women more caring wives or better mothers than they are now? "

Mrs. White interrupted, "Would anyone like some tea? I suggest that we change the subject. Since these are Dr. Bailey's last days with us, we should be asking about his plans." She rose to get the teapot.

Margaret looked surprised. "Last days? I didn't know you were leaving."

Talking more to Margaret, Dr. White interjected, "This is another problem. Jason Lee never liked the idea that I invited Dr. Bailey into my home to review his study of medicine. See, this is an example. We need doctors here in the Willamette Valley, but Lee is selfish."

"Dear," Mrs. White held out a cup. "It seems we are back on the same subject. Please, Dr. Bailey, tell us your plans."

"Well, I'm going up to my cabin. I'll clean it up a bit, stock up the woodpile for winter, and keep going out to practice medicine whenever someone needs care. There isn't much else to tell."

Margaret sighed. "With whom will I talk fauna and flora?" She faced

Bailey to say, "No one else wants to go riding like you. I'll miss you."

"I'm not far. My place is a few miles north of here. I invite you to visit and help with my plant collection. You would find it to be a pleasant cabin. It has an ash bark roof, clay and stick chimney, and a long front porch. I have a black hawthorn in the yard with plump, dark, purple berries." Bailey stopped and puzzled that Margaret seemed not to be listening.

Margaret gazed at her hands in her lap. When she looked up with a distraught face, she suggested, "Surely you will come for the Sunday services. We could sit together and go for a horseback ride afterwards."

A couple of weeks passed before Bailey awoke to a Sunday without sick patients, but he was tired from working most of the previous night to save a man attacked by a cougar. He stretched under the blanket before reaching for his timepiece hanging from the bedpost. "I'm late!"

Determined not to miss seeing Margaret at the Sunday service, he quickly dressed and saddled his horse. In that morning ride to the Mission, Margaret occupied his thoughts, and he was filled with hopes that were dashed upon his entrance into the Sunday services. Margaret was sitting with Willson. Bailey found a seat next to Mrs. White and whispered to ask her if there was something going on with Margaret and Willson.

Mrs. White told him that Mr. Willson had proposed to Margaret, "But I understand that she refused the proposal."

Throughout the service, Bailey sat with slumped shoulders and a drooping head in obvious disappointment.

Mrs. White and Bailey left together and walked from the services toward her house.

She said, "Let me be outspoken, Dr. Bailey. I like you and want to help. I can see you fancy Miss Smith. But you didn't let her know. She thinks of you only as a friend." She stopped and turned to him. "Did you ever kiss her?"

"No, ma'am. I couldn't tell if she wanted me to."

"Well, don't run off like a wounded pup. I don't believe she loves Mr. Willson. I can tell these things. You need to keep coming around and to invite her horseback riding, like she asked."

Meanwhile, Margaret agonized over her situation day in and day out. *I can't stop feeling that my Lord abandoned me. I caused the death of an innocent boy. Why did He let that happen? I came to teach the word of God to these children, and they are gone. What is my purpose in life?* Frustrated, she did what she always did – she made more problems for herself. During the day, she continued to complain in writing about Mr. Leslie to Jason Lee. During the night, unknown to anyone, she slept with Willson. Any frustrations she endured during the day were assuaged during the night.

An upset Mr. Leslie wrote to her:

> Miss Smith: I know that you are accusing me in letters and notes to Jason Lee, although I have not seen the documents. My fear is that you have exaggerated our disagreements. Can we not talk more?
>
> Signed,
> Rev. Daniel Leslie

Margaret answered and thrived on defending herself. At this point, what had started all the fighting was a distant memory and had little significance here at the Mission. If she had stopped to think, she would have realized she was upset for the same reason that Mr. Leslie was; they each felt slandered by the other.

Jason Lee insisted that he would have the two of them meet face-to-face in front of all the members of the Mission to explain both sides of the grievance.

Margaret refused to go to any such meeting, overlooking the authority of Jason Lee, the head of the Mission where she wanted to do the calling of her Lord. She wanted the whole affair to be presented in front of missionaries who were not already biased – those who would come to the Mission in the future. She brought it to a stalemate, at least for the moment.

By the time Jason Lee left on his trip, she had made a confirmed enemy of Mr. Leslie – the man becoming a very influential person in Oregon Country and the man in charge of the Methodist Mission while Jason Lee traveled to the East to raise support.

Margaret's time at the Mission had come full circle. She had arrived at the

Mission being perceived as a maniac; she gained appreciation through teaching the native children; and then she caused the death of the little boy and added more problems with her continual criticism of Mr. Leslie. The missionaries finally ostracized her.

When she fell from a horse and was bedridden for three weeks, none of the missionaries brought her food. Sawala noticed and hid roasted potatoes in her skirt to bring to Margaret. When Mrs. Leslie – the kind soul who never faltered in her Christian practices – heard of Margaret not being able to get out of bed, she sent an apple pie, not knowing that Margaret was without proper daily food. During those three weeks, Margaret looked inward again, facing her problems, especially the death of the boy from her camas cakes. She accepted her fate as a punishment from her Lord and even abstained from bedding with Willson.

Time passed and Margaret healed. With her body well, her sexual desires returned, and she invited Willson back to her bed. But the critical opinions of her among the missionaries did not mend. When she returned to daily chores, she was reprimanded first by Brother Shepard for cutting a piece of soap to wash girls' clothing, next by Mr. Whitcomb for borrowing a wash tub when he needed to use it, and finally by one of the women for offering food to visitors. She was also scolded for using an old, discarded tin pan to remove ashes from the fireplace. Someone hid the molasses from her after she had used it over her blackberries. With Mr. Leslie's approval, the women locked away the pumpkins so she couldn't cook them for the children. They placed rocks too heavy for her to lift on top of the barrels of salted meat and refused to give her tea or coffee, citing shortages.

On top of all these conflicts, she was frustrated with William Willson, who made daily proposals of marriage to her, which she refused. He could not understand how a woman who slept with him each night would refuse to marry.

It was apparent to Margaret that everyone at the Mission was annoyed with her, and so she left for a respite at Fort Vancouver, where she was welcomed. In her journal, she wrote:

> Have today come to Vancouver for a little relaxation and rest from trouble – and also to be relieved from the importunities of Mr.

Willson. Though I respect him, and believe he would make a *kind* husband, yet he is not possessed of that strength of intellect and sedateness of mind which I should wish to find in a man with whom I am destined to be engaged in missionary labors. And besides, the duty I owe to my parents and to the Methodist Education Society would, perhaps, make it necessary for me to decline his offers.

In Fort Vancouver, different families invited Margaret to dinner, and she went riding, as in the past, with Dr. Tolmie. Many of the Fort's upper-class society pastimes, such as having tea with the ladies, bored her; she missed her missionary work. So she decided to look for lost souls to save.

After venturing out of the Fort one afternoon, she found herself in the village of the French Canadians. As she walked, odors of horses, cows, pigs, chickens, and large English sheep wafted past her. She met families on the streets and spoke with them in Chinook Jargon.

She stopped to chat at one house where a woman who sitting on her doorstep told Margaret that she had been traded for a horse. Margaret asked, "Are you married?"

Without hesitation, the woman said that there were no priests here to do that. "My man is a French Canadian and Catholic. We need a priest to be married." Margaret suggested that the missionaries could marry her, and the woman said that God would not accept that. Margaret smiled and walked on.

Surrounding Fort Vancouver were four main streets, one for each ethnic group – the English, the French Canadians, the Kanakas, and the Americans. When Margaret walked in the French Canadian section, she saw many houses in obvious decay due to the wet Oregon climate. Deserted by their partners, native women and *Métis* children remained living in these homes after their fur-traders returned to Canada. Smells of dried salmon, duck, sweet bread, and bannock lingered in the air.

In another house, Margaret met an old woman, decrepit with age, making moccasins. Her dark face had deep creases and her braids were all white. Many children sat on her floor and they stared at the visitor. Not wanting to sit in the dirt, Margaret stood to watch the old woman use an awl and thread. After some conversation, Margaret attempted to guide the conversation toward topics of afterlife and God, inquiring, "At your age, do you realize that you may not have much more time in this world?"

"Yes," the old woman replied, "I must hurry to finish these moccasins."

The room filled with laughter as the children and the old one chuckled at her cleverness.

In the next home, Margaret met another woman – almost dead with consumption – trimming a dress with different colored ribbons. Margaret spoke about this world and the next, saying, "There are so many sick and dying. Do you realize there is a place where sickness never comes?"

The old woman scratched her head. "That good. Where is it?"

Margaret explained, "Through prayer you get there."

"Prayer?" The old lady looked at the others in the room. "Where is prayer?"

Margaret had no success saving any souls on her venture out of the Fort.

On another day, she walked down the Hawaiian street. People of all ages were busy working: repairing the roads, herding swine, weeding the gardens, and doing woodwork. She stepped over and around people busy with their tasks. From a distance, she saw children beating dust from furs, chasing crows from crops, and working in the gristmill turning the grindstone. She yearned to teach these children, but spoke to no one that day.

The following morning, Margaret went to a man in charge of education at the Fort. "I would like to inquire if I could attempt to instruct the native and *Métis* children here."

"What a worthy undertaking that would be, but I'm afraid that there is no place for such classes. If it would be agreeable to you, I am sure I could find a home where you could give classes to many ladies, including my wife and some of the young girls who are daughters of our officers. We surely are in need of this."

Margaret argued about the need to teach these underprivileged children in the name of God. She received a lecture about Chief Factor McLoughlin's philosophy.

"My dear, your ideas are grand, but not realistic. The Hudson's Bay Company is a business and we must manage the manufacture of barges, canoes, carts, furniture, window frames and – need I go on? To succeed, Dr. McLoughlin provides food, shelter, and clothing for all his employees. It is care from cradle to grave. When parents are killed or die, this organization takes over the care of the children. He has a soft place for children – he has raised eighteen orphans in his own home. We have schools to teach various forms of manual education, such as farming. We tried to teach reading and writing, but it did not work. You must understand that McLoughlin knows what is best for his employees and their families."

"I see. I do need sufficient employment to defray the expense of my board here, so I accept your offer to teach the wives and daughters of the officers. And I thank you for your time."

About a week later, the McLoughlins invited Margaret to dine again. Upon her arrival, she found it odd that she was the only guest. During the evening the reason became apparent. Dr. McLoughlin reminded her that as a single woman she should not talk to men who have not been introduced to her.

Defending herself she explained, "I have only been talking with the women who live outside the Fort."

McLoughlin huffed, "And you must not walk alone or leave the Fort without a chaperone."

She began to feel depressed and lonely after that evening. *Why can't I get along with others? I don't want much, only to teach the heathens about the Lord.*

And time passed.

When Margaret started her school for the wives and daughters at Fort Vancouver, she had no books containing exercises. Most of the women had no ink boxes or even goose quills to write lessons. So she taught her students by singing, reading from books she found at the Fort, and teaching portions from the scriptures.

After school one day, the cheerful Mrs. McLoughlin invited the whole class to have a walk around the Fort and afterwards to take tea on the grass surrounding the Chief Factor's home. After tea, they played a game called stick and sign. Margaret was bored. *What frivolity! What a waste. What satisfaction do these girls and women get from doing activities with no end result? They could be weaving, knitting, sewing, or preparing food for the coming winter.* Margaret excused herself from the game, saying she was tired, and reclined on the grass with her head on a log. *Look at the heavens, and how the tops of the tall green firs contrast with the blue sky and white clouds. Yes, these girls could write a poem about this beauty – the stillness, purity, grandeur, and glory of the works of God.* She turned her gaze to the buildings and the mud in the street. *Do these girls and women even see the works of God, especially when contrasted with the works of man?*

The next day, Margaret took her class to gather wildflowers. Back in the classroom, she assigned each to write a poem about the beauty of God in nature. "I've borrowed ink and pen for each of you. Before you begin writing, gaze deeply into your mind to remember the beauty we saw outside the walls of the Fort, or pick up your flower and see the details that God has produced in something so small." As she walked between the women struggling to start or find a rhyme, she talked to her Lord. *Is this why I came to Oregon? Am I not of more use than this? How can they forbid me to go among the people outside the Fort and share your words?*

And her time at Fort Vancouver dragged by.

At the end of June in 1838, Mr. Leslie arrived at the Fort from the Mission. He came with the sad news that Jason Lee's wife and newborn child had died. He requested to send a message to Jason Lee, who was still traveling across land. McLoughlin agreed to send some of his riders to find the party of travelers.

That evening after dinner with the McLoughlins, Mr. Leslie requested to walk Margaret back to her quarters. "Miss Smith, I want to invite you to return to the Mission." He didn't wait for any response, but continued, "We should set aside our differences. My wife urged that I offer you board at our home, if you would like. Brother Shepard and his family have moved out of the Mission buildings and are keeping house by themselves. Your room is still available. I am sure you would be more comfortable with us than here, and I hope you haven't shared any of our private matters while you have been here."

Margaret studied his words. *I see I have an opportunity here. I shall ignore his last comment; he need never know if I did or did not talk about him and the Methodist Mission.*

They strolled without words for a few steps, and then Margaret stopped to let a few people walking inside the Fort pass them. Margaret looked up to see broken clouds pass over the full moon. The air was crisp at this late hour, and she pulled her shawl tighter around her shoulders before turning to face him. She chose her words carefully. "After all the problems I have caused you, why are you making this offer?"

Taking a deep breath, Mr. Leslie said, "This is a cloudy matter; however, I shall be honest and candid. It was not my idea and never would have been. My wife sees more of the good in people than I do. As I said before, Mrs. Leslie insisted that I extend this offer. She noticed all that you did for the young students at the Mission."

"Thank you, I appreciate your honesty. Now I shall be candid as well. My mind has been exceedingly troubled in consequence of being unable to benefit the natives. When I consider that for many years the predominant desire of my heart has been to devote my life to the good of the Indians, I feel a great sadness knowing I haven't helped them. I am grateful to have the opportunity to return to the Mission. Nevertheless, I must think before making a decision. Can we please talk more in the morning?"

"Of course."

The next morning, Margaret agreed to return to the Mission under certain considerations. "Mr. Leslie, I want you to understand what I would like to accomplish. There are many adult Kalapuyans in the huts around the Mission, many females who are quite destitute – indeed I can scarcely bear to go among them in consequence of their nudity. I would like to resolve the problem of the native women's clothing, and this is what I propose: In my leisure time, I could assemble a circle of Kalapuyan woman and teach them to sew and knit for themselves. If you would give me old garments and anything to help cover them, I could teach them to cut and sew clothing for themselves. Also, I would like to form a group, called the Oregon Female Benevolent Society with the purpose of clothing destitute females. I would write letters to people in the East to request contributions in the form of clothing, fabric, needles and thread. You understand, any material that would help these women to sew." Margaret looked over at Mr. Leslie to await his reply.

He was generous. "I think those are pious ideas and worthy of consideration. I have no objections at this time, but I would need to present the ideas to everyone on the Mission Board."

Margaret returned south to the Mission. Although she would work long and hard hours on her Oregon Female Benevolent Society, not much would come of it: Margaret's time at the Mission was nearing an end.

Once Margaret unpacked and settled into her old room, placing her Bible and ink box out on a table, she went looking for Sawala. The girl was nowhere to be found. While Margaret was wandering around the grounds, Mr. Willson found her and told her how happy he was to see her back at the Mission. She was curt and excused herself. "I am looking for the girl called Sawala. She has blonde hair and a flattened forehead. Have you seen her?"

He said he didn't know where she was.

During dinner with the Leslies, Margaret asked Mrs. Leslie about Sawala and was told the girl was at the hospital. "Miss Smith, she is quite ill."

"Oh my! I must go see her. What is wrong with her?

Mr. Leslie replied, "I really can't say. She didn't fall or have an injury. She is just sick. I think it would be best to talk with Dr. White. And I'm sure it will interest you that we have given her a Christian name of Sally Soule."

With a serious face, Margaret commented, "Maybe I shall visit her after we finish eating."

"It is quite late. If you go in the morning, I will accompany you," Mrs. Leslie suggested.

"That would be agreeable with me. You said her new name is Sally Soule?" Margaret asked, "How does one spell that name?"

"Well, you know how to spell Sally and the last name is S-O-U-L-E."

Margaret brightened. "How beautiful and appropriate for a Christian name to have the word 'soul' contained in it. How did this occur?"

"Brother Shepard received correspondence from back east asking to have a child named after this woman, Sally Soule, who died. Her last wishes were that her schoolbooks, of which she has many, be sent to our Oregon Mission, and that a native child might be called by her name. Everyone feels that we chose the correct child."

"I do as well, and will enjoy calling her Sally." Margaret wiped her mouth with her napkin. "So we shall visit her tomorrow at the hospital. I hope she has nothing that can't be cured."

The next day, Margaret and Mrs. Leslie walked to the hospital. Margaret asked the doctor, "What is wrong with Sawala? I mean, Sally Soule?"

"She has dropsy of the chest. I think she has had it for months or maybe years."

"And?"

"She needs to stay here for a while and rest. She should not run around or exert herself. I'll examine her from time to time in the future, but she'll be better in a few days."

"Oh, I am so happy to hear that. May I visit her now?"

Sawala smiled when she saw Margaret. "I happy."

"I am so happy to see you, too. I missed talking with you." Margaret asked, "Can I bring you something?"

Sawala talked in whispers, "Please, my cat fur and baby doll."

"Of course. But your book?"

Sawala knew Margaret liked to teach. "Yes. My book. Learn me to talk on paper?"

Margaret encouraged her, "I'll come tomorrow and every day. Yes, you can learn to write on paper."

"I like. Come with box to talk on paper?"

"Yes, I'll bring my ink box. You must eat and get well so we can go to look for wasp nests." Margaret turned to explain to Dr. White, "When Sally told me the word for springtime – *am plaatowa* – she told me of looking for wasp nests. She likes to eat little wasps."

Sawala beamed, "Yes, I say."

The return of Margaret helped rejuvenate Sawala. Very soon, she was better and back at the Mission. Margaret made sure the girl had hot soup and good food. One day, over a bowl of oatmeal, Margaret said to her, "I learned what Sawala means. Do you know what your name means?"

"Yes, it big flower!" With her arms, Sawala made a circle. "Middle black."

Margaret said, "Wait, I show you," and rushed from the table to get a handful of seeds from the storeroom, "Look, Sawala means sunflower seed." And Margaret made a little circle with her fingers, "Seeds! Sunflower seed, not the big flower."

"I know."

"I'm going to make a pumpkin pie and roast sunflower seeds for you when we give thanks for the harvest this year."

"Too much words."

Margaret erased the air with her hand and started again, "I cook for you," and she pointed to Sawala and then the pumpkin before saying, "I cook big pumpkin and little seeds for you."

"Cook with Sally? New name, Sally."

Margaret hugged her. "Sawala is Sally Soule."

One Sunday, when the days turned colder, the missionaries cooked an extra chicken, baked pumpkin pies, and said prayers for their harvest. In this way, the day of Thanksgiving came and went. Margaret made sure that Sawala, little Sally, had some pumpkin pie and kept warm. Margaret had taken one of her woolen dresses and sewed a coat for the girl.

Still in secret, Margaret kept herself warm in bed with Willson, and to stop his daily insistence to marry him, she finally agreed they were engaged. But he was not allowed to tell anyone until they set a date. She knew that she didn't love him and was adamant when she told him, "Mr. Willson, do not pressure me to marry you. I shall tell you when I am ready. This is not the time."

Willson begged, "Please pick a date."

"Can't you understand? I'm busy with God's work. I want my society for Kalapuyan women to be successful. It would be selfish to worry about a wedding so please stop asking to set a date."

From time to time, Bailey traveled south from his cabin to visit Dr. White.

He always found Margaret and invited her to go riding. Without hesitation, she would go. The rides were enjoyable and their friendship grew, but the rides were rather uneventful until one December day.

"Miss Smith, you have never come to visit me at my house. You should see my plant collection. I have collected so many more." They had stopped for him to collect some mistletoe that had fallen due to the coldness of the season. "This is a good specimen."

"I am sorry I have not visited, but I am so busy." She squatted next to him to see the plant.

"This mistletoe is part of the sandalwood family. Do you know that this one plant has both the male and female individuals together?" He sat and picked off a dried flower. "You can't see it now, but the female flowers are a light pink to yellowish color and make these berries. See, they aren't round – they're spherical." He turned and handed her a berry.

Taking it in her fingers, she said, "A female berry? How strange."

They were so close. Remembering what Mrs. White had said, he leaned into the few inches of space where their breath clouded the cold air and kissed her. It was a short but warm kiss. Holding out a piece of mistletoe, he asked in a nonchalant manner, "Would you like some of this for decoration? It is the season."

She kissed him back – a long kiss with her hands on each side of his head. "Yes, I would like some for Christmas decorating," she replied, in the same nonchalant tone.

He smiled at her and tried to remain calm. "Do you know that this plant is a parasite that lives off the tree?"

"Hmm," she pondered, "are you saying that this male and female plant needs the tree?" She pushed him back against the tree trunk, "Like this female and male against the tree." Leaning with her chest against him, she placed a long, firm sensual kiss on his mouth.

When she finished, they peered into each other eyes a long time. Beautiful green eyes met gorgeous blue ones. They laughed, and Margaret stood to brush dried leaves from her skirt.

"I see," she said. "Shall we continue our journey? I am anxious to see how little Arnaud has grown."

Oh, the happiness his heart felt.

On their next ride, they became more passionate, but they continued their casual interplay. They touched and kissed. Yet talked, as friends.

"Have you heard that the Catholic Bishop has come to Oregon?" She asked between little kisses to his face. He was trying to get a cutting from a fir tree.

"Yes, Bishop François Norbert Blanchet, to be exact. Quite a name, isn't it? Exactness can be important, you know." For emphasis, he hesitated before saying, "For example, that last kiss missed my ear and landed on my beard, I do believe. You need more practice. More exactness!"

She planted a firm kiss to his earlobe. "Not your ear – the earlobe to be exact."

He stood, placing the specimen into his *parflèche,* and pulled her up next to him.

"I see. I mean, I feel. No, I felt it on my earlobe and *stand corrected.*" With his hands free, he wrapped his arms about her waist, encircling her back, and pulled her close.

Face to face, they smiled. "Yes, you *stand corrected.* Quite humorous."

They melted into each other and kissed and kissed and kissed.

Margaret tried to concentrate on her missionary work, but the happiness her heart felt with Bailey, created a confusing desire, so she still slept with Willson each night. She could not focus on what was right, and whenever she stopped to think about the great sins she was committing, she asked the Lord for help, "Lord, please lead me away from my carnal desires and return me to the path of my destiny."

Soon her prayers would be answered and her nights with Willson would end.

A special day unfolded, answering not only Margaret's prayers but also the prayers of most people in Oregon Country. The Catholic Bishop François Norbert Blanchet arrived at the Methodist Mission to perform marriages and baptisms. The event was larger than Christmas. Dozens of French Canadians and their families came in wagons filled with food to celebrate after the ceremonies.

"Joseph Gervais and Mrs. Marguerite!" Bailey shouted when he saw them. "I bet I know why you are here."

Gervais rushed to his friend Bailey, with a sheepish grin. "Yes, finally a Catholic priest to marry us. Me and my bride will have a honeymoon tonight."

"You are a devil, you old man," Bailey slapped him on the back. "Mrs. Marguerite you should marry me, not this old man."

She giggled, "No, you too late. I love old man."

Many other French Canadians came with their native wives and *Métis* children. This was the first opportunity in Oregon Country for Catholic families to obtain official marriages and baptisms so they could live without sin in the eyes of their church.

Monsieur Bugat asked Bailey, "Are you ready to be godfather to our son?"

"I am! And I'm the happiest man here because you asked me." Bailey held the little boy in his arms. "Look at you, Arnaud, you are almost two and so big."

"I two," he said, as he held up two fingers.

Such a crowd! Word had spread great distances. No matter how far, the people didn't find the miles too great for this long-awaited event. Reverend Leslie had agreed to host the Catholic Bishop, reasoning that both religions have but one God, and the Methodist Mission was the only place to have church services for such a large crowd. He opened the doors of the Mission and the whole countryside came.

Sawala had seen excitement like this at gatherings of the Kalapuyan tribes in the big lodge. She noted that much of the food was different, but in the same abundance. She ate roasted goose and pig like the Kalapuyans served, but also the delicious beef and pumpkin pies that she knew from her life with the missionaries. With her fingers sticky from sweets and greasy from meats, she squeezed between all the tall people. Her bonnet kept falling down her back, but the ribbon tied around her neck held on. Ducking under someone's arms to get closer to the front where a man dressed like a woman was performing some special ceremony, she stepped into an opening where she could see it all.

This man – dressed in skirts of red and white with gold braids sewn from the top to the bottom – was beside the river. "There is Dr. Bailey," she whispered. A radiant energy filled her face and ran through her body; her small hands clutched her skirt and she squeezed to contain the joy. She wanted to run to him and shout his name, but she knew she could not. For the moment, she murmured his name again, "Dr. Bailey."

With fear, she watched the strange happenings. It looked like they were going to drown the little boy in Dr. Bailey's arms as they leaned into the waters. *Do these white people kill little children like this?* Before she had another thought, Dr. Bailey lifted the child out of the water and hugged him. A woman wrapped a blanket around the child and everyone cheered.

Relieved at what she saw, Sawala moved closer. *This is a special ceremony. I wonder what it means?*

At that moment, Bailey and some others rushed toward the buildings, and Sawala slipped in behind Bailey when he passed with the child. She had to run to keep up with him, so she reached out and held onto the back of his coat to help stay with him. He didn't seem to notice.

Once inside, Bailey laid the child on one of the tables and pulled off his wet clothes. People crowded around them.

"Arnaud, Arnaud!" Sawala heard people saying. She stood against the table with her face next to the little boy whose red hair was wet and matted down against his head. Bailey rubbed a cloth on the boy's head to dry him.

In that instant, Sawala saw!

With her small hand, she reached up and parted some hairs to see again. *There it is! The black oak leaf! My son! My son! My son!*

She glanced at Bailey's face while he talked and laughed with the boy. She could understand no words, only happiness and love. *Does Dr. Bailey know this is his son?*

Sawala turned back to relish the sight of her child. *His hair is the color of the big round pumpkin that Miss Smith cooked for me. His eyes are like mine – some of the sky dropped into them.*

Now Bailey stood Arnaud on the table while getting his clothes buttoned and the child played with Bailey's beard. *Their hearts are woven together like a basket.*

When Bailey raised the child into his arms, Sawala had an idea and ran off to her room. She picked up her lynx fur and rushed back to the crowd. Squeezing and wiggling between people who towered over her small frame, she made her way back to where Bailey still stood with the child. She wanted to look proper as Margaret had taught her, so she flipped her braids down her back and put her bonnet on again, tying and arranging the bow under her chin – it covered all her hair around her face and her high, flat forehead. She tugged on Bailey's coattails, and he turned to look down to her.

Holding up the lynx fur, she said, "For Arnaud. Gift for Arnaud," and then repeated, "For Arnaud."

With all the conversations and excitement in the room, he could not hear. Bailey squatted and was eye to eye with her.

Sawala repeated, "For Arnaud."

He heard and took the lynx fur. Bailey ran his hand over the soft fur, marveling at the colors of the hairs – from blonde and golden to white and a few black. Bailey knew it was a prize to own one. He looked into her face and had a flash of recognition. He wondered how he knew her but he didn't remember.

Sawala explained, "For Arnaud to sleep."

"Yes, thank you. I'll give this to him when he sleeps." Bailey stood and showed Monsieur and Mrs. Bugat the gift. "This little girl gives Arnaud a gift. What is your name?"

Standing as tall as she could in her paisley blue dress and bonnet, she said, "Sally Soule." Not the name he knew.

As Bailey turned, the lynx fur flipped and Sawala could see her message to her son – the message that took her days to write after practicing on paper with Margaret's metal pens from the ink box. In a corner on the smooth back of the hide and in the script of a child with crooked, but legible letters, were the words, "For My Son" in all capital letters.

Your mother named Sunflower Seed grew a boy with a pumpkin head. She liked her silly thought. *My searching is finished. The hollow tree trunk within my chest has been filled with a feeling of flapping birds and their songs. The white man has a word for this. Miss Smith said it is being happy.* Watching her son disappear with Bailey, she hoped to see him again, yet knew she might not.

Among all the festivities and happiness, Margaret stood at a distance from those crowding around Bailey. She was sulking on the outside and happy on the inside. Looking at her two Williams, first Willson with disdain and then Bailey with a glow in her breast, she found amazement in how her Lord had shaped her life. *Later, I must open the Bible and see what words of God appear upon the page to explain what happened today.* She had learned earlier from Willson's own mouth that he had written a letter, months ago, and sent it with Jason Lee. In that letter, he had proposed marriage to a Miss Chloe Clark.

The whole scene echoed in her mind. Willson had told her, "I tried to get the letter back before Reverend Lee could deliver it." Willson had wrung his hands and wiped his brow as he said, "When they sent word to Lee of his wife's death, I wrote to him to return my letter. He hasn't answered me. Please marry me, Miss Smith. It doesn't matter about her. When she comes, she can marry someone else. It doesn't matter."

Haughty and tall, Margaret told him, "I shall never marry you. You proposed to her first. She is your choice. For me, our relationship is over." And she thought, *He proposed to her before he had carnal knowledge of me, and it didn't stop him. How is it possible that two men have done this to me? Jeremy and now Willson.*

Margaret thought that she had ended her relationship with Willson. Obviously, she didn't realize the power of the men at the Mission. This was not the end of the sordid matter.

Poisonous Death-Camas blooms among the Violet-Blue Camas Lilies

CHAPTER 9

DARK EVENTS
1839 Begins

In Margaret's opinion, people who assumed that she came to Oregon Country to marry were foolish. She had told everyone over and over that she had a calling from the Lord to help the less fortunate and to teach God's ways. Therefore, she saw her refusal to marry William Willson as logical and understandable.

On the day following the visit from the Catholic priest, Willson confronted her in anger and declared, "You must marry me!"

Margaret saw his devastation, but insisted, "You have no right to speak in anger to me." With her head high, she reminded him, "What of your proposal to Miss Chloe Clark?"

"You and I have lived as husband and wife, so we can never marry another." With that thought, he used his trump card. "If you refuse me and receive the addresses of another man, I'll expose what we have done. And I shall give you a cup of sorrow from which you will have to drink the dregs."

Margaret tried to remain calm, saying, "You cannot change my decision." Then she walked away.

Later, she searched the Bible for the place that Willson had quoted and saw that he had changed it a bit. In Isaiah 51:22, she read:

Thus saith thy Lord the LORD, and thy God that pleadeth the cause of his people, Behold, I have taken out of thine hand the cup of trembling, even the dregs of the cup of my fury; thou shalt no more drink it again.

Unbeknownst to Margaret, Mr. Beers, the blacksmith, found Willson crying outside under a tree and stopped to listen to his problem. Willson reached out to Beers – the first person to ask and listen.

Willson opened up and his words spilled forth. "I am in the most unfortunate situation in regards to Miss Chloe Clark of Boston. In a letter, I requested that she come to Oregon to marry me. In the meantime, I became engaged to Miss Smith. So I sent a rider to withdraw the letter from Reverend Jason Lee on his journey. You see, it gives me great pain to admit my sin, but I must confess that I have been intimate with Miss Smith so I should marry her instead of Miss Clark. Do you see?"

"Yes, I see."

"But Miss Smith learned of my letter and my proposal. Now she refuses my hand in marriage, saying Miss Clark was requested first. I disagree, don't you?"

Soon Reverend Leslie knew of Margaret's intimate relations with Willson.

By the next day, Margaret realized that Leslie held her future in his hands. She saw determination in his eyes when he approached her with Willson by his side. "I have come to you on an unpleasant errand. I know everything you have done. Nevertheless, all of this will be passed over in the ways of the church if you marry Mr. Willson."

"I shall do no such thing," Margaret huffed.

The three were sitting in a corner of the busy breakfast area with people bustling around them. Although everyone seemed to be minding their own business, anyone who listened could hear this conversation.

Leslie was adamant. "With my authority as your pastor, I must say that if you have committed the crime of fornication with Mr. Willson, you must marry. In that way it no longer will be considered a sin."

"How dare you assume that this happened!"

Leslie turned to Willson. "Are you guilty of committing the crime of fornication with Miss Smith?"

With shame Willson looked at Margaret and tried to utter his answer. "Dear me, I, I am in the, the hands of my brethren. They, I mean, you may do as one plea, pleases with me."

And so began Leslie speaking with his *'twould* and *'twill* as he did when preaching. He turned back to face Margaret. "I must tell you 'twould not hurt you at all. Your brethren would forgive, but you must confess and marry. I know of two Methodist ministers who were guilty of this error before marriage, but they confessed it and all was passed over."

Margaret sat stiffly and lied, "I am not inclined to confess any wrong act of which I am not guilty. I fully and freely confess that I was wrong in keeping company with Mr. Willson after he had proposed improper intercourse. But I refused him and have never committed that crime with him or any other."

A silence fell.

Leslie, who had never stopped staring at Margaret's face, cleared his throat and emphasized, "Please, 'twill not do. You must acknowledge this, for the brethren will be satisfied with nothing else!" He stood and walked away.

With wrath, Margaret looked at Willson before standing and walking outside. Once away from the other missionaries, pain filled her heart. *I lied! I say I follow the Lord's words, and yet I do despicable things.*

She had not walked far when she found a group of native children bending over someone. Margaret parted those standing on the outside of the circle. "Sally!" she cried upon seeing Sawala on the ground, gasping for breath. "Children, help me carry her to the doctor."

A couple of the larger boys lifted Sawala and carried her across the fields. Margaret took off Sawala's bonnet, hoping she could breathe easier without it.

"Can we go faster? She looks quite ill. I'll hurry ahead to tell the doctor." Margaret gathered her skirts and took off in a run.

When Sawala was resting on a cot, the doctor explained, "Sally, I am going to let you stay here for today. You will be fine. I'll have my wife bring some steam for you to breathe. Shh! No talking until I say so."

He took Margaret by the elbow, and they left the room. "As you know, I diagnosed her with dropsy of the chest quite a while ago. Her disease has existed for months or, more likely, for years. She is quite sick. Have you noticed any different behavior lately?"

"She has been more sedate but has not complained. She seemed more interested in her books and in learning to write."

"I see. Well, I cannot predict, but no matter what my efforts, she will not recover to her prior liveliness. Dropsy of the chest is serious."

Margaret's hand went to her mouth. "Oh, no." She leaned toward him and whispered, "I hear more than what your words say. Am I correct?"

He nodded.

"How long?"

He rubbed his chin, thinking. "Maybe a few months."

But he was wrong.

The next day dawned with more difficulties. Leslie approached Margaret while she sat on a bench under a tree reading her Bible. She saw his stern face as he came toward her.

"Good morning, Sister Smith."

"Good morning, Reverend."

At first, he remained standing and extended his hand. "You have a letter from the East."

Margaret took it.

Leslie continued, "And I have brought a paper for you to sign." He handed her the paper and sat beside her. She read:

To the Methodist Episcopalian Church in Oregon:

Dear Brethren,

With deep regret I have to acknowledge to you that I have been guilty of the crime of fornication, and hope that God is to forgive me.

Margaret stood and thrust the paper back into his hands. "I have told you I am not guilty." She walked off.

Leslie followed, preaching again, "As I told you yesterday, knowledge of what you have done 'twould never leave this Mission and 'twould be forgotten."

Margaret made no attempt to answer and kept walking.

He stopped walking and raised his voice with the distance growing between them. "Do you think you will be allowed to labor here if you refuse to confess? Can you imagine having it known that you were expelled for such a crime as this?"

One of the hardships of life in Oregon Country was the passage of time before a message or information arrived from the East. Margaret opened the letter and learned that her father had died after she had been gone from her family for one year. She left in January 1837 and he died in January 1838, yet she did not know of his passing until almost another year later. The news of his death was heaped upon her pile of problems.

Pensive, she folded the letter slowly and slipped it into her Bible. She stood at the edge of the Willamette River, gazing over the view and seeing nothing. Life in Oregon was changing her.

All day she worried about the possibility of having to leave the Mission and not being able to teach the children. *I was chosen to do this work. I know I was. How could it be that I have so many obstacles? Lord, please guide me. Why did this letter come at this moment? Lord, are you trying to tell me something? My father died, and I was sure he had many years left. You, Lord, led me here for missionary work. Was it wrong not to be with my father in his last days?*

That evening, Margaret went to Sawala, who was back from the hospital and resting in the loft. Margaret gave her a short lesson about going to heaven – a lesson about being a good person and being rewarded by going to heaven. *It is as if I am talking to myself about my carnal sin. I have such a burden on my shoulders. I have sinned with yet another man. Four men! And I said I would never do this again. And here I tell this innocent child to ask for forgiveness so she can go to heaven. What has she ever done compared with my sins?*

Margaret sat at Sawala's bedside for quite a while after the girl had drifted into sleep. She put her head on the blanket covering Sawala and cried. *Am I crying for this sweet child leaving me, or crying for myself? With whom can I talk? No one! This little girl gave me such joy. What am I to do? I am losing her.*

After Margaret retired to her own bedroom, she heard a knock on her door. She covered her shoulders with a blanket and answered the door. Reverend Leslie stood in her doorway, his extended hand held the same paper to be signed. "All your brethren are below, awaiting your acknowledgment of this error in question."

In despair, she blurted, "If I sign this, may I continue in my same role at the Mission?"

"Of course, my dear."

Margaret went to her ink box, slipped the box cover back, and chose a wide writing nib to mount in the holder to make a bold signature. As she sat and opened the ink bottle, Leslie came in. He watched her sign the paper *Margaret J. Smith*.

Walking out, he said, "The committee will meet first thing in the morning to discuss this paper. I expect you to be there."

Margaret closed the door without responding and returned to her desk. To relieve her upset at Willson's betrayal – *doing what any gentleman would not*, she thought – she composed a little poem:

> He said his prayers and learned the creed,
> And went to sea, and knew to read,
> And whiskers wore cravat and glove,
> And blew the flute, and talked of love,
> And tailored some, then took to teaching,
> And coopered more, then went to preaching;
> But losing favor as a rector,
> He next resolved to be a doctor,
> And studied "Thomas," "Bell," and "Burns,"
> And "Cooper's Surgery" by turns,
> And made some pills, but still was he
> As feeble minds will always be,
> Puny and poor when all was done,
> Like a plant in shade which seeks the sun.

The next morning, Margaret climbed to the loft and approached Sawala's bedside. The girl was weak and could barely talk above a whisper, nevertheless she seemed in good spirits, "I want talk."

Margaret caressed the top of her head, smoothing the hair from her face. "Yes, I want to talk with you. Do you understand life and death?"

"Yes."

"Our Lord waits for you after death. Do you know this?"

"Yes."

Margaret came closer to her face, asking, "Which makes you happier? To go to school and play, or to die and go to God?"

"To die and be in ground."

Margaret sat up straighter, quite pleased.

Sawala whispered, "Now I talk. Please." She began to cough and when the hacking relented, she continued, "Important." She rested a moment. The talking took great effort, "Tell Dr. Bailey. He father Arnaud." She stopped to rest again.

Margaret puzzled. *Does she think a godfather is the same as a father?* So she asked, "Yes, Dr. Bailey is godfather for Arnaud."

"No. I mother. Dr. Bailey father. You tell Dr. Bailey."

Margaret reached down and picked up the baby doll, saying, "Here is your baby."

Sawala insisted, "No, not baby doll. Arnaud my baby. He have black leaf here." She touched her own head in the hairline above her forehead. "Arnaud inside me. He come out and I see black leaf. Dr. Bailey take him. *Tsaal an tatsa* – snow on ground." Sawala rested a moment and then tried to sit up. "You tell Dr. Bailey?"

Margaret eased her back in bed. She knew that *tsaal an tatsa* was wintertime in Kalapuyan, but what Margaret heard sounded so absurd – black leaves and this girl a mother. Too many things Sawala said made little sense; snow was rare in the Willamette valley. The missionaries never knew the ages of the children, but they had guessed Sawala to be near ten years old when she came to the Mission – too young to have had a child. Margaret nodded and promised, "Yes."

Margaret kissed Sawala's forehead to soothe her. *I don't want to leave her at this moment!* But she said, "I must go to a meeting. I'll come back."

After Margaret had entered the next cabin, one of the girls rushed up from behind to tug at her skirt. "Come!"

Margaret returned to the loft.

Although Margaret was no expert, she knew death was coming. Sawala inhaled in deep guttural gasps. Margaret sat on the bed and placed Sawala's head on her lap and called to her, "Sally, Sally Soule can you hear me? Give your heart and soul to God and you will enter the gates of heaven." There was no response from the girl. Margaret pulled the small blonde head to her breast. "Sawala, do you hear me? Do you know I love you? Sawala, I don't want you to leave me." Just then, Margaret's heart jumped. *She is not baptized! Oh, why did I not think of this before?*

Margaret lifted Sawala and said to one of the little girls, "Bring the baby doll for me," and she took Sawala downstairs to her own bed, where she gently laid her down. She then rushed to the waiting brethren, and called them to the girl's bedside. In haste, Reverend Leslie sent one of the children for a cup of water so he could perform a simple baptism. Afterwards, all the missionaries recited the Lord's Prayer, encouraging the children to join them. Margaret went to her knees at the bedside during the ceremony and continued to pray when the others filed from the room.

On his way out, Leslie tapped Margaret's shoulder and spoke in a low voice, "I shall go for Dr. White. Let us postpone your meeting until after she has passed."

All day and all night, Margaret sat with Sawala, who never regained consciousness. Margaret sat in the darkness, trying to understand the words that Sawala had told her. In the girl's voice, Margaret recollected:

Tell Dr. Bailey.
He father
I mother. Dr. Bailey father.
You tell Dr. Bailey.
Arnaud my baby.
He have black leaf here.
Arnaud inside me.
He come out.
I see black leaf.
Dr. Bailey take him.
Tsaal an tatsa – *snow on ground.*

After much thought, Margaret decided that Sally Soule had been delirious – the words made no sense. *Maybe this girl knows that Dr. Bailey collects leaves. Maybe the baptism looked like something the Kalapuyans do, and it made Dr. Bailey a father figure. I don't understand. Why did she talk about snow?* In spite of her promise to tell Bailey, and even though in her mind she could still hear Sawala asking, "You tell Dr. Bailey?" Margaret decided to say nothing to Bailey. But she wanted to write it down so she lit the lamp to make an entry in her journal. She wrote what Sawala had said, word for word. When finished, Margaret extinguished the light and sat on the bed. She took the blonde head onto her lap again and stroked the hair. *With the loss of this girl a light will be extinguished in my life.*

Like the moon, which shone as feebly as the life in Margaret's arms and disappeared with the coming light of day, Sawala faded from life. Margaret held her for many minutes before she stood to go and tell the missionaries. Before she left her room, her eyes went to Sawala's baby doll and she picked it up. Hugging the doll, Margaret cried, and then she replaced Sawala's beloved baby doll in the corner of her bedroom.

The stone in the mission graveyard, where many native children were buried, would be marked, "Good bye, Sally Soule." In the springtime – *am plaatowa* – and above the small grave, Sawala would burst forth as yellow flowers – *pookwa am plaatowa.*

With these deaths – the little boy from her camas cakes, her father in her absence, and now Sawala – some arrogance in Margaret died as well.

Leslie postponed his long-delayed meeting with Margaret and the other missionaries again. Instead, he scheduled a revival.

David Leslie was becoming well-known for saving souls with his revival sermons. So during this winter evening in early March, Dr. Bailey decided to go to the Mission to hear one of Leslie's sermons. He hoped to see Margaret although as far as he knew she still was engaged to Willson.

The cold, rainy, and muddy night didn't stop people from coming to the revival. Quite a few wagons, carriages, and horses were outside when Dr. Bailey rode up. He had arrived late. The sermon had started and he heard a fire-and-brimstone lecture echoing from the windows as he loosened the saddle and tied his horse to a tree.

He shook the water from his wide-brimmed hat before entering. There was a blaze roaring in the fireplace on one side, and Reverend Leslie was roaring at the end of the room on a raised platform built especially for this occasion. Whale oil lamps on tables along the walls glowed and smelled of the sea, and every hook on the back wall held a dripping coat. Bailey stepped inside, avoiding a puddle on the floor. He nodded to several people as he looked for a seat, and then he saw Margaret. She was sitting alone on a bench in the middle of the room while people crowded onto other benches. He slid in next to her as he slipped off his leather jacket and nodded a silent greeting, wondering why her bench was empty.

Suddenly, lightning flashed and thunder exploded instantly afterwards. Some worshippers jumped with the loud crack and others responded with a squeal. Thunderstorms were not typical in Oregon.

Leslie threw his arms high. "Are we hearing from the heavens in response to my words? Yes, 'twas a sign." He raised his voice and with authority preached, "I am telling you as I have told you many times, God does not think kindly of sinners who do not repent their wicked ways."

And the thunder crashed again!

"Who is so foolish not to hear their Lord exploding in frustration? Exploding over you the sinner! Tonight is the night to repent and give your soul to your Savior. He gave his life for you and now 'tis time for you to step forward and show him that 'twas not done in vain. 'Twould be another sin not to listen to the call of God from nature's loudest feats. Come, 'twill lift you up. You will feel your Lord walking with you when you come forward and admit to your sins. I shan't tell you how gratifying you will feel."

Leslie's voice seemed to diminish in sound when Bailey leaned toward Margaret to ask, "Have you been saved?"

She whispered, "Oh yes, but not by Reverend Leslie. I was saved back East during a revival near Boston."

Bailey scooted closer to hear her, "You were saved back East, you said?"

She reciprocated and slid closer to him until their clothing touched, then whispered, "We shouldn't be talking."

"Yes, of course."

The rain increased. It pounded the roof and blew in through the glassless windows. A few women moved away from the incoming water. A couple of the missionaries got up to secure the deerskin covers; there were nails around the windows on which to hook them.

Margaret started to get up to help, and Bailey pulled her back onto the bench, saying, "Please don't disturb the moment. I am listening to the

Reverend." He pulled her closer than before. Warmth came from her against his legs.

Across the room, Willson groaned loudly and stood. "I am with sin. Dear Lord, forgive me." He put his hands to his face and began to weep.

Leslie called to him, "Come! Come to your Lord. Come kneel beside me."

And Willson went to the front and fell to his knees, groaning.

Leslie's voice boomed out above the rain, "Now is the time. Come, you sinners! There is no better time. You know in your heart it is the right thing to do. Come forward and kneel before me to give your life to Christ."

Bailey whispered to her without turning his head, "I have sinned. Killed two innocent Indians. I should go."

Margaret bobbed her head in agreement. "You will find relief and be filled with goodness." As she watched Bailey walk to the front, she had a realization that made her face contort in pain. *I have killed an innocent Indian, too. A little boy!*

Bailey stood in the front with the three others who were taking a step to redemption.

At the end of the service, hymns were sung and hot tea served.

Margaret commended Bailey for going forward to be saved. "I congratulate you."

"Thank you." Then Bailey asked with puzzlement, "What was Willson doing across the room from you? Why were you sitting alone? Aren't you engaged?"

Margaret set down her tea. "I must go. Perhaps we could talk another day about all this," and she walked away.

Confused, yet aware something was amiss, he watched her disappear through a door in the direction of her room. He put down his cup and looked around for Dr. White. Not seeing him, he left and went to the White's home.

Distraught, Margaret had sensations of lightheadedness and dizziness on her way to her room and she bumped a wall while passing one of the other bedrooms. To calm the swirling in her head, she stopped and leaned against the logs of the cabin. It was then that she noticed women's voices coming from the room across from her. She heard, "Margaret," and again, someone else said, "Margaret," followed by words she could not understand.

Margaret gasped. *They are talking about me!* She held her breath and closed her eyes to better hear what they were saying.

One of the women said, "Check a second time to make sure you ripped out all the pages."

"I don't like tearing up my journal, but I do tear out letters that I have written to be mailed, so there were torn remnants of pages even before I began to rid it of Margaret."

Silence. It lasted a while.

"I looked through it all. I don't think the name Margaret is anywhere now."

Another voice said, "I checked my husband's journal, too. He had quite a few pages, so I dripped ink over the references to her. You can't see her name anywhere now."

"And I have Anna Pittman Lee's journal that was here. I removed everything about Margaret."

Margaret gathered her skirts and rushed off. She had heard enough. *Why do they want to remove me from their journal entries?* Once in her room, she closed her door and leaned her back against it, not wanting to move. Although she stared across her room, her eyes saw nothing – not the glass with brown water and wilted spring flowers, not her ink box with an unfinished letter on top, not her Bible open to a favorite verse, and not Sawala's baby doll, which she had placed in the corner some days ago. Trembling, she began to think about her problems with others. Taking a slow step, she moved to her bed and kneeled to pray. It was not her usual prayer:

"Dear Lord, please hear my words. I cannot claim to be someone who has served You in strict purity, but I do claim to be one who believes in You, and this belief has been the guiding star of my life. If not for my belief, I could not have endured the intense burdens I have experienced since I first embarked on the ship to come here. I feel disposed to lay my finger to my lips and confess that I now distrust my own judgment. It has failed me many times. Forgive my lust and impulsive pride. My sins are many; the greatest surely stands now at your side in the form of the child who, in his hunger for sustenance, ate my poisoned cakes."

Her voice cracked with emotion, and she stopped praying. The wind rustled leaves outside her window and rain started to patter against the cabin. Still on her knees, she sat back on her heels and put her head to the bed, too distraught to properly climb into bed.

At the hospital, Bailey learned of Margaret's signed confession and asked, "When is this meeting with her and the missionaries?"

Dr. White said, "Tomorrow morning after breakfast. I must be there."

"I think I'll come. Now, don't tell me I can't. I'll make it appear that I am coincidently dropping by to talk to Reverend Leslie about my experience of being saved tonight." Bailey took Dr. White's hand with both his hands and shook goodnight. "I have some patients I need to see in this neck of the woods tomorrow, anyway. I won't stay long."

Outside the White's place, Bailey sat in his saddle ready to ride away, but hesitated. He looked around at the still night. Just then, the clouds moved away, and he saw the stars peeking from their edges. Suddenly, he felt invigorated and decided that he had been hiding behind clouds. *It's time to go to Margaret. It's now or never.*

In the time it took to ride the mile back to the Mission, the sky had cleared of all clouds. The Mission was dark and peaceful when he approached. Once outside her window, still on his horse, Bailey whispered, "Miss Smith, Miss Smith."

Her face appeared at the window and she asked, "What is the matter? Why are you here?"

Bailey lifted his hat, brushed back his black hair from his forehead, and cleared his throat. With both of his hands on the brim of his hat, he leaned forward and said, "Miss Smith, will you marry me?"

He could barely see her face, so he could not see her expression.

She made no sound.

The wind rattled dried leaves clinging to some oak trees since last season. Bailey's heart rattled as well, and he knew he needed to say more, "I have never felt for a woman as I do for you. From the time I first saw you during the dinner at Fort Vancouver, I haven't had a day without you on my mind. Margaret, please accept my hand in marriage."

At last, she smiled. "I do, Dr. Bailey. May I call you Willy?"

"Yes." His smile flashed from his dark whiskers. He stepped his horse closer to the window and precariously leaned to her. With one hand he reached for the back of her head after she stepped up on her bed to lean out to him. They kissed.

Still gazing at her face, he said, "I'll come tomorrow."

Margaret touched his whiskers. "Good night, Willy."

Unknown to them, Willson had been standing outside her door, planning to walk in and sleep with her. He had hoped with her confession signed that she would marry him. But with what he overheard, his hopes were dashed.

Early the next morning, Willson shared the knowledge of Dr. Bailey's proposal with Reverend Leslie and asked, "Wouldn't it be wrong if Dr. Bailey married her not knowing of her confession? I would think that it is the responsibility of the leaders of the church to inform him before he marries."

Leslie agreed. When everyone gathered for the meeting with Margaret, he explained to her, "Your confession was read by all here and has been burned. Your brethren have forgiven you as I have said we would do. But we feel that you must marry Mr. Willson."

"I thought I had made myself quite clear."

"My dear, my dear, do not interrupt me! As I was saying, if you do not marry Mr. Willson and choose someone else, I cannot condone you to marry that person without making that person acquainted with the circumstances in your confession. And I am sure you realize that there is no other official who could marry you here in Oregon Country."

"How dare you!"

"Please, you are interrupting me again. It is my understanding that there is a person expecting to marry you, and it is my responsibility to tell him."

Dr. Bailey walked into the meeting. With deliberation, he said, "Excuse my interruption, Reverend Leslie." He removed his hat before nodding to the other missionaries. "Good morning. Did I overhear that you would like to inform me about my intended?"

Since only Leslie and Willson knew of the proposal, looks of confusion and surprise appeared on faces.

Bailey continued, "I came to schedule the marriage of Miss Smith and myself and to confirm that you burned her confession. I also want to inform you that none of the facts I have learned or rumors I heard have lessened the esteem I entertain for Miss Smith."

Silence prevailed in the room.

Finally, Leslie stood and walked toward Bailey with his hand extended and said, "May I congratulate you? Yes, the paper is burned and all is forgiven." Enjoying his good fortune to soon be rid of the torments and problems of Margaret, he turned to the others, "This meeting, on the third day of March in the year eighteen thirty-nine, is adjourned."

On Monday, the fourth of March, Bailey arrived at the Mission in the late afternoon for his wedding. He came with two horses, two leather hats, and two capote blanket coats.

Bailey had shaved for the occasion and his facial scar, extending from his upper lip down through his chin and neck, looked ghastly. Margaret wore a dark green merino dress and had a black and green handkerchief tucked around her neckline where a white collar would normally be worn. She had no clean white collars.

Since the mission families had learned of Margaret's affair with Willson and wanted nothing to do with her, only three persons from the Mission attended: one missionary assigned to be the witness, Reverend Leslie to conduct the ceremony, and Mrs. Leslie, always kind and fair.

The wedding commenced soon after Bailey arrived, and Margaret found the ceremony to be as dismal as a funeral. On her march to the altar, Margaret had to circle the buildings in the rain and pass where pigs and chickens ran across her path and dogs barked at her. She kept remembering the scripture she had read that morning when she opened her Bible.

Why gaddest thou about so much to change thy way?
Thou shalt be ashamed of Egypt as thou hast been of Assyria – yea thou shalt go forth from him and thy hands upon thy head.

Jeremiah 2:36-37

Margaret had stood wide-eyed, thinking, *The Lord means for me to leave the Mission and marry.*

After the ceremony finished, William kissed his wife and they walked to the Mission's doors. He reached to the hooks on the back wall and placed one of the wide-brimmed leather hats on his own head and the other on hers. With two of his fingers, he tucked some of her dark curls under the rim and then reached for one capote, explaining, "You are going to live with me on the French Prairie among the French Canadians. They know how to make life more comfortable in many ways, such as this capote. Do you know about them?" After she shook her head, he continued, "It's a coat made from a wool blanket. All the French Canadian trappers use them; they're usually made them from a Hudson's Bay Company point blankets. They keep you dry in this weather." He draped it around her shoulders and closed it around her neck with a loop over a button. He gave his new wife a quick kiss on her cheek and then opened the door to go outside to his waiting horses. "Get in the saddle and let me arrange the capote around your legs to keep you dry."

Not used to someone fussing over her, she hesitated but then decided that she might enjoy it. She kissed him back before raising herself into the saddle.

Bailey tucked her skirts under the capote and pulled it down to her shoes. He furled his own capote around his shoulders and mounted. They began the trip through mud and rain up the Willamette Valley to his cabin that he had purchased for one hundred dollars.

William John Bailey was an alcoholic and he knew it. A year of sobriety did not change the fact that he would be a cantankerous drunkard if he started. He knew that with drink he would return to his former ugly self – a man who had no regard for others and could shoot innocent Indians. He felt grateful to Dr. White for giving him the opportunity to remain sober, the opportunity to be a physician again, and the opportunity to meet and know Margaret. He never wanted to touch another drink in his life.

Margaret was an enigma, even to herself. She was devout, but took the freedom of choice when it suited her. She was ignorant when it came to delicate human relations, yet she was exceedingly intelligent in her range of knowledge. She saw that men and women had basic roles in life, but she believed herself equal to any man. She also saw herself as proper, although no proper woman spoke her opinions. She loved her Lord, believed all the words of her Savior and the Bible, but had let her instincts and primal desires give in to men. Now, for the first time in her life, she believed the Lord had chosen the right man for her. She wanted carnal knowledge of no one ever again, except William J. Bailey.

They each had seen only one side of the other. Margaret had never seen him mean and drunk. Bailey had never seen her stubborn and opinionated.

The time would come when they would meet the other side of their personalities, but many fulfilling years awaited them.

William J. Bailey and Margaret J. Bailey in Silhouette as Envisioned by the Author

CHAPTER 10

MARRIED BLISS
1839-1840

Leaving the Mission, they trotted side by side, heading north for twelve miles to Bailey's cabin; the rainy March evening darkened. The couple rode without words for the first few miles, but Bailey wore a grin on his face.

Margaret had packed a small bundle and her Bible for the night; Bailey had put them in his *parflèche* to keep them dry. They planned to borrow a wagon and return to the Mission the next day for her trunks stuffed with clothing, seeds, books, papers, and her ink box.

Bailey broke the silence. "After I get the fire stoked up, I'll prepare dinner. There should be coals from this morning." He hesitated and began again, "You mustn't expect too much. I don't have much."

Margaret looked over at him and smiled at his apparent concern. "I don't expect anything. We shall make do. Isn't that right?"

He nodded.

She saw his relief and continued, "You must remember that I am not bringing much of anything to this marriage. I do have some pay coming from my work at the Mission, however," she let out a laugh, "I have no idea how much."

"Well, that's your money to spend how you please."

"Thank you, but we shall see. I want you to know that I am hoping to get back to missionary teaching when Jason Lee returns. I spoke with Dr. White, and he thinks you could get an assignment as the doctor at one of the other mission locations here in Oregon Country. If that is so, I could continue my work teaching the native children."

"Don't expect that to happen, Margaret, you are asking to be disappointed. Lee and I don't see matters eye to eye, so I don't think he would ever give me a position. Besides, after how they treated you, why would you want to work for those people?"

"Willy, I am saying we could go somewhere else with different missionaries."

He thought. *But how do you know they would be different?* But said, "Let's not think about this until Lee returns. He won't be back for more than a year. For now, don't worry. I don't make much from doctoring, but we won't go hungry. People pay me with a chicken or flour, sometimes a pie or berries. Right now, I have some eggs waiting for us. A family not far from here paid me this morning with those eggs, so they're fresh."

"I promise not to worry. Oh, you should not have talked of food. My stomach heard and is rumbling to eat."

His face turned serious, "They were rude at the Mission not to offer a meal to us."

"Not that I am one to defend them, but they spoke the truth when they said they didn't have enough to spare. Willy, they are so disorganized and don't know how to conserve. I should not start discussing this."

"But Margaret, this is our wedding day, and they didn't act like Christians." He stopped, at a loss for words. "You have the best idea. Let's not start talking about this." He changed the subject. "I must tell you that I asked a neighbor to make us a table for eating." He chuckled, "I told you I don't have much. Listen, I'm going to ride over there to see if it's ready. His name is Quesnal. Perhaps he will let us use his wagon to bring the table home, and then I could use the wagon to get your trunks tomorrow."

Surprised, Margaret asked, "You are going to ride off and leave me? Right now?"

Bailey sat up straighter in the saddle and turned to face her. He raised his brow to appear puzzled. "Does my Margaret sound scared? That is not the Margaret I know – the brave woman who came alone from the East to save the Indians, the single woman who defies the scowls and gossip of other missionaries, the only missionary to learn the language of the Indians." He stopped. "Need I go on?"

His words, his praises, his obvious love flooded her emotions and she glanced over, trying to see his eyes in the night. After all that praise, she disliked sounding meek, yet she protested, "But I don't know the way to your cabin."

"Do you know the Big Dipper?"

She looked up. "Willy! The sky is covered in clouds!"

"Yeah, that's right. Just keep going straight for a mile. I'll be right back." He disappeared, slipping away between the falling rain.

Margaret reined in her horse and softly called out, "Willy?" She strained to hear his hoof beats, but they were already gone. "Willy? You have not really gone, have you?" She waited a bit more before shouting, "Willy, where are you? Please, don't tease me." Her heartbeats quickened. She looked ahead and then back at where he had gone. "He said to keep going straight. How will I know if I am going straight?"

The horse complained with a whinny, and the situation became clear to her. She laughed and addressed the animal, "Oh, I imagine that you know your way home." She nudged the horse and loosened her hold on the reins. "Take me home, please," she said, and off they went at a steady trot.

She rode beneath tall and abundant trees until passing into open meadows and fields owned by French and Irish settlers who had once been trappers for the Hudson's Bay Company. Noticing the increase of wind, she pulled on her sleeves to tuck her fingers inside.

It appeared that the horse was taking her to Bailey's cabin; nevertheless, Margaret decided to pray. "Praying will relax me," she told her gray mare before beginning the Lord's Prayer aloud. "Our Father, who art in heaven," she interrupted the prayer, over and over, with complaints. "How could Willy ride off?" She started again, "Hallowed be thy name," and stopped to say, "He didn't even tell me that the horse knew the way." The rain fell steadily as she trotted along, praying, "Thy will be done." Minutes passed and the night grew darker while she bobbed along in the saddle. She had no idea how many times she repeated the prayer as she continued to let the horse lead the way.

All of a sudden, Bailey appeared at her side. "Our table's not ready. Guess we eat sitting on the bed." With the mention of the bed, he stopped talking abruptly. He glanced at her, and she smiled coyly. He nodded with a grin and made an effort to keep his talk casual, "The Quesnals send their congratulations and have invited us to dinner on Friday. His wife is Marie Tchalis. Is there anything on our calendar?"

She smiled at his attempt at humor, and answered, "Well, I don't know, dear. I'll look in my Farmer's Almanac to see if the moon is in the correct phase to go visiting."

He laughed and took off at a gallop. "Come on, there's home!"

They stopped at a lean-to shed built on the side of the house, and he assisted her down from the horse. After removing their saddles and bridles, Bailey threw out some hay into a feed trough. "I'm going to make better accommodations for my horses – a barn – and I'd like to have some other animals someday. I'd like a few cattle for beef and maybe chickens and a pig."

Margaret suggested, "And a cow for milk, because that means butter and cheese, too." At that moment, she decided to use her pay to buy a cow.

When Margaret approached their cabin, she began mental notes of changes she wanted to make. A front porch ran the length of the house; she planned to put chairs on it and a small table. Inside, the hearth was wide but lacked any forged metal hangings. Margaret decided to talk to the blacksmith at the Mission to make some metal hooks to hang pots over the fire. However, she saw no pots; they needed to get a cast iron Dutch oven since she only saw a tin kettle and a griddle.

"Here, let me help you," Bailey said, as she removed the capote and hat. She saw no place to hang them and made another note.

Taking the wet things, he pulled one of his two chairs closer to the hearth and draped both capotes over the back; they were too bunched up to dry well, so Margaret straightened them. He pulled up his only other chair. "Come sit here, it's still warm." He stirred the embers and placed new kindling on.

"Oh, it is warm. Thank you." The fire started to flame.

He continued to chat while he went to one of the deep windowsills and removed a bowl with some eggs. "First, I should get the kettle going," he said as he placed it on some red embers that he had pulled to one side. "I filled the kettle before I left this morning. I only have one tin cup, so we can share or I can wait until you have finished drinking your tea."

"Let's share. Where's the tea? I can help."

"No, tonight you need a special meal. It's your wedding night, and I'm the person to make it." He laughed, "Well, 'special' is defined as 'unusual or different' for now." He put black English tea into the kettle to steep, pulled up the other chair, and sat on the wet clothes to be next to her. They both faced the fire. Bending down to a shallow tin plate on the floor, he cracked six eggs into it and tossed the eggshells into the fire. "I have some bacon! I almost forgot. This is going to be a wedding feast!" Up he jumped and went back to the windowsill. Under a cloth, laying over another tin plate, were the rashers of bacon.

In amazement, Margaret said, "Look at that meat. There is almost no fat!"

"An Irishman, who lives not far from here, paid me with this back bacon. That's what he called it. Look, there are three slices for each of us. I had planned to give you four, but now you said we are sharing." He tossed the six rashers on the griddle and placed it on the embers next to the kettle.

Margaret gave him a little push. "Be quiet or I'll change my mind and eat it all."

He was whipping the eggs with a fork in the shallow tin, and with her push, some started to spill over the side. He tilted the tin plate back to save the frothy yellow mixture. "Hey, don't spill it! If you do, it won't be my portion!"

Laughter lingered on their faces while the bacon began to sizzle. He turned each piece with his fork and then pushed them to one side before pouring in the eggs. He stirred nonstop while they cooked. "I was thinking that the lowest shelf on the wall might be a better place to eat, rather than sitting on the bed. The shelf would make a good table." He raised the griddle of cooked eggs and bacon off the fire and stood. "Surely, we must be proper," he said, raising an eyebrow.

"Yes, I suppose you heard the story of my first dinner in the Willamette Valley when I made a fool of myself at the McKay's home, saying that I would send them a proper teapot."

"I did indeed." He placed the steaming griddle on one of the higher wooden shelves and then went back to get a chair.

She stood, turned to look at him, and kissed him. "Let's promise to never hide anything from each other. So I must know, why did you shave off your beard?"

"Like you said, I didn't want to hide anything and figured that, if you would marry me with this lopsided face, you must really want me."

She hugged him around the neck and kissed him again. "Well, now that we're married, you can grow it back."

"I guess I need not ask which way you like me best."

Margaret took some of the eggs with her fingers and said, "I don't think you do. So far, I think I'm going to like you in all ways."

He put his arm around her waist, walked with her to the other chair, and said, "Mrs. Bailey, dinner is served. Wait! I forgot." He went for the kettle, tin cup, and sugar, arranging them on the shelf before he handed her the fork and poured the tea. "And I have a spoon, too." He turned and reached into a corner of the windowsill.

Margaret began eating while he stirred sugar into her tea. "This food is so good. I thank you for my wedding dinner." She passed the fork to him.

"You are welcome, ma'am."

Soon they were working on the bottom of the griddle. "I like these crisp brown scrapings the best. Let's get them all," he told her, "so it'll be clean enough for cooking breakfast on it. We get six more eggs, but no bacon, in the morning."

"Do you have flour? I could make some pan bread."

"No, I don't. We'll get some tomorrow. I want to go to see the Bugats; they would lend us some."

Margaret poured herself more tea.

"Come in the bedroom and drink that sitting on the bed." He picked up the lantern and a magazine before motioning for her to follow him to the bedroom. He had a bedstead made with high posts and sideboards in a dark rich wood, nicely finished and quite stylish for Oregon Country. "A farmer made this for me when you were only a hope in my mind."

In amazement, Margaret stood a little taller and looked directly at him.

"I told him how I wanted it built. I had to borrow this straw-filled mattress. Do you think you could sew one? I'll let you pick out the fabric you want. I have plenty of straw to fill the one you sew and then I'll return this."

Margaret nodded. She looked at the one pillow covered with a fur deerskin.

"I had to borrow blankets, too. I always use my spare capote, but I knew it would come home wet tonight."

"Thank you for this impressive bridal bed." She sat on the side with her cup of tea.

"Here, if you sit on this side, you can use the windowsill for your cup. I'm going to read for a while." He pulled off his boots and sprawled on the bed, opened his English magazine, and started to read out loud. "Listen to this." He read an article about fox hunting and another one about King William IV. "I brought this magazine with me when I left England. That was before the reign of Queen Victoria."

Margaret added, "Now you are ruled by the Rain of Oregon."

They both were comfortably lolling on the bed and laughed.

All of a sudden, the lantern sputtered out. They were silent a moment in the dark before he said, "Well, I used exactly the right amount of oil, it seems." He reached across the bed in the darkness to touch her, and she was not there. He searched the mattress here and there with his hand.

"I'm standing over here, half undressed already," she whispered. "Hurry!"

The bed creaked as he got out on the other side. She heard his belt buckle hit the floor.

She dropped her hairpins onto the windowsill and climbed back onto the bed. It creaked again. "Hurry, it's cold without you."

The only light came from the fire in the other room as it danced on the walls. They could not see each other as he slipped under the cover next to her.

After breakfast, Bailey asked, "Would you like to see the land? We could walk around the edge of the property. And I'll show you what kinds of trees we have."

"Oh, I'd love that. It's not raining and the air is mild." But fifteen minutes later when they were under one of those trees making love, they wished they had a capote to put under and over them. It began to drizzle.

As soon as they returned to the cabin, they saddled the horses to go visit the Bugats.

Monsieur Bugat showed surprise at the wedding news. "Why you no invite us to your wedding? What we do?"

Bailey stood next to Monsieur Bugat and draped his arm around the shoulders of the small man. "Please understand. There was no time. I proposed to Margaret at midnight on Sunday, and we were married Monday. That was yesterday, and you are the first friends we have visited, so you have that honor."

Mrs. Bugat spoke to her husband in French, and they both turned to look at Margaret's belly. Margaret gave a sidelong glance to her Willy and nudged him with her elbow.

Monsieur Bugat shook Bailey's hand. "We understand and congratulate you. You must eat our dinner with us. It ready soon. Go now play with Arnaud."

After dinner, Margaret and William rode to their other neighbor to pick up their table and drove the borrowed wagon to the Mission for her trunks. Bailey commented on the way home, "We are rather poor."

"In terms of worldly goods, we may be poor, but that doesn't matter. We are intelligent and willing to work. I have been told that you are an excellent physician and surgeon, besides being the doctor of choice with the French settlers." She could not resist teasing him, "Of course, you are the *only* doctor in these parts. Dr. White works for the Mission. I guess not everyone has a choice."

"You are right. I am all they have. And they complain at my fee of a dollar a day. I tell them that it includes the expense for my horse, but they still complain.

So began their life as Dr. and Mrs. Bailey.

Dr. Bailey enjoyed practicing his profession among the settlers on the French Prairie. And Margaret practiced what she liked – organizing and improving their life. She bought her cow, milked it every day, and made fresh cheese, butter, and hasty pudding. They took a live chicken and then a second and third in payment for his doctoring. She built a pen, and they got a pig. She placed rails to outline her garden that first spring, using seeds that she had brought from Massachusetts. Her potatoes, onions, cabbage, corn, and cucumbers emerged from the soil and were beautiful. Beautiful, that is, until a frost came and she learned not to plant outdoors until May.

Slowly, Margaret made the place a home. It was a squared log house with two rooms on the first floor, four windows, a flight of stairs up to a garret, and a front porch. She had put a table, stump chairs and flowers on the porch. Each day she filled the house with smells of cooking, and Willy filled it with his ardent love for her.

Visitors were welcomed. One day, Dr. Bailey returned home with Mr. Thomas Farnham, a journalist, who had traveled from the East to record the happenings in Oregon Country.

Bailey handed Margaret some portions of beaver meat wrapped in cornhusks. "I was paid by a woman today with this, and she said it would make a good stew if you cooked it long enough."

"Mr. Farnham, excuse me while I start the stew pot. I shall return shortly to show you around our homestead."

They walked around and Mr. Farnham seemed to enjoy seeing the animals. However, the garden he found special. "My oh my, I am impressed with your flowers and vegetables."

"Luckily I didn't use all my seed and was able to replant after a late frost, and again after the chickens pecked and ate the first seeds. That's why I built the fence. I know my plants are growing mixed together in as much confusion as if they had blown from the skies in a gale of wind. But I am proud of my gardens."

Her guest agreed, "You should be. I understand you only arrived here in March, and look at what you have accomplished."

That evening, after Margaret served a dinner of cooked cabbage and beaver stew with potatoes, Mr. Farnham asked to be excused to write.

Margaret opened her eyes extra wide when he pulled several sheets of paper from his portfolio. She said, "I beg your pardon. Please do not think me rude, but I must tell you that paper is one item that is impossible for me to obtain." She gave a small giggle as she added conspiratorially "I can't seem to grow it in my garden."

The gentleman needed no prompting, "It would please me so if you would accept some of my paper." He gathered an inch stack and placed it on her table.

Bailey turned to him to say, "You have given my wife something better than gold, for she lives to write. She used her last piece of paper a few weeks ago. Thank you. And while you write your report, I am sure she will be eager to add to her journal." He turned to Margaret, "I have never written to my mother about our marriage. At least one sheet is mine."

Quietly all three of them sat and wrote at the same table, the only table inside the cabin. Bailey wrote to tell his mother that he was married, but he also wanted her to know where he lived; seven years ago, he had disappeared without telling her his plans.

With the opportunity of a mail messenger sitting in her home, Margaret wrote to her family as well. She told them of her marriage and her lack of simple things such as a towel, teapot, and shoes. But mainly she wanted to describe her garden – her pride and joy of the moment. She wrote:

> I introduced the seeds as thick as grains of flour in happy porridge. The seeds were those I brought from you and were many of them two or three years old, so that I did not expect them to germinate, but they came up like a host and could not grow for fighting. So Master Frost thought he would remedy the matter, and passing over the beds one night, I found in the morning the potatoes, and corn, and beans, and vines, all black with wrath...they were dead.

Mr. Farnham was a visitor passing through Oregon and they would never see him again, but he wrote in his report a few sentences that recorded their lives for centuries to come:

> I traveled a circuitous track through a heavy forest of fir and pine, and emerged into a beautiful little prairie, at the side of which stood the doctor's neat hewn log cabin, sending its cheerful smoke among the lofty pine tops in its rear. We soon sat by a blazing fire, and the storm that had pelted us all the way, lost its unpleasantness in the delightful society of my worthy host and his amiable wife. I passed the night with them. The doctor is a Scot and his wife a Yankee and a happy little family they were.

Within a few months and as a result of letters to friends and family, first one wooden crate arrived from Oahu, and then a wooden barrel. She had opened the crate alone and was pleased with the gifts – bars of soap, towels, molasses, writing paper, nibs and ink, a beautiful bonnet for Sunday wear, and a variety of fabric. When the barrel came, she waited for her Willy to open it with her. As well as a set of china with four settings, her family had sent knives, forks and spoons, a tablecloth and napkins, and a teapot with six cups and saucers.

"Willy, look, books to read! And shoes for me! You men can get shoes from the Hudson's Bay Company, but they have nothing for me. I imagine that the women and wives who live there buy out all the shoes that are sent from the East." Margaret sensed that he was not as pleased with the presents as she was. "What's wrong, Willy?"

"I know I should be happy and grateful, but this makes me feel like we are poor and I am not giving you what you need."

"Oh, Willy, these are wedding gifts, not handouts to the poor. Look at what we have, compared to what was here when I first came – our animals and all our improvements. Our hands did everything, and I am proud of what we have done. I would not want to return back East to live like I used to live." She pulled her chair close to his and placed her head on his shoulder. "We live as God wants. We are close to Him and all that he made. I never want to return and live like my parents. If I do have a dream, it is to return to teach the native children."

"Just forget that, Margaret!" He stood, frowned, and started to pace the room. "Jason Lee knows how I feel about him. He knows I think him a hypocritical bastard who has no right to be considered a Christian leader or a person to help save the Kalapuyans."

Margaret let him rant. When he stopped, she began in a soft voice, "We all have our faults as well as our good aspects. With some of us the scale tips more one way than the other, but we all have good and bad. In my opinion and from what I have seen, the Reverend Jason Lee was a good man and possessed the true missionary spirit. He was devotedly pious, ardent and dauntless, but deficient in judgment; easily influenced by those whom he considered his superiors, but obstinate and unyielding to his inferiors. His great forte was in talking. He could keep a whole body of people around him, listening to his conversation and waiting for his nod, but he could not set them to work or decide on any work for himself. Hence, affairs at the

Mission were generally in the condition of confusion.

"The fact was that he could not with a glance see what should be done. He had located the Mission in the wrong place – in the summer, the mosquitoes; with the rain, the erosion; and at this river location, no waterpower for mills. He was unable to determine how to get out of all that. Others too easily influenced him, leaving his mind ever vacillating and fluctuating. The wish to fulfill the intentions of the board, and to perform his duty as a missionary, rendered him tardy in complying with the wishes of the mission family. One of them wanted to farm, another wanted an orchard, another a band of cattle, et cetera. One could not be sent to a remote place to start a mission for he wanted his children schooled.

"Thus we see mismanagement and waste, but that does not mean that Jason Lee is a bad person. He just is not good at running a mission."

Bailey had stopped pacing when she started talking and leaned against a wall with his arms crossed over his chest. When she stopped talking, he approached her while she still sat in the chair, with all the new spoons and plates at her feet. He took her hands and carefully back-stepped away from all the gifts. "Margaret, Margaret, what a woman you are. Let me ask, could you give such a forgiving and lengthy discourse about Reverend Leslie after all he has done against you? And Willson?"

They stood face to face and could feel the warmth of the other's breath. Looking into his green eyes, she saw no challenge, only satisfaction with her, his wife.

She put her hand to his face and lightly touched her lips to his before answering, "I hope I could forgive him. Today I would, but tomorrow might find me not as forgiving. I have to ask the Lord to help me to be a good Christian every day, but I am not always so logical and understanding."

Although they had not yet eaten dinner, they went to the bedroom. "We can eat later," he said.

Margaret still douched with vinegar. Every now and then, she would forget or not want to venture out in the rain to their outhouse, but most of the time she took care of the matter. She was not ready to have children.

Bailey had noticed that after lovemaking, she often left their bed to use the outhouse. He thought nothing of it.

A year would pass before he would learn of her vinegar douching, but for now each was busy with their daily tasks. If they talked of a child at all, they spoke of Arnaud.

One day, Bailey came home with Arnaud. "His mother and father are both sick, so I brought him home to be with us."

Margaret took the boy from the saddle and hugged him. "Arnaud, we can make pictures in the dirt, and you can help me pick the beans in the garden."

"I big now. I three," he said holding up his fingers.

Margaret looked up to her husband. "I decided to cook pea soup today with the last of the peas and it's a good thing I did! Arnaud likes pea soup. Don't you?"

The boy nodded with a grin and patted his belly.

Margaret took his hand. "Arnaud, I must go milk the cow. You come and help."

Bailey leaned over and touched her shoulder.

She looked up and saw a serious face on him.

He said, "Margaret, before you two rush away to the barn, I should tell you that Brother Cyrus Shepard died at the Mission. He had an abscessed knee. Dr. White had drained it several times, but it would not heal and became infected. He died of blood poisoning."

"Oh, dear me." Anguish flooded her face. "I never get to the Mission anymore. I had not heard he was ill. I am so busy all day with my chores." She wiped her palms on her apron and composed herself before taking Arnaud's little hand in hers. "Brother Shepard, without a doubt, would do anything to help at the Mission. He washed, baked, scoured, mended, and taught the native boys." She hesitated a moment. "I'm so busy with my new life that I never think about the Mission. It's like another life that is gone and forgotten."

What she said was true. Thoughts about the Methodist Mission were not a daily occurrence. Nor did she think about the promised made to Sawala.

"Willy, I never go worship. It seems so far now that the bridge is out. Why don't they mend that bridge?"

Bailey, still sitting on his horse, said. "Margaret, who do you mean by *they*? The first time someone needs to use the bridge for their crops or animals, it will be repaired. Not before."

"I guess I knew that."

Now Bailey turned his horse. "Let me get the horse fed. I'll come to the barn to help with your chores. I know I don't help enough. Maybe you can get down to worship this Sunday. Arnaud, don't drink all the milk before I get to the barn."

That evening after they had eaten and cleared the table, Margaret slipped a little wooden box off the top shelf. It was the box that had contained the bars of soap from her friends. Margaret had filled it with sand. She dribbled some water over the sand and put the box in front of Arnaud. She had cut a stick from a tree and placed it on top the sand. "Look, Arnaud, you can make pictures in the sand." With the stick, she made a circle with two eyes and a smile.

Arnaud looked up to her face. "Mar-gert, for me? I draw?" He heard English only when he was with the Baileys, and her name had too many syllables for him to pronounce.

Margaret was determined that he would learn to speak English well. Although he didn't yet know it, this was to be his first lesson. "Yes, I made this for you. Please call me Mar-Mar." She handed him the stick. "Be careful not to spill the sand or we'll have to go to the river to get more."

Arnaud's pudgy hand held the stick in a fist, and Margaret gently opened his fingers. "Here is how you hold the stick to make pictures." She slipped it between his thumb and index finger to make him hold it like a pen. "Now make a line. Go on!"

Bailey showed him that a pointed mountain with a line across it made an A for the first letter of his name. "Do it again, Arnaud."

The boy smoothed the sand to erase the jumble of lines and made another mountain. He made two little holes in the sand at the base of his mountain. "Mar-Mar, I make bear. See?"

Before his bedtime, he had made an X and an A as well as a mountain, an unrecognizable tree, and other designs.

After Margaret told him a story, Bailey placed the lynx fur next to him. "He likes to sleep with this."

The fur looked familiar to Margaret, but she didn't know where she had seen it. She decided perhaps in the Bugats' home. She had no memory of seeing it at the Mission. Back then, Sawala had rarely taken it outside or away from her bed. The Baileys did not notice the words "For My Son," that Sawala had written on it. And the Bugats could not read. Sawala's childlike scribbles remained a message undelivered.

In a few days, Dr. Bailey rode off to check on the Bugats. When he returned home, he reported that they were well enough to care for Arnaud, "Let's kill a chicken and take them some food."

"What a wonderful idea." Margaret fried the pieces of chicken. She and Arnaud then worked to make chicken soup with the bones; the boy cracked carrots into smaller pieces with his hands and dropped them into the pot. Laughing, they cried over slicing the onions before they threw them into the soup pot and ran to wash the smell from their hands. "Don't touch your face before we wash," she warned him. She fried pan bread; Arnaud dropped blackberries into the cakes while frying. They worked all afternoon preparing for the following day's trip.

At the Bugats and after a fine meal, Margaret took advantage of the situation. Mrs. Bugat was resting in her bed and Margaret asked, "I know some Kalapuyan words, can you teach me more? I would like to know all the months of the year and what they mean in English."

"Yes, I tell you, but I not know if we had words for all. We not have months, like you."

"Of course, but you have words for the seasons." Margaret used a piece of her precious paper to record what she heard. She wrote:

January – *t'saal an t'atsa* – burned breast. A time of cold when the old people sat too close to the fire and burned their breasts.

February – *tuuu pyan* – pretty near springtime.

March – *am plaatowa* – it buds out, like leaves and stems.

April – *pyan* (Mrs. Bugat could not remember the meaning.)

May – *pookwa am plaatowa* – time of flowers.

June had no translation.

July – *tu wilfo am meek wa* – half-summertime.

August – *tahapunaeq* – time to dig the camas root.

September had no translation.

October – *tin tan kwa* – hair falls out, like leaves fall from plants and trees.

November and December had no translation either.

Margaret exclaimed, "I knew *tin tan kwa* meant the fall of the year, but not what it meant literally. Oh, that's humorous that they call a time of year 'hair falls out.' If you ever remember more, please let me know."

With the comings and goings of missionaries and the many visitors to the Methodist Mission, news arrived more easily to the Mission than to the Bailey homestead. So in the fall of 1840, when the Baileys finally took a trip to the Mission, there were many surprises in store for them.

The Mission had changed since Margaret had left. Jason Lee had returned from the East on the ship *Lausanne*, bringing fifty-one people to work at the Mission. Only thirty-four were at the Mission the day Margaret and Bailey visited: twenty-six missionaries, three *Métis*, four Kalapuyans, and one Hawaiian.

The Baileys had tea with some of the new missionaries and heard many complaints about Jason Lee and his management. After tea and while they walked toward Dr. White's house, Margaret mentioned, "It's amazing all that has changed. And the Mission is moving away from here! I don't know where this new place is. What did they call it?"

"I think they called it Mission Mill. It is farther south, ten miles more or less. Although it is near the Willamette River, evidently it's a place that will not flood, like this one. It's the same place that Hoxie went. Remember Webley Hauxhurst with the gristmill? He has the nickname Hoxie."

She nodded. "I remember him, but I didn't know that he moved."

"He sold his mill last year to one of the McKays. Maybe I do remember; they call this new place Mill Creek. It's supposed to have a fine waterway for a mill."

"So Webley moved. Did you hear about all the trouble between Dr. White and Jason Lee?" asked Margaret.

"Some of it. Dr. White and Lee have had troubles from the moment the doctor arrived back in 'thirty-seven. But this! No, I heard today that they gave White a trial and found him guilty." Bailey snorted in disgust.

"Evidently the trial was only days ago." Margaret replied, "My goodness, embezzlement of church funds is serious! I wonder how White feels being expelled from the Methodist Church? Of course, this could not have happened if Lee had not brought another physician to replace him. Perhaps Lee planned all along to replace him. Did you meet this Dr. Ira Babcock?"

"Not yet."

They arrived at the Whites and listened to Dr. White's version. "They charged me with disobedience to the church's orders, dishonesty, and imprudent conduct. Lee wanted me out because I disagreed on how to spend money. I spent only to help the health of the Indians. While he was gone I made choices he didn't like. He has always wanted me out, and now he has done it."

Bailey looked forlorn. "Where will you go?"

"I'm determined to remove Lee as head of the Mission. I'll go back to the East and tell them the truth about Lee's incompetence. They held an official trial against me, just days ago. How dare he! We leave in a couple of days, on September fifteenth."

After dark, the Baileys started their trip back home, traveling slowly in the pleasant warm air. Bailey shook his head. "So many changes." He turned to look at his wife and inquired, "How did you feel when you heard that your two favorite missionaries, Willson and Leslie, were sent up to Puget Sound to start a branch mission?"

"I felt relief that they were no longer living here to gossip about me with the new missionaries. Willson and Leslie should be happy together.

Humph, one of the new women I spoke with today mentioned that Miss Chloe Clark refused to marry Willson, so he went to Puget Sound without a wife."

Bailey interrupted. "Now I remember what they call this new place where the Mission is relocating. It is Chemeketa Prairie. But it is also known as Mill Creek and Mission Mill."

The new Methodist Mission would later expand to become the city of Salem, Oregon. William Willson would create the street plan for Salem, and Jason Lee would build the first house in 1841. The following year, Lee would start a school for native children that would later become the first university west of the Mississippi River, Willamette University.

Jason Lee's House (first structure built in Salem, Oregon)
Built for Methodist Mission to house four families

Location today: Willamette Heritage Center at Mission Mill Museum

SALEM, OREGON

CHAPTER 11

LOVE AMID DEATH, SICKNESS, AND PAIN
End of 1840 through 1842

One morning, soon after the shipments of wedding gifts had arrived, Bailey awoke with an idea. "Margaret, I am going to do what you did and write letters to my medical friends in England, telling them about my medical profession and my needs. If I can elicit some interest, maybe I'll be surprised one day by the arrival of a box of medical supplies."

Margaret's face lit up. "Oh, Willy, I that would be wonderful."

"Wait, there's more. I want to build a two-bed hospital, like Dr. White's at the Mission. You help so much that you are like my nurse, but we shouldn't be using our home."

"Willy, we cannot afford to build a hospital!"

He sat up and leaned against the wooden headboard. "Just listen! I have figured it all out. For twenty dollars, anyone can have a membership in the hospital. If they cannot pay, they can cut down trees to give lumber or work building the hospital. What do you think?"

She leaned across the bed. "I think my husband is a resourceful and clever man. His only fault is that, because of all the sick people demanding his attentions, he spends too little time in bed with his wife."

"I am considered an expert for what is ailing you. Let me show you my remedy."

Their yellow curtains with pink rosebuds fluttered in the window and then blew out above the bed with a gust of wind. The day was pleasantly mild as so often happens before winter sets in. The Baileys kissed oblivious to the hundreds of Canada geese honking high above them.

Sure enough, months later a crate of surgical instruments and medicines arrived from Bailey's friends in England while he was constructing the hospital.

In 1840, Mrs. Marguerite died one night of diphtheria, leaving Joseph Gervais to grieve with six children – some grown to adulthood. At the funeral, the Baileys stood with rain dripping from their hats and rolling down their backs.

Bailey felt a great loss and remembered how Mrs. Marguerite attended to his tomahawk wound when he first arrived in the Willamette Valley. *And we spent a lot of time together, sharing healing herbs. She was a fine woman.* For the first time in years, Bailey's thoughts drifted to the little virgin Indian with the blonde hair; the girl Mrs. Marguerite had brought to him one evening. *What was her name? Ah, yes, Sawala.* It was a fond memory. *Sawala.*

Mrs. Marguerite had been Gervais's second wife and had bore four of his six children. He told the Baileys, "In Oregon Country, a man needs a woman." Within months, he married a third time to Marie Angelique who would give him one more child. "My new woman is Chinook."

Margaret got sick that winter. By January 1841, she was confined to bed for two weeks. She became despondent. Whenever her fever subsided, she would reach for her ink box. One such day, she wrote:

> Time flies and 'tis but little good I do in the world. Have been confined to my room with my husband my only attendant when he waits on me in the morning and late in the evening after he returns from seeing the sick. Poor man! He has a hard task riding in the rain and mud, cooking for himself when at home, and waiting on me.

Another day, she wrote a poem:

> I have no joy – how strange the tale –
> Though fed and housed in lovely dale;
> Tho' clothed, and blessed with husband true,
> And earthly wants remain but few.
>
> The birds, nor flowers, nor lovely sky;

Nor grass, nor grounds, nor stars on high;
Nor sin, nor saints, me ease can give
While such a useless life I live.

While Margaret was bedridden, a French Canadian neighbor came each morning to feed their animals and milk the cow. She let him take most of the milk home in payment for his help. Bailey locked the house each day when he left, not trusting this particular man, and told Margaret, "He keeps several native women at his place. I think they all serve as his wives, so I'm not taking any chances with you becoming one of his conquests."

Late one day, when Margaret felt stronger, she wanted some milk, so she dressed and went to the barn. While milking, she heard hoof beats and a wagon approaching. Peering out the barn door, she saw Ewing Young riding up in a wagon with one horse pulling and two horses hitched behind. She walked out to greet him.

"Ewing Young, I haven't seen you in so long. Glad you came by. Tie up over at the water trough and help yourself to some feed for the horses. I shall put on the kettle."

"Thanks, Mrs. Bailey. Be right in. Is William around?"

Feeling dizzy from her exertion, she turned at the door to her house, set the pail of milk down, and leaned against the doorjamb. "No, he is still out with patients. Come in and we can talk."

Ewing didn't smile and pulled at the reins in an undecided manner. The horse sashayed this way and that. "When do you think he'll be back?"

But Margaret had gone inside and didn't hear his question. She needed to sit and rest. Ewing took a few minutes outside before he came in. She ended her rest and reached for the cups and saucers. The sugar and tin with tea were on the table. "I have some pan bread from last night that I'm going to heat. If you are hungrier, I can fry some eggs."

Ewing looked strange to her – worried or haggard.

He flopped in a chair without taking off his coat and then stood to remove it, placing it on a bench to one side of the table. He sighed, "Tea and bread is enough. I need to talk to Bailey. When do you think he'll be here?"

"I never know if he'll come at sundown or midnight. Depends on how sick his patients are. Can I help you?" She sprinkled some tea into her teapot and went to the hearth for the kettle of hot water. Instantly, the aroma of delicious English tea filled the room. "This is tea my mother sent us as a wedding gift."

Ewing didn't seem to hear. He rubbed his forehead before looking up and saying, "Listen, I want to give this wagon to you and Bailey for a wedding gift. I owe him the two horses, too. And I left the whip in the wagon. Bailey always admired that whip. I brought it up from Mexico. The Mexicans know how to make all these designs in leather, and they stained the leather in colors. It's beautiful."

Surprised, Margaret stood to look out the window at the gifts. "Mr. Young, that's too generous of you. But, heaven knows, we sure could use a wagon. My Willy tried to borrow one the other day and our fool of a neighbor told him that one of the wheels belonged to someone else so he needed to ask the other owner before lending it out. Can you believe that?"

Again, Ewing didn't respond. He stood and looked like he hadn't heard.

"Mr. Young, are you all right?"

"I'm going to look to see if he's coming." He went to the door. "While the tea steeps, I'm going to put your two horses in the barn. Is there room?" Before she had a chance to answer, he repeated, "I'm going to put your two horses in the barn. I'll be back."

Margaret got out some jam, a mix of blackberries and salmon berries, that she had made when the wild berries were ripe last fall. Ewing was taking a long time. She walked to the window and didn't see him, so she slipped a capote over her shoulders and went to the barn.

The two horses were in a stall eating feed, and Ewing was sitting on the milking stool. Margaret went to him and put her hand on his shoulder. "What's wrong?"

"Not much. I felt a bit lightheaded and thought I'd sit a spell."

Margaret pulled up a wooden box and sat next to him. "I'm tired, too. I'll sit with you."

Ewing gazed out at nothing in particular and murmured, "I was sitting here remembering a cold, dark night when Bailey and me went out to raise money for the cattle run to California. We came upon this squaw. He ever tell you 'bout that night?"

Margaret searched her mind for what he meant and answered him, "No, I don't think so."

"What a night! In the distance, we saw her with unbraided black hair flying in the wind. She was ready to crush the head of this baby. Guess it was hers. We heard the baby screaming, and we came to a dead stop right in front of the huge boulder holding the naked babe. Holding that large flat stone above her head, she stood with a look of surprise. Then she screamed, heaved the stone away, and ran. Bailey got down and put the baby inside his shirt, directly against his skin to warm him. The little boy was all covered with blood from his birth." He stopped and turned to Margaret. "You ain't heard this story from Bailey?"

She shook her head, too amazed to speak.

Ewing turned to gaze into the distance again and continued, "We never found the squaw, and so we took the baby boy to these people. I forget their name. He's an old retired fur trader named Bu, Bu, something."

"Bugat?"

"Yeah, that's the name. So you do know this story."

Margaret shook her head and said, "No, this is the first time I heard it. I do know the little boy, and Willy told me he would tell me this story, but I forgot to ask."

Ewing got up. "I think I better be going. I want to get down to Hoxie's place before dark."

"That's down by the Mission's new location, right?"

He stood and headed outside. "Yeah. Sorry I troubled you to make tea."

Margaret walked by his side. "No trouble at all. But Willy won't be happy that he missed you."

Adding to his unusual behavior, Ewing turned and hugged Margaret – something he had never done. Getting into the saddle, he said, "Tell Bailey I was here," and he rode away.

Margaret stood watching him disappear and wondered what was wrong with him. *I'm exhausted. This was more walking and talking than I've done in a couple of weeks.* And the surprise of hearing Arnaud's story took more of her energy. *I need to drink some milk and go back to bed.*

When Bailey got home, a couple of hours later, he was irritated, "You should have made Ewing wait for me."

"Willy, I never know when you're going to be here."

"I've been coming home early since you've been sick. You should've kept him here."

Confused, Margaret asked, "Is there something I don't know? Why is it so important to see Ewing tonight?"

"I don't know. I haven't seen him in a long time, and now he's gone."

Now Margaret felt irritated, "There's something you're not telling me. In fact, Ewing told me the story of you finding baby Arnaud. Why didn't you ever tell me that story?"

"I told you a long time ago."

"No, you didn't!"

Now Bailey was angry and shouted, "You calling me a liar or something?"

She sat up in bed, staring at him in silence. The wind was whistling and knocking something against the porch. It went thump, thump, thump, then it would stop for a time. A minute passed and the thump, thump, thump occurred again.

They both stared at the other.

He turned to go see. "Damn it! What's out there making that noise?"

"Don't you walk away from me," she insisted. "We aren't finished." She raised her voice and hands to shake at him, "You are so factious!"

He stopped abruptly in the doorway, as if he had bumped into the wall, and turned. "And you, my dear, are captious. Extremely captious! It can drive me crazy!"

Silence held sway while they tried to outstare the other.

She broke the quiet, "You exasperate me so much of the time!"

Without hesitation, he answered, "You exaggerate so many things!"

Margaret whispered, "You are too arrogant."

His body tensed as he answered, "You are too intelligent for your own good."

She sat up straighter in the bed and suppressed a smile. "If you weren't so diligent and fair, you wouldn't work so hard."

His muscles relaxed. "If you weren't so militant with beautiful hair, I'd stay mad at you."

Now she could not hide her growing smile. "That makes no sense."

He grinned. "That may be so. But if you want to talk about sense," he hesitated. "All my senses love what I see, smell, touch," he was walking to the bed, "and especially taste. Yes, I love your taste." With his knee on the bed, he gently rolled onto the bed, pulling her into his arms with a kiss.

Afterwards, while they remained in a tangle together, he said, "I heard that Ewing was sick. That's what I didn't tell you. I'm going to ride down there."

"Oh, stay. You can go tomorrow. Please. Dr. Babcock is there and can care for him."

The next morning, Bailey rode south toward Mission Mill. He filled the trip with his memories – all his times with Ewing. He remembered how he had hated him down in California when he lost the surgeon job because Ewing had lied about him. He thought about suturing Ewing's leg wound, his first surgery in Oregon. He recalled the time Ewing helped deliver the Bugats' dead baby, and how they delivered a live one to them. He savored that story for quite a while, thinking of little Arnaud. When his mind returned to his many adventures with Ewing Young, he gritted his teeth replaying the scene with Ewing yelling at him for shooting that innocent Indian on the cattle drive. "When am I going to get there?" he screamed to the tall firs. "How can this be only ten miles? Surely it is more!"

When Bailey found his friend, he was too late. Bailey stood at the front door of Jason Lee's house, where Ewing had died, and asked, "How?"

He was told that Ewing "just died."

Bailey left, and it wasn't long before someone offered him a drink. He had not drunk liquor since the cattle run from California. Before long, he had another and another. By the end of the day, he had started a fistfight with a stranger, broke a glass window in Jason Lee's house, and was chased away from the Methodist Mission by angry missionaries. Then he wandered off toward the Kalapuyans who were sleeping nearby in lean-tos. He fell to sleep with the natives.

Margaret worried about him on and off throughout the day, but she was too sick to get out of bed and slept most the day. She awakened once and remembered Ewing's story of the baby ready to be crushed on a boulder. When she slept again her thoughts changed into delirious dreams with the rock falling on the child's head and blood flying in droplets up toward the trees and sky. The blood-red skies became a sunset with a black-haired woman running, silhouetted against the horizon and screaming, *"t'saal an t'atsa"* until suddenly the woman's chest burst into flames. Margaret awoke in a sweat.

She couldn't get Ewing's story out of her mind.

At times, the fever subsided and she reflected on Ewing's story with clarity, wondering about Sawala. *Was Sawala there? How did she know this story of the baby Arnaud being found by Willy and Ewing? Ewing didn't say it was snowing. I should have asked him. But little Sally Soule may have been delirious when she told me that she was the mother. Ewing described a squaw with unbraided black hair, not a little blonde-headed girl. I am so confused and tired. And where is Willy?*

The day faded and she had no idea how much time had passed. She didn't know if it was the evening or the middle of the night, for the sky darkened early in February. Once she struggled to the chamber pot, thinking she felt the need to urinate, but not much was released from her dehydrated body. *Willy said I must drink, but I have no cup of water here.* A drink was too difficult to obtain, for she couldn't get herself out of bed again in the cold, fireless house. Eventually, she fell asleep.

Bailey awoke at dawn under a tree, soaked inside from the booze and outside from the February rain. He rolled over and found his horse munching grass a few feet away. "What luck! You didn't run home. Shit! My head hurts!" His hat was filled with rainwater and sat by his side. He stood with the help of the tree trunk, and then leaned against the tree while he poured the water out of his hat. When he put the hat on his head, he remembered Margaret being so sick. He stumbled to his horse and quickly rode back north to his cabin.

Upon his arrival home, his head felt heavy with pain, but he slipped from his horse and rushed to the door. It was locked and he couldn't find his key. "Margaret," he called and went to the bedroom window and climbed in, busting the deerskin covering when he fell to the floor.

Margaret turned over in the bed and screamed.

"It's me! It's just me." Bailey crawled on his knees with his shoulder throbbing from the fall. Standing, he rubbed his upper arm, leaned over the bed, and climbed in. Reaching for her, he said, "Margaret, I feared you were dead." He buried his head in her soft breasts and felt her fever; she was burning up. She was so hot that he sobered. "Margaret, I must cool you down."

Struggling to push him away, Margaret managed a grimace and in a weak voice said, "You stink! Willy, you're drunk! You reek of spirits. Please take the bar of soap and go wash." She placed her hand to her chest. A deep pain surged, but she said nothing.

He went to the wooden water pail and soaked a small cloth, placing it on her forehead before he took the pail outside. Stripping off his clothes, he nearly fell. "Damn, I'm still drunk!" So he sat on the porch step to finish the removal of his pants. Once naked, he poured half the water over his head and began to soap up from head to toes. "I'm icing up!" He emptied the bucket to rinse and realized he had no towel. Leaving the pile of stinking clothes on the porch, he rushed in, dried himself, and slipped into bed with Margaret. Pulling her burning fevered body to his, he held her. "This is the doctor's remedy to cool you down," he said between kisses to her forehead, cheeks, nose, and eyelids. Sleep, my sweet. And forgive me." They slept in each other's arms.

Fearing to upset Margaret with the news of Ewing's death, days passed while he waited for her to get better.

When he finally told her, she covered her mouth with the back of her hand. "No, oh no, Willy! He looked strange when I saw him, but I had no idea he was near death. He must have known, because he brought us our wedding gift and the two horses he owed you."

"We'll never know if he knew. But one thing is sure, I am grateful he settled up what he owed me – those horses. Did you realize that he was one of the richer settlers here?"

"How did he get so rich, and we aren't?" She gave Bailey a little push in his side with her finger. "Are you hiding some of our riches?"

"Let me finish. You are joking with me; you know Ewing owns more than us. He has the gristmill and sawmill. He had horses when he first came and then cattle from our run. I had no money to invest. But what you don't know is that he was a rich man before he came here. He was married to a woman named Maria down near Mexico where he made lots of money."

"Really? You never told me."

Bailey brightened, "Now I remember what I needed to tell you. Ewing didn't leave a will and has no kin around here. This is a problem, because there are no laws on how to handle his estate. Dr. Babcock was assigned as judge to determine what to do with all his debts, the money owed to him, and his assets. So everyone is saying that we need some laws written for Oregon. When you fell asleep early last night, I went to a meeting, and they elected me chairman of a committee to form a constitution and code of laws for our community."

"Willy, that's wonderful! Well, maybe it's not so wonderful. It's more work and time away from our home. Well, we can have the meetings here."

But for the time being, nothing came of the committee.

Margaret got better with the spring weather, but not completely well. The hospital was finished not too far from their house, and Margaret's life became busier. Besides the care of her garden, animals, and home, when Bailey was making calls somewhere in the French Prairie, she took care of the sick in the hospital.

She lamented that the Mission's new location was so much farther away. For fifteen months she had not received the Lord's Supper on the Sabbath. One Sunday, she tried to attend church by driving alone in the wagon. She had to stop and lie down twice to recover her strength. *Will I ever get well?* Finally, she went no farther and returned home.

One month in the summer, Bailey came home with a little French girl who had suffered ill treatment from her aunt. The young girl had a dreadful contusion on her head and forehead, besides a broken collarbone.

Before Dr. Bailey would even take her into the hospital, he sat the thin girl in the yard and asked Margaret to cut her hair.

"She's in pain and needs to be in bed, Willy."

Exhausted and needing sleep, he explained, "Yes, well, she has lice. Actually don't cut her hair. Get my shaving blade. Shave her head and wash all of her with lye soap. I must go sleep for an hour or two. Another thing, I asked Monsieur Quesnal to bring his sick wife here, but I told him that he is to take care of her. He will feed her, change her clothes, take her to relieve herself, and do whatever else she needs. Not you! You have enough work. They will arrive soon." Bailey went inside to sleep.

Alone in the front yard among the flower garden and a goat nibbling some of the blooms, Margaret spoke gently to the French girl, trying to explain, "I want to remove all your clothes and wash you before the Frenchman arrives with his wife. You can wear my cotton nightgown while I boil all your clothes. But first, I have to cut away all your hair to get rid of the vermin." They spoke together in Chinook Jargon.

The girl began to cry.

As she watched the girl's long brown hair slip down her naked body and fall to the ground, Margaret was grateful for the warm day. Wounds on her back, one breast, and a shoulder made the task more difficult. One wound on her right thigh was recent and began to bleed when Margaret washed her. The girl stood shivering from fear in the beautiful yard of flowers. Margaret kept talking, but kind words and pink hydrangeas could not assuage the French girl's past torments. Her name was Angeline.

Later, Margaret took two bowls to the hospital. She always had soup cooking on the hearth in their cabin to feed the patients. She had to spoon-feed Angeline. Monsieur Quesnal was feeding his wife Marie Tchalis who rested in the next cot. No one spoke.

That evening Margaret asked, "Willy, what happened to Angeline's fingernails and toenails? They look like they are nearly torn off. How could that have happened?"

Bailey took a bite and spoke with his mouth full. "I saw her fingernails and thought she bit them. With her shoes on, I didn't see her feet." He put down his spoon. "Margaret, I cannot describe the hateful and dirty conditions of her life with her aunt. I cannot guess what happened." He put his elbows on the table and let his head fall into his hands. "Sorry, Margaret, I'm not too hungry. I think I'll go check on my patients."

"I'm coming, too."

Within two days, Margaret realized that Angeline needed constant care, so they moved her into their house for convenience. Margaret talked with her about God and the afterlife. The girl listened, but rarely spoke, and never smiled.

A day later, Monsieur Quesnal's wife died, and they arranged for her burial in St. Paul. A few friends came to follow the cart that carried the corpse to the cemetery. As Margaret walked, she remembered going to Quesnal's home years ago to get the table he had made for them. She reached for her handkerchief in the reticule tied to her waist, but before a tear came to her eyes, two of the men in the procession of six persons stopped to look at the wheat in the field, and anger grabbed her. Those men remained behind hanging over the fence and looking at the crop. They never arrived at the gravesite.

Margaret thought. *This shows what the overriding passion is here in Oregon. People value crops more than they do other people.*

With the end of summer came the end of Angeline's life. They buried her not far from their house. No one came to her burial. Margaret read aloud from the Bible and silently hoped that Angeline made it to heaven to be among the angels.

By the start of the fall, Margaret went to bed again with her sickness deep in her lungs.

Bailey said frequently, "Margaret, this cool damp weather is keeping you ill. We should return to the States. Nothing here is so important. I can't lose you."

"Willy, I do not want to go. My heart is knit to these people, although I do so little to help them. How gladly I would like to spend a long life here and bring them to God."

So they put off the idea of leaving for the time being.

During this period of death and illness, the Baileys found their joy in Arnaud. When they had not been to visit the Bugats in a while, the Bugats came to see them.

Sitting around the table having tea, Mrs. Bugat told them, "Arnaud miss you. He talk about you all the time." Margaret excused herself and went to her bed to rest.

The boy was prone on his belly near the hearth with his sand box and stick. "I'm almost five. How I make five?"

Bailey sat on the floor next to the boy. He moved the boy's hand and made a five in the sand. "Now make your name like you did last time you were here." Bailey turned to the Bugats to mention, "He's learning to read and write. Did he tell you?"

"Yes, and he go out for leaves and make them flat, too."

From her bed, Margaret had a direct view of the table and hearth. She called out, "Willy, are you teaching him to collect leaves?"

Bailey said a simple, "Yes," but she saw the pride in his face. After all their time together, they knew each other well, inferring meaning from the other's looks. "I gave him that old English magazine for the leaves." Bailey asked Arnaud, "Did you find something to press the pages and leaves flat?"

Arnaud, concentrating on writing in the sandbox, answered, "Yes." He asked, "Dr. Bailey, is this right for the letter 'd' or is it backwards?"

"It's backwards."

The boy smoothed the sand over his mistake and continued writing A-R-N-A-U-D.

Bailey smiled at the finished name, "Show Mar-Mar and then we can go to the hospital. I'll show you how to hear our hearts beating."

As Christmas of 1841 approached, the weather was unusually dry and warm, and Margaret felt better. She and Arnaud decided to decorate the house and surprise Bailey. They gathered colored berries, strung them on thread, and draped them across the windows. Using an old magazine, they tore out sheets, folded them, and cut snowflakes to hang from the rafters. They cooked hasty pudding with cornmeal, poured it into teacups when it was a hot porridge consistency, and made it festive by sprinkling sugar and cinnamon on top.

Margaret saved the best activity until last; they made sugar candy by pouring sugar in the iron skillet. They cooked it until it was a thick brown liquid. "Now I'll use a spoon and make shapes on this tin sheet. Arnaud, this is really hot and can burn you, so don't get close while I pour. Look, I made a snowman. Quick, now drop the kernels of wheat where his eyes go. And make a mouth, but don't touch the candy. It is still hot."

When he finished with the snowman, he exclaimed, "Make another turtle, they look good!"

"Yes, the turtle shape is the best. The ears on the rabbits will probably break when we pick them up. Guess we'll have to eat those broken ears." They giggled.

"Will you make me some sugar candy for my birthday next month?"

"Of course," she said.

But she wasn't able to. She got sick again.

The pain in her chest increased. Bailey urged that they travel back East for her health. Again, Margaret refused to commit to this plan and prayed to get well.

While Margaret rested in bed trying to recover during February in the winter of 1842, Bailey came in from his doctoring and told her, "Mrs. Leslie died."

"Willy, no! They have five girls who need a mother. She was the only true Christian I have known here in Oregon. I guess you knew that she was sick before they came here. Did she have consumption?"

He seemed weary, thinner, and sad. He sat on the side of the bed. "Margaret, I don't know. I never examined her, but I think she did."

"Willy, tell me true. Do I have consumption? Am I going to die soon?"

He pulled her to his chest and hugged. "I don't know. But I am sick with worry. At least you are not losing weight and are not spitting up blood. Margaret, please let's go back to the East and get you well. I think you need a dryer climate and some rest. This farm makes you work too hard. Please."

She looked at his pleading eyes, "All right. This summer."

"Promise me. You and I know that you get better from time to time, especially in the summer. Even if you are feeling better, promise me that we'll go."

"But, Willy, your practice and all my work on our farm!"

"Margaret, we are talking about your life. Promise me!"

"I promise."

By spring she felt better than she had in a long time, but they continued their plans for a summer journey to Boston. Gradually, they began to sell animals and possessions, not knowing if they would ever return.

She lamented one day upon hearing some news, "A literary and debating society called the Oregon Lyceum is being formed. Oh, Willy, I regret that we'll not be here to join. They will discuss literature and scientific pursuits; it is perfect for us."

"Yes, I heard. I don't know if they would welcome a woman into their midst."

"Well, I talked to the man in charge, Mr. Robert Newell, who also is the director of the Oregon Printing Association. I discussed the book I am reading, *The Shortest Way of Ending Disputes about Religion*, by Manning. Since there is agitation between the Catholics and Methodists here, he agreed that all should read this book. And he asked that I send him some of my poetry. He was very encouraging about my writing."

Bailey responded, "We must bring back more books and reading material for us to share with others. All of our reading material is so old. You have been reading and rereading the *Methodist Preacher Periodical* from 1832. I let you cut up all my old magazines with Arnaud," he hesitated because they knew they might not return. That would mean he would never see Arnaud again. Without finishing his sentence, he walked outside. *Margaret must be well for us to have any future plans.*

Before long, Margaret sent her poem *Indian Missions* to Robert Newell in hopes of some recognition. As she folded the sheet and wrote the address on the back of the paper, she recalled the day she had given this same poem to Willy, years ago. With that memory, her skin rippled and a warm sensation passed from her head to her toes.

Physically Margaret felt better and had energy to make love. One afternoon after sweet intercourse, she jumped from the bed and reached for her clothes.

With a gentle touch, he held her arm. "Use the chamber pot and don't hurry away. I want to relax with you and hold you longer."

"I'll be back quickly. I must go douche." As soon as she said it, she regretted her words. He looked puzzled, "Why do you have to douche?"

She climbed back onto the bed, crouched on her knees, and took his hands. "I am not ready for children. I need to be healthy and want to teach the natives about God. And I desire to write a book."

He began to laugh a belly-busting laugh. "Have you learned a way to stop pregnancy that no one in the medical profession knows?"

Puzzled, Margaret stood. "I have been douching with vinegar for years and have not gotten pregnant. You must know about douching with vinegar."

Turning on his side in the bed, he doubled over with his knees to his chest and continued his laughter. "I should have wondered where all the vinegar went because we never had any gherkins on the table." His eyes watered and his laughter continued until, like the end of the play when the curtain comes down and the actor ends the forced guffaws of the scene, Bailey's laughter stopped abruptly. The humor of the situation vanished in an instant and he froze.

Margaret saw his face fill with anguish. "What's wrong?"

Her statement echoed in his mind: I have been douching with vinegar for years and have not gotten pregnant.

Suddenly, he realized that Margaret was oblivious to the underlying meaning of her words. He rambled, "I have been so busy. We never talked. I was waiting for the day when you would say our child was coming." He ran his hand through his hair. "It's not that I sit and think of having children." He hesitated. "Well, maybe on a ride home in the dark." He stopped and looked at her. His voice cracked, "How could I not realize? You told me you've known other men besides Willson. Have you? I mean, have you ever lost," with that unfinished sentence, he frowned and looked away.

"What do you mean?"

Swallowing, he cleared his throat, to explain, "Margaret, douching with vinegar is only to clean the vagina. Nothing more."

Her eyes widened, and she repeated, "What do you mean?"

"I mean that douching with vinegar does not stop pregnancies. I want to know have you ever been pregnant?"

"How insulting!" She huffed, "No!"

"Never had a natural abortion? What I'm asking is have ever lost a fetus?"

"Willy, why are you asking all this?" The indignant look on her face changed to a frantic one, and she gasped, "You think I cannot have a child?"

The curtain dropped and the first act of their life together came to an end.

William Bailey had always been filled with elation whenever he rode on his horse in Oregon. He enjoyed letting his eyes sweep across the prairie to see the abundance of flora and feeling the refreshing rain upon his face. He never thought he would leave.

Gradually, his mind stopped seeing the terrain when he rode; he shifted to thoughts of next winter, when Margaret would be bedridden again, sick and coughing, too tired to stand or walk, and hot with fever for days. At those times, he remembered the death of his forty-year-old friend Ewing, a man too young to die, and he realized he could lose Margaret, too.

He became despondent. Day in and day out, with his conflicting feelings and sadness, he began to dwell on another burden – the likelihood of never having children.

He started to spend many hours drinking.

Margaret had stopped douching, and as the months passed with no pregnancy she slowly came to the same realization, that she could have no children.

She started to spend many hours trying to accept herself – a different person than before. All her life she had thought that she could teach the native people about the Lord, make a man happy if he was the right man, and have a child when she was ready. She was no longer that woman.

One evening, when Bailey arrived home after seeing patients in their homes, Margaret saw that he had been tipping the bottle.

Margaret was furious. "If you think I am going to put up with you coming home drunk, you are wrong. You can serve your own dinner. I am going to write in my journal." She went to the bedroom and returned with her ink box. She placed it on the table and reached behind her back to untie her apron.

Bailey swayed in the same spot where he had been when she left the room, near the open front door. But now he moved with speed and without words. He rushed to the table and picked up the ink box. Raising it above his head, he hurled it across the room and against the wall. As it hit, the box shattered, sending splinters of wood, nibs, and ink bottles flying. Not satisfied with his destruction, he walked over to the mess on the floor – ink dripped from one uncorked bottle – and smashed with his heel any object he saw. He crushed the nibs and the wooden holders, flattened the sealing wax, and cracked the blotter to pieces before going outside to his flask on the porch table. He emptied it in one swallow.

Through the crashing, crunching, and pounding, Margaret had whimpered in fear. After he went outside, she sobbed into her hands. When she had the strength to face it, she kneeled in the debris, looking for anything not broken. *I hate him! I hate him!* She found one ink bottle under a chair – unbroken and still full of the blue ink – the penknife and paper was still in the closed slim drawer that had not opened. *He purposely destroyed my favorite object. Maybe he hates me because I can't have children.* Suddenly she stopped. Her hands wiped away the tears. *One should not covet anything as much as I did this ink box.* She inhaled deeply and began to calm herself, whispering, "I can make quills from goose feathers. I still have my pen knife to cut the points." And she told herself, "I'll go to the Bugats and ask for some big feathers from their goose." She gathered the wooden scraps scattered everywhere and saw that the ink box was beyond repair. Her nose dripped, and she could no longer stop the tears from overflowing. *I should not cry over spilled milk.*

The next day he had a hangover but was sober; he begged her forgiveness. He promised that nothing like this would ever happen again. He cried, and she cried. Soon they were making love.

But his promise would go unfulfilled.

One Sunday in the summer, Margaret went alone in the wagon to the

Mission for the Sabbath. Upon her return, she found Willy sitting outside on the porch with a bottle on the table again. Several crows were complaining with their *caaws* and other *squawks* as she pulled the horse to a stop in front of Bailey. She asked, "Will you get the harness off the horse? If you do, I can start our meal." Just then, a red-tailed hawk took off from the top of a fir tree, spreading and flashing the cinnamon tail as it circled overhead and flew away. Looking up at the bird, Margaret shaded her eyes and watched it disappear to the west.

Bailey stood weaving, and leaned on the table as she passed into the house. Raising his arm to take a swig, he fell against the house and sat back down.

Margaret removed her bonnet and rubbed her forehead, murmuring, "If only I could fly off to the west, like a bird, away from our disagreements." She didn't want to start an argument. Changing from her silk Sunday dress, she lamented. *And I don't want to anger him like I did the time he threw my ink box.* She glanced out the window while tying her apron. He was coming back from the barn with his whip, the beautiful Mexican whip that Ewing had given to him. As he walked, he snapped it in the air, he snapped it under a tree, and when he reached the porch he snapped it against the logs on the house. Margaret jumped at the loud sound it made, hitting the wood. CRACK!

Not wanting an encounter, she busied herself at the hearth. She kept hearing the snap of the whip or the crack when it hit something. She gave a little start when it hit the house again. Then she noticed the sound was farther away and glanced out the window. She saw Willy practicing by whipping the heads off her flowers. His efforts were precise; the pink, blue, and yellow petals flew. She hurried with the preparation of the meal, knowing that food would be sobering for him.

Carrying the two plates of hotcakes with a dollop of jam on top, she went out to the porch. She placed their plates on the table before reaching for his bottle of booze. Wanting to hide the glass flask, she started to set it on the floorboards by her chair, but out of the corner of her eye she saw him approaching.

Snap! The whip snapped in the air.

"What are you doing with my bottle, Margaret?"

Snap!

"Here, give it to me," he insisted with an outstretched hand. He let the whip in his other hand coil through the air again.

Snap!

Standing at the edge of the porch, Margaret turned the bottle upside down, and with a protruding lower lip, she said, "No! I can never hand the spirits to you to drink." With both her hands she held the slim bottle with the vile, brown liquid spilling to the dirt between her petunias.

CRACK!

Events seemed to happen in the wrong order for Margaret. Her mind could not grasp what she saw. A red liquid was falling with the brown liquor! She felt the hot sting of pain and saw the black tip of the whip as it flipped off her hands. And then she saw two slits across the backs of her hands opening wider with blood gushing from them. She dropped the glass flask covered in her red blood and watched it fall among her red petunias. Before she fainted, she wondered if the petunias were really red or if her blood had stained them.

I've heard it said you're quarrelsome:
Of this I've not a doubt!
And so is fire – when water's thrown
On it – to put it out.

Display of old store in Champoeg State Heritage Area

CHAPTER 12

GOING IN CIRCLES
1842-1846

Margaret pondered. *Isn't forgiveness a part of being married?* She sat next to her Willy in a bateau on the way to Fort Vancouver, where they would board a ship to the Sandwich Islands. From there, they would continue south around Cape Horn to the east coast of the United States.

Her bandaged hands were covered in her nicest pair of gloves. She gently ran her fingers over the scabbed area; it was itching. *Willy said it is healing when it begins to itch. He has been so attentive and loving since that incident.* She shook her head and sighed. *I married two men – one is a devoted husband and doctor, the other is a demon who explodes from nowhere once he starts to drink.* Reflecting on his two outbursts, Margaret was not sure. *Which hurt me more: the breaking of my ink box or his whipping my hands?* Gradually, the beauty of nature distracted her, and she let the river and the flora along the banks soothe her mind. She did not want to leave Oregon, either.

Margaret had two sides as well. The Margaret living on the French Prairie, alone with nature and her farm, was a different person than the woman she had been at the Mission and while traveling on vessels. When she was among many other personalities, her captious nature oozed out. On her sailing trip in 1837, she had been testy and rash, stubborn and faultfinding of Mr. Leslie. And she had been a recluse.

Now it was 1842 and the hand of fate dealt Margaret a losing set of cards again. When the Baileys arrived at Fort Vancouver, they learned that Mr. Leslie and two other families from the Mission were to be their traveling companions aboard the ship.

Once they sailed, the other passengers avoided Margaret. She told Willy, "I spoke with a woman today to introduce myself. She stood up and walked away, saying nothing. Willy, it has been years since I had to face the accusations of being a maniac or a woman of loose morals."

"Margaret, you're strong. Ignore them." Bailey laughed, "A stranger was talking with me on the aft deck, not knowing whom I was, and he nodded in your direction to tell me that you were a troublemaker." Recollecting the incident, Bailey laughed some more, "That's when I let him know that I was well aware of your character and had much experience dealing with you. He looked puzzled until I told him that you were my wife."

Margaret frowned and did not see the humor.

Bailey continued, "He turned as red as a lobster in boiling water. He knew he was in hot water and excused himself, stammering an apology. He admitted that it was nothing more than hearsay and gossip." Bailey pulled Margaret to him for a hug. "I can't stop laughing at the memory of his face. Come on, you are strong. More important, you are not a hypocrite as they are." They were standing in their stateroom with low ceilings and little round windows. He tilted her chin upward and kissed her. "This is the time to record all these incidents for your book. It might hurt right now, but it will make good reading some day."

"Oh, Willy, what were the chances that I would be on a ship again with Mr. Leslie? I hear he is taking his two older daughters to Oahu to go to school. Without his loving wife to tame his tongue, I am in for a long and hateful trip. Poor Mrs. Leslie, may God rest her soul." Margaret spent a lot of time in their cabin and wrote one evening in her journal:

Three sly, slandering, venom-tipped tongues on board, with which I as much dread to come in contact as with the poison of asps. With the character of two I have been acquainted in former days, and another soon discovered itself to be of the same woof, by stinging in my presence the fair reputation of some with whom I happened to be acquainted.

Bailey enjoyed approaching anyone and everyone, even those enemies of Margaret, and starting conversations. His gregarious nature attracted people to gather around him. When he told stories, laughter followed. Most times, if Margaret appeared on deck, he went to her side and everyone would casually disperse.

Before they arrived at the Sandwich Islands, they missed Oregon so greatly that they talked of returning. Once at Oahu, they found another ship leaving by way of Tahiti. "Let's take it to avoid those disagreeable missionaries."

Margaret was grateful for his idea. "Listen Willy, once we are in Tahiti you could go back to Oregon while I continue. I see that you miss Oregon so much. When I am well, I'll return to Oregon to be with you." So they changed their original plans and separated; Bailey put Margaret on a ship for the Boston.

Once at sea, she noticed less pain in her chest. She concluded that the weeks on Oahu and Tahiti in the warm and fresh air had allowed her to start healing. But she had a new pain, one she had never felt; she missed Willy. They had not been separated like this since they were married. She wrote letter after letter to him:

My dear husband: Although we have been separated but two days, I would rather see you this evening than any other person of whom I think. I am quite unhappy.

And another day, she wrote again:

Dear W. J., how I wish I could see you and, instead of writing, tell you what I would like to express ...

Oh, it begins to hail and greatly darkens my sky-light, so good-night. I must again go lonely to bed, when I should be so happy to sleep in your arms. God bless you my dear, dear husband! If any person breaks the seal of this letter who has no right to do, let him or her consider it is written from a wife to her husband, and therefore all expressions therein contained are lawful.

Dearest;
Although we have had a very good passage thus far, time passes slowly, and the remaining two months, which must elapse before I reach Boston, seems like a long time in anticipation.

I think that going to sea alone must produce a bad effect upon the memory – perhaps good, I should say – as I have forgotten all the causes of disquietude that ever existed between us, and I can only think of your kindness and love – which recollections afford me much pleasure.

I am almost constantly brooding over the unwelcome thought that some unforeseen event will prevent us from meeting again in Oregon, and am most anxious to reach the United States that I may hear from you in a letter via Java.

Margaret had six weeks with her family and no letters from her husband. She worried what could have happened until word came that he was in New York. He had followed her on the first boat possible, not wanting to return to Oregon Country without her. She said goodbye to her family in the Boston area and went to be with him and his family in New York.

On their first night in bed together in months, Margaret told him, "Your mother said that she had thought she would never see you again in her lifetime. I feared the same. I don't want to be away from you again."

He examined her. "I hear no problems in your lungs. I think you're well." He raised himself on an elbow and leaned over to face her, "But I should clarify my first examination and listen again. Please remove all your clothes."

She grinned and obliged the doctor.

They decided to return to Oregon as quickly as possible.

Confined during the seven-month journey back to Oregon on a ship with no garden or animals to fill her time, Margaret became melancholy and prone to exaggerate her problems. Her only outlet was her pen. She wrote:

EVENING NODS

To bed to bed, I go,
Kind place for secret woe;
And here I weep, and sometimes sleep,
Till morn doth peep up o'er the deep;
And ope my eyes to view the skies,

While o'er them hies such beauteous dyes
As charms my soul within me;
Then sleep must go, and whining too,
And sorrows which do sting me.

Life speed, life speed away;
And come, thou perfect day,
When shall begin life free from sin,
And all within my God shall win –
And all I do be offered through
His love most true who died for you
And I – who reads believes me;
O! glorious hour bring near thy power –
Lord, let me cease to grieve thee.

They had made many purchases in New York and now had books to pass the time on board. Margaret was sitting on deck engrossed in *Scenes in a Court of Justice*, when Bailey plopped into a chair next to her.

"Margaret, this will lift your spirits. You must read this," he said and handed her the book *An Irish Hulaballoo*. He started laughing to himself, "I put my bookmark in the place I thought the best." He leaned over and placed his hand on her cheek, "No one is near, kiss me!"

After that kiss and then another, Bailey got up to go play cards with some of the gents, and Margaret watched him disappear into the playing salon. *He has such a jaunty step! Where does he find his happiness while confined on this endless ocean? Do I love this man? I really don't know what love for a man is. I know I love my Lord.* She frowned with the memory of her splintered ink box. *I hated him at that moment. In my mind I screamed that I hated him, but I don't.* And she wrote:

TRUE LOVE

Long years have past and gone
Since we in heart were one –
Changes have gone to come,

My dearest dear.

Yet still I feel thee mine –
My heart doth round thee twine,
Nor can it yet repine
Thy love to share.

Before they arrived in Oahu, Margaret would dwell on dismal thoughts and feel sorry for herself. Her mind went in emotional circles. She obsessed about her worries, seeing only the negative.

William was the opposite – he saw logical solutions to difficulties. He looked for places to find pleasure and laughter. Even when a fire broke out on their vessel as they waited for the second leg of their journey in Oahu, he eventually found humor in the tragedy.

At the time of the fire, they were in the garden of friends whom they had met on Oahu. They were looking at the harbor when William and his host saw the flames whipping in the air on the main deck of their ship. They jumped up from their lounge chairs and rushed down the hill.

Bailey shouted during the descent, "I believe there is a good supply of gun powder on board. We must hurry! I don't see anyone doing anything."

"I'll go to the offices and inform them, you try to find the Captain!"

Huffing, Bailey shouted, "What bad luck! We were to sail tomorrow."

Within the hour, the Captain and Bailey stood side by side watching the ship sink in the bay. Bailey commented, "With all the other vessels it put in danger, I can see why you scuttled it."

The Captain nodded as he spoke, "Yes, I had no other choice. Tomorrow, we'll raise her and see the damage. From what I saw when the men hacked holes into the sides, we'll be delayed a month for repairs. I'm hoping that most of your supplies are recoverable."

Sunk in the deep waters were all of the Baileys' new furniture, clothes, books, medicines, and stacks of blank paper that would never receive Margaret's words. Yet Bailey was jovial during dinner that night, telling of the sailor who had swung at the hull and missed. "He followed his axe into one of the holes in the ship. In two seconds, he was frantically trying to climb back out before it sank. His feet were hanging out of the hole, and he was kicking like he was trying to swim out." Bailey laughed so hard at his own story that his eyes watered. He took the napkin and dabbed them. When he could speak again, he finished the story. "He made it out only minutes before she sank."

Margaret took a bite of her serving of fish. *How different we are. Imagine if we were alike and were both always complaining and writing sad poems. He is good for me.* She smiled to herself. When she looked up, she noticed that her hostess had seen her smile. "What a delight is your fish," Margaret remarked.

Back in Oregon at last, Margaret said to Bailey, "Our trip seemed so short, but in fact we were gone from October 1842 until May 1844."

Willy gave some logic to her feelings, "Of course, you don't mean the voyage was short. Our time in Boston and New York was the only short part." Margaret had spent a couple of months in Boston and Willy a few weeks. "If you look at all the changes in Oregon since we left, aren't you amazed? I don't know how so much could have happened in a year and seven months."

When they left Oregon, the non-native population of Oregon Country comprised sixty retired fur trappers, both French Canadians and Irish; one hundred American and British settlers; and a handful of Hawaiians. Upon their return, the first overland wagon train on the Oregon Trail had arrived. Bailey told his wife, "McLoughlin says the Oregon Trail has brought nine hundred settlers to the Willamette Valley."

Attitudes had changed. Patience with neighbors diminished. Prejudices increased and swirled like oil on water for all to see.

Margaret told Willy, "Joseph Gervais said that some of these new people insulted him and his wife when he went to have his wheat ground. They said loudly, for others to hear, that they didn't want to stand next to a smelly savage."

Willy shook his head.

Margaret continued, "Although it no longer seems important, I heard that Miss Chloe Clark finally married William Willson in Puget Sound in the year 'forty-two, if I'm remembering right. And Jason Lee's leadership of the Methodist Mission was questioned by his other missionaries, so he was forced to return to the States to defend his position." She stopped and asked, "Had you heard this?"

Bailey nodded and finished the story, "Yes, while he was still at sea, the missionary board in the East relieved him of his command."

For $700, Bailey bought back their property – cabin, barn, hospital, and the land with their original animals. Margaret's gardens were in disarray, but the plants and flowers had reseeded themselves so she could begin again.

The Baileys heard so much news that they had trouble remembering what to tell one another. One such evening, Bailey came home from treating a woman farther north in the French Prairie. "Margaret, today I found out that everyone is calling the French Prairie by the name Champoeg now. Don't ask me how to spell it; I heard several suggestions. Anyway, they built a town with streets and named them.

"Do you remember my friend Hoxie, who sold his gristmill to a man named McKay? Well, that mill is gone! They had a flood. The waters rose to the second story window of the mill – with the miller still inside. Someone came in a canoe to help him out of a window."

Margaret was at the hearth with a wooden spoon in her hand.

"In fact," Bailey told Margaret, "I forgot to tell you something amazing! There's a ferry across the Willamette now. A man named Matheny built it down by the old Methodist Mission. This Matheny bought Applegate's boat and then built a larger barge; he hitched up ropes and cables to his mules to pull the barge across the river."

"Willy, all of this is so exciting." She put silverware on the table. "Keep talking while I serve our food."

Bailey found it hard to eat and talk, "I thought of something else. I have so much to tell. Margaret, I can't believe that McLoughlin didn't describe this huge warehouse he built in Champoeg. It's twenty feet by forty. I saw it. Now the farmers can take their wheat, corn, and any other crops to this warehouse that's so close. And Hudson's Bay Company built a store in Champoeg as well. We can go there to buy supplies. We won't need to go all the way up to the Fort." He stopped to eat. Margaret had made a good chicken stew.

"That sounds wonderful, Willy. I want to go see. Let's go soon."

Bailey wasn't finished, "I can't believe so much building happened while we were gone. After McLoughlin built his granary warehouse, another man built one. At the foot of Maple Street, a man named Pettygrove established a granary and also a store to compete against the Hudson's Bay Company. Can you believe his gumption?"

Margaret had an idea, "Let's take our wagon tomorrow to see Arnaud, and then we can go up to Champoeg." With the passage of almost two years, little Arnaud was seven and a half years old.

The Bugats allowed the boy to spend many days with the Baileys. After their trip to see Champoeg, Margaret recommenced lessons with Arnaud. With his maturity and eagerness, he was reading and writing within a week; nevertheless, Margaret knew what Arnaud really wanted was to be working in the hospital with Dr. Bailey, asking him endless questions.

One day, more or less, a month after their return, they were turning the soil in their vegetable garden when Margaret stopped to wipe her brow, "I am so glad that we returned in time to make a garden. Willy, I am so glad to be home."

He grunted and turned over another shovelful.

She began to work again and then stopped, "Willy, when we were back in United States, did you hear all the animosities against the Indians? So many of the tribes in the East were being sent to reservations."

Bailey shoved his blade in the ground and stood resting his arm on the handle. "I did, Margaret. I remember thinking that I was proud to live here in Oregon. The Indians walk up to our house, you serve them tea and chat with them in that pidgin. The French are our friends. The native wives of fur trappers like Gervais and Bugat, and even John McLoughlin, are gracious, loving women who are accepted into our society. And their children are wonderful and productive."

Margaret interrupted, "Willy, you're speaking of Arnaud, and how it was before we left on our trip. I don't think you saw what I did when I taught at the Mission. Sometimes, the *Métis* children have hard times. The natives do not accept them and the whites don't respect them. But I started telling you this because I see how different the situation is now. These new settlers coming by wagon train seem to think that this land is theirs for the taking. Perhaps they were told something like that before they started their journey."

Bailey started digging again. "That's it, Margaret. Land! Before, there weren't many of us competing for this land. Now, people look at the natives and think they don't deserve the land."

Margaret finished his sentence, "Because they don't farm it. Oh, Willy, while we were at Fort Vancouver I overheard someone saying the wandering tribes don't need land. They talked hatefully about the *Métis* and their families, claiming they're not Americans and don't deserve the land."

Bailey stopped to rest again. "Did you hear McLoughlin telling me that forty conspirators signed a written agreement to drive out the retired fur traders and their families? When they finally had a meeting in March this year to get it started," he said, slapping his thigh with a hoot. "Most of the people who came were the Canadians and Frenchies whom they wanted to drive away, and that ended that. Their plot failed."

"Thank heavens!"

"One more thing of interest McLoughlin said. He told me that he expected this day to come since as long ago as eighteen twenty-eight, and from that time he started warning his fur traders that one day this would belong to the United States." Amused, Bailey continued talking, "He said that most of them told him that they didn't care and would be glad to be rid of the British government. I can hear Gervais or Bugat saying that. Can't you?"

"Yes, I can." She didn't smile; she had serious thoughts. "Willy, the new settlers are irritated that the retired fur traders own the best land especially since they don't even speak English. I hear Irish, French, and Chinook Jargon more than English when I go to visit our friends. And I know I find much fault with the Catholic Church, but I don't dislike the Catholics themselves. I think the new settlers look unfavorably on people because they have a different faith. I feel all their prejudice."

Bailey nodded. "This new committee I'm on to form a provisional government has a lot of work to do."

Margaret stopped working the soil and went to sit on a large rock at the edge of the garden plot. She picked up her water cup, which she had placed in the shade of the rock, took a long swig, and then held out her arm to offer Bailey a drink. He took the cup and drank before he sat next to her. He wiped his whole face with his shirtsleeve, leaving smudges of dirt streaked on his cheeks. She used her apron to dab the dirt from his face.

She tucked some stray strands of hair out of her face and broke the quiet, speaking in a soft, slow voice, "All of us here in Oregon are like grains from our fields: some are wheat, others barley, and many corn. We each have our distinct taste and value. You never see a field growing all the grains together – the wheat field has no corn but if a stray stalk grows, it does no harm. A few plants of a different grain growing among another crop isn't bad; it shows that someone can be an individual among other kinds." She paused for another drink. "All the grains are important, and in time, they travel to the mill to be improved. For, it is the grist that benefits us most. Once we have the grist – the flour and cornmeal – we have sustenance. We all need to have our rough and tough edges ground down. We all need to know the weight of the millstone to value what we have and what we are becoming. We are the Grist of Oregon."

A woodpecker hammered against a conifer tree. Distracted, Margaret ended her discourse and stood up to see a pileated woodpecker – a bird almost the size of a crow and with a bright red crest. She pointed, and William looked up. Without words, they shared the moment before getting back to their work of turning the soil.

There was one change in Oregon that Bailey had kept from his wife. It was another first, like the ferry and the Hudson's Bay Company warehouse. Up in Champoeg the first gaming and drinking establishment in the valley, Howard's Tavern, had opened its doors the same month that they returned. When he had a sick person to see in the vicinity, Bailey would go to Howard's. One such evening, he returned home late and found he had visitors.

When Bailey came in the door, Margaret – not wanting to rile him – ignored his condition and said, "Look, Joseph Gervais, Marie Angelique, and their new baby Rosalie have come to visit. They stopped in to welcome us back to Oregon. I invited them to join us for dinner." She stood to get another cup and saucer for Bailey. "We can finish our tea and then dinner will be ready. I'll see if the potatoes are done." She stuck a fork into one. "Not quite."

Bailey reeked of the spirits and swayed in his walk. "Goodth to see yah," Bailey slurred and went to sit with his friends. He tried to extend his hand to steady himself before sitting, but fell onto the chair.

Margaret sat in the chair next to him and placed the cup and saucer on the table. "I'll pour you some tea."

"I don'th wanth tea," he mumbled.

Gervais spoke up, "We happy you are back, Dr. Bailey, both you and the missus. You must come see us. We not sick, but you come anyway."

Margaret agreed, "We shall ride over next Sabbath, if that agrees with you."

Marie Angelique nodded, "Yes, come."

Margaret finished stirring sugar into Bailey's tea and added a few drops of milk. She raised the cup to hand to him.

Bailey was adamant, "I saidth no tea."

As she started to say something, Bailey stood. He pulled back his arm and applied a fisticuff to her face – right to her nose. The teacup clattered to the floor, and Margaret's chair started to topple from the force of the blow. Gervais jumped up to catch the chair with Margaret, but missed. She fell backwards, hitting her head on the floor. Blood flowed from her nose as Gervais knelt to help her. She appeared stunned from the impact of her head on the floor.

Bailey stood, weaving on his feet, and stumbled toward the door. Once outside, he fell flat on his face and didn't move.

Marie Angelique moved fast and pulled a towel from the side of the hearth. She doused it in the water pail, wringing it out before returning to Margaret who remained stretched out on the floor. Carefully, she pressed the wet cloth to Margaret's face to contain the bleeding.

Gervais righted the overturned chair and went to check on Bailey. When he came back inside the house he told them, "I turned him over. He's out cold and too big for me to help up."

Margaret tried to sit up but turned to her side and retched on the floor.

Gervais and Marie Angelique stayed the night with them. In the morning, Bailey did not remember hitting his wife. Margaret sat quietly under some fruit trees most of the day, trying not to move too much. She refused to let Bailey near her to see if her swollen nose was broken.

To Gervais, she lamented that the relationship was back where it had been before the trip back East, "My head is spinning, my heart is turning, and my life goes in circles."

Tragic as it was, this incident kept Bailey sober for years and the Baileys prospered.

By the end of the next summer, Bailey counted their cows as he turned them out to pasture; they had twenty-one cows with newborn calves. Margaret had starting by buying the one cow with her pay from the Methodist Mission. With so many cows producing milk and Margaret making cheese and butter to sell to neighbors, the cattle were profitable. They also had thirty horses and eighty-six sheep, including the lambs.

These animals were a lot of work, but the Baileys had little helpers; their family had expanded in the form of two young girls, Sarah and Eliza Flett. A while back, McLoughlin had referred to the girls as orphans when he asked the Baileys to raise them. Actually, their father, Mr. Flett, was alive, but his wife had died and he felt that girls needed to be raised under the care of a woman. The girls were nine and ten years old, and Arnaud was near their age. The three youngsters became the best of friends.

These were some of Margaret's happiest years.

The next year, Bailey ran for Governor. Much to Margaret's relief, he did not win. "Willy, I guess I'm selfish. I want more time with you. You are busy enough being a physician." But he still went to meetings, wanting to help plan the future of Oregon.

The Baileys heard that Jason Lee died back East, in 1845; they rarely spoke of him again.

Dr. Bailey had an extensive practice and most of the settlers preferred him to any of the newer physicians who came to the area. "He has more business than he needs. And his patients pay their bills, if they can," Margaret told George Gay and his wife La Louisa when they came to visit one day. "Oh,"

Margaret interrupted herself and changed topics, "I'm remembering that I heard you built a brick home. I would love to come see it."

"Our house is so warm in the winter. I enjoy it so," La Louisa commented.

George explained, "We made all our bricks. Since I had no one to help me learn how, I had to do a lot of experimenting. It was hard work making the bricks, but easy to build a house with them.

Bailey ambled in with the three youngsters, Arnaud, Sarah, and Eliza. "My goodness, George Gay and La Louisa! The children came to the hospital to tell me you were here. I couldn't believe it."

Margaret interjected, "I'm going to go pick some ripe apples to make a pie or two for dinner."

George jumped up, "Get the bushels and we'll all help." They talked and told stories as they picked and soon they had emptied the apples from one tree into two bushels.

"I had to have a fruit cellar dug under the shed to store all our potatoes and apples," Margaret explained.

Arnaud asked, "Can we go get the cart and not hitch the horse? We three want to be the horses." And so the three children stepped between the wooden hames and held onto the leather- padded breast collar on the front of the cart. They leaned into their load and pulled the two-wheel cart with two bushels up the slope. Within minutes the cart returned, going downhill, with one child pulling the other two. "We'll put the cart away after we play a while," Arnaud yelled as he sped past.

La Louisa beamed, "He's a beautiful child with his red curly hair. Did you say he's a half-breed?"

Margaret straightened, "No, I didn't say and never would. In God's eyes, people are people. Have you heard that a law was passed to expel Negroes from Oregon and to prevent anyone with black skin from coming? To me, it was as ludicrous as if they had made a law that all the redheads must be banned."

La Louisa looked stunned at the outburst.

Margaret took La Louisa's hand and explained, "Don't mind me! I hate putting a label on people, and I should never talk politics. I can be severe. Please pay me no mind and help me pare apples for some pies. I want to send a couple pies home with you tonight."

As they returned to the house, La Louisa admired the flowers, "How do you do this? I have never seen a garden so orderly. The short flowers are near the path and the tall foxgloves and gladiolas stand tall behind them. It is delightful." She hesitated, "Do you have any extra seeds that I might plant?"

Margaret explained, "It is not time to gather the seeds. I can save some for you and come visit to see your brick house. I understand it is the first and only one in Oregon. How proud you must be."

One day in 1846, Margaret received a letter, telling her that the *Oregon Spectator* newspaper in Oregon City wanted to publish some of her poems. Publishing under her initials, MJB, the first one appeared in the February 5th edition, making her the first local poet to be published west of the Rocky Mountains. Her poem was short:

LOVE

My heart it is burdened and sad,
What can I perform for relief?
Conversation where can it be had?
And comfort for internal grief?
The birds they are joyous in air,
The beasts in the field find delight;
All insects in liveliness share,
And flowers are smiling and bright.

But me – ah! My heart is the seat
Of sorrow intense and forlorn
Love's saplings lie dead at my feet!
Her tendrils are parted and torn!
Blest Gardener! In mercy draw near;
Ingraft me anew into Thee,
Lest, blasted too soon I appear,
Nor fruit to perfection can see.

By MJB

The second poem appeared in the March 4, 1846 issue. It read:

AFFLICTION

Behind some logs an iris grew.
A roof withheld the falling dew,
And once I wondered much to see
A drop as pure as drop can be,
Sit laughingly upon each leaf
Like joy upon the eye of grief.

Whence they had come I could not tell,
Till I the storm remembered well
Which late had swept the teeming earth
Of bud and flower just in their birth,
And towering pine of many a bough
Which lay, like fallen tyrants—low.

I've known a form as iris—fair,
Defenseless as the iris there;
Begirt with foes , like logs, as dead
To kindness, pleasant most in need,
Who as a roof shut out Fame's sun,
And Friendship's dew so few have won.

And in that form a mind serene
And equal as the iris green,
From woe – cull rapture – pain – relief,
And flourish in the midst of grief,
And blessings gain from every harm
Like dew drops gathered from the storm.

By MJB

The sorrow in her poems was not without reason. A month before they were printed, in January 1846, Bailey arrived intoxicated and belligerent late one evening. Sarah and Eliza sat with Margaret at the table while they made lace. Bailey wavered to and fro in the doorway without closing the door from the winter cold. His face had the blank stare of a drunk, and for no apparent reason he tapped the pocket on his shirt where a cigar protruded.

"Willy, come in and close the door," Margaret suggested.

He slammed the door, and as he took off his coat, it slipped to the floor. On his way to their bedroom, he insisted, "Margaret, come to bed." He still wore his hat.

Trying to sound nonchalant, Margaret answered, "It's a bit early. Come here. I'll make you some food."

"No! You come to bed. Now!"

Margaret sensed disaster coming. With a soft voice, she said, "Girls, hurry up the stairs to your bed. Close the door and lock it." But before they had gathered their lace work, he was there.

With his fist, he banged the table. "What did you say to them?"

Margaret stood between the girls and Bailey. "I asked if they wanted something to eat, like I asked you."

He growled, "Get to bed, you two. No one needs anything to eat."

Pleased because the girls had already had dinner, Margaret watched Bailey as he returned to the bedroom. The girls started up the stairs.

Shouting, he called out, "Well, are you coming to bed, Margaret?"

"No, Willy, not at the moment. I have things to do."

He bolted out of the bedroom again, seething. "I know how to make you come to bed!" He headed for the musket that he kept loaded in the corner of the room and grabbed it.

Margaret looked upstairs and saw the girls' frantic faces before they closed their door. When she heard the bolt latch on their door, she turned to see him aiming the gun at her. She screamed and fled the house, running to the barn. Without saddling the horse, she threw her leg over the wide brown back, clutched the mane, and left in a gallop. When she rode past the house, Bailey stood silhouetted in the doorway with the musket pointing at her. She prayed he would not fire.

She rode and rode. *Where do I go? It's dark and cold and here I am with no coat or protection. What makes him like this? What happens to Willy? It has been years with no incident and then when I least expect it, he goes crazy like this. Do I have no reason to think the girls are not safe?* She slowed to look behind and knew he would not be following in his drunken condition. *I'll go to Gervais. He will understand. He has seen Willy like this. And Gervais could go get the girls.*

The next day, Bailey went looking for her at different neighbors and finally arrived at the home of Gervais. He begged her to return; she refused. She and the girls stayed three days with Gervais and his new wife, Marie Angelique, and each day Bailey came to apologize.

At last, he gave a solemn promise, "Margaret, you mean everything to me. I promise to treat you as you deserve. Please forgive me and come home. I am so ashamed of myself. I promise not to drink." They were sitting outside on the hewn bench that Gervais had made so many years ago. Their backs leaned against the cabin, and they looked out toward the meadow that would fill with camas in the springtime. Normally a sunny January day would brighten the disposition of anyone living in Oregon – but not Margaret and William on this day.

"Willy, you are a different person when you drink. I need to know why you do this to me. Do you hate me because I cannot bear a child?"

"No, Margaret, do not think that."

"Tell me, Willy. Are you sad that you don't have a child?"

He remained quiet a while. When he turned to face her, his green eyes seemed iridescent in the sunlight, "Margaret, I honestly don't think about this. I know that we both would have liked to have had a child. My pain is no greater than yours."

Margaret swallowed and bobbed her head. "Willy, I'll come home, but if I see you drink again, I'll leave you forever. I promise you."

He nodded, "I understand." He truly believed her and knew that she would leave him.

Neither moved. They were emotionally drained, but the sun warmed them.

They had a pact, an understanding, and there were many content years ahead for them.

The people of Oregon Country had a pact as well. In August 1846, a treaty was signed that made the Oregon Territory an official part of the United States, whose boundaries became all the land south of the 49th parallel.

Stone Implements of Kalapuyans

Polk County Historical Museum
RICKREALL, OREGON

CHAPTER 13

SCENES FROM OREGON
End of 1847-1852

During this time, Margaret entered in her journal:

Our life has taken a normal course.

As soon as she wrote that sentence, she realized that no one could call life in Oregon normal. *"Normal" means lucid, sane, or rational. Those of us who came to Oregon are anything but normal. Those who came wanted to be strong, adventuresome, and determined. We are people who wanted an Eden and something beyond normality.*

After returning from a two-day jaunt around the countryside caring for the sick, Bailey sat with Margaret having breakfast.

"Oh, Willy, listen! The meadowlarks are singing. Yesterday, some blackbirds came to our yard. I find their song to be the sweetest and prettiest of all."

Bailey was reading some documents that had been sent to him; he was on a number of committees that were drafting the laws of the provisional government, which still prevailed as the governing body even though Oregon Country was now a territory of the United States. He looked up with a blank face, "Yes, I agree."

Margaret flicked her finger at the papers he read, "You agree with what?"

"What you said!"

"Willy, you didn't even hear me. I yearn to talk with you and share what has happened in my days, boring as that may be to you."

He nodded, "I understand. So tell me."

"I was telling of the blackbirds. They alighted in the yard this morning – dozens of them. You should have seen the chickens run straight at them until they flew." Margaret laughed, "It was to no avail because those blackbirds returned quickly to feast upon the chicken feed."

"That must have been amusing." He bowed his head to read again.

"Even if you don't listen, I'll keep on talking. Unlike you, I have no other adults to talk with and need to talk this morning."

He grunted and looked up to smile. He had not heard.

"I enjoy this weather so – yesterday brought a heavy autumn shower, but today feels of summer. I love the forest trees changing their green dresses to colorful ones. And I have been venturing out to walk within the woods, now that the bushes and undergrowth have lost their leaves. When they lose their leaves, I lose my fear of a bear, wolf, or cougar surprising me. I pass sometimes an hour meditating and praying in a forest grove. Little birds come and sing, but in my loneliness I know no pleasure."

"Margaret, do I hear self-pity or is this one of your exaggerations?"

She smiled, "Ah, Willy. So you are listening." She stood to kiss his forehead. "I'll stop chattering and let you finish that paper while I clean away our breakfast. I want to be ready to go help in the hospital." She tied on her apron again. She always removed it to sit and eat; she still held fast to being proper.

The summer harvests had been abundant for all; barns were overflowing. The Hudson's Bay Company was no longer taking any wheat because their granaries were bursting, but the Bailey's had sold theirs earlier – eleven hundred bushels for sixty cents each. As they walked to see the patients in the hospital, Bailey told her, "With the good harvests, everyone has money to pay me. I collected most of the fees that were owed yesterday."

They worked side by side with two patients for forty-five minutes, changing dressings on a wound, checking foreheads for fevers, and giving out medications.

After Bailey rode away to make rounds, Margaret looked up to see her old friend, the Kalapuyan called Oofaaf. He had gone blind and no longer remembered what his name meant, but he still loved sugar. He often stopped by her house to ask for some. They spoke in Chinook Jargon.

"All my friends have left to join their parents, grandparents, and children who have died. They are with all the others who disappeared because of sickness. In my last days, all I want in the world is the sweetness from these white grains of sweet sand."

"Oofaaf, I understand. Let me make you some tea to put the sugar in."

"No, I want only sweetness. I brought a grinding stone to pay."

"Please, eat some bread and have some tea."

"No," he insisted.

"Well, I am going to get you some thread and a needle so you can mend your breeches. Winter is coming. Did you know they were torn?"

"It better you mend," and he took off his clothes and sat on the ground to wait in his nakedness. "I eat sugar while you mend."

When Margaret went inside for the sugar, she saw that Eliza and Sarah had stopped making bread and were giggling at the window. *I didn't see a man's parts until I saw the professor naked when I was in my twenties. This is a better way to learn.* She took Oofaaf some sugar in a folded scrap of paper.

When Oofaaf walked away in mended clothes, still sucking on sweetness, Margaret went to feed the pair of sheep that Bailey had acquired against her wishes. *We have so many animals. I didn't need more sheep to feed.*

As she approached the fenced area behind the barn, she heard bleating and found the male tangled in the fence with his mate nowhere to be seen. "Look at you, you foolish ram! You failed at your escape." She gently worked him free. He couldn't stand on one of his legs and hobbled on three, bleating in pain. "I think your leg is broken." She threw her arms in the air, "Listen to me! I am talking to an animal." She called Sarah and Eliza to bring the cart. Working together, they got the ram to the hospital where they had an enclosure for sick animals.

In three weeks, when the ram recovered, they put him out in his fenced pasture, where the ewe was back with a lamb. "Sarah and Eliza, come see what we have here!"

The lamb became a pet for the girls. Margaret sewed a collar and leash for the girls to use, but soon it wasn't needed. Little Lizzy Sar-sar, as they called the lamb, followed them everywhere. Watching the three playing, Margaret often bit her tongue so as not to complain about flowers disappearing from her garden. *More will bloom, but the girls will never be this age again.*

One night the Baileys awoke to the sound of an approaching rider. They got out of bed just as someone began to beat on their door.

"Dr. Bailey, Dr. Bailey!"

One of McLoughlin's workers stood at the door. Bailey knew the young man, "Come in, Jacques."

Margaret had already gone to the hearth to heat water.

Soon they were seated around the table with some hot tea and Bailey contended, "I'm confused. McLoughlin's son is hurt down south of here. Why didn't McLoughlin go with his own physician to handle this?"

"McLoughlin didn't go because he wants you to go. He said to tell you that he has more confidence in you. Besides, you live closer."

Bailey held up his hand to interrupt, "Let me understand this correctly. McLoughlin's oldest son Joseph fell from a cliff in the Umpqua region – miles south of here. Obviously, a rider must have gone north to Oregon City to tell McLoughlin, who sent you back south to tell me."

"That's how it is. Joseph is asking for his father, but his father said he can't make the trip right now."

After twenty-two years as Chief Factor of the Hudson's Bay Company, John McLoughlin had resigned a year ago. He retired near the Willamette Falls, in the place he had established twenty years before, now called Oregon City.

Margaret shook her head. "Willy, in my opinion, since Dr. McLoughlin no longer is working, he should go."

"Mrs. Bailey, please don't give me your opinion. I know it will be different than mine, and it will waste our time. I'm going to get dressed."

Dr. Bailey was gone for three days. Joseph McLoughlin died at the age of thirty-nine from that fall.

And such was life in Oregon.

In July 1847, the newspaper *Oregon Spectator* published another of Margaret's poems. There were small joys and some hardships, but life was good. Although the Baileys passed their time with the events of farming and doctoring, upheavals were happening all around them.

Bailey came home one night with sad news. "Margaret, John Turner accidentally killed himself with a discharge from his own gun. You remember him, don't you? He helped carry me after I was injured with that tomahawk." Bailey rubbed his scar beneath his beard and started rambling, talking more to himself than her, "How long ago was it that his Cayuse wife died, and he up and sold his land? He's been down in California since then. Up here, he had been in charge of all the cattle that the Mission bought when we brought those six hundred or so animals up from California. He tended their herd and was their butcher, too." He looked up to see Margaret's face. "You do remember him and his wife, don't you?"

"I do, Willy." She came and sat next to him. "I remember the time we went to visit. John and Mai-yi had a place a few miles from the Mission. While we were visiting, he slaughtered a young heifer, and she served us some of that meat. It was so tender. He took the rest over to the Mission, and you reminded him not to tell them that the Baileys were eating their stock."

Bailey nodded his head.

"That wasn't a bad way to die, Willy. Better than being killed by someone else or starving."

Bailey agreed.

One evening in late November of 1847, they heard of other deaths. Several men from the legislative committee had gathered at the Baileys' house for their regular meeting, but the agenda was ignored. A horrible event had occurred. Although it was too soon to know all the facts, the violence created fear throughout Oregon Territory.

"Those Cayuse Indians killed everyone!"

Someone else maintained, "I heard that both of the Whitmans were killed, along with twelve others."

"Don't just say 'killed' – it was a massacre at the Whitmans' Mission. Marcus and Narcissa Whitman were brutally mutilated, and those Cayuse are holding sixty prisoners."

Near the hearth, Margaret prepared some coffee to serve the men and listened intently. She didn't know the Whitmans personally; they had arrived overland and set up a Presbyterian mission up the gorge at Waiilatpu, quite a distance east of Fort Vancouver, very near to Fort Walla

Walla. Margaret had never gone there.

One of the men asked, "What could have made the Cayuse go crazy like that?"

Someone said, "I heard that there were rumors among the Indians that Marcus had put arsenic poison in melons in his patch to make the poachers sick. And they say that Narcissa was too stern a teacher for the *Métis* women."

Bailey interjected, "Let's not talk about rumors."

"Well, this isn't a rumor; I know for a fact that Marcus Whitman was dismembered and mangled beyond recognition."

"And his wife Narcissa was riddled with gunshots and died on the ground, outside her house."

Margaret felt sick and frightened. She excused herself and retired for the night.

The men talked for another hour, never discussing the agenda of the legislative committee.

As the story spread, Margaret was not alone in her reaction. During the coming days and weeks, fears rippled through all of Oregon. The incident soon became known as The Whitman Massacre. The white people no longer felt safe. The reasons for the attack would never be resolved, although some settlers had heard that the Cayuse became suspicious when Whitman had cared for children with measles but only the whites recovered. The natives blamed the "Shaman Whitman" for the deaths.

One day in 1848, when Margaret went to Champoeg to get some flour and other supplies, all the talk was about gold. A clerk at the general store mentioned to her, "I see these mean, dirty fellows, just ignorant low-life, return from California bragging about pockets full of gold."

Margaret replied, "But 'tis pleasant to see the poor have an opportunity to enjoy the good things in life as well as do their former taskmasters."

"I guess," he said while wrapping her hanks of thread and needles in some old paper. He tied the package with string, and Margaret dropped it into her basket.

Walking around the community of Champoeg, Margaret talked with people she met and learned that Howard's Tavern was having gambling nights more frequently. She was told, "Howard is digging his gold right off his gambling tables."

Margaret laughed on the outside, but not on the inside. She said a little prayer that Willy would continue to stay away from Howard's Tavern.

Margaret was thankful that Willy seemed to have no interest in gambling, whether it was looking for gold in California or gaming in Champoeg. Financially, they were prospering, but Margaret didn't find their financial prosperity a comfort when she was left at home alone. Bailey spent more time away than home, often sleeping overnight at a patient's house.

After she returned from shopping and they sat having supper, Margaret said to Willy, "Since the news of California's gold rush reached here, men are crazy with greed. People don't talk about anything else. Men ride away and leave with their whole family, leaving their life and their land. Willy, won't they lose their claim to the land? It's insane!"

He finished his meal and leaned back in his chair. "I know, Margaret. When they abandon their life and land, they're fools. Yes, they will lose the land. We have such a good life here." He frowned and shook his head. "I heard that the Hudson's Bay Company has lost one hundred fifty men to the gold rush. They deserted their posts to go looking for gold."

Margaret hesitated, not wanting to upset Willy, "Joseph Gervais left, too. Did you hear?"

"Yes, I couldn't believe he went, at his age. At least his wife will care for his place and he won't lose it. I'll stop by from time to time to see if she needs anything. I will always owe him for how he helped me." Gervais would return to his cabin in two years but not a cent richer.

One winter morning, Margaret wandered through their woods of oak and fir trees. The cold was greater than had ever experienced. Dead birds were on the ground wherever she looked. She feared for her garden and returned home quickly to ask Willy for help. They built a roof over her flowerbeds using some old rails and placed boughs of fir over the trimmed roses. Two days later it snowed. This was the first hard snow she had seen in Oregon, and she had been there eleven years; it remained on the ground for nine days.

When Willy came home one of those snowy nights, he found two rails sticking out of the fireplace. He greeted her and the two girls before turning to point to the fire, "Margaret, what is this?" He chuckled as he hung his coat.

"Remember that you helped me gather rails to build coverings for my garden? We forgot that I needed firewood. I tried to split an oak log and nearly cut off my foot. So I used these rails."

He walked closer to the rails. One end of each was stuck in the flaming fireplace and the other end was propped on a chair to keep it angled into the fire. The rails were over four feet long. He hugged his wife and laughed, "What ingenuity! Listen, I'll go split a good stack for you after I thaw a little and get some food in me."

"Good!" She kissed him before she turned to serve his dinner. "I won't tell you the name of the man who came by today and laughed, just like you, at my fire. He insulted me saying that the only difference between an Indian and a bear is that a bear can't build a fire." She put her one hand on a hip and turned with a wooden spoon waving in the other hand, "I guess he thought me a bear."

Bailey let out a guffaw.

"Don't you laugh! He didn't even offer to cut any wood for me, and I didn't ask. I wanted him and his insults out of here."

Spring was unusually warm that year. Bailey had an idea, "Margaret, for the first time in a long time, there are no patients in the hospital. Let's take the children on a trip to the ocean. I talked with Solomon Smith at the meeting last week, and he invited us. Arnaud has never been to the ocean. Have you, girls?"

"No! Let's go, let's go." Eliza chanted. Sarah joined her, jumping up and down.

"Well, you girls don't know Solomon Smith and Mrs. Ellen, but you will. They live up at the mouth of the Columbia River. That's right on the ocean in Clatsop country. We'll spend the whole week there. We should leave for their place on Friday. We can stay overnight at Fort Vancouver before we continue on Saturday. On Sunday we can go to see the ocean."

Margaret turned to the girls, "We'll need to pack food for this trip. We can work on that tomorrow."

The girls held hands and danced in a circle.

Bailey continued, "So I'll bring Arnaud here. Hope the Bugats have no plans for him."

When Arnaud arrived, he wore what he always wore. He was dressed like most *Métis* boys in clothing with braided, beaded or embroidered leggings of gay colored cloth. Mrs. Bugat prided herself on making intricate designs. Margaret decided that this trip was the time to dress Arnaud in some clothes she had been making for him. She pulled out two pairs of somber, homemade blue and brown denim broadfalls – similar to the breeches that Bailey wore.

"Thank you, Mar-Mar, I look like Dr. Bailey now." He hugged Margaret, and she noticed that he had grown as high as her shoulders since his last visit. And she was a tall woman,

After two days of traveling to arrive at the Smiths' homestead, Solomon promised a trip to the beach the very next day.

Early that morning they left for the shore with two wagons: behind Margaret and William sat the three children; Solomon Smith had his wife, Mrs. Ellen, and some friends in his wagon. When they started down the sunny beach, Solomon stopped his horses with a quick jerk of the reins. He stood up, put his hand over his eyes, and peered out along the waves. Bailey saw where he was looking; there was a dark object far down the beach.

Solomon gave a whoop, jumped down into the sand, and came running back to the Baileys, "Look! I think it's a beached whale. Let's make tracks. I want some of that meat."

The children hung over the sides straining to see while the horses went at a gallop and sped down the beach. It was a bright sunny day. The sea left long tendrils of seaweed among foam that the wagons plowed over; sand matted on the wheels and sprayed fine grains into the air and onto the children in the wagon bed; birds, running with skinny legs, took flight to avoid the on-coming horses; and the huge black whale draped across the beach grew larger and larger with each minute. The anticipation was making Margaret giddy, and she shouted above the sound of surf and gulls, "I am as excited to see a whale as the children are. I never thought I would see one in my lifetime!" The brim of her sunhat, tied on with a scarf, flopped in the wind.

When they reined in the horses and everyone gathered around the majestic animal of the deep, Solomon told them, "This is actually a rather common occurrence. No one understands why whales come to shore and die, but there are a few each year."

Red men had begun to cut into the whale meat. Margaret went to talk to them in Chinook Jargon.

Solomon turned to Bailey, "Your wife is amazing! She learned to speak the Jargon and I even heard her give a talk in Kalapuyan once, many years ago."

Bailey said with pride, "I know."

Bailey walked around the carcass and reached out to touch the huge whale.

Margaret came over to them, "They said that anyone who is here can have some of the meat. That is their way."

Solomon took out his jackknife and staked his claim by tracing the portion he wanted. He had to pull his arm back and thrust with quite a force to cut through the tough skin to mark their portion. "I'll get enough for all of us."

Margaret began talking to the natives again, and she laughed with them before they turned back to continue cutting. "They said that we shouldn't cut it off now. They are going to cut around our marked meat, so we can go enjoy the sun and beach. They laughed and told me that they don't want us to get sick, like the white man makes sickness for them. That's why they said not to cut the meat off until we are ready to leave."

Margaret walked over to Mrs. Ellen, "Do you know how to cook this meat? I surely do not."

"You can learn when we cook it tonight. Let's sit together on the ride to our house, so we can talk. We have not talked for a long time."

The years passed with every season different – the harvest bountiful one year and skimpy the next; the winter severe one year and generously mild the next; a spring with a surprise frost and flowers that bloom through it all;

and an early fall with bursts of colors brighter than usual and migrating geese in diminishing numbers.

Margaret had no time to sit on the porch and write in her journal like she had done in years past. She was busy with their homestead yet determined to record at least a sentence on most days. One such evening, after a whole week of no entries, she decided to record what had been happening. She dipped her goose quill into the ink bottle and wrote:

It's 1849: one hundred and eleven fruit trees to prune.

The wrens built nests in three corners of the house. Martins dart here and there constantly feeding off the insects.

Willy went away for two weeks on political business. He returned home with the news that he had been elected a member of the legislature again. He gets no pay for this, loses his patients to other doctors while he is gone, and leaves me alone. We argued.

The woods echo with the notes of mourning doves and other birds, singing charmingly their morning songs.

Impossible to milk our twenty-three cows, so I take the milk when I need it and let the calves drink the rest of the time.

The father of Sarah and Eliza came for his daughters. They were happy to go with him, but he said he would bring them back if he could not manage financially. He expressed how much he really missed them. And he asked if they had learned cooking and mending from me. I told him that they had.

The sheriff from Oregon City and a gentleman in pursuit of a murderer stopped for some refreshments, and I offered some coffee. They told me, "Ma'am, we saw your milk cows. Do you have any buttermilk? I obliged them.

We got a dog and named him Caesar.

It's calving time, so tomorrow, Willy and I plan to ride out together to locate the young ones. Willy and I haven't worked together for years. I hope we don't argue. I must remember to take Caesar along.

In January 1850, discontent was in the air. Margaret wrote:

Winters in Oregon allow feelings of discontent to fester with the lengthy darkness of the nights. Without the sun to dry the dampness and wet, people's minds get soggy.

But the discontent was more than the darkness. Bailey found some cattle killed and fine colts missing. He burst into the cabin, seething. "I found a carcass cut apart. The fools! Only half was taken away – the rest left rotting on the ground. Remember when you found one of our hogs in the same condition a few weeks ago? I wonder if the same culprits did both slaughters." With a loud thud, he slammed his fist on the table. "How can people do that?"

Margaret jumped from the noise. She was in a rocker, doing some mending, and knew there was nothing to say.

Bailey started pacing the room. "Today I find our fine dun mare on the prairie with her neck broken. Someone must have done that. They probably were riding her and pushing her too hard. She must have reared up and flipped backwards. How else could she break her neck? I hope to hell whoever was on her got plenty hurt."

Margaret rocked nervously.

He blurted, "I want to sell out and get out of here. I need a trip back to New York."

So Bailey started to spread the word that he was selling his place, and he began to eliminate the animals. He sold the band of twenty mares and colts at twenty-five dollars per head.

Margaret reminded him, "Remember, twelve to fourteen of them were mine, Willy."

"I know, Margaret."

"I don't mind that you sold them. We always had such a hard time finding feed for them in the winter, and they would suffer so."

Bailey received $2,500 for his beef cattle, which he sold at the same price as the horses.

"All our milk cows came from those three cows that we started with. Remember, I bought the first one with the money I earned at the Mission. And Willy, don't forget that it was my labor, milking and putting them out to pasture each day, that made the herd grow."

"I know, Margaret."

Margaret decided to keep a purse of her own. She told him, "I still have the silver dollar from my father, four dollars given me from friends for a bonnet that I never bought, and thirteen particles of gold dust that I cleaned up off the floor after someone paid you. I should like to put my money from the animals into my purse as well."

"I know, Margaret."

In the first months of 1850, Margaret began to write in earnest, in hopes of finishing and publishing her book, the dream she had had for years and years. The happiness and satisfaction that she derived from writing was overshadowed by the arrival of Bailey's brother James, who came to Oregon from the East. He moved in with them.

With his brother there, Bailey began to drink more heavily every day.

And Margaret began to write more than ever. She decided that her book would be a memoir based on her journal entries and poetry, but also a novel.

The idea of writing a novel came to her on a day when Bailey and his brother were full of verbal abuse toward her. It was a spring day when the flowers were so beautiful that she decided to ride away from the house with all of her writing supplies. During the ride, she realized that she had an opportunity that few had. She could write the story of her life and tell all. She found a lovely place to sit under a tree and began to write.

After a few hours, she was satisfied with her writing and returned home, knowing that Willy and his brother would still be drunk. They were.

She worked on her book as much as possible while they packed, sold, and prepared for the journey to the east coast by ship. After the sale of all the animals, house, buildings, and three hundred and twenty acres of land, all three Baileys – Margaret, William, and James – sailed south in the Pacific Ocean during April in 1850.

And as with William's previous trips to the States, after a month or two in the East, he missed the lush green land and the life of the West. They returned to Oregon in December 1851.

The Baileys had physically returned to the land of Oregon, but they would never again return to a contented relationship.

Copy of original letter written by Margaret Jewett Bailey on May 17, 1852

CHAPTER 14

THE PRICE OF DREAMS
1852-1854

Arriving back in Oregon Territory in December 1851, Margaret and William were without a home. They went to the newly incorporated City of Portland, which had only three businesses: a sawmill run by steam, the *Weekly Oregonian* newspaper, and a log cabin hotel. There were also homes that served meals, homes that took in boarders, and one home with a room set aside a drinking establishment. About eight hundred inhabitants lived in the area.

When the Baileys registered at the hotel, the proprietor told them, "Yep, we are officially the City of Portland. Can you believe the name Portland was chosen with a toss of a penny?"

Margaret smiled politely. Bailey had his head down in the registry and made no response. Minutes before, they had quarreled as they often did, over nothing important, and Bailey was still angry. In their room, they didn't speak. Exhausted by the journey and excessive bickering during the voyage, Margaret closed the curtains, removed her muddy shoes, and collapsed on the bed.

"I'm going out," Bailey said. And he walked out.

Tired as she was, Margaret remembered that they had important business to do the next day so she struggled up and put on her shoes. She had no doubt that he was going to get drunk. At the desk, she asked the proprietor where the nearest drinking establishment was.

"Your husband asked the same, and I told him it was two blocks down on the right. You can't miss it." So she went out to wander down the wooden sidewalks in the dark.

Unable to find Willy, Margaret returned to the hotel. She slept soundly and did not hear when he came in.

Bailey slept the whole next day.

They stayed at the Portland hotel all of January and February of 1852.

Off and on, they took trips south to start getting their life together. Bailey purchased four fine horses for their travels, bought nine vacant lots in Champoeg, and hired workers to build a house on one lot. Every time they went south, they visited Arnaud and the Bugats.

On the first visit, the Baileys surprised the Bugats.

Monsieur Bugat stood outside grooming his horse on the sunny winter day. When he saw the Baileys in the distance, he ran to his house and shouted in the front door, "Come look who is here!"

Out came Mrs. Bugat and a tall young man.

By the time that they reached the house, Margaret and William realized that the young man was fifteen-year-old Arnaud. As soon as Bailey slipped from the saddle, Mrs. Bugat rushed to his side, hugging him. Their dog Caesar ran up, barking and prancing in circles around Margaret.

"You surprised us! Where you live now?"

Bailey looked over at Arnaud, "I am the one surprised. Look at my godson. A grown man!" Monsieur Bugat took Bailey's hand and pumped it up and down. Margaret hugged Mrs. Bugat. Finally, Bailey took a step toward Arnaud; they stood eye to eye. The dog continued to jump and bark, going from one person to the next. After savoring a long moment gazing at each other, at last, Bailey and Arnaud threw their arms around each other, slapping their backs as men do.

Arnaud asked in a deep mature voice, "Are you back for good?"

"I am."

"I'm glad." After hugging Margaret, Arnaud added, "I missed you both." Turning to face Bailey, he said, "I want you to know that I read all the medical books you gave me. Did you bring me more?"

"I did."

Bailey grabbed his *parflèche* as they walked into the house.

"Still your same *parflèche*," Mrs. Bugat said.

Bailey nodded. Margaret kept patting the dog.

Arnaud could not contain his excitement, "I'll get my plant collection out. I hope you brought a good plant classification book with you, too."

Bailey could not stop smiling. "I did. Your English is better than when I left. How did? I mean, who helped you?"

Arnaud knew the question before he heard it, "I've been working with

Solomon Smith. I make the hundred-mile trip back here once a month, stay three days, and then go back to work up in Astoria. I leave tomorrow. Did you know that he has stores and a sawmill? He lets me help with sales, do the books, cut lumber, and everything. He speaks well and is always helping me. He has some good books, too."

"Yes, Solomon is an educated man. Hey, let's travel together tomorrow when you head back north on your way to Astoria. I was going to be bored down here because Mrs. Bailey is going to stay and do things for our house. She's buying fabric for curtains or something – woman's work."

Whenever Bailey was away on business, Margaret used her time in the Portland hotel to continue writing her book. She *was* telling all – her affairs with the three men before she left for Oregon, her innermost feelings and thoughts, her own faults as well as those of others, incidents that occurred in Oregon Country, and facts about the people she had known. She realized that many persons would be upset by what she was writing, but she didn't care. *In my eyes, this is the truth, although I am changing people's names and taking some author's license at times.*

One evening, after Margaret and William had eaten dinner at a boarding house in Portland during which Bailey had downed a bottle of wine, they returned to the hotel. For Bailey, the hotel room was only for sleep. No sooner had he entered the room and took a warmer coat than he left again, saying nothing. There was nothing particularly wrong, and they hadn't fought. This was how their life was now; the rapport they used to have was gone.

She listened to his footsteps disappear down the hallway. *Bailey keeps talking of his hope that, when we settle down in Champoeg, we can get back to how our marriage was. I don't know if that's possible. He wants to start practicing medicine, but he is drinking so much. He needs to be sober to be a doctor.* Margaret went to the window and saw him heading for the little drinking establishment. She decided it was useless to go after him, but she looked out the window to watch him. He walked a half-block and stopped to converse with a woman who seemed to be a prostitute. The two were standing in a darkened doorway. Margaret saw him take a cigar out of his inside coat pocket; he struck a Lucifer match, puffing to get the cigar lit and laughing at the same time. *What could he be saying that is so humorous?* With the light of the match, Margaret saw the woman's face – a young Indian woman.

Margaret pushed the window open and put her head out, "Willy!" He couldn't hear her, so she rushed outside and hurried along the wooden sidewalks to the doorway. She screamed at him, "Haven't we done enough to the native women? You have a venereal disease and cannot consider this."

He jerked his arm back and plowed his fist in her face, shouting, "I do not! You saw blisters on me from shingles!"

The impact from his blow rammed Margaret against the brick building, and she fell to the ground. The prostitute slipped back through a door and a bolt clicked in place.

Bailey, still full of rage, reached for the front of her dress to raise her up. With his hands clenching the ruffled lace across her chest, he bashed her against the wall over and over. "Margaret, you're driving me crazy! Why couldn't you leave me alone tonight?" He banged her again until his face contorted with a look of shock, and he whispered to himself. "What am I doing? God help me." He let go of his wife, covered his face, and started to bawl.

Margaret fell into the dirt next to the wooden walkways. With bloody cheeks and stunned from the blows to the back of her head, she remained there, limp. The ripped lace hung in tatters.

Bailey, still crying, leaned back onto the brick wall and slumped down next to her. He threw his head back to shout again, "God, help me!"

People passed, making a wide circle around them and scurrying away.

Margaret groaned in pain and tried to clear her head. She heard his plea to God and was pleased he felt remorse, but she was tired of his mistreatment. Struggling to sit up, she slipped and fell back down. Unmoving, she took a moment to give her throbbing head some rest before she spoke. "Damn you, Willy, an Indian woman."

Disgruntled, he mumbled, "I wasn't going to fool around. When I saw her tonight, I was remembering my first time with an Indian." With that thought he hesitated, and when he began talking again he had a dreamy voice. "I thought of my first time with a sweet little *Métis* girl." His eyes seemed to gaze into the past, and his face showed pleasure. "She had a flattened forehead and blonde hair. She was a virgin." Now, he remembered more and smiled. "Gervais's wife, Mrs. Marguerite, brought her to me. I remember the girl's name was Sawala."

Unnoticed by Bailey, Margaret jerked with surprise. He kept talking but she was no longer listening. Her heart pounded like it would explode. *Sawala! It has to be my Sawala. With blonde hair, he said. What was it that Sawala said on her deathbed?* Margaret struggled to her feet and rested against the bricks before stumbling back to the hotel. *My journals are all in my trunks in the hotel. I must read what I wrote the night that Sawala died. Could it possibly be true what she told me? Oh, my head hurts. I must rest and think about all this.*

The next morning, Bailey still slept when she got out of bed. Margaret had a swollen cheekbone and a blackened eye. *I can't take any more of this. I want out of this life with him. I must get out of this marriage.* Her whole body ached from last night's bashing while she hobbled around the hotel room going through her trunks and looking for her journal with Sawala's words. Bending into a trunk, she found it!

She slumped against the wall next to the trunk and read. *So Willy got Sawala pregnant, she gave birth and a black-headed squaw tried to smash the baby's head. It all fits. Willy saved the baby and gave him to Mrs. Bugat, who had delivered a stillborn child. Sawala must have come to the Mission, looking for Willy, because she saw him take the baby. The only thing I don't understand is the black leaf on his head.* Margaret stood up and looked in the mirror, putting her hand to her head. *Sawala touched her head where her hair grew above her forehead. I wonder what she meant.*

Margaret turned to look at William sleeping and then back to the mirror to gaze at her own reflected eyes. *Am I going to make him happy and tell him that Arnaud is his child?* She pursed her lips tightly and rotated her aching head left to right. *No!*

As the black and blue around her eye became more vivid and the pain in her head intensified, she decided that when they were in their new house in Champoeg, she would go to Salem, the new capitol city of the Oregon Territory, and start divorce proceedings.

No sooner had they settled into their house in Champoeg than springtime arrived. Bailey bought fourteen cows and calves. And in Margaret's name, he bought another house and four lots in Butteville, a settlement a couple miles north of Champoeg along the Willamette River. Bailey did not have a working medical practice just yet, but he had started a store and was supplying another store in Oregon City with purchases he had made in the East. They had income from the stores and money they had saved, but Margaret was not aware of the exact amount. Bailey was spending a lot with purchases, banking a lot at Hudson's Bay Company, and losing a lot through drinking.

Unknown to Bailey, Margaret was working on divorce proceedings. She was nervous, yet felt justified, and hoped the laws of Oregon would help her live on her own. Margaret's lawyer, Mr. Mathew Deady, had informed her that half of the property of married couples was to be held by the wife.

One day while alone in the house in Butteville, she received an upsetting letter from her lawyer. It was a dark, rainy day so she walked to a window to have more light. Within a moment of unfolding the paper and reading a few lines, she cried out, "No!" Talking aloud in an irate and frustrated tone, "He misinformed me! How could my lawyer not know this before? Now he tells me that the act of Congress states that the lands must be owned before 1850, resided upon, and cultivated in order for the wife to have half ownership. I have no rights to anything Willy has been buying since we returned. My goodness, it's 1852 and our laws only benefit men. By law, I can't even buy property!" She let her hands fall to her sides and crumpled the letter in her fist. She turned her gaze outside and saw Mount Hood. *At least no one can take the beauty of nature from me.*

Nevertheless, Margaret continued the divorce preparations with hopes that the court would award her what she believed was her due.

One day Arnaud came to visit their Butteville home on his three-day leave from Astoria. Arnaud exclaimed in his new, deep voice, "This is a great house, Mar-Mar. Which do you like better, living here in Butteville or Champoeg?"

"Arnaud, I love Oregon and enjoy wherever we live. But come look out this window at our view of Mount Hood."

Standing side-by-side and peering at the majestic volcanic mountain covered in snow, they said nothing. Finally, Margaret touched his arm and said, "Follow me. I'll show you the bedroom where you will sleep."

Arnaud grabbed his bedroll and walked across the main room.

Margaret opened the windows. "There's no view of Mount Hood from this window, only rolling hills of green. But I love this view as much as the view of the mountain." As she tied back the curtains, he unfurled his bedding onto the mattress. She saw the lynx fur and picked it up. "Oh, this is a beautiful piece. It's so soft. What animal is it?"

"It's a lynx."

She asked, "Where did you get it?"

At that moment, Bailey popped his head into the room, "Hurry, Arnaud, it looks like rain, and I want to show you the property."

Now the three of them were in the bedroom; Arnaud reached for the fur. He puzzled a moment, "I've had this all my life, and I don't know how I got it." He looked up. "I never asked my parents."

Without hesitation, Bailey answered, "You got it at your baptism. A short, young Indian girl living at the Mission gave it to you. Her name was Sally, ah, Sally something."

Margaret interjected, "Sally Soule?"

"Yes, that's the name."

Bailey added, "She seemed to like your red hair and jostled it. She was quite taken with you. Come on, let's go."

They left and Margaret picked up the lynx again. *Sawala gave this to her son. She jostled his hair. Yes, I remember seeing her with Willy after they returned from the baptism at the river.* Margaret ran her hands over the lynx fur and even put it up to her nose to smell. *I like the smell. Earthy and maybe a bit of Sawala and Arnaud.* When she went to place it on the bed, the corner flipped, and she saw the scrawled writing of Sawala. Margaret looked closer. Satisfaction flooded her face as she recalled teaching at the Mission. With a choked voice, she whispered to Sawala, "Surely you are watching from heaven. You wrote FOR MY SON. Yes, Sawala, I only taught you the capital letters. Are you pleased with your handsome son?"

349

When Bailey and Arnaud returned, the day had changed. "This is Oregon; rain one minute and sun the next."

With the sun out, the air felt unusually warm. Arnaud asked Bailey, "I want to jump in the river. You want to come with me, like we used to do when I was little?"

"Yeah, let's go!"

Margaret liked the idea of them going swimming and made a plan for when they returned.

They came back dripping, and she had a towel draped over a chair and ready to use. "Arnaud, it is my turn to do something like we did when you were little. Let me dry your hair a bit." She rubbed the towel through his hair, looking above his forehead in the hairs. With his wet hair, the birthmark was easy to see. *There it is! The black leaf.* She said aloud, "Oh, you have a birthmark."

Bailey replied, "Yes, I saw the oval black mark when he was born, but it doesn't show now with all the hair he has."

Arnaud touched it and looked at Bailey. "I forgot that you were there when I was born."

Now Margaret understood everything Sawala had spoken on her deathbed. She handed Arnaud the towel and could not resist a mischievous impulse. Margaret took her hands and smoothed down all the curls in the wet hair on Arnaud's head before she said, "Willy, look how much Arnaud looks like you with his wet hair. The red turns dark." She pressed the hair straighter. "Come here. Both of you stand side by side and look in the mirror."

Arnaud reacted and quipped, "Hey, I do look like you. I always wanted to be as tall and handsome as you. Now I am!"

Margaret could see Bailey puzzled over the similarity. He quickly stepped away from the reflection. She saw the brief pain in his face. *I should tell him.* She gritted her teeth and walked away. *If he is good to me, maybe I will. But not today.*

Later during dinner, Margaret wanted to tell Arnaud about himself. She had worked out a way to do it indirectly. She removed her apron and sat down at the table before she turned to Arnaud, "You are a grown man, working and earning money, and living away from your family. I want to talk to you as a grown man."

Arnaud looked at her while he chewed his food. He waited, not having any idea what she was going to say.

She began. "Please continue eating while I speak. As you know, you are *Métis*."

Bailey grumbled, "Margaret, why do you want to talk about that?"

"Willy, let me speak!" She turned back to Arnaud, "One who is born *Métis* has little worth among the Indians. Did you know this?"

Arnaud's mouth was full again, "Maybe – what do you mean?"

"I mean that, when living among their own people, those born *Métis* are often sold or traded to become slaves." Margaret hesitated to emphasize her next sentence, "Like Sally Soule who gave you the lynx fur. She was born into a different tribe and traded to the Kalapuyans as a slave. Her life was hard before she came to the Mission. She was very intelligent and learned to speak English and write a little. She died from dropsy before she was your age."

Arnaud showed no curiosity.

Bailey complained again. "Margaret, why are you telling him this?"

She ignored Bailey, "On the other hand, a *Métis* born within the French Canadians, Irish, or other Whites, like you, is raised with the richness of different cultures. The sons and daughters of John McLoughlin are an example of this, too. To be successful and prosperous, the *Métis* children living with the white men depend upon the experiences of their childhood and the interest of the adults who raise them.

"But this is not to imply that all the *Métis* have blended in and are accepted. There is much prejudice and even hatred from some of the new American settlers. Has your mother or father talked with you about this? Or have you encountered prejudice?"

Arnaud said, "My mother told me once that she had found the white man's tongue is better for lies."

Margaret was disappointed. She wasn't sure what she had wanted to accomplish other than letting Arnaud know more about his birth mother. She finished by saying, "Be strong and proud of whom you are. You can accomplish all that you dream."

That night, while the men slept, Margaret sat and pondered. *Am I glad I said all that to Arnaud? Someday he might remember and benefit from my words. With Willy the way he is now, my thoughts are all I have now.* She rose from the bed and opened her journal to write:

> My mind to me a treasure is, and affords me sweet repast by day and night.

She lifted her quill to dip it into the ink bottle and stopped to gather her thoughts. *So many groups of people have difficulties to overcome; not only the Métis but also we women who are so mistreated.* Placing the feather's tip to paper, she wrote:

> I long that my sex should be emancipated from the thralldom of erroneous public opinion – her worth appear in its true light – her injuries be redressed, and herself occupy that position in society, which she is capable of adorning. I wish not to see her a mere bauble – a doll – to dress fine and lay by in a drawer – suitable to be seen and used only as a pastime – but disrobed of the imputation of weakness and unchastity, and adorned with the confidence and estimation of the opposite sex, which she deserves.

After many meetings with her lawyer, Mathew Deady, a court decree was prepared from her dictation:

DIVORCE DECREE

> That sometime in the spring of 1850, complainant (MJB) overheard defendant and his brother, James Bailey, making arrangements to take what money there was in the house and go to the gold mines in California and abandon complainant (MJB) without the means of subsistence, whereupon your complainant (MJB) removed the money to another part of the house. Defendant demanded the money of complainant (MJB),

and ran her out of the house. Defendant then followed complainant (MJB) out of doors, and whilst threatening to take her life, caught complainant (MJB) by the hair of her head and dragged her into the house, and abused her brutally. Defendant injured complainant's hip at this time so that complainant (MJB) was for a long time unable to walk upon it, and to this time has not wholly recovered from the effects of said treatment.

That in the summer of 1851 whilst complainant (MJB) and defendant were on the visit to New York, complainant (MJB) went to visit her mother, while defendant remained in the city of New York. That during this time (about seven weeks) defendant squandered in dissipation and licentiousness about three thousand dollars, and as complainant (MJB) has good reason to believe, contracted a venereal disease.

That defendant afterwards by fair promises for the future, and a pretended repentance for the past, induced complainant (MJB) to return to Oregon with him.

That in the month of January AD 1852 at the town of Portland defendant without any provocation on the part of complainant (MJB) seized a stick of wood and drawing it over complainant's head said to complainant (MJB) "God damn you I'll kill you."

That sometime in the month of February 1852 complainant (MJB) detected defendant taking indecent liberties with another female and making proposals of criminal intercourse, and when complainant (MJB) spoke about it, the defendant struck complainant (MJB) with his fist and knocked her down and otherwise cruelly abused complainant (MJB).

Margaret sat in the office of her lawyer and read the whole decree before signing it. *Well, I shall not put this into my memoirs. My, my, I must go back and read what I wrote during the spring of 1850. I was wise to decide to write a novel. Heaven knows I have written some scandalous scenes of my past into the book, but I do not want to hang all my dirty laundry out. Yes, it will be a novel. I know a good name for myself – Ruth Rover – a good biblical name with a surname that depicts my life of roaming.*

When Bailey was served with the divorce papers, he exploded. They were upstairs in their Champoeg house. He picked up a gun and pointed it to her head.

"Get out of my house before I kill you!"

Margaret went to her trunk. "I'll get my clothes and papers before going."

"No! You don't get anything. Get out!"

She scurried down the stairs with him following.

"And don't come back!"

Margaret hurried away and returned later, after she had seen him leave. He had locked the doors with padlocks, and she could find no way inside the house. When evening approached, she took a horse blanket from the stables and went to one of their sheds to sleep. In the morning, she saw a stranger arrive and she used the opportunity to go in to get her clothes.

As she entered, she said, "Good morning, I will get my clothes right now."

Bailey displayed no embarrassment in front of this other gentleman and stood to block her way. "No, you might take some of my things. Get out. I'll put your clothes outside the door later. Now, get out!"

She waited for hours. After his visitor left, William placed a bundle outside the door. Margaret knocked on the door and walked in to tell him, "Willy, I want my papers, too. And you packed only two dresses. I need other clothing."

He seized the bundle. "If you're not happy with this, go without. In fact, I'll sell everything, so you will have nothing. I'll leave you broke."

Margaret went to neighbors to live; she worked for her board by mending and washing. She used the little money she had to buy a couple dresses and other needs. And the months passed.

Then out of the blue, Bailey wrote to her:

To Mrs. Bailey:

My dear wife, I wish you to return to me and to your home, and if you will do so, I will tell you what I pledge myself to do. In the first place, I will certainly drink no more liquor for at least one year, hoping that if I can refrain that long, I may be able to refrain forever. I acknowledge I have treated you with undeserved severity, and if ever it should come to pass that I should put you from home again, I promise to let you have half my property for your support.

I also promise to request those storekeepers who refused to trust you on my credit – to let you have anything you want while my credit is good. And I will try to correct any false impressions that I have made about you.

Your affectionate husband,
William J. Bailey

Margaret dropped the divorce proceedings in July 1852.

By September 1852, their life had deteriorated again. He drank more frequently, so she secretly started to remove all her valuable journals, manuscripts, and papers from the house, little by little. One day as she sorted through papers, she found a letter that put fear into her. *This means that Willy corresponded with his family in the East about our troubles. No, look at the date! He must have talked badly about me to them while we were back there!*
She held a letter from Bailey's sister:

March 8, 1852

I would like to know how Beauty gets along. I think she is a smart hussy. I can imagine I can see her – the long, tall banshee – particularly when she is eating. I think you must abhor the sight of her.

She stopped herself and took a deep breath. *I am jumping to conclusions.*

Maybe his brother James told lies about me. But one thing I know for sure; I have seen Willy influenced by his siblings. When James is with him, Willy treats me the worst. Why didn't Willy show me this letter and laugh in the manner that he does when someone criticizes me? Tears came to her eyes. *Is Willy planning something horrible for me?*

Margaret packed up and left. Only some of her old or extra clothing remained at their house. She headed for Butteville to stay at their other house and learned that he had sold it. *How could he not have told me? I think I made a good decision to move out.* She got a room in a boardinghouse. This time she would not return to him, but she was afraid to see a lawyer. She told Willy that they needed to live apart, and he accepted her decision. With small jobs teaching and doing sewing, she supported herself. What's more, she had time every evening to work on her manuscript.

A year went by and then in September 1853, Bailey wrote a note to Margaret:

My dear,

I have suffered yesterday from fire in our house in Champoeg. It burnt to the ground and nothing was saved.

From,
Willy

On September 13th, Margaret read more details in the *Oregon Statesman*. The newspaper article described how all the furniture, furnishings, supplies for their stores, and clothing – most items purchased during their New York trip – were destroyed. The article noted that the doctor had removed his supplies of medicines and equipment, which he placed in his yard, but a runaway horse trampled everything, leaving nothing salvageable. In the last sentence of the article, Margaret read that they suspected a cigar started the fire. *A drunk Willy with a cigar, they mean.*

356

A week later, Margaret decided that there was no hope for their marriage and filed for divorce again.

On October 18, 1853, Bailey made the newspaper again when he and a man named Beale had gotten drunk on wine, quarreled, and then fought. Beale clubbed Dr. Bailey on the head and knifed him near the shoulder. Dr. Bailey got a pistol and fired at Beale, but missed. The courts acquitted Beale in the assault suit, and no charges were filed against Bailey.

In April 1854, the divorce went to court and was granted. Soon after that, Margaret wrote a letter to Bailey, who had gone to Astoria to stay until his house was rebuilt. He was living with Solomon Smith and Arnaud, who still worked at the mill. On the day Margaret's letter arrived, Bailey and Arnaud were working together in the gristmill.

A rider delivered the letter to him. Bailey wiped the dust from his face with the back of his arm before taking the letter and sitting down on a bench near the millstone. He broke the red wax seal with the pressed M, pushed the hair from his forehead, and began to read:

Dear Willy,

Well, when you receive this, I can say that we are finally divorced. I think it is for the best; of course, I can say that now – without knowing what the court has awarded to me. I thought it best to write to you while my Lord sits at my side to urge me to do what is right. When I learn the final decision of the Judge and know what I receive from this marriage, I might find myself wallowing in the self-pity and hatred, which you so often saw. But I have said enough on that subject.

I am writing because I want to say that you are a good man. Of course, I am referring to the sober William J. Bailey. When sober, you are the best man I have ever known. Remember when we spoke about Jason Lee, and you were amazed that I could find good in him? Willy, we all have good in us, but I wanted to let you know that I think you can return to be the best; you only need to stop drinking.

You know and I know that you can stop because you have done it before. When we married, you had not drunk for a long time, years. Dr. White had given you the reason to stop. You had to have a reason, didn't you? This time, I hope to give you the reason to stop (you will learn what it is at the end of this letter).

Next, I wish you to know that you helped me to reach my dream. You encouraged me to be the best I could and to accomplish my dreams. I wanted to thank you and tell you that my book is to be published soon. I paid Carter and Austin of Portland to print it. The title is *The Grains, or Passages in the Life of Ruth Rover, with Occasional Pictures of Oregon, Natural and Moral.* Are you laughing at the length of my title, or maybe at my lack of courage to use my own name? I am Ruth Rover in this book; I choose to call it a novel, but it is mostly the truth of my life.

Finally, here is the reason to help you stop drinking:

I shall start by saying – although you may disagree – that I think one of the reasons you drank was because we could not have children. You may say I am wrong, but that matters not, because I know you would agree that you wanted children. If you are not sitting, please do sit before you read the next two sentences.

You have a child.

Arnaud is your son.

It is a complex story how I learned this; it was bit-by-bit and over many years. Actually, in Portland, it was you who told me when you said that you had intercourse with a little virgin called Sawala. You never knew, but I lived with Sawala when I first arrived at the Mission. I was so angry with you that night in Portland that I said nothing. Sawala was Sally Soule; the missionaries renamed her. At first, she could speak no English and I no Kalapuyan, so she and I needed time to learn to communicate. I believe that she came to the Mission to find you and her baby. Yes, she had your son. She was on her deathbed when she made me promise to tell you something that sounded like delirium. Since it made no sense, I never told you, but I wrote it down – as you know, I recorded everything. Sawala said:

Tell Dr. Bailey.
He father
I mother. Dr. Bailey father.
You tell Dr. Bailey.
Arnaud my baby.
He have black leaf here.
Arnaud inside me.
Then I see black leaf.
Dr. Bailey take him.
Tsaal an tatsa – snow on ground.

When Ewing told me the story of Arnaud's birth, I had one piece of the puzzle, but I knew of no connection between you and Sawala. Ewing didn't tell me of the snow that night; the brightness of white snow made me understand how you could see the hair color of the woman who wanted to smash the child's head. When I asked you to tell the story, you said nothing about the "black leaf." Remember the day that you swam with Arnaud and I dried his hair? I found the last piece of the puzzle when I saw his birthmark beneath his red hair. I knew where to look because Sawala had touched her head when she said, "I see black leaf." Willy, you are his father, without a doubt.

May God be with you,
MJB

P.S. Look on the back of Arnaud's lynx fur to see how I taught Sawala to write. She wrote her son a message.

As Bailey finished the letter, goose pimples rippled down his flesh and a warm flush covered his face. He reread the last parts of the letter. When finished and while wiping his shirtsleeve across his brow, he looked up to see Arnaud coming toward him from across the mill. They peered at each other through glittering grist particles suspended in sunbeams.

With their eyes locked, Dr. William J. Bailey watched Arnaud approaching and worried. *My son! He's my son, but how will I explain?*

Footprints in the spilled grist and grains formed behind Arnaud; they appeared smaller in the distance growing bigger as he came closer, like footsteps progressing through the years and leading to his father.

Arnaud stopped an arm's length away and a grin spread across his face, "Don't worry, Dad, Mar-Mar already told me the whole story – or should I call you 'Pa' now?"

EPILOGUE

Margaret Jewett Bailey published her novel *The Grains or Passages in the Life of Ruth Rover, with Occasional Pictures of Oregon, Natural and Moral* in two volumes during 1854. The reviews were not complimentary; one reviewer stated, "Who in the dickens cares about the existence of a fly, or in whose pan of molasses the insect disappeared." Although it is not known how many copies were printed, the outraged citizens in Oregon made an effort to destroy all of her books.

In 1944, two copies of Volume II, purchased in 1922 by the Oregon State University Library, were found. Later, one incomplete copy of Volume I came to light in the Yale University Library. In 1986, Oregon State University Press reconstructed and reprinted both volumes of *The Grains* into a single book.

In 1855, Margaret married Mr. Francis Waddle and had a second unsatisfactory marriage; it ended in divorce in 1859. The Waddles were estranged early on, and during the separation in 1856, Margaret bought property in Salem on Commercial Street, on the west side of the street between Court and State Streets. Interestingly, she purchased it from Chloe Willson, née Clark then was in charge of selling property that had been owned by the Methodist Mission. In 1871, Margaret also bought a lot in Gervais and another in Hubbard. In the 1870 census in Salem, Oregon, she had a twenty-year-old student named Martha Hyatt living with her as well as a five-year-old girl born in Oregon (no name). The *Statesman* newspaper ran two items, in 1869 and 1872, that referred to Margaret as Mrs. Bailey: one stated, "More stores! Mrs. Bailey has moved back the wooden building on her lot, north of Starkey's and will immediately proceed to erect brick stores on the same site"; the other article announced that Mrs. Bailey's piano was for sale. Margaret married a third time, to a Mr. Crane, but nothing is known about him or about that part of her life.

In 1855, William John Bailey married Julia Nagel Shiel, the widow of Dr. James Shiel, who had practiced medicine on the French Prairie. Not much is known about his life after the divorce from Margaret. He continued to practice medicine and ran unsuccessfully for the Democratic gubernatorial candidate in 1855. He converted to Catholicism in 1870, died in 1876 and was buried in St. Paul, Oregon.

In 1882, when Margaret was seventy years old, she wrote to Dr. Tolmie, the doctor who had worked for the Hudson's Bay Company and attended Bailey when he had his 1833 tomahawk injury. Margaret was trying to find William Bailey. But Margaret died on May 16, 1882 from "lung fever" (pneumonia) in Seattle, never having learned that her Willy had already died.

On May 19, 1882, the *Puget Sound Weekly Courier* ran her obituary:

> Mrs. Margaret J. Crane, author of *Ruth Rover*, a novel that created a great sensation in Oregon in early days, died in Seattle Tuesday night of pneumonia and was buried from Brown Church, Rev. J.F. Damon, officiating.

What this obituary neglected to mention was that Margaret Jewett Bailey was the first published poet in Oregon, the first published novelist in the Northwest, and possibly the first woman to successfully sue for divorce, although she was granted only her clothes, her piano, and one hundred dollars from the proceeds.

Some changes to Oregon law during Margaret Jewett Bailey's lifetime:

1859: Women were not subject to husband's debts if a husband died and left her with the estate.

1866: Unmarried women could own property.

1878: Women could vote in school elections.

1882: Women could practice law.

Advances of germ theories in medicine during Dr. William John Bailey's lifetime:

1847: Ignas Semmelweis from Hungary popularized the practice of doctors washing hands in chlorinated lime water.

1854: John Snow from England contributed to germ theory in his work with cholera.

1860-1864: Louis Pasteur from France proved the existence of microorganisms in unboiled broth, leading to the practice of pasteurizing liquids such as milk.

Contents Of Letters Of MJB

Letter shown in Chapter 14:
Linn City – May 17th 1852

Mr. Deady – Sir – I understand that Mr. Bailey and his brother are preparing soon to leave for California with the proceeds of their trade in Portland which must amount to five or six thousand dollars in cash. I thought I had better inform you as I wished to inquire what my course should be this summer in relation to the expected trial. Will I be expected merely to prove the statements I have already made [to] you – or should I be prepared to [missing word] them of another? & is it of any use to [smeared ink] sp[eak] of abuses & irregularities which I cannot [missing word] by a third person? I wish you would confer [wh]en you find it convenient – with Mr. Gaffin of Portland, Mrs. Mary Clane of Linn City & Mrs. Watt of Lafayette. Mrs Watt was on our place a few years ago & learned considerable of our difficulties. The others witnessed the disturbance in Portland.

I shall endeavor to move here this week, when I hope you will write me.

Respectively – Margaret J. Bailey

Mr. Robert Newhall of Champooiah [Robert Newell of Champoeg] can also tell you much – he has letters on the subject received from Dr. Bailey.

Letter shown in Chapter 2:
June 1st 1852

Mr. Deady – Sir – Enclosed is a notice as you will perceive for me to appear at Portland on the 9th of June [?] – if I shall please. I am anxious to be present & also wish you should be there. Will it be possible for you to attend? & will you send me word!

If you write please divert to the care of Mr. Weston – Canemah [?].

Respectively – Margaret J. Bailey

Letter to her lawyer, Mr. Mathew Deady in June 1852 (original not shown in GRIST):

"I am compelled to trouble you again, to my regret. Dr. Bailey passed here yesterday on his way to Buteville. He has closed his business at Portland, & is on his way to the [gold] Mines with his brother. I am satisfied that it is his intention to avoid the Court, giving me means of support, & allowing me to have the remainder of my effects at Buteville. You will best know if there is any remedy, if there be – it must be found immediately, or it 'twill be of no avail. I presume you will without my urging you, do what you can, at once."

ACKNOWLEDGEMENTS

My gratitude is profound and overflowing to those who gave of their ideas, knowledge, and time to assist in the making of this novel *GRIST*. My fingers may have typed the words and structured the story; nevertheless, the final product was a result of the support of many people.

The editing took longer than the creation of the original manuscript, and I am indebted to everyone who toiled to verify the accuracy of this story. My editor Dave Picray has an eye that finds discrepancies and errors like no one I know; he sees what others miss. My brother Charles J. Marlen, M.D. attended to all the medical scenes, editing with a bedside manner like he must have had when he was a practicing radiologist. Lori Shafer appeared at the last moment and expertly did the final editing; I can't thank her enough. The publisher Kristi Negri searched for logic and flow, embarrassing *faux pas* that I needed to remove, and overall coherency; she is an expert. Todd Silverstein, Ph.D. combed through the manuscript, editing and advising me; he supported me in my efforts to make *GRIST* my best accomplishment. Finally, the historical experts Donna and Mark Hinds, who are volunteer interpretive hosts at the Champoeg State Heritage Area, know the era of Oregon's history in my novel as if they had lived it; I am happily in their debt for all their pages and pages of comments.

Others gave important pieces to add to the fullness of the story: Tom Beatty, the horticulture technician at Bush Park in Salem, first mentioned the poisonous, white death-camas plants and lent me a book to learn more. Arnaud Bugat, my longtime friend in France, gave me his name to use. Bruce Gordon, a fan and friend, told me of the Kalapuyan display in the Polk County museum. Kay Demlow, of Lavender's Green Historic Clothing, graciously answered my endless questions about fabrics and clothing of the mid-eighteen hundreds. The people working at the Marion County Historical Society helped with time and resources, and Scott Daniels from Oregon's Historical Society in Portland assisted me by scanning letters by Margaret Jewett Bailey.

Everything began because of the Hinds, mentioned above, and two others:

David R. Brauner, Ph.D. (Professor, Anthropologist, and Archaeologist), whom I met at an archaeological dig on the Champoeg site. He gave me information, words of encouragement, and two lengthy historical papers to read. I cannot thank him enough.

And

Cindy Crosby, my dear friend, who introduced me to Margaret and started my quest.

These are the main books and papers that I used to develop the history and views of Oregon: David Brauner, Rebecca McClelland, and James Bell, *Eden's Gate: Champoeg State Park Historic Sites Archaeological Project 1990-1992* (1985); Caroline Dobbs, *Men of Champoeg* (1993); John A. Hussy, *Champoeg: A Place of Transition – A Disputed History* (1967); Harold Mackey Ph.D., *The Kalapuyans: A Sourcebook on the Indians of the Willamette Valley* (2004); Jim Pojar and Andy Mackinnon, *Plants of the Pacific Northwest Coast: Washington, Oregon, British Columbia, and* Alaska (1994); Juliet Thelma Pollard, *The Making of the* Métis *in the Pacific Northwest Fur Trade Children: Race, Class, and Gender* (1990); William Sullivan, *Hiking Oregon's History* (1999);

and, of course,

Margaret Jewett Bailey, *The Grains or Passages in the Life of Ruth Rover, with Occasional Pictures of Oregon, Natural and Moral* (1854).